SEASON OF LIES

Dennis Hetzel

Publisher Page
an imprint of Headline Books, Inc.
Terra Alta, WV

Season of Lies

by Dennis Hetzel

To order additional copies of this book or for book publishing information, or to contact the author:

Headline Books, Inc.
P.O. Box 52
Terra Alta, WV 26764
www.HeadlineBooks.com

Tel: 304-789-3001
Email: mybook@headlinebooks.com

Publisher Page is an imprint of Headline Books

ISBN 13: 978-1-882658-94-7

Library of Congress Control Number: 017932963

PRINTED IN THE UNITED STATES OF AMERICA

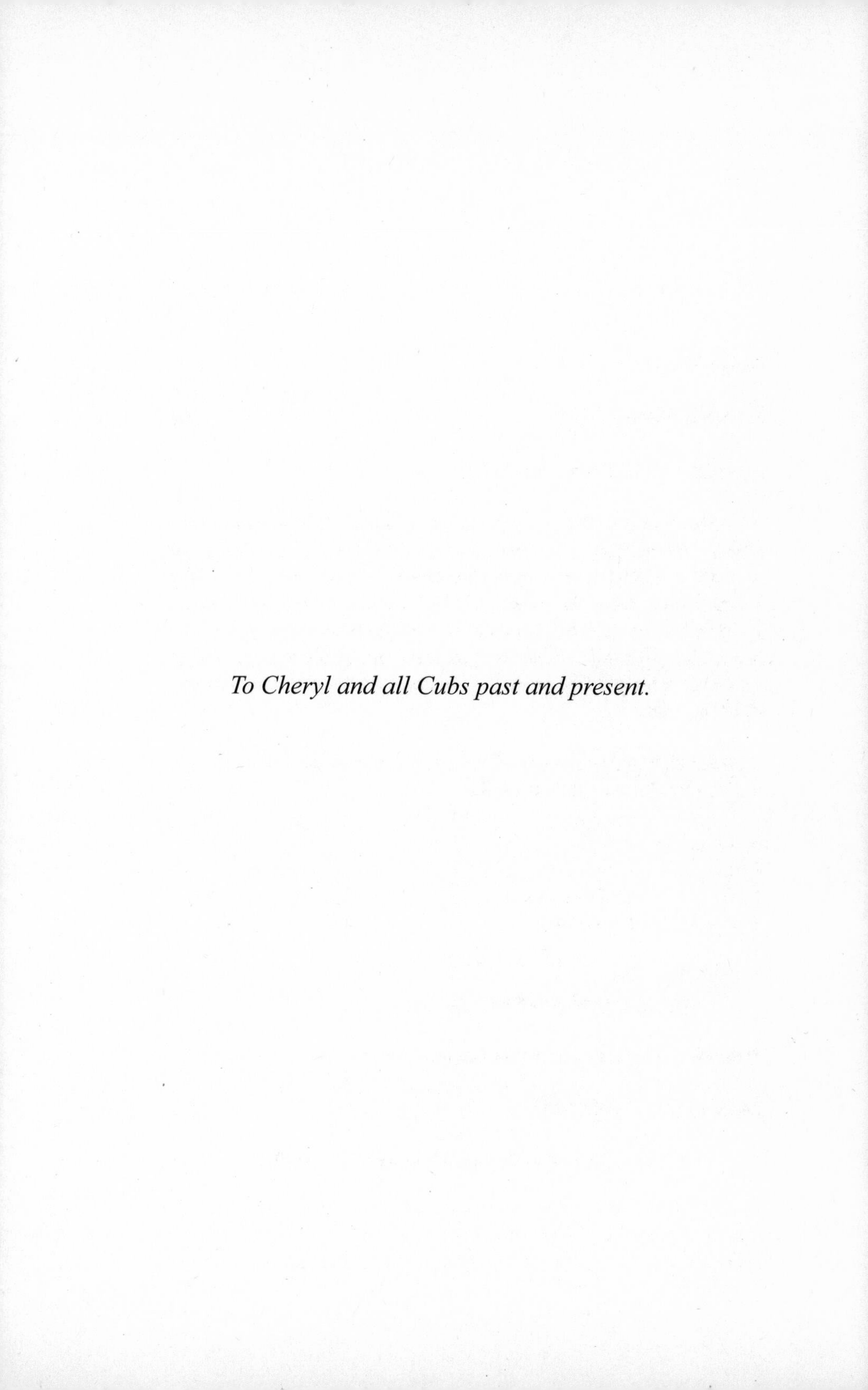

To Cheryl and all Cubs past and present.

"The heavens proclaim the glory of God, and the sky above proclaims His handiwork."

Psalm 19:1, English Standard Version

"If dreams were lightning, thunder was desire..."

John Prine, lyric from "Angels of Montgomery"

PART ONE
LUKE & TREY

1

Cascade Mountains
One Year Before The Election

It was a perfect night to watch a comet.

Moments after Reginald Preston Fox spotted the potential campsite along a hiking trail in Oregon's Cascade Mountains, he looked up. They had hiked an extra hour to find a perfect position to see the sky that night. The surrounding mountains and sparse terrain formed an oblong basin around a heavenly stage. He wanted to fully appreciate the panorama about to unfold in a night sky that promised cloudless, remarkable clarity free from the intrusion of the lights of civilization.

"Yeah," he said aloud, even though his hiking companion hadn't caught up yet. "Yeah. It's perfect."

They were there to view a rare lunar eclipse, but not just any eclipse. What made this night unique by all accounts was the proximity of a comet to the event. The recently discovered object, named 695 Esaias by the scientist who discovered it, would fly in the path of the eclipse. Such a fascinating, rare coincidence had attracted millions, maybe billions, to observation sites or live broadcasts from around the globe. Astronomers predicted the comet's tail would be quite visible and its flight would mingle with the Earth's shadow falling over the full moon that was still fully visible in the crisp, mountain air.

For Reggie Fox, the timing was perfect, too. Influencing the political process was his life but astronomical events formed his hobby passion; especially when he could hike to a remote spot like this. He needed time away to clear his head—to decide whether to sit out this election or actively work to prevent Luke Murphy from winning a second term as president.

Of course, Fox could have plenty of impact without all the stress by doing what all unemployed consultants seemed to do—spout off on cable news.

"He needs to spend more time thinking about Christians and less time thinking about the Cubs, even when they're playing in the World Series" was Fox's latest talk-show line, a reference to the president's moderate political views and unabashed enthusiasm for his hometown team, baseball's Chicago Cubs, who were playing in the seventh game of the World Series on this night—an opportunity for their first championship since 1908.

Fox had a lifelong fascination with Christianity along with a personal faith that fluctuated the way some rivers vacillated from roaring rapids to drought and back. Critics, especially from the left, called him a phony, wondering how a political hardball artist could align the ruthlessness required to win a national election with Christian values. Those closest to him knew it wasn't quite that simple. To be sure, Fox knew how to exploit any weakness of his political foes, but he felt pings, twinges and even an occasional deep regret at the tactics he deployed for the perceived greater good. Usually, he got over such twinges quickly.

Astronomy offered a respite; a place where he could relax and touch the sky. It filled him with wonder for creation and, he admitted, probably kept him from falling completely into the sociopathic abyss of self-justification where too many political operatives landed eventually.

He discovered political consulting almost as a fluke, years after he stopped studying for the priesthood. ("After all," he said in his stock speech, at the going rate of $50,000 or more, "whose childhood dream involves political consulting?") Four things, he said, convinced him to leave the seminary before it was too late. The first was the disappointing but realistic recognition that his faith was neither deep nor profound enough to sustain such a career choice. All three of the other reasons were attractive females.

"I was either going to be a frustrated celibate or a fraud to the vows," he had said the previous night to his backpacking friend and business partner, Trent Schuller. "If you can't imagine giving something up under any circumstances, then you're a fool to follow that path," Fox said. "Instead of beating up on myself, I followed a different path."

Schuller nodded in affirmation. They had spent a beautiful Pacific Northwest day in the late fall hiking to this spot from a base camp. They were almost above the tree line, low enough in altitude to have a site with shade from a few scrubby pines that formed an arc around a flat area just large enough for a lightweight, two-person tent. A stream about 100 yards away provided a thin but usable ribbon of water.

It was very late in the season for the Cascades, nearly the end of October, and they were fortunate to have picked days without snow in the air. The opportunity to hike without snowshoes and other winter gear wouldn't last much longer. They had built a small fire to stay warm in the high-elevation chill and they mixed splashes of Maker's Mark bourbon from a small flask with the water they had purified at the campsite.

Schuller was tall and lanky. He worked hard to look good and stay in shape. He attracted attention, but he was 100 percent loyal to his wife, and he treasured their two small children even if he had to go long stretches without seeing them.

Fox hadn't been quite as fortunate in that department. Married and divorced twice, he had put long-term relationships on hold. He was built like the college wrestler he had been. He was short—five feet, eight inches tall—and stubby with powerful arms and legs. He had lost most of his hair before he turned 50, so he shaved his head. He had recently added a "soul patch" of hair under his lower lip, which made him more distinctive during frequent guest appearances on political talk shows.

"What's that comet name again?" Schuller asked, stretching back across the boulder that had been serving as his outdoor seat, looking to the sky as they awaited the start of the eclipse. He shivered slightly in the night chill. He moved to finish extinguishing the fire to eliminate any intrusive light. A few remaining campfire embers flickered to a halt.

"Esaias," Fox said, spelling out the word and correctly pronouncing it Is-Eye-Us in the soft drawl of his native Kentucky. "It's the New Testament Greek name for the prophet Isaiah. Think about the meaning. This namesake object travels through the heavens and now crosses the path of the Earth, sun and moon at this precise moment. And think about the coincidence that the astronomer who discovered it would have Esaias as his middle name. They name comets after their discoverers, you know. And this guy insisted they use his middle name, because of the symbolism. In other words, this rocky, frozen snowball is named after the one Biblical prophet whose vision should still astound us. It's almost uncanny.

"Well," Fox quickly added. "Correct that. Take 'almost' out of the sentence. Isaiah's prophecies were flat-out uncanny in foretelling the life and work of Jesus. So, you've got to wonder, just what is Esaias predicting on this night?"

"Refresh my memory," Schuller said, sipping on the bourbon, letting its warmth take the edge off the cool night. "To put it mildly, my Bible study is rusty."

"Well, there are many examples. First of all, Isaiah said the Messiah would be born of a virgin," Fox said. "Jesus was born of a virgin. Isaiah said there would be a ministry in Galilee, an heir to David's throne. Jesus ministered in Galilee and was related to David. Isaiah prophesized that the Messiah would be disfigured and suffer. He would be widely rejected. He would accept our guilt and punishment for our sins. This, of course, is what all Christians believe. And, remind you, this was in the 8th Century B.C. These words were being studied hundreds of years before the birth of Christ."

Fox continued after a pause. "I don't have the deepest faith in the world, but Isaiah's prophecies have always filled me with wonder. It makes me think, well, maybe this book really is the revealed world of God. At least parts of it. So, yeah, Trent—it's worth your time to read the book of Is-Eye-Us."

"That's pretty wild," was all Schuller said.

The need for silence seemed to touch both at once. They stretched out on their backs and stared at the moon, their heads now resting on rocks they had set side by side. The eclipse was only a few minutes away, getting ready to dim the bright, full moon that illuminated the nearby, volcanic peaks of the Three Sisters mountains. From their campsite, they would have a short hike in the morning, weather permitting, to the top of one of the Sisters, arriving in time for a backpack lunch with plenty of time to get back to the campsite before dark.

The lunar eclipse began as expected, initially seen as a sliver of black, as though God Himself was busily carving crescent-shaped chunks into the moon. The Earth cast a shadow as it came between the sun and the moon. Then the chunks grew bigger as blackness spread across the moon's face.

The global frenzy of sky watching had started after astronomers predicted Esaias' long tail would be faintly visible just before it crossed behind the moon and then appear brighter on the other side as the comet pointed into the inky darkness of space. Esaias also would approach at an odd angle because of its trajectory. The relatively small chunk of rock itself wouldn't be visible to the naked eye but millions might see the tail that spewed out for thousands of miles behind as Esaias sped across the sky.

None of the predictions came close to reality. What Schuller and Fox saw caused them and millions of others to gasp in amazement and contemplate the hand of God.

Their account squared with what millions of others witnessed: The diverging tails appeared to form a cross moving across the sky. The blackness of the eclipse absorbed the faint apex of the cross first, then the arms and finally the base as though the void itself needed to consume humanity's most powerful symbol of suffering, death, redemption, and grace. The comet rapidly sped to the other side of the eclipse. As the visible tail emerged, the cross-shape brightened. Some observers swore it flashed like a beacon, like a strobe-signal from God Himself. Videos failed to provide definitive evidence. In the aftermath, endless debates would rage about what was real, what was illusion and what was in the eyes of beholders.

Scientists agreed the cross image was possible. The two parts of a comet's tail—one made of dust and the other made of gas—could bend in different directions. The unusual trajectory created the perception of a cross shape for many observers.

Still, there was no scientific formula for the shock, fear and wonder the comet inspired. Or, what it might unleash.

Being truly surprised was a rare emotion for Fox. Not this time. "It's a sign," Fox finally said. "It has to be."

"What are we supposed to do with that sign?" Schuller said in a soft, barely audible voice. "What does it mean?"

"I don't know yet," Fox said. "But I guarantee you that we're not the only ones asking these questions tonight."

2

Wrigley Field, Chicago
After Game Seven of The World Series

The manager of the Chicago Cubs knew he should be a lot happier than he actually felt. After all, his team had just won the World Series. Maybe it was more in spite of him than because of him.

When a security guard opened the door for Mike Surrey, he winced. He knew what would happen next as the hinges emitted the somewhat loud, pained-sounding squeak that he remembered from the cheesy horror movies of his youth. Remembering his wife's advice to "stop slouching in public," Surrey sucked in his gut just a bit, pushed his arms back and tried to look natural, instead of looking like he was making a conscious effort to walk tall.

Today the door's screech provided a fitting introduction. Surrey steeled himself before sitting at a table that provided an electronic nest for at least 15 microphones. A blue banner peppered with the familiar round logos of the Chicago Cubs formed the backdrop. He stood still for a moment, peering into a swarm of reporters jammed into the packed room where news conferences were held at Wrigley Field, the home of Chicago's National League baseball team.

Surrey had toyed with a philosophical opening that quoted Herbert Bayard Swope Sr., a reporter and editor sometimes called the greatest journalist of his era. He invented the term

"Cold War" to describe the tension between the United States and its allies versus the Soviet Union following World War II. In 1917, Swope won the first Pulitzer Prize in reporting for his dispatches from Germany during World War I. This was Swope's best-known quote:

> *"I can't give you a sure-fire formula for success, but I can give you a formula for failure: try to please everybody all the time."*

Swope had expressed a thought that had remained with Surrey since he first studied him during a college class on journalism and the two world wars. It certainly fit the status of a Major League Baseball manager; a position that invited second-guessing that would escalate to a frenzy on this day.

The way the Cubs had won this pivotal game was absurd, so weird you almost had to laugh, as though the curse gods who had haunted the team for decades had looked in a funhouse mirror and twisted things around. Now the joke was on him. Surrey quickly concluded the subtlety of a quote involving an obscure journalist wouldn't work. He knew what the fans in Chicago and across Cubs Nation wanted: A big damn smile and a fervent apology for decisions and behavior that almost cost them the championship.

Call it dumb pride, but he couldn't take a full ride on the apology train. He wouldn't please everybody.

Instead, he considered talking a bit about the curse's downfall. After all, that would be the story long after fans forgot his meltdown. The Cubs hadn't won a championship since 1908 and missed opportunities in countless bizarre and baffling ways for decades, involving everything from goats to Gatorade; from black cats to Steve Bartman.

The goat was denied entry to the 1945 World Series—the last time the Cubs played for baseball's world championship. The goat's owner, Billy Sianis of Chicago's famed Billy Goat Tavern, placed a curse on the team, which went on to lose the Series. Bartman was the fan who reached out to grab a foul ball that arguably could have been caught by Cubs' outfielder Moises Alou. He got the blame for the Cubs missing a chance to go to the World Series in 2003, even though an on-field collapse by the Cubs in the rest of the inning had far more impact.

By now, Surrey had heard all the tales of jinxes and odd events, including the more obscure ones—like Gatorade spilled on first baseman Leon Durham's glove in the dugout during a 1984 playoff game against San Diego. The 1984 team seemed to have the combination of talent, confidence, and intangible mojo to finally kill the curse. In the next inning, Durham made an error at a critical moment. The Cubs lost the game and the series.

All these incidents combined into the kind of stew that boiled into a legend. The Cubs could make the firmest atheist believe in Biblical curses. Until tonight.

Surrey fast-forwarded through the last few hours as he prepared to answer the questions.

First, his team had won the most extraordinary World Series game ever played. It was the only time in Series history that the last game had to be played twice. The Cubs and the Boston Red Sox had tied at three games each in the best-of-seven battle for the World Championship.

That was when crazed fan Tommy Czerski had entered the picture. And, so did President Luke Murphy, whose passion for the Cubs was legendary since his days as a young Congressman from suburban Chicago. Radical environmentalists exploited Czerski's willingness to do anything to ensure a Cubs victory as part of a larger plot to assassinate Murphy during Game Seven if Murphy refused to cooperate with their demands. They manipulated Murphy's childhood friend, Bob Walters, to get him close to Murphy. The intense pressure they put on Walters included kidnapping and abusing his daughter, Aimee.

If the Cubs lost, Czerski threatened even greater carnage. The FBI and Secret Service decided the game had to be fixed to ensure the Cubs would win, but in ways the public in general and Czerski in particular wouldn't notice. Even then, the Cubs were losing late in the game, causing Czerski to trigger a huge explosion at the Navy Pier Ferris wheel. Innocent children died.

Still, Chicago won the bogus game in the end. The plot against Murphy failed and Czerski died as well, but the terrorist ringleader remained unidentified and at large.

A fixed game couldn't stand as a defining moment. So, the leaders of Major League Baseball ordained a do-over. The "real" Game Seven quickly became the biggest sporting event in American history, magnified by the presence of the Cubs and the Red Sox.

The only recent Series that came remotely close was the Series of 2004 when Boston shed its own curse and won the championship; their first since 1918. That was known as "the Curse of the Bambino," hearkening to the trade of immortal home-run hitter Babe Ruth, who had been a star pitcher for Boston, to the New York Yankees, in 1919.

For once, Surrey agreed with Walters, a bombastic talk-show host on Chicago radio station WCO who spent many hours ripping the Cubs. Walters had recently said this, "Only the Cubs could almost lose a game that was fixed for them."

Now, in the game that mattered, they had accomplished what generations of Chicago fans thought they'd never see—and many of their parents and grandparents never did.

Surrey knew he'd be a primary target of the media swarm; the guy who had to explain another historically weird ending for the Cubs. It was going live on ESPN and it could quickly turn into a media "gotcha" fest with him playing the role of piñata.

He decided to go with a lightly humorous curse reference before the questioning began. Plus, the more he said at the beginning, the faster he might be able to leave the room, using the time-tested response to reporters' questions, "I believe I covered that in my opening comments."

He awaited predictable questions. The better-informed, more-serious reporters viewed a press conference as somewhere between a sincere opportunity to ask relevant questions and armed combat. Some reporters specialized in serving up questions with juicy bait they hoped he would take by saying something stupid that nowadays translated into thousands of instant tweets and digital clicks.

Members of the other group were more interested in how they looked asking their questions than they were in his answers. He reserved particular scorn for the perky blonde-in-a-bottle female reporters and their pretty-boy colleagues from television networks like "E," who probably thought a suicide squeeze was what happened when a celebrity's girlfriend killed herself.

Still, shallow journalism had advantages. The questions would be easy and some would be inane. Cliché answers were good enough. (His personal, recent favorite, "So, Mike, do you wish the team had scored enough runs to win?")

With television lights glaring, he took off his baseball cap and stared for just a moment at the red letter "C" with the white border centered above the bill of the medium-blue cap; a symbol that meant so much to millions of Chicago fans. Surrey ran a hand through his sandy-brown hair. Then he tugged on the closely cropped goatee he had grown during mid-season. It was mainly gray, but Lisa thought it was a good look and that worked for him. He was an attractive man in his early 50s who looked like someone Hollywood would pick to play a baseball manager in a film. His liberal arts degree made him an unusual person in the closed world of baseball and his unconventional managerial decisions made him a target of plenty of critics. He expected plenty of that in coming days.

"Well, as you folks know, I've always pooh-poohed the idea that the Cubs are dealing with some sort of silly curse," he said, speaking slowly into the microphone.

"Still, recent events made me wonder," he continued. "After today, either the curse took its last gasp, or it moved from the team to me." He flashed a barely visible grin; then tried to read the room to see if he got much reaction and was pleased to see at least a few nods. "I'm not proud about getting kicked out of the game," he added, "but if that's what it took to finally win a World Series for Chicago and our fans, it was worth it."

He started to say more, but already the shouts from the media corps overwhelmed any scripted dialogue he had in mind.

"Mike, Mike," yelled out a voice he recognized as belonging to Jimmy Constable from the suburban *Herald*. "Walk us through what happened in the ninth inning with Minser."

The reference was to Matt Minser, the relief pitcher Surrey had brought into the game in the top of the ninth inning with the Cubs leading 2-1 and the World Series on the line.

"You saw it same as I did, Jimbo," Surrey said. "Maybe we should have delayed the game so everyone could watch the damn eclipse."

Surrey caught himself just in time, having almost dropped an f-bomb instead of "damn" on live, national television.

Boston had two outs and two runners on base. The latest runner was a batter Minser had walked on a disputed call that almost got the pitcher ejected for barking too loudly at the home-plate umpire, Andy Cassidy, after the ump called "Ball Four" loudly and decisively. Minser was certain his slider had nipped the outside corner of the plate and should have been called a strike. For good measure, Cassidy show-boated the call, adding some expansive arm gestures and a big, swooping motion that ended with his index finger pointing the batter to first base.

"What, are you a fucking clown?" Minser snorted under his breath after the call. He also took added offense at the umpire's extra effort at loudly stretching out the words "ball four" so that it sounded like "bahhhhhhawllll forrrrr."

Seeing he was rattled, Minser's catcher, Armando Martinez, quickly called time and walked to the pitcher's mound to help settle his pitcher only to be greeted by another string of profanities, starting with "dickwad ump maybe just cost us the fuckin' World Series."

As Martinez approached the mound, Surrey left the dugout to talk to his pitcher, hoping to avert a crisis, which is exactly what losing his best available pitcher would be.

"You gotta settle down man," Martinez said, drawing on the key English phrases he had learned. Simple, confident proclamations usually worked best with stressed-out pitchers of any ethnicity. "We need you in this game. That call; it was bad man. But move on. Gotta move on."

As the dialogue progressed, Cassidy walked to the mound to tell the players to get things moving. When Minser saw the umpire, they made eye contact. It spoke volumes. Cassidy already had been lip reading.

"Do you got something you want to say to me, Minser?" Cassidy said. "My advice is to button it. Let's go."

Surrey quickly grabbed Minser's arm to keep him from talking. The manager was seething, too. Cassidy's ball-and-strike calls had annoyed him for the whole game and the umpire already had warned him to tone things down in the sixth inning.

Surrey knew better, but he couldn't help himself.

"You fucking missed it, Andy," Surrey said. "This is the seventh game of the World Series. You picked a damn bad time to have a bad game."

"You know what, Mike" Cassidy said. "Boo-fucking-who. Get out. You're ejected."

"You can't eject me," Surrey claimed.

"What the fuck Andy," Minser said. "He was just standing up for me."

"You're gone, too, Minser." Cassidy then pointed at both of them, and to emphasize his disgust to the screaming crowd, he extended his arm in a flourish toward the dugout and the clubhouse door. The Wrigley Field crowd exploded. The announcers scurried to learn if a manager and a critical player ever had both been ejected in the ninth inning of the seventh game of the World Series.

On the way off the field, Surrey kicked first base so hard it popped out and had to be replaced. He turned back and gestured once more at Cassidy.

Entering the dugout, the consequences hit him. He turned to his bench coach, Greg Clare, and whispered, "Man, I screwed up Greg. Put in Crawford and hope for the best."

After the game, replays seemed to confirm it was a close call, but most observers agreed with Minser: The ump should have shouted "Strike Three" to end the game.

"So, Mike, you've had a chance to see the replays. Was that a bad 'Ball Four,' call against Minser?" shouted another reporter at the press conference.

"Yeah, I think so," Surrey said. "But I shouldn't have lost my cool. I hurt the team."

Surrey thought for a moment, trying to decide if he wanted to add a comment. *What the hell, it's the end of season,* he thought. *We aren't playing again for six months.*

"I might be fined by the League for adding this, but I think what really got to Matt was it seemed like Andy went out of his way to embarrass him on that 'Ball Four,' call. You saw him showboat it. Nobody likes to be shown up," Surrey said as reporters held their voice recorders a little higher and scribbled furiously, energized by Surrey's willingness to chomp on their bait. A manager criticizing the umpire with a World Series at stake—that was a juicy nugget. Gazing at the activity in the media multitude, Surrey realized he had violated his rule about ever letting his heart rule his head during a press conference. All he could do now was move to another topic as fast as possible.

"Look," he continued as the question cacophony elevated, and Surrey suppressed a vision of clowns piling into a circus car. "I still haven't finished Jim's first question. Let me anticipate where this is headed and maybe we'll come back to that.

"First of all, you want to know why I used Minser. Why did we use a middle reliever in that spot instead of our number one reliever in the ninth? You want to know that, right?" Surrey quizzed the group, raising his eyebrows as though he was genuinely interested in their feedback.

"Yeah, Mike, you know we want to know that," was the condescending, unspoken consensus.

"Okay," Surrey said. "The one secret was we didn't think that Crawford's blister healed enough for him to pitch. He opened it up again warming up on the sidelines yesterday. We didn't want to use him."

That got their attention and calls of "what blister?" filled the room from a few of the reporters who weren't regulars.

Surrey was referring to Kirby Crawford, who had stayed in the "fixed" seventh game despite a growing blister on his right, index finger—a critical spot for someone relying on the split-finger fastball. The "splitter" was wickedly evil to hit when thrown well. The ball left the pitcher's hand looking like a normal fastball only to drop sharply like a darting fish as it reached home plate. But the blister caused one of Crawford's splitters to flatten out—like a fat worm to a hungry batter. With the help of a burst bulb in the outfield lights that blinded an outfielder, Crawford gave up an inside-the-park home run that led to Boston taking the lead in the top of the ninth inning of the fixed Game Seven.

"Now that our little deception is out, maybe some of you can stop ripping Kirby for that pitch," Surrey said. "He did his best. The way some of you put it, you'd think Kirby personally climbed into that light tower and made the bulb explode."

The manager shook his head, reliving another moment certainly to fight for top billing in the lore of Cub curses. "So, anyway," he continued, "that's why Minser was my best choice. And, besides, what happened wasn't his fault either."

For that, Cub fans could forever blame Surrey, Crawford and outfielder Darrin Cain.

Surrey, who was often criticized for letting his starting pitchers stay in games too long, had done the opposite in this game, frequently switching pitchers to get the best match-ups. With options limited, Crawford was the best remaining choice. The unexpected ejection gave Crawford extra time to warm up before he faced Boston's pinch hitter, Cesar Hidalgo.

Hidalgo looked helpless on Crawford's first two pitches. He had left the bat on his shoulder, fooled completely by a slow, change-of-pace that seemed to slither into the strike zone at the last possible second. Crawford followed that pitch with a perfectly placed slider and tried to avoid obviously wincing as the rub of the ball's leather cover opened up his blister again. He'd have to finish on instinct and deception. The Cubs were one pitch away from their first championship since 1908.

Hidalgo anchored himself at the plate, knowing that the World Series was on the line as well as the passionate prayers of everyone in Red Sox Nation and all New England; not to mention his native Dominican Republic. He crossed himself quickly and called time out to interrupt Crawford's pace. The runner on first, Austin Dugan, lengthened his leadoff, looking for an edge to score the potential winning run and trying to distract the Chicago pitcher.

Crawford decided that heat—his best fastball—was his best option and a pitch he could control.

For decades, baseball players have been convinced that some fastballs "hopped," jumping perceptibly just as they reached the plate. Physics and motion experts denied it was possible, claiming the hop was an illusion of perception. Crawford had a decent fastball and because it seemed to rise, batters tended to hit under the ball, causing lots of high pop-ups and fly balls that were easy outs.

Surrey knew what questions were coming.

"Before we talk about Cain missing that easy pop fly from Hidalgo," Surrey said, "maybe we should talk about why maybe it would have been a good idea to delay the game a little longer so everyone could watch the comet crossing."

Surrey immediately realized that sounded defensive. If he and his pitcher hadn't lost their cool, the game might have been over before what happened next.

Raised a Baptist in a devout Christian home, Darren Cain knew exactly why he allowed himself to be distracted, but he doubted he would ever stop hating himself for losing focus; victory was the only forgiveness. It didn't change the reality that he'd always be known as the guy who stared at the shimmering, cross-shaped tail flying across the night sky a split second before Crawford delivered his next pitch to Hidalgo.

"Wow. Holy Shit," he recalled thinking at that moment. More than 40,000 people crammed into Wrigley Field reinforced his inner thoughts, suffering from the same momentary distraction as loud "ahs" filled the park. Thousands of index fingers pointed skyward.

Crawford, laser-focused on the task, figured it was the perfect time to pitch. Hidalgo, no less apt in total concentration, swung at the rising fastball but popped it up.

Cain, having stared briefly at the show in the sky, left a half second later than he normally would have. He knew he was the only fielder with a chance to reach the ball; it would be too far into shallow right field for an infielder to catch it. He sprinted frantically toward the grassy area behind first and second bases. He needed to leap.

The ball seemed to drop more like a boulder than a baseball. It skidded off the edge of his outstretched glove and then rolled behind him for several more yards as he fell.

Because Cain was prone on the ground from his futile leap, both runners scored. Dugan got a great start leaving first base and slid safely under the catcher's futile tag. Hidalgo, meanwhile, ended up on third base.

Crawford convinced the next batter to swing at a dipping pitch out of the strike zone. The result was a weakly hit groundball that the first baseman handled for an easy out. The Red Sox were ahead 3-2, ready to face the Cubs in the bottom of the ninth inning with their ace relief pitcher, Mack Lewis. Their starting pitcher, Trey Van Ohmann, had pitched a masterful eight innings. Millions of Cubs fans cursed Surrey, Minser, Crawford, and Cain as they mourned the inevitable end.

But this team was different and Greg Clare showed he knew how to manage. The cliché of the ball having eyes proved to be true. The first batter blooped a hit into short centerfield. The second batter bunted the ball and was safe at first when the third baseman's throw pulled the first baseman's foot off first base at the last moment.

Lewis buckled down and struck out the next two batters, including the unfortunate Cain. The next batter, Randy Hickman, doubled into the area of leftfield where the wall jutted out at an unusual angle. The Boston outfielder, not used to playing in Wrigley Field, misplayed the ball.

Both runners scored and the Cubs improbably were World Champions. Just like that.

Surrey endured 20 minutes more of questions about the baseball gods, pitching changes, curses, crosses, and a mind-numbing assortment of other queries. Finally, the communications director shouted "last question" to the media throng.

"So, Mike," asked one local TV reporter, Randy Flynn, a guy he liked pretty well. "I hate to ask this, and I know it's a weird question after you just won the Series, but is your job safe? I mean, you made a lot of questionable moves, not just today but all season. You've had your ups and downs with the owners. And, you've talked openly about whether the Cubs winning the Series would be the right time to step aside."

Surrey sighed and shook his head. He wasn't prepared to ponder it just yet.

"Look," he finally said. "I'm just thrilled we won. The goal now is to put this mythical curse to bed for all time. These guys want to come back next year and do it again. When you get to my age, you always take a minute to assess, but who wouldn't want to be part of what we have going here?"

He took a merciful exit to his office to do something he only did at work on rare occasions. He opened the bottom drawer of the wooden desk and stared at the metal flask with an embossed logo that said "Woodford Reserve."

A long, hard pull of good Kentucky bourbon helped. But not much. The last question haunted him and he was more conflicted than he wanted to admit in public. He knew he wanted to redeem himself, but he knew it wouldn't be easy to repeat. The team surely would lose some key pieces, including at least two starting pitchers, to free agency. You couldn't blame the players for seeking top dollars, especially pitchers, who always were one pitch away from career-ending injuries.

"Okay," he said aloud, tapping a pen three times against the Woodford Reserve bottle. "Let the celebration begin."

3

Washington D.C.
Moments After The World Series

"Holy Cow."

Luke Murphy contemplated those words, the catch-phrase of Harry Caray, the late, legendary Cubs announcer. That's how he felt. At this moment, he was thankful to be with the one person in the world who could hear whatever was on his mind, unfiltered, without having to worry about the implications. It wasn't his wife; certainly not lately. It was Col. Charley Rayburn, his closest friend and chief of staff.

"Nixon, President Goddam Richard Nixon said it: 'I don't know a lot about politics, but I do know a lot about baseball,'" Murphy said. "Me and Nixon. Go figure. I'm thrilled, but shouldn't I be more focused on world peace or something? When it comes to the Cubbies, I'm just another sad schmuck with a cold beer and a dream."

It was 10 minutes after the end of the game. Those were the first words the president had uttered after a "holy shit" he blurted when he saw video of the comet's tail, which was stunning in and of itself, and then watched what happened during the game.

As he talked to Rayburn, Murphy peered intently at the post-game highlights on the state-of-the-art television in the White House movie theater. The scrolling text interplayed the joy of Cubs' historic win with headlines like "Surrey's Fury" and "Cain's not Able."

Murphy let out a sigh. "What's it say that I can't imagine anything worse than the Cubs losing a World Series and anything better than what just happened," he said, then realized how his critics could twist that comment coming from a man who had to deal with a crashing comet along with other assorted crises and world evils.

"Don't ever repeat that," he added as he finally made eye contact with Rayburn. He also adopted a tone of mock authority. "You know what I mean," he said. "But I like that 'schmuck with a cold beer and a dream' line. We can use that sometime when you guys tell me I need to show my human, everyday-guy side."

"Yes, Mr. President," Rayburn said in a tone of mock respect. "Or, should I say Mr. Schmuck?"

Rayburn was one of the few people who could speak harsh truth to power and that was his job now.

"Sir, I'm sorry to interrupt your excitement for Chicago's National League baseball team, but we really need to focus on the consequences of this comet," Rayburn said. "Social media and the networks are going nuts. Every religious kook in the world is going to take some sort of twisted meaning from it."

"You're right Charley, as usual," Murphy said, reluctantly shifting focus to the words of his trusted friend. "When things settle down in a few days, though, make a note that I should call Mike Surrey and wish him well. I hope he keeps his job. Not too many managers get fired after winning the World Series, but it's happened."

"Will do, sir," Rayburn said. "Do you want to know what my biggest fear was with this comet?"

"Yeah. Absolutely."

"None. Zip. We knew it wasn't going to hit our little planet, so I wrote it off as an interesting moment in the name of science. That was before all this Christian symbolism that just played out before billions of people. Nobody saw that coming."

Despite Murphy's joking claims about being a superficial baseball fan, Rayburn was sure the president had been contemplating the same thing.

"Let's have a status briefing as soon as you can assemble the advisors first thing in the morning. Wake me up if you have to," Murphy said after a brief pause. "Based on what I just saw in Chicago, I can believe God is in a weird, message-sending mood today."

***

Upstairs in the White House, Alison Murphy looked at herself in a full-length mirror and tapped in the phone number of her sister in Indiana.

She had just finished a hard, late-night workout in the White House gym. She had tossed off her T-shirt and shorts, so that she was wearing only a sports bra and tiny, light-blue panties. She could see she was still sweaty and her chestnut brown hair with fresh blonde highlights was pulled back in a short ponytail. There were flaws to be sure. While she was in great shape for her age, she scowled at some new, noticeable sags in one or two key spots, some veins that were more obvious and a fresh crease in her forehead.

She had felt an urge just to call Sue and say hello. Her sister's first question was asked in fun with no obvious intent to be critical. "Why aren't you with Luke during his big moment?" Alison could almost see Sue's eyebrows raise and she heard a touch of sarcasm in her tone.

"These men and their sports obsessions. I know how it feels," Sue said. "The only difference is I switched from American baseball to British soccer when I married Clive. Don't show up in our rec room right after Manchester United loses an important match."

Alison really didn't want to drill into the depths the question implied; she just wanted to chat. It would take too long and the time wasn't right to explain: The presidential couple could still put on a good show in public. Privately they struggled to maintain a civil and, at times, even pleasant rapport. Still, any sparks of passion barely qualified as flickers and it had been that way for months. Their relationship felt like a family car with 200,000 miles that had aged past the time when it was anything more than reliable transportation with dents no longer worth fixing. No smart woman wanted to be little more than a useful appendage; like a taxi service you ignore until you need a ride.

Their relationship puzzled her and she had to fight obsessing about it. She thought sometimes there might be more to it, but she dismissed the hypothesis of an affair. Where would he find the time? *Well, JFK and Clinton seemed to squeeze it in,* she thought. *Yeah, pun intended.*

Still, such dalliances didn't fit the character of Luke Murphy, at least as much as a spouse could tell.

"Oh, Sue," she finally said to her sister, complete with a practiced, wry chuckle. "It's the same as with Clive. I can't stand to be around Luke when the Cubs are involved—even when they win. He's impossible. Plus, I'm really not that interested in baseball, and I think it drives him crazy to see me reading a book when he thinks I should be watching the game or listening to him go over the same old ground. I left the room in the sixth inning to get ready to exercise and I don't think he even noticed."

The phone conversation drifted to other sibling topics. Alison Murphy had just reached her milestone 50th birthday—12 years younger than her husband—and she only revealed her age if it really mattered. She acknowledged it was a silly affectation. The age of one of the world's most prominent women hardly was a secret.

"It's a yin-and-yang thing," she said to Sue. "Middle-aged women might say they wished they were 10, 20 or 30 years younger in terms of appearance, but who the hell would want to re-learn what you've already learned?"

"Well, you still look gorgeous," Sue offered. "If I didn't love you like a sister, I'd be jealous. Actually, I am jealous. I'm starving myself with kale chips while you eat nachos and still could pass for someone 15 years younger. Oh, and don't forget you were a brilliant scientist."

As Sue continued talking, Alison stared at her image in a full-length bedroom mirror. Her green-flecked, brown eyes still lit up a room, her figure was trim, her breasts still firm. She needed only a small amount of hair coloring and she could go light with makeup in a pinch.

The amount of cosmetic work on her body was minimal, too, though she had been advised to do more. She told those consultants to get lost; it was her minor protest in support of a woman's right to age with a bit of grace. She had agreed to just a few pulls and tugs under her chin and around her eyes before Luke's last campaign, plus some treatment to get rid of some obvious blue veins emerging on her trim, muscled legs.

"Well, it could be worse," Alison said. "Hey, at least you don't have to spend hours getting ready tomorrow for another formal dinner. Snore."

"Take care Sis," Sue said, ending the call.

She tried to push aside her concerns about her relationship with Luke. Alison didn't just feel neglected as a spouse. For someone with a doctorate in information technology and strong opinions about what the country needed to be doing that it wasn't accomplishing, she felt very underemployed.

But her marriage was the immediate problem. Hard exercise was the most productive way she knew to deflect increasing depression that she hid from everyone—including herself at times. She loved how pushing herself physically made her feel alive. Exercise aroused her in other ways, too. Usually she simply suppressed her urges and passions, but it wasn't always easy after months of deprivation. She shrugged. No intellectual, emotional or sexual fulfillment was going to come from Luke for as far into the future as she could see. She yearned to accept that reality.

She took a long, slow drink from a bottle of orange juice she had brought into her bedroom after the workout. Now she felt relief. There would be no need for at least 12 hours to compose a happy face for the façade of their public lives.

She shrugged inwardly and walked into the master bathroom. She ran the water for the shower to the right temperature; then she stripped and entered. After the shower, she grabbed a towel and dried herself with fast, hard pressure, as though she could soak up her sadness along with the dripping water.

As soon as she exited, she enjoyed a glass of well-chilled chardonnay. That definitely helped, at least for the moment. She enjoyed it well enough to pour herself a second.

***

As Alison Murphy showered, her husband again contemplated the note that his predecessor had left for him in the Oval Office—a tradition that crossed party lines as the outgoing chief executive provided words of wisdom for his successor. For probably the 50th time, he read the copy he had made of the letter, which he kept in the small study where he worked at night in the private part of the White House.

The original remained in the Oval. Nearly four years ago, Murphy had carefully placed it in the center drawer of the sturdy wooden desk used by his hero, President Dwight David Eisenhower. Eight consecutive presidents had used this desk, starting with William Howard Taft, although craftsmen made it for Theodore Roosevelt in 1902. It was a bipartisan desk, too, having served both Democrats and Republicans. That, Murphy mused to himself, made the desk an anachronism in the highly polarized world of Washington today.

The note said this:

> *Dear President Murphy (Luke):*
>
> *One thing I learned in this damn job was that leadership won't mean what you think it means very often. All presidents come into office thinking it means accomplishing the things you hoped to do, or the things you said you would do. Good luck with that.*

Most often, it will mean dealing with all the things you didn't predict, many of which you couldn't possibly predict, though you'll be criticized for your failure to see the future. No one wants to hear that you're not God. But I truly believe successful leaders create the conditions to either minimize the damages or maximize the opportunities that the unexpected things present. If you're really good (and lucky), you will accomplish both those things sometimes.

I only wish I could give you advice on how to get more rest and add more hours to the day, though that would make cable news and social media last even longer than 24 hours a day, so maybe that's not such a good idea.

With the stress, constant criticism and demands on your time, you'll be surprised how easy it is to forget that the presidency is an honor and a privilege only a few will ever know. There were times when I failed to remember that and didn't do enough to suppress selfishness, defensive self-pity or acts based on pure political calculations. You won't be perfect at this either. You wouldn't have this job if you didn't know how to be a self-absorbed, manipulative SOB, but you must try hard to stay away from the dark places—no matter how screwed up, infuriating or weird everything—and I do mean "everything"—will seem at certain moments. You need someone who can kick you in the ass when that's what it takes to push you back to the right place.

Most of all, you must make time to tend to your faith, your family and the handful of friends you know you can trust. This will see you through when all else fails.

Godspeed, and good luck.

Richard Thompson

The letter was signed in the nearly illegible scrawl of President Thompson. Murphy wondered for a moment what he might write when he was done being president—hopefully after completing two full terms. He leaned back in his chair and pulled his arms behind his head in a vain attempt to loosen a kink in his neck, letting a frustrated sigh escape. He stood up and started his walk to the presidential bedroom, pondering his relationship with his wife and other things that even presidents couldn't predict.

"Like comets, crosses and the Cubs," Murphy said out loud a few minutes later as he put on his pajamas. Talk about a totally unpredictable event. He knew the slightest nudge of "bad"—bad news, bad luck or bad reactions—would spin events rapidly out of control. The cable commentators and talk-radio hosts already couldn't resist sensationalizing something that was sensational enough already.

The World Series hadn't ended until almost midnight, and he felt the exhaustion of a long day. He needed a few hours of sleep, finding some comfort that extremely capable people would monitor the world's reaction to the comet.

Alison entered from the bathroom. "I'm going to read for a few minutes before turning in," she said.

"Sure. That's fine," he replied.

Murphy took note of his wife as she sat in the corner chair reading a Vince Flynn political thriller—the types of books that were her guilty pleasure.

"You know, we really can't solve all our foreign problems with cowboy military operatives," he said to her with a patronizing tone he hadn't intended—or maybe he did.

"Flynn knew how to tell a great story, though," she said, annoyed by Luke's barb but having neither the energy nor desire to unearth the passive aggression already buried for the day. "It's a shame he died so young with so many more books left to write. Cancer is evil."

Alison offered a slight wink and crawled into bed next to him. She didn't say anything except a mumbled, "G'night Luke." The First Couple exchanged respectful pecks on one another's cheeks before turning their backs to one another in the king-size bed.

4

Washington D.C.
The Morning After The World Series

"If a big comet hit the Earth, it would cause great devastation. It might cause huge tidal waves and fires and put so much dust and soot in the air that most of the sunlight would be blocked, and plants would die and animals would have nothing to eat. Such events are very rare, however."

Science Line website, University of California Santa Barbara

Murphy shook his head in wonder as he tugged at his tie while skimming the daily news and national security brief prepared by his staff, including expressions of relief that there were no comet-impact scenarios necessary. *The natural world always provides infinite variety and reminders that kept humans in their place,* he thought. It was only 3:45 a.m., 20 minutes after the bedside phone ran and the operator told him Col. Rayburn had scheduled a one-on-one meeting and then a full briefing within an hour.

"So, how is the leader of the free world feeling on this late-fall morning?" Rayburn asked after observing the president had digested the briefing paper.

"Groggy," Murphy answered. "It's bad enough we had to get up this early. I had a lot of trouble getting to sleep last night."

"Is there another crisis that was not brought to the attention of your key advisor?"

"No," Murphy said, too tired for the moment to offer a witty comeback. "No, it wasn't that, and it wasn't the Cubs almost losing because of the comet. Actually, Alison and I had a fight after that endless luncheon yesterday before the game. You know, the lunch saluting some of our Middle Eastern friends—the guys with the oil and the centuries-old grudges among themselves."

"Yeah, I know," Rayburn said. "I started getting the nods before dessert, fought it like a strong, old soldier and didn't do anything to violate protocol. I don't mean to pry, but if you want to talk about things, I'm around."

Murphy paused for a moment and Rayburn could tell his friend was fighting his usual instinct not to get terribly introspective.

"Well, isn't it funny how, with all the bullshit going on in the world, personal stuff still keeps you up at night more often?" Murphy finally said. "Let's just say I'm not exactly living up to her expectations in a certain department. I imagine it took a lot for her to even bring it up. It really wasn't about sex as much as, well, she senses we just aren't the team we used to be. I guess she has a point. I gave her the 'Gee, sorry, I'm the busy, stressed-out Leader of the Free World' excuse."

"I'm not taking sides between two people I like," Rayburn said. "But, you have a high-stress job and you're just past 60 now. I mean, we all have problems from time to time. No biggie—I admit that pun was intended."

"Well, aren't you the comic genius," Murphy offered. "Let's just leave it at that."

"Okay, but remember I'm here."

"So, what do you make of this cross thing?" he asked, gladly changing the subject. "Is it just going to be one of those oddball stories that makes us all stand at attention for a few minutes and then we move on? Or, is some fringe group going to seize on this as their call to do something radical in the name of religion?"

"It'll be a real problem," Rayburn said with a tone of certitude. "The only question is the intensity of the reaction.

And it's not hard to understand why. Once you see this, it's something you never forget. It's haunting. Spiritual. I can understand how people would see it as a sign from God. It looks like the crucifix is ready to melt into the side of the blackened moon. The astronomers say it's more than a one-in-a-billion-years coincidence that this would happen at the same time as an eclipse. On top of that, it's a damn comet named after Christianity's most famous, most accurate prophet.

"So, yeah, that's why we had to get going this morning. We've juggled your schedule. A more complete briefing is first up after we're done with our one-on-one."

Murphy had watched the video several times as well before going to bed. He nodded in agreement with every word Rayburn had said.

"The cross adds whole new layers of complexities," Murphy said. "Who knew? It's a weird problem we couldn't have predicted. All we were concerned about was whether there was even a remote chance that the impact calculations were wrong and it might hit us."

"I know. You asked everyone over and over," Rayburn recalled.

***

They had gathered in one of the White House briefing rooms about a month earlier. Everyone stood when Murphy walked into the room.

"At ease," he said with a slight grin as he eased into the chair at the head of the long table. "President Thompson warned me there would be days like this and he was right. Sometimes this job amazes me. You run for office on the economy, the debt and working for world peace, but you never really know what's going to blow. Now, we have to be experts on the geology and trajectory of comets. Help me."

That was a nod to Dr. Mary Hempfling, his chief science advisor, whose team had been working non-stop for three days to understand and explain comet behavior after some self-styled, amateur scientists hypothesized that solar activity might cause Esaias to make an orbit change that could send it crashing into the planet.

Reputable astronomers quickly refuted the reports and there was speculation that the "amateur scientists" actually were fake news hoaxsters from Belarus. It didn't matter. Once social media amplified the reports into tidal waves of fear-sharing, global news organizations followed with endless hours of barely informed speculation. Billions of people panicked. Quotes from the Biblical book of Revelations started trending on Google and Twitter.

"We've been playing catch-up," Hempfling said, quickly and crisply pronouncing every word in a clipped monotone practiced during years of serving in the military and giving scientific presentations. "We're playing catch-up not only in terms of the science involved but also with public opinion. Too many people don't believe the calculations. We do. To put it succinctly, Mr. President, we believe it'll be quite a show for observers, particularly because the comet is so unusually close. But, that's it. We do not—repeat "not"—see an impact event that will send the world back into an Ice Age or anything like that."

"Talk to me about the science of these things," Murphy said. "Give me the basics."

"First of all, comet hits are rare; way rarer than meteors hitting the Earth," the science advisor said and then paused. "Sir, we prepared a few slides. It'll be easier just to follow along with what NASA provided."

"Here," she said, putting on-screen the photos, computer graphics and artists' renderings she had received from the U.S. space agency that went along with her prepared text:

> A comet's nucleus is like a dirty snowball made of ice. As the comet gets closer to the Sun, some of the ice starts to melt and boil off, along with particles of dust. These particles and gases make a cloud around the nucleus, called a coma. The coma is lit by the Sun.

> The sunlight also pushes this material into the beautiful brightly lit tail of the comet. …
>
> The very black material on the surface is carbon-based material similar to the greasy black goo that burns onto your barbecue grill. The comet originally formed from ices (mostly water ice), silicate dust (like powdered beach sand), and this type of black space gunk.
>
> Some parts of the nucleus are smooth and young, while other areas are cratered and old.

"Now, we know quite a bit about comets from recent space explorations, but obviously we aren't able to study comets in person. We'd like to know more about the internal materials, for example. Are they hard as diamonds, squishy as mud or something in between?" she said.

"So, just out of curiosity, do we know what happens if one of these collides with the planet?" Rayburn asked. "Could the hype we're seeing from some of the extremists and Armageddon types have any chance of being true?"

"Well, unfortunately, it's not far from the truth conceptually. Given the right conditions, conditions that don't exist in this case, it could be very bad," Hempfling said. "We hear more about asteroids and meteorites, because there are more of them. The way to look at it, really simplified, is that an asteroid is a big chunk of rock with some ice, and a comet is a big chunk of ice with some rock.

"But, as a practical matter, it really doesn't matter if either one hits the surface head-on," she continued. "Scientists believe it could be unbelievably devastating. And a comet could hit at three times the speed of an asteroid, magnifying the power of the impact."

"What are we talking about? Ice Age? Extinction?" Murphy asked.

"I won't sugar-coat it, sir," Hempfling said. "Maybe it wouldn't be that bad, but it would be awful, and that's before you consider the economic impacts of everything from pure panic to global crop failures and darkened, ash-filled skies for maybe years. These things have nuclei around 10 miles wide. Their tails can be hundreds of thousands, millions, of miles long. Any object 10-miles wide is going to do a lot of damage. Now, imagine it slamming into a populated area at a speed of 37 miles per second."

As though the moment had been scripted, everyone in the room paused.

***

Murphy pushed his mind back to the business of the morning. "What else is up?" he asked Rayburn, almost too abruptly as it visibly jarred the chief of staff, who was busily looking at text messages.

"The Number Two story is still the famine in China," Rayburn said. "Speaking of the end of days, the Chinese are enduring a drought that would be of Biblical proportions if all their leaders weren't atheists—at least publicly. Our negotiators are working with them, but we have scarcity issues of our own. They don't like the prices we're quoting. Of course, the companies that include several major campaign contributors love these prices."

"I'm sure they do," Murphy said. "I told the schedulers to avoid any events in which I'm in earshot of these CEOs until this settles down. We can't be seen to be profiteering."

"The price of corn already has tripled in the past month," Rayburn said. "That ripples out into everything. And, of course, selling more corn to China will drive up prices in the USA."

Murphy knew that was true. Few everyday citizens understood the economics of corn. You could make a case that skyrocketing corn prices damaged the economy more than oil prices. Corn and its byproducts went into everything from food and cattle feed to plastics and ethanol gasoline. It just wasn't as sexy a topic.

The Chinese situation was dominating world news. Parts of China hadn't had measurable rain for two growing seasons. For all China's economic explosion had brought its people, the drought bluntly exposed the Chinese leaders as helpless against this force of nature.

"Without a favorable deal from trading partners, they can't feed their own people without creating inflation that would shake their stability," Rayburn reminded Murphy. "These guys are really, really nervous. Nervous guys that own more than a trillion of our debt and also own nuclear weapons with working missiles make ME nervous."

"Agreed," Murphy said. "Charley, I'm up way too early to be having this conversation. You're holding out on me. What's next?"

"What's next is the full briefing on the comet aftermath," Rayburn said.

"By the way, I said I want to make a personal call to Mike Surrey later today," Murphy said. "Get that on my schedule."

"Oh, yeah, that's your top priority," Rayburn said. "Aren't you glad I can get away with being sarcastic with the Leader of the Free World? Remember, I'm the guy who can kick you in the ass when you need it."

"Be careful. I might ask Surrey to take your job," Murphy responded.

"You've seen how he manages. I'd be a little concerned with his strategic thinking," Rayburn said. Murphy gave him a look that said, "Touché."

A sharp knock on the door interrupted them just as Rayburn started to rise from his seat.

"Yes," Rayburn said. "What is it?"

A military aide entered, looked at the two men and shrugged his shoulders with a "pardon-the-interruption" gesture but quickly got to the point as he was trained to do in emergencies, which everyone understood.

"Mr. President, Col. Rayburn," he said. "They asked me to inform you immediately about a Bali situation."

"A Bali situation?" Murphy asked. "What do you mean?"

The aide handed Rayburn a mini iPad and Murphy could see it had four or five sentences of text. After reading it, Rayburn uttered a long, drawn out, "Shit."

"This is unbelievable," he said.

"What?" Murphy asked, growing impatient.

"A damn meteor. A meteor no one knew about just hit something in Bali," Rayburn replied, his voice sounding tense and concerned at a level Murphy rarely heard. "So, first we've got a comet with a tail shaped like a damn cross and now we have damage in an area targeted by Islamic extremists. To make matters worse, it's in Indonesia, which just happens to be the country with the world's largest Muslim population."

Rayburn looked directly at Murphy until he made strong eye contact. "The symbolism of this is more than scary Mr. President," Rayburn said. "There will be strong reactions. My advice is to buckle up and sneak in some rest when you can for the next few days."

5

Oregon | The Day After The World Series

When he was hiking in the mountains, Reggie Fox made it a point to stay "off the grid" as much he could. Political consulting could completely consume someone, with the only goal to win at any cost.

It also was very measurable. While you could build your practice by doing "better than expectations" with candidates who weren't given much of a chance, the consultants whose candidates won were the ones who stayed busy and got rich. Consultants to winning campaigns also were the ones whose egos got stoked by talk-show appearances, Politico.com articles, foreign consulting junkets and $50,000 speaking engagements.

Fox's success with conservative candidates in particular had given him enough of a name that he could hop off the grid now and then, as long as he didn't do so too often. He wanted a break during this election cycle.

With that in mind, he had kept his cell phone with him but turned off for most of the hike through the Cascades. To not have one with him, especially this late in the fall, would be stupid. A phone could save your life in the wilderness. But, short of an emergency, he had no plans to engage with the world until he and Trent reached the parking lot in the state forest where he had parked his new Land Rover. After they packed the backpacks, tent, sleeping bags and other gear, they stood outside the SUV for another minute, soaking in a final moment of clear, mountain views and sweet air before returning to Seattle.

As soon as he had settled into the tan leather driver's seat, he activated his Korean phone, which reminded him of how lobbying advice he gave that corporation not only paid well and protected their patents but ensured he had the latest, greatest products.

"Wow," Fox said. "Unreal."

"What's up?" Trent Schuller asked.

"I have a lot of voicemails. I mean, I always have a lot of voicemails if I'm out of action a couple days, but this is crazy," he said. "Basically, my mailbox is full. I think there are a few hundred texts, too."

One text particularly caught his attention.

"It's Lydia," he said. "I have a text from freakin' Lydia Nicks. She sent me a text. All it says is 'Call Me.'"

"The Senator from Wisconsin?" Schuller said. "I thought you and her were on the outs."

"Yeah, me too. Too much history and we just disagreed too much on her positions and her strategy," Fox added as he quickly scrolled through texts and voicemails to see if there were any urgent names or numbers he recognized.

Schuller was in the act of lighting a Cuban cigar; the last one he had with him as a reward for completing a strenuous hike. He placed his arm on the sill of the rolled-down window. He took a long drag off the Cuban and swiveled his head to look directly at Fox.

"Reg, how long have we been together?"

"Ten years," Fox replied in a distracted voice. "Probably more. Why?"

"Would you say I know you as well as anyone."

"You know me as well as anyone."

"There's no reason for us to move this car out of this parking space until you call her," Schuller said. "You aren't going to be worth shit until you find out what she wants."

Fox glared at Schuller for a moment. The memories and reasons for his feelings about Nicks weren't all that pleasant—well, that wasn't 100 percent true as he recalled one adventurous night they both agreed would not be mentioned again. Then he finished processing his partner's words.

"Yeah," he conceded. "Yeah. Okay. Do you mind going outside for a minute?"

"Sure. I just hope a ranger doesn't see me smoking in a no-smoking zone, which I think is everywhere in Oregon these days except your kitchen between 10:10 and 10:20 p.m."

Fox tapped the icon for Lydia Nicks' number as Schuller exited the car. He activated the driver's side switch so that the passenger-side power window would go back up. Standing outside in the empty parking lot, amid the tall pines and the audible trickle of a mountain stream just to the south, Schuller observed Fox talking for less than a minute. Then the passenger window powered back down.

"Okay," Fox said to Schuller through the open window. "Let's go."

"Don't play games, Reg. You know I'm dying to know what she had to say."

"Well, it's pretty basic," Fox said. "I'm going to Wisconsin, to her home outside Appleton actually, as soon as I can make the arrangements."

"You're going to Wisconsin?"

"There's an echo in here."

"Okay, I'll bite. Why?"

"Total, 100 percent secrecy."

"Agreed. Of course."

"I remember exactly what she said. She said, 'Reg, we need to talk. Have you seen the news? After what happened last night, I've made a decision. We're going to take down Luke Murphy. You're the best person to help us do this. I know a sign when I see it. I'm supposed to run for president. I'm the one who can keep the world from going to hell.'"

6

Chicago | The Day After The World Series

Sleep wouldn't come for either Boston's star pitcher or the Chicago manager, though for very different reasons.

Mike Surrey sat at his kitchen table, already on his third cup of coffee at 8 a.m. after a fitful, restless night, tapping the beat to a song by the late guitarist Danny Gatton on his tabletop. Gatton, sometimes called "the world's greatest unknown guitarist," was a legend among those who obsessed great blues and rock guitarists—people like Surrey. Gatton often used a foaming beer bottle instead of a conventional glass slide on his left hand to play slide guitar at his live shows. How could you not like a guy like that? Music always offered Surrey's best and most effective escape from the stresses of reality.

The song was a fun one—Gatton's cover of the theme song to "The Simpsons" television show, which seemed somehow wildly appropriate at the moment. Sometimes Surrey felt like Lisa Simpson, the daughter of the satirical cartoon family. She was bright, sensitive and a bit misunderstood. She usually turned out to be right. Today, however, he felt more like the idiot father, Homer Simpson, who messed up even when he was trying to help.

He knew that, in the eyes of many, the Cubs had won the National League title and ultimately the World Series in spite of him, not because of him. Talk radio hosts like Walters were happy to pounce on every opportunity to second-guess and he had just handed them a long match after pouring jet fuel on himself.

He knew what was coming: His players weren't as prepared as they should have been. He didn't know how to manage his pitchers. Sometimes he let his temper get the best of him. Other times, he wasn't emotional enough, the stand-offish guy with the Ivy League degree. They said he coddled his players; that he made too many unconventional decisions. And he was really going to hear about it from the League office for his postgame comments about the umpiring.

You tuned out as much as you could, but you still heard it. The Cubs had given him a great opportunity and he felt as though he had delivered—their first World Series appearance since 1945 and first title since 1908. He wanted to be the guy who turned one-time success into a dynasty.

Being a coach or manager in professional sports was an occupation like no other. "Imagine," he once told an interviewer, "taking a job knowing there was a 90 percent probability of being fired in five years or less? That's what we do. Of course, it's also a profession where most of us keep finding ways to get hired again no matter how often we've been fired. We're recycled more than the glass in a beer bottle."

He shook his head and laughed. The interviewer did, too.

Leaving on your own terms was almost as rare as, well, the Cubs winning the World Series.

Meanwhile, Trey Van Ohmann, Boston's star pitcher, sat in the Starbucks next door to the downtown Chicago hotel where the Red Sox had stayed. Functioning on about three hours of sleep. Van Ohmann sought strong coffee and time to collect his thoughts before the flight back to Boston and the inevitable second-guessing.

He was wearing sunglasses and a "Bass Pro Shop" baseball hat. Many hours of fly fishing in his home state of Idaho and nearby Montana had weathered the hat and faded its once-bright orange into more of a milky yellow. The brim was bent into a deep, inverted "U" shape that covered much of his face. There weren't many people around either. He loved the solitude and pure beauty of fly fishing, almost as much as he loved the memories the hat evoked of his late father teaching him how to tie flies and master the touch to casting as a young boy. The hat had traveled with him at every stop in his career and served him well now that he was a reluctant star in sports-celebrity nation.

He enjoyed the anonymity the early morning brought in Chicago. In Boston, autograph-seekers already would have formed a line outside the coffee-shop door. Even though he usually was quite comfortable in solitude, he had felt the walls of his hotel room closing in on him during this particular morning. Still, he craved privacy for the thoughts he needed to sift. Sitting in the corner at Starbucks, he made a show of looking as absorbed as possible, staring intently at his phone or taking gulps from his cup of black coffee.

What he saw surprised him. On his phone, he skimmed the headlines. He hadn't turned on the television before heading out. He expected to see a lot of commentary about how maybe the curse had shifted back to Boston.

There also was a lot about what happened after the game—from Bali. He saw videos from Indonesia that showed flames, people screaming and outbursts of religious fervor from both Christians and Muslims. The Islamic voices shouting "call for jihad" and Christian voices shouting "end of days" submerged any voices of reason. Suddenly the comet Esaias was much more than an ironic sports story that almost gave the Red Sox the World Championship.

It was disturbing, but he felt exhausted and had other things to think about, so his mind drifted back to his immediate concerns.

He had said all the right things to the media about "trying my best to win for my Dad." However, only a handful of people, mainly FBI agents and the Secret Service, knew that the unexpected death of Don Van Ohmann before Game Six of the World Series wasn't a heart attack along a lonely stretch of Idaho highway as many suspected but likely a murder by a hacker who got into the pickup truck's OnStar system and caused the truck to barrel into the Lochsa River west of Missoula, Montana. It would all come out soon enough, unleashing a media frenzy that Van Ohmann hoped to avoid as much as possible.

He knew it was all somehow connected to the reason the teams had to play Game Seven twice. The crazed fan who probably killed Van Ohmann's dad logically assumed that the star represented Boston's best chance to win and either wouldn't pitch at all or be able to stay focused if he tried to take the mound. Tommy Czerski almost succeeded. Pitching in those games was the hardest thing he had ever done.

The authorities told him on the morning of the "real" Game Seven they were still trying to piece everything together.

"So, who is going to be accountable for killing my father?" Van Ohmann had asked FBI Agent William Beatrice in an early-morning call.

"Czerski, the guy who probably did it, is dead," Beatrice said in his best, measured agent's monotone. He pronounced the name SHUR-skee, with the accent on the first syllable. "We know he was connected to the eco-terror group that tried to kill the president, but we don't know if this was their direction, his solo effort or some combination of both.

"So, no one else is going to be held accountable?"

"Trey, it's too early," Beatrice responded. "But, you know, Czerski was motivated enough and skilled enough to do that on his own. There may be no one else to hold directly accountable."

"All due respect, that's not good enough, Agent Beatrice," Van Ohmann said, trying to put some firmness into his voice. "Not for me or my brothers back in Idaho."

"I'm telling it straight with you, Trey," Beatrice said. "That's basically what we know. If we learn more that we can possibly share, you'll know that, too. These guys we arrested say that part was all Czerski, but maybe they know more than they're saying. My advice is to grieve your father and then give yourself a break. We won't stop working on it."

After Beatrice ended the call, Van Ohmann continued to analyze the price of fame. If he hadn't sought fortune throwing a baseball, he'd be back in Idaho. His father would be alive. In fact, his widowed father—his best friend and biggest fan—was hurrying to get to Missoula in case he needed to catch a plane to Chicago to watch Trey pitch Game Seven.

So, yeah. It was sort of his fault.

Van Ohmann went back to his phone and tapped to the "most recent" call list until he saw the mobile number for his agent, Adam Zerbey.

Zerbey answered the call and it was obvious the call interrupted a good night's sleep, because it was two hours earlier in San Diego. Van Ohmann pushed aside a brief moment of jealousy for anyone who felt well rested.

"Yo, Trey," Zerbey said. "Hey, I'm so sorry you guys couldn't pull it out at the end. That comet. Craziest thing I've ever seen.". Zerbey stopped at that point, realizing he hadn't talked to Van Ohmann since just after his father's death. "Hey, I'm so sorry about your Dad, man. I'll be at the funeral and be there for anything else you need. Are you doing okay?"

"Couldn't sleep much," he said, then quickly got to the point, as was his habit. "What if I took next season off?"

There was a long pause.

"This is more about your Dad than losing the game, right?" he finally said.

"Yeah, Adam, it is."

"Trey, you know I have a financial interest in you, so I'm conflicted," Zerbey said. "Keep that in mind when I say I don't think that's a good idea. Christ, you haven't had time to even mourn. Take some time now. Go home; spend some time with your brothers. Think about it some more before you make a final decision. Can you do that?"

"Yeah," Van Ohmann replied. "I can. I owe you that much and I'd hate to see you go hungry."

7

Washington D.C.
The Day After The World Series

As news of the Esaias cross and the meteorite strike that quickly followed swept across the globe, Charley Rayburn led a hastily prepared briefing.

"Until yesterday, few Americans knew anything about the island of Bali," Rayburn stated, looking at Murphy. "The ones who did, like me and probably you, probably had a vague memory of a 2002 Islamic terrorist bombing that killed 202 people."

"Bali!" the president exclaimed to Rayburn, forgetting for a moment his recent resolve to swear less as he grasped the implications of the comet's crash. "I'll tell you my question: 'You're kidding me, right?'"

"Yeah," Rayburn said. "Bali. And it gets worse."

"Worse?"

"Well, we know a few things that haven't been reported yet, but it won't be long. The meteorite was big, probably tons, so there was a lot left even after it burned up in the atmosphere. And, yeah, in case you're wondering, there's precedent for them to go undiscovered."

Rayburn started down at the briefing memo on his iPad and continued, reading aloud, "In early 2013, a meteor that weighed more than 500 kilotons exploded over Chelyabinsk in central Russia. About 1,500 people were injured and buildings were damaged from the explosion. Astronomers didn't see it because it was relatively small—and it was coming in with the sun glare behind it, blinding telescopes. They pulled a 1,300-pound fragment out of a nearby lake a few months later."

Rayburn looked up before continuing.

"Thank God the Bali meteor wasn't that big, but this time we have fatalities. Some big chunks landed. They fell right at the spot of the bombing memorial. I don't have the whole death toll yet and there were fires and building collapses. We know that the debris killed six young Muslim men from Jakarta who had stopped at the memorial after hanging out on the beach. I'm sure you can see the symbolism. We're still sorting it all out."

"So, after a comet shaped like a cross shocked the world, a meteor caused the deaths of a bunch of Muslims at the site of one of the worst bombings ever carried out after the World Trade Center attacks in 2001." Murphy summarized. "And I also suppose you're going to tell me that, far as we know, the victims were solid citizens."

"It's all true," Rayburn said, unable to suppress a sharp outward breath as he processed all the twists events might be taking. "They were college students. Four of them were studying to be teachers even. They come from good, devout families with no overt suspicions about terrorist ties. The other two—we're not so sure—but they look solid, too. You'll learn more as soon as we do."

"What's the reaction so far?" Murphy said in a terse, clipped tone.

"Well, the Muslim world is one thing. In some ways, our own country maybe worries me more. The crazy-right, fundamentalist blogs already are seeing symbolism; they're already quoting verses from Revelations," Rayburn said, gazing down at a piece of paper. "One verse flying around is Revelations Chapter 8, Verse 10. Let me read you part of it."

Rayburn lifted a Bible from his lap. Murphy could see he had bookmarked the spot as Rayburn fanned open the pages. Rayburn's voice was unusually quiet as he read.

"It goes like this, 'the third angel sounded his trumpet and a great star, blazing like a torch, fell from the sky,' and then it goes on to say, 'and many people died from the waters that had become bitter.'"

Rayburn looked up at his friend, the commander-in-chief of the greatest military force the world had ever known and leader of a nation that seemed increasingly at war with itself, polarized with no consensus on any direction on the major issues of the day. Neither man needed to comment as they pondered the power of spiritual forces—real or imagined; Christian or Muslim.

"We've prepared some background on Bali that you might want to look at to refresh yourself, sir. A bunch of people have worked pretty hard in the last few hours to pull this together for you."

"It must be serious," Murphy said, trying to lighten his own mood as much as Rayburn's. "You just called me 'sir,' and you never do that unless it's serious."

With that, Murphy skimmed through the briefing paper, reminding himself to find time to concentrate in more depth later, though knowing that the time to actually do that was unlikely to materialize.

He remembered a few details of the 2002 Bali incident from his time in Congress. The island was one of the most popular tourist areas in Asia. The briefing paper described the dramatic transformation of the Kuta district in southern Bali from sleepy fishing villages into a major resort area attracting tourists from around the world. In particular, gorgeous beaches and big waves drew Australian surfers like sun-drenched magnets.

With a population of more than 4 million, more than 8 out of 10 Bali residents were Hindu. Islam practitioners numbered 13 percent and Christians made up only 2 percent of the population.

On Oct 12, 2002, Jemaah Islamiyah, a violent, extremist Islamist group, exploded three bombs, targeting an area that, to them, symbolized Western decadence. A suicide bomber with a backpack device entered the Kuta nightclub district and blew himself up. Then a large car bomb exploded. A small device also exploded outside the U.S. consulate further away, but it didn't do much damage.

However, the bombs in the nightclub district were devastating. The attack killed 202 people, including 88 Australians, 38 Indonesians, 27 Britons, seven Americans, six Swedes and three Danes. Another 240 people were injured. A cassette tape—perhaps the voice of Osama bin Laden himself—stated the bombings had two purposes: Punish Indonesia for supporting the war on terror and send a message to Australia for its role in liberating the southeast Asian nation of East Timor, another place of frequent violent clashes between warring factions.

Then, in 2005, a second Bali bombing killed another 26 people.

Officials had erected a memorial site across the street from the demolished Sari Club. Now, once again, thanks to Esaias, chaos marked the same spot.

Murphy pondered the implications of the latest State Department assessment in the report. His experts suggested that Bali's economy had recovered nicely since 2005. Indonesian officials received accolades for rooting out militants; they believed the bombing perpetrators had been brought to justice. Tourism started booming again. Worldwide conferences and conventions returned, using a new international airport terminal. A toll road opened to exclusive resort areas.

But recently, the report said in the dry, bureaucratic-speak of government officials everywhere, "numerous variables, events and circumstantial evidence have caused us to project that desirable regional stability and economic progress are likely to be threatened by heightened risk factors."

Murphy read that sentence and immediately recalled how much Rayburn hated reports that buried the message under passive prose. A military man who knew lives could be lost when reports lacked clarity, Rayburn always did his best to help Murphy decipher not only the words but the level of urgency those words implied. He glanced at the yellow sticky note Rayburn had placed on that page of the report and stifled a brief grin. He had seen that hand-written line before; a shorthand summary meant for Murphy's eyes only that used the PM (President Murphy) and CR (Charley Rayburn) abbreviations they initialed for each other:

"Translation for PM: Things appear headed down the crapper. CR"

Murphy had to agree. Terrorism still lurked in Bali's shadows. The latest CIA analysis accentuated concerns in the State Department report, noting "increasing evidence that radical Islamists are returning to Bali after operating with jihadists in Syria and Iraq."

The final page of the briefing report noted that events could trigger new rounds of violence far less dramatic than the comet, so repercussions appeared likely.

"Well, it really doesn't seem fair," Murphy said, looking up at Rayburn. "At least they can't blame a meteor on us."

"Don't be so sure," Rayburn said. "Not that these misguided assholes need provocation, but there will be people on our side who, unintentionally or not, are going to exploit this. No matter how many condolences and how much help we offer the Indonesians, the ripples have started. They could be more like tidal waves."

8

Chicago | Two Days After The World Series

Bob Walters was a humbler man these days, but he mostly tried to keep it to himself. Still, it was obvious to a handful of others that included Aimee, Mickey, and his colleague from childhood, Scott "Moose" Skowron. He realized "Humbler Bob" was no secret to those he saw at Alcoholics Anonymous meetings. He had attended three sessions in the past few days and was feeling proud for going again, though he knew excessive pride could spell danger for a boozer.

Heavily promoted on Chicago radio station WCO as "the man Cub fans love to hate," he still had a public image to maintain. The events at the end of the World Series had nearly resulted in Aimee's death and she still was dealing with the physical injuries and trauma of the kidnapping. He couldn't put the events out of his mind and doubted he ever could. The bastards had made him watch. They had hung her nearly naked by the arms while a black-masked operative brutally administered a bullwhip with promises of greater pain to come. The goal: Manipulate him into helping an assassination plot against President Murphy, his boyhood friend from the Chicago suburb of Palatine. They almost succeeded.

The weird irony—so weird that it felt wrong to even acknowledge it—was that Aimee's ordeal had created a chance to restore relations with Mickey, his second ex-wife and Aimee's mom. He didn't know to act on those feelings, or even if he should, but he wanted to win her back. Mickey had returned to her job teaching film studies at Western Illinois University in Macomb, a small town in rural, downstate Illinois. In the immediate aftermath, he sensed that Mickey, too, felt a glimmer of respect for him; something he hadn't come close to detecting since Aimee's sister had died in an accident caused by his drunken driving.

On the air, though, no one was interested in mellow, thoughtful, talk-show hosts who saw the nuances and gray shades of life. And, in a sports-mad town like Chicago, there always was plenty to scream and shout about. The Cubs' success at finally winning the World Series simply amplified the volume.

"How long? How long? How long?" he repeated into the microphone during his afternoon show. "How long does Mike Surrey last as the manager? How long does management put up with this Ivy Leaguer who might have a lot of book smarts but gets an 'F' in baseball knowledge? How long? What do you think, my listeners? The lines are open! Let's start with Billy from Berwyn."

"Yo, Bob," said Billy on the air. "I don't see how you can blame Surrey for Cain's brain-freeze in the outfield."

"Get off the Surrey Train. It's called coaching and teaching focus, Billy," Walters responded. "Great players NEVER, and I mean NEVER, lose their focus. Great managers TEACH IT. Cain catches the ball and the Cubs don't need a miracle finish. Am I right?"

"Seems like a stretch," Billy from Berwyn said.

"You seem like a stretch, Billy, but thanks for the call," Bob said with his "radio laugh" backing it up—a low-register chuckle punctuated by a "humph" sound.

"Okay, we've got to sell some Buicks and Cadillacs for Tony Singleton, Chicagoland's greatest car dealer, during the next break while I check with Moose for more of Mike Surrey's shameful statistics," Walters said. "We'll be right back."

As soon as the "on air" light dimmed, Walters buzzed Scott "Moose" Skowron, who was sitting in the adjoining room feverishly working at a keyboard surrounded by three large monitors. Walters could see some type of complicated Excel spreadsheet on one screen and unflattering pictures of Mike Surrey through the years that Moose must have been preparing for the "B-Walt" sports blog that was by far the most popular part of WCO's otherwise pedestrian efforts to stay relevant in the digital age.

Walter's relationship with Skowron was beyond complicated. Nicknamed "Moose" for his athletic prowess and a build similar to "Moose" Skowron, a Major League baseball star from an earlier era, Skowron became wheelchair bound in a childhood skirmish with Walters, Murphy and their friend Meg Williamson. Skowron had started it with a bullying taunt. Murphy clobbered Skowron with an icy snowball that caused Skowron to hit his head on a sidewalk. Walters took the blame to protect his friend and spent most of his eighth-grade year in a juvenile home.

Years later, Skowron approached Walters to reconnect. He had channeled his sports passions into number-crunching and computer-based research skills that Walters thought the CIA could've used to stop bin Laden a year or two faster. Working with Walters had made Skowron a celebrity, particularly now that Murphy's childhood secret had been exposed.

What had started out as a fair trade for childhood sins had grown into a reasonable proximity of friendship. Professionally, Skowron had been a godsend for Walters. Moose's quick mental reflexes, knowledge of sports and tech skills meant Walters had access to the freshest, best, funniest and most provocative material on sports-talk radio. Skowron had turned down numerous job offers from ESPN and several national sports websites.

Just lately, Walters had been toying with the idea of asking Skowron if he wanted to switch from sports to political talk, an increasingly tired radio format that was badly in need of fresh approaches. Murphy imagined the two of them moving beyond the confines of Chicago radio. Stations across the country would gobble them up. They might even get a segment on cable news. The comet-and-meteor incident was a good example of an issue they could tackle. Religious zealots and demagogues already were stroking it for maximum impact. Muslim fundamentalists had just attacked a Christian family in Bali. So far, the U.S. government had done nothing but send sympathy for the victims.

But the immediate challenge was the next show.

"Moose," Walters said over the intercom. "Have you finished the stats on Surrey?"

"Bob, this is good stuff," Skowron said in his slow-but-steady speech pattern, an outgrowth of the paralysis and long recovery from the childhood injury. "What I'm sending is a top-ten list I'm calling 'Mike's Managerial Miscues.' We'll start, of course, with the way he used his pitching staff in the World Series."

"That'll work," Walters said. "I'll go with that as soon as we're back on air. And it'll be a great one for the blog and social media. I can use that live from Eger's Pub the next time we're over there, too. The crowd will turn it up a notch."

"Check on all that," Skowron replied. "Hey, hang on, one of my tipsters is on the phone."

Skowron answered his cellphone and saw on the caller ID that it was one of his sources, a member of the Cubs' staff. Like most Major League teams, the Cubs had their own group of computer and statistics geeks who analyzed performance of players in the Cubs' system, young prospects they might draft or players on other teams that could interest them.

Helping Moose Skowron or Bob Walters would get you fired from the Cubs, but sports-statistics freaks naturally gravitated to one another. Skowron had carefully cultivated that interest with Jason Conkle, a young data analyst, by passing along some names of interesting prospects he had uncovered that the Cubs' brain trust had missed.

Skowron found one prospect, Devon Dozier, based on a few stories about him in an African-American newspaper in Cleveland. Scouts now pegged Dozier as a sure-fire star and the top shortstop prospect in all of baseball. Skowron let Conkle take credit for the find, which had elevated Conkle's organizational status greatly. To return the favor, Conkle offered tips under rules of strict confidentiality. Even Walters didn't know Jason Conkle was Moose Skowron's primary source for Cubs gossip.

"Hey, Moose. It's Jason," Conkle said. "I'm giving you a 60-minute heads up and then you have to forget where you heard it."

"Sure, Jason," Skowron said. "I know the drill. What's up."

"Mike Surrey will be fired as the manager. I just saw the draft of the news release. Take it to the bank. They're talking to him now."

9

Chicago | One Week After The Surrey Firing

During the last commercial break before the end of his show, Walters' phone buzzed with a text message from the station manager, Davis Bryant. "Stop by ASAP after show" was all it said.

Curious, Walters walked down the hall of the WCO studios to Bryant's corner office, slightly limping because his bad knee—the one he hurt in the accident that killed his daughter—was bothering him.

"He's expecting me," Walters said, walking past Bryant's assistant, Shawna Riggs, and opening the door without knocking or waiting.

Bryant peered up from his monitor, giving him a mock glare that would have been scary to an outsider since he had a shaved, bald head and the build of an NFL linebacker. "Why should you have to knock or be asked in like everyone else?" he said.

"Hey, 'Big D,' I think that's in the contract when you're a ratings champ, especially after a big scoop like the Surrey firing," Walters said.

"Yeah, just remember, this is radio. You can move from superstar to a drooling idiot with one bad ratings book. Things that go up come down and the fall ain't fun," Bryant said, sitting back in his chair and pausing for a moment. "Anyway, I can't believe I'm asking you for advice, but I have an idea you need to keep to yourself for now."

"Wow, this is a crazy day," Walters said. "First, Surrey gets axed, and I always thought you only liked me for my looks."

"Yeah, you're my wet dream for sure. Let's see. You're divorced. Twice. You're out of shape. You smoke too much. You're 10 years older than me. And, oh yeah, we're the same sex. I'm hot already," Bryant said. "Seriously, Bob, we all know your show is going well, but the station needs another fresh voice. I've got to get those two idiots in the morning replaced before we get sued for broadcast malpractice, or I get fired."

Bryant was referring to Trevor Brunson and Billy Terwilliger. "Their ratings are in the dumps," Bryant said. "That's actually a good description of what happens when you combine toilet humor and sports clichés."

"I've been telling you that for six months," Walters responded. "Your predecessor bought low and they went lower."

"So, I've got an idea. It's in the spirit of the crazy idea that Emilio Profita had when he owned this station. Remember? He got disgusted with the Cubs and rescued you from being a newspaper columnist. How'd you like to be in the roll-it-up-and-throw-it-in-the-driveway business today? You'd be begging me to come over for half of what I'm paying you. Maybe we should've waited."

"Okay," Walters said, immediately bored with that line of discussion. "Where are you going with this?"

"Surrey."

"Surrey?"

"Mike Surrey. Exclusively on WCO," Bryant pronounced, using the deep voice of a radio announcer. "Think about it. The Cubs just canned him. He's got an Ivy League degree in history. He's smart. He's witty. He's candid. Look how he called out that idiot umpire at the end of the Series. He's a big name. I think he'd like to stay in Chicago. And obviously, he's going to be looking for a job. We need to use Moose more, too. He can help Mike. Or maybe Aimee. Your daughter's knowledge of sports equals yours and her looks certainly trump yours. I'm thinking we move you to the morning drive, let you mix politics more with sports like you want to do, and put Surrey and Aimee on right after."

"No argument about Aimee," Walters said, warming to the idea with Bryant dangling extra-large carrots: a great gig for Aimee and the show he wanted to do at the most important time of the day for any radio station. "Well, there's just one thing about all this," he added. "I think Surrey would kill himself by shoving a baseball bat up his ass before he'd work anywhere I was working."

"And that's exactly why you and Mike Surrey are having dinner tonight at my place," Bryant said. "I have my ways to reach people, too. No one else knows about this. I expect you to behave. I expect you to help convince him there's room for both of you at WCO."

For once, Walters didn't know what to say. He stared at Bryant, nodded his agreement, and left the office. He instinctively reached for a Marlboro in his shirt pocket as he moved past Shawna Riggs. He couldn't resist borrowing a line from the movie "Airplane."

"Shit, Shawna, guess I picked a bad time to quit smoking and drinking. At least I can still swear."

***

"Living large in Lincolnshire." Using that line was a quick way for Walters to annoy Bryant on the rare occasions when he received and accepted invitations to the mini-mansion.

Bryant's rich-guy suburban lifestyle with an acre of yard to maintain and nightmare daily commutes to the west edge of Chicago's downtown Loop didn't square with Walters' preference for urban living. Still, Walters enjoyed the trappings of success, too, such as a black Lexus LS. It stickered at $71,000, but he had a much better deal: a ridiculous $125 monthly lease from Rodney Baker at Lakefront Lexus. Rod advertised on the station and Walters often mentioned how much he liked his Lexus in some of his "offhand" on-air comments.

This had led to one of the biggest blow-ups between Bryant and Walters, because the exclusive auto advertiser on Walters' program at the time was Tony Singleton Buick-Cadillac and Tony didn't appreciate Walters talking about "my sweet-riding Lexus." Meanwhile, Baker still expected on-air love. Two angry auto advertisers equaled any radio station manager's nightmare.

"Okay, okay," Walters finally said during that heated exchange. "I deserve the ass-kicking for this one."

An hour later, Bryant met with Walters and Baker and floored Walters with his negotiating skills by brokering a deal in which Baker not only agreed to cool it with Walters until Singleton's contract ran out, but also agreed to spend more money with the station.

A few weeks later, Bryant also sweet-talked Tony Singleton into advertising more, including a prime sponsorship of Walters' blog on the WCO website.

It was an ancient radio sales joke—you needed to be pretty damn good to sell empty air. "Davis, I think you could sell Bibles to Al Qaeda," was all Walters could say.

With that episode in mind, Walters wasn't surprised to see a new, pearl-white Cadillac Escalade with a Singleton license-plate frame occupying one of the four bays in Bryant's immaculate garage, which had a vine-wrapped trellis over the path connecting the detached garage to a rear entrance.

Walters turned his Lexus into Bryant's semi-circular driveway; one of those driveways designed to mimic the entrance to larger estates—the kind in which servants and valets met you at the door.

The plantation effect was accentuated by the tall columns that reached from the base of the front porch that ran the length of the house to the start of the roofline, two stories up. Walters saw large windows on either side of the double entrance doors. Lush, carefully tended landscaping in front of each window included a fountain centering the window to Bryant's study. The fountain quietly trickled water out of a frog's mouth.

Walters pulled behind a dusty, green Honda Ridgeline pickup truck with a Wrigley Field parking pass in one corner of the rear window and a "Cubs" logo in the other. He assumed the pickup belonged to Mike Surrey.

Talking to Moose Skowron a few hours earlier, he broke Bryant's vow of confidentiality and described the evening plans, noting he hadn't had an actual conversation with Surrey for several years.

"I've pretty much spent Surrey's entire time as manager painting him as an incompetent shithead. I've made him the butt of hundreds of snarky jokes," Walters said. "Not that we have anything to apologize for. Price of fame makes you fair game. He knows that."

"And don't forget I helped," Skowron added.

Once, at Wrigley Field, he had passed Surrey's wife, Lisa, in the walkway behind the press box. He had been drinking a lot during that period. Determined to keep walking and in a hurry to grab some coffee and sober up a bit, he wanted to pass by with no more than a glare from her.

But she stopped him, grabbing his elbow with a surprisingly strong grip and staring straight at him.

"I knew when Mike took this job there would be criticism. I knew there would be assholes like you, but you take despicable to a new level," she said in a soft voice barely above audible level so no one else would hear. "And Mike would die if he knew I was even having a conversation with you."

Walters started to open his mouth, but she shushed him. If anything, she gripped his elbow harder and the cliché "fire in your eyes" came to mind.

"Don't," she said. "Just shut the hell up. It's bad enough you've made a good man's job harder. Even our kids get hate mail. I read up on you. I know what you did to your family. You killed your daughter driving drunk. Why don't you make jokes on your show about THAT? Maybe you should think about what being such a dick does to our family."

That froze Walters in place for a moment. He wasn't much for inward analysis to begin with. The booze made him angrier and even more defensive. He started a rapid internal debate about whether to just give her the heat-in-the-kitchen line. He was sober enough to conclude that wasn't a good idea, but he still felt he had to respond.

"Look," he started to say, not sure what he was going to say next.

But, before Walters could say another word, she loosened her grip on his elbow, turned 90 degrees and walked away.

***

A few minutes later, with drinks in hand, Surrey and Walters eyed each other. Bryant sipped a Makers Mark bourbon and water, Surrey drank a craft ale from a bottle and Walters settled for a Diet Sprite. Surrey appeared to be having mixed success at trying not to look like an unfed, caged cheetah. Walters tried to shake off the sheepish feeling of a bully forced to confront his target on a level playing field.

Bryant's outdoor porch looked like a set for HGTV. It had the latest, greatest trappings—a propane-fueled heater to cut into the chill of a late fall evening, a full-service bar, an outdoor kitchen and a 50-inch flat-screen television hanging on a wall behind the covered bar, protected from the elements. The sound was off and the TV was playing a Blackhawks hockey game while, quite appropriately, Walters thought, Bryant's Sirius radio stream had Marvin Gaye's "What's Going On" playing in the background.

Bryant tossed some thick steaks on the hot grill, sending flames shooting through the cast-iron grates.

"Guys, let's sit down," he said, motioning to the chairs around the glass-topped patio furniture. He pulled a barstool over to the grill. "I need to stay close to the heat so I can tend to these bad boys."

Surrey and Walters sat across from each other, neither exactly sure what to say. Walters finally decided it was his job to thaw the conversation.

"Mike, I'm going to lay it out there," Walters said. "You probably figured out that Davis wants us to make nice. I just want to say two things. I know I was really hard on you and probably overdid it at times. But I also think it would be a good thing for you and for WCO if you came over. You've got the chops to do really well. I think it's a good idea."

Surrey stared at Walters, saying nothing, and gave a head turn toward Bryant, who was busily shifting the steaks so the meat could dodge arching flares of dancing fire.

Instead of responding to Walters, the ex-manager decided to take a different path, the way he'd deflect a question he didn't like at a press conference.

"You know, Davis, everyone says when you're grilling steaks you should be moving them around as little as possible," Surrey finally said. "Keeps the juices locked in. Best thing is to go a few minutes on each side. You turn 'em once, get 'em off and let 'em rest."

"I know. I've got some serious flare-up problems," Bryant said. "The damn grill actually gets too hot."

"Well, to be honest, that's not too different than how I feel," Surrey said. "Hot. Too damn hot. I'm flaring up. Too much has happened in the past few days. Let's talk about families, politics, anything but baseball or the media until after we eat. Then I'll see how I feel about even getting into this conversation."

Three days later, Surrey said he'd take the job. Once again, Bryant's salesmanship skills impressed Walters.

Five days later, Surrey had signed a contract to go on the air later that winter in Bob Walters' time slot with Walters moving to "morning drive," the lucrative time of day when people listened while trapped in rush-hour traffic.

A major part of the announcement was Bryant's decision to pair Surrey with Aimee Walters. The more Bryant thought about it, the more he liked the idea. It wasn't just because she was young and attractive, though she obviously was both those things, and those things never hurt.

A college dropout with a sharp wit, pleasant personality and no immediate direction in her life, Aimee had found work as a bartender at Eger's Sports Pub in Chicago's Wrigleyville neighborhood. Her dad, a close friend of the proprietor, Geoff Eger, helped her get started with a positive word, but she quickly proved herself. She could hold her own with any guy when it came to sports trivia and statistics. When Walters started live broadcasts from Eger's, Aimee joined him as the perfect foil to his bombast and quickly demonstrated natural ability for broadcasting while filling Eger's bar with paying customers.

And now she was nationally famous—a fact not lost on the WCO station manager. The public knew about Aimee's kidnapping and beating but had neither heard nor seen all the gory details—at least not yet. The video that showed it all was on her father's cell phone and potential evidence in the pending cases against the two lower-level operatives who had been arrested in the assassination plot.

She prayed the prosecutors would never release the video or play it in open court. Still, she knew she was an unwilling star in a reality show, and she wasn't naïve enough to believe it would never surface, most likely on social media for every sicko to watch. The authorities already had received dozens of requests to release the records they were holding in the case.

"Fame is very much a double-edged sword," the actor Kevin Bacon once said. Aimee knew exactly what Bacon meant when she stumbled on that quote. Now she had the opportunity of a lifetime. She finally decided she was tough enough to handle whatever happened. Otherwise, the bad guys would get another undeserved win. Doing this was even a way to let them know she could prosper while they spent years as someone's prison bitches.

The announcement of Bob Walters' new time and the unveiling of the "Mike and Aimee Show" was a big story on a slow news day in Chicago.

"My wife said it was about time someone got on WCO who could undue whatever damage Bob Walters is doing as soon as possible," Surrey said at the press conference. "Maybe I can be Triage Mike or Mike the Fixer."

Aimee laughed. Bob laughed. Everyone laughed.

10

Lewiston, Idaho
Two Weeks Before Christmas

Trey Van Ohmann walked silently in his father's back yard, standing in knee-deep snow. His boots easily pierced the fresh, top layer, the latest deposit of the long Idaho winter. His feet crunched through another layer before he walked to the spot he sought. He knew from a thousand other moments in the yard that he was standing where he wanted to be; the place where they had scattered his father's ashes.

It was Don Van Ohmann's garden, where he took pride in growing Idaho's tastiest tomatoes, or at least that was what he bragged. Trey still missed the spaghetti sauce his mom made from the garden tomatoes before cancer made her too weak to cook or can and, eventually, claimed her life.

Trey's brother, Travis, waited patiently, standing just outside the screened porch in the back yard. It had been his idea to get Trey to come home. Only an hour earlier, he had picked Trey up at Lewiston's small regional airport.

"I'm glad I came," Trey said. "I need to get a feel for what happened."

They had started at Don's auto parts shop, which specialized in hard-to-find parts for collector cars. Trey realized he had missed talking with Ray Scheid, Don's long-time partner and best friend from his days as an auto racer. All the Van Ohmann boys saw Ray as almost a second father. Ray still blamed himself for telling Don to keep driving after the pickup truck started acting oddly on a remote stretch of U.S. Highway 12 near the Montana line. When Don called, Ray told him it sounded like a minor glitch; something to check again in Missoula.

The following day, weather permitting, Trey planned to rent an SUV to retrace Don's final drive; to see the spot where the Don-Ray Automotive pickup truck careened into the Lochsa River.

Now he could sense Travis watching him as he walked back to the porch. He hadn't planned to stop at the house. The "for sale" sign in the front yard made him sad, but his brothers, both farmers outside Lewiston, urged him to stop for a final look.

"It was a good idea," he said. "I really miss him. Probably will for a long time."

"We all miss him Trey," was Travis' response.

Later, talking over dinner, the third Van Ohmann brother, Tom, joined them and they shared memories before turning back to the accident. None of them could grasp how Don Van Ohmann, a careful, experienced driver with a racer's reflexes, would lose control of a vehicle. They had no trouble believing that somehow the killer had hijacked control of the vehicle's OnStar unit. With OnStar, the truck's precise position would have been known through its always-on GPS. By taking control of the brakes and the accelerator at the point of a curve, the killer forced the truck into the river.

"Ray still feels awful," Travis Van Ohmann said.

"Ray shouldn't blame himself. We tried to tell him that," Trey said. "Heck, Dad was hustling to Missoula so he could fly to Chicago to see me pitch. Ray knew that seeing me pitch in the World Series would be Dad's priority. I want to drive that road. I need to see it. Have you been to the spot?"

"No," Travis replied. "Actually, I'd like to go with you."

Trey's phone beeped. It was a text from Zerbey. "Call me ASAP."

"Hey, I've got to make a call," he told his brothers. "Be right with you." He turned around in his chair and tapped Zerbey's number to return the call.

"Adam, what's up?"

"Trey, you sitting down?"

"Actually, I am. I'm at dinner with my brothers in Lewiston in fact."

"Hey, good. Well, stay sitting down. You just got traded to the Chicago Cubs. You need to be in Chicago tomorrow. Forget my financial stake in your future. Friend to friend, I really don't think you should quit. They have no idea you're even considering that, so you have to decide pronto. Think about it. There could be no bigger buzz than being the main man for the hottest team in professional sports. The fans want a dynasty now. You'll be the key."

"Well, shit," Van Ohmann replied, not knowing what else to say. Zerbey waited, knowing his client was thoughtful and would want a few seconds of pondering time. Then the agent heard what he wanted to hear.

"Okay. Yeah. My Dad would want me to do this and he'd remind me I have no known skills to be an Idaho farmer. I'll give it a try. At least one more season."

11

Appleton, Wisconsin
Two Weeks Before Christmas

Lydia Nicks seemed confident, even cocky, but Reggie Fox wasn't. Given the timing and reality of presidential politics, it might already be too late for her to declare, especially against an incumbent. Luke Murphy certainly wasn't the most popular president of recent times, but Fox had a hard time seeing how Murphy could lose the nomination of his own party.

"We've lined up a lot of support from the people who matter, the people who write big checks—and their friends who write big checks to places that can't be tracked," she said. "Until I declare, it's a big advantage. Legally, we can work directly with those groups."

She was right, Fox knew. Under the Byzantine rules of campaign finance, candidates couldn't legally coordinate with the advocacy groups supporting them. Until you were a declared candidate, though, the messaging could be aligned between your "exploratory committee" and the dark-money groups that had little or no accountability.

The two sat in a coffee shop outside her home town of Appleton, Wisconsin. It seemed like everyone knew Lydia Nicks in Appleton; and courteous Appleton neighbors still granted her privacy, not making too much of a fuss when she was around.

At 64 years old, she knew this election likely was her last, best shot to reach the White House, and recent events had handed her an incredible opening.

Wisconsin's heartland formed her base. Arguably, no other state was as politically schizoid. The Badger State produced Sen. Robert "Fighting Bob" LaFollette, the champion of liberal progressivism in the early 20th Century, and creator of the "Wisconsin idea" that education should have influence far beyond the classroom. There was even a symbolic visual connection with direct sight lines down State Street in Madison between the entrance to the state capitol building and the University of Wisconsin campus.

Less than 50 years after the LaFollette era, Wisconsin elected a very different United State senator—Joe McCarthy of Appleton, a demagogue who saw Communists in every corner of the U.S. government in the 1950s before he went too far with blacklists and unfounded allegations that destroyed people's lives. McCarthy died in 1957, an angry and defeated man, from a combination of hepatitis and alcoholism.

Statewide candidates knew that once you got beyond the glue of Packers football and the University of Wisconsin, there were three different Wisconsins. The first Wisconsin was centered in the two largest cities, Madison and Milwaukee, with pockets of Scandinavian liberalism elsewhere, particularly in university towns like La Crosse and Stevens Point. Madison was a snow-belt twin of Austin, Texas, both state capitals with major universities. "Mad City" had a long history of radical, left-wing politics. Urban Milwaukee represented a textbook urban stew of unions and minorities that usually voted strongly Democratic. These were the places where Democrats needed huge majorities to win statewide elections.

The second Wisconsin included conventional Republicans in the Milwaukee suburbs and just outside the smaller cities across the state. The southeastern corner included the Lake Michigan cities of Racine and Kenosha where union manufacturing jobs were mainly memories. While the urban cores with their dwindling numbers of Democratic voters fought decline, the outlying areas grew with corridors of huge warehouses and shopping centers. Countless subdivisions filled with white, middle-class commuters who left each morning for jobs in the Milwaukee area and the spreading, northern sprawl of the Chicago metropolitan area.

The third Wisconsin had, for decades, been a Wisconsin of the more isolated cities and rural areas. Many of these people were conservative and inherently suspicious of anything government was doing. At the most extreme, Wisconsin had been a breeding ground of the Posse Comitatus, a white-supremacist, Christian-claiming survivalist group that holed up in bunker-like compounds. Many Posse members believed an international Jewish conspiracy had gained control of the U.S. government.

Lydia Nicks never could hope for traction with the first Wisconsin, so she had spent her political career cultivating the second and third versions while annoying the first. One way she did it was by playing to the unusually entrenched and influential conservative talk radio hosts in Milwaukee.

"People elsewhere have no idea what this state is really like," she had said on a recent show, criticizing the pro-choice abortion policies of the state's Democratic governor. "I like the Packers, ice fishing and farmer's markets, too, and I even like visiting Madison. But Madison is an island surrounded by reality. It's time the rest of the country understood that Wisconsin is a lot more than that."

Fox and Nicks sipped their coffee for a few moments without saying anything, both lost in thought about the effort it would take to unseat Luke Murphy.

"You know, Reg, I've even been working on my body," she said, showing a hint of a smile. "Frumpy females have extra challenges. Someone did a study and found out that online comments, usually snarky, about the appearance of prominent females out-number comments about guys something like 20-to-1. Do you believe that?"

"Yeah," Fox said. "I do. It's actually a tactic when you run against a woman candidate. You find sneaky ways to raise questions about how badly she's aging, or you get someone to go on Facebook and ask if she's had Botox. All that stuff. Of course, you can't do it yourself, or you get accused of sexism and bullying. But there are plenty of ways around it."

"I'm not trying to look younger than I am," she said. "I'm proud to be my age. But I want people to say, 'Damn, she looks good for her age.'"

"You're there Lydia," Fox said, doing a mock size-up with his eyes. He saw a woman who indeed looked like a mature, wise woman who also wouldn't have a problem at the target range –a hobby of hers—or running a 5k for charity.

"How about the family?" Fox asked. "Any skeletons hiding in closets I don't know about?"

"No, really," she said. "There's nothing of any consequence that isn't out there already. The first marriage. The divorce. It was an adult divorce. We both moved on. We just weren't happy. Then came Christ in my life. I'm not afraid to talk about it. Second marriage. Two kids. Both doing well. Neither of them are convicted of anything or having kids out of wedlock. Three grandkids. They're fine. And, yeah, I do miss John. Not afraid to say so publicly either. People like it, actually. He's still my biggest asset."

Her eyes misted a bit when she finished the sentence. John Nicks, her second husband and a successful business executive, had died of Hodgkin's lymphoma five years earlier.

"I know your next question," she said. "I'm not seeing anyone; don't know that I ever will. There just isn't anything at all to talk about in that department."

"You're going to have to try to keep it that way," Fox said. "Once you declare, Murphy and the Democrats are going to go after everything. Everything. I'm sure they already are."

"So, I guess that means you're taking the job?" she said.

Fox spent a few seconds giving the offer a final mulling. "I guess I am," he finally said. "I owe you that and frankly, I got bored faster than I thought I would this year. But you have to understand the toll this will take, not only on you but maybe the country: The only way you win is to fire up the religious base.

You're going to have to be Luke Murphy's worst nightmare in the Senate. You're going to have to play off that comet for all it's worth. It's a sign from God. The meteor that followed is a sign of the threat of radical Islam. The media will paint you as a demagogue.

"How do you stir turnout in the early primary states? How do you win the Iowa caucuses?" he asked rhetorically. "You're going to have to open boxes of prejudice and even hate that might be best closed to get elected. You'll probably lose a lot of the business Republicans until they see you're going to unseat him, and their only option is some Democrat who wants to end the greed party on Wall Street for good. Meanwhile, of course, their nominee will be privately assuring them that it's all just campaign rhetoric; don't get too overheated. Can you do that to become the first woman president of the United States?"

"Oh, yeah," she said, and then switched her tone of voice so quickly it startled Fox. "I can. Screw Wall Street. They'll have no choice. And I'm not worried too much about Murphy either."

"And why's that?" said Fox, who thought he knew everything there was to know about Murphy. "That childhood-secret stuff is going to be old news and he got a lot of sympathy with that crazy Cub fan and his terrorist friends going after him."

"A guy like that—he's got other secrets," Nicks said. "He has to. Once I'm running, you can bet we'll hear about them, or we'll come up with something ourselves."

12

Washington D.C.
Late January Of Election Year

Sitting in the Oval Office, Murphy and Rayburn watched the Lydia Nicks announcement that all the cable networks were broadcasting live from the Fox Cities Performing Arts Center in Appleton.

"I have decided," she said, extending her hands palms out for silence as the crowd cheered her on, knowing her decision was no secret. "I have decided. I have decided to run for president of the United States as the only true conservative nominee of the Republican Party."

A deafening roar followed, balloons dropped and the sound system started playing "Have A Little Faith," a song by country artist Kaitlyn Baker that Nicks had adopted as an anthem for her campaign.

"I do this with confidence but a heavy heart," she continued. "My heart is heavy, because it is not an easy decision to challenge an incumbent president of your own political party.

"I bear no ill will toward Luke Murphy," she said, then had to pause as a chorus of boos erupted when she said Murphy's name. "But Luke Murphy is not the right man for the job at this moment. Not in a world in which America's exceptional place in the world is under attack. Not in a world when we're giving sweetheart deals to China while too many of our own citizens go hungry. Not in a world that ignores an unequivocal, an unambiguous and an undeniable sign from our awesome God. The message couldn't be clearer. It's the challenge and, yes, the mandate of our times to defeat Islamic terrorism, not negotiate with those who openly call for our destruction."

In Washington, Murphy shook his head.

"She's good," he said. "She could unlock something powerful, especially with Reggie Fox pulling the strings. Purse strings, too. Her buddies have raised a pile of dark money. A damn big pile. And, face it, the world is pretty messed up right now. We've got starving Chinese that we've tried to help. Somehow that makes me soft. We've got Christians thinking God told them to go after Muslims. We've got Muslims who were on the fence over terrorism. Now, after this, the gloves are off."

"We've still got a case to make," Rayburn said, wanting to limit Murphy's tendency to take long hikes down the pessimism trail. "The rational voters will be there. And, believe me, we can raise plenty of money. We'll make Lydia Nicks look like a Christian crazy ready to start a nuclear war over astronomy. Not that she isn't doing that herself already. Plus, the other party's candidate is going to be wildly left most likely. You're in the sweet spot. Most Americans really want to vote for a moderate, reasonable adult. You know: A guy like you."

Murphy nodded in grudging agreement. Rayburn paused for a moment before adding another thought, "On the other hand, we can't let her have own the social conservatives. We don't need all of 'em, but we need some of 'em. We'll remind them that you're against gay marriage; that you're only for abortion as an option for incest, rape and the life of the mother. Hey, maybe you could carry an assault weapon inscribed with a Bible verse everywhere you go."

"Can you get that on Amazon Prime for me? I might point it at you," Murphy said, then turned serious. "Charley, it's amazing how often these calculations have nothing to do with what you actually believe or don't believe. Some of this stuff, like my abortion position, is what I actually believe. The other items, well, I'm not so sure. If I ever was."

"Shh," Rayburn said, making a "cut" sign by sliding his index finger horizontally across his neck. "I didn't hear that. Those positions have brought you a long way. And, remember, you can't do anything for the greater good unless you actually win."

"Well, maybe I can get a job on WCO after the 'Mike and Aimee Show' if this president thing doesn't work out," he said.

"Yeah, sports talk is exactly where you should be if you want to encourage people to keep their priorities in order," Rayburn said.

"And, by the way, Col. Rayburn, I still haven't given you a formal reprimand for ignoring a direct presidential order," Murphy said.

"And that would be?"

"Mike Surrey," Murphy said. "I haven't forgotten that we didn't get a call to Surrey on my calendar.

"Now that he has a new job, maybe I should even go on his show," Murphy added, knowing that would get a rise out of Rayburn. "This is the kind of passive aggression that will go in your file, Colonel. Consider yourself on double-secret probation."

"Duly noted, sir. It was my judgment that your blood pressure couldn't handle the tension of focusing on the Cubs at the same time the world was going to hell. Would you like me to write the reprimand myself?"

"That won't be necessary," Murphy said. Then he slapped his friend on the back and moved his other arm around Rayburn's shoulders in a near-hug, an effusive display from a man who rarely showed emotion other than the fake affection demanded by public appearances. "Charley, I know you've got my best interests at heart. Still, I enjoy talking to Surrey. It's a welcome break to tell you the truth. Let's do his show at an opportune time."

"Also duly noted, sir."

"I mean it this time," Murphy said, adding a hint of mock presidential command. "No shit. You think I don't know how you operate? Ignore his non-essential requests the first time unless he asks again. Anyway, I'm headed upstairs for lunch with Alison."

Rayburn made eye contact with Murphy and raised an eyebrow, knowing the First Couple rarely had lunch together.

Murphy said nothing, but he raised an eyebrow in return, added a shrug and headed upstairs.

***

Alison Murphy already was sitting at the small table in the casual, private dining area in the family kitchen of the residence area on the second floor of the White House. She took a triangle of pita bread from a basket and stabbed one end into a shallow bowl of red-pepper hummus before turning her attention to one of the two Greek salads on the table.

"Do you want my olives?" Murphy said in a monotone, eyeing his salad while pointing to four fat black olives that formed the corners of a square surrounding an impressive amount of feta cheese. "The chefs know I love feta and they know I hate olives, but like to share them with you, because you love olives. Sometimes I wonder how the hell they know all this stuff."

"Sure," she said. "Toss 'em over."

Luke took his seat and shared the olives. The couple ate quietly for several minutes. The only noise came from Fox News at low volume on a small, flat-screen television under a nearby counter. Several talking heads shared meaningless chatter about Lydia Nicks' announcement before dissecting Luke Murphy's presidency.

"Luke, do you mind turning that off? I'm sure you're not hearing anything you don't know already and we need to talk," Alison said. "It's taken me a long time to get my head together on what I want to say. A quiet lunch in the kitchen is the best place to get your attention."

"Sure," Luke said. As he switched off the television, he added, "I don't have a lot of time before my next meeting, but they gave me 15 more minutes than usual for a private lunch. When you said you wanted to talk, I figured something was up."

"Well, that was very thoughtful of you," she said, trying to control a flare of frustration and temper.

"Sarcasm doesn't suit you, Alison," Luke said.

"And, it doesn't suit you to act like you're doing me a big goddam favor by giving me 15 more minutes," Alison responded. "This is exactly what we need to be talking about."

"You asked for the lunch," he said, his voice turning colder. "Let's not start with a fight."

"Luke, this is bullshit. Our marriage is nothing. Our relationship is nothing."

"Is this about no children again?" Luke said, staring down at his hand, suddenly finding it to be a fascinating object of interest.

"Luke, goddam it, look at me like I matter," she said, raising her voice. "That's more bullshit. We agreed about that a long time ago. We enjoy my nieces and nephews. They pose for pictures for the press even. We talked publicly about my quote-unquote difficulty in having children, because, my goodness, the American people expect their First Couples to have beautiful children. It's fine. It worked for both of us. For both of our careers."

Now Luke felt defensive. "Look, I know I'm kind of distant, but cut me some slack here. I don't like to play the president card, but dammit, it's a pretty hard job."

"I realize that," she said, her tone getting icier. "But we're not partners now in any sense of the word. Not physically, not emotionally and not intellectually. I can live without sex if I have to and I can even live without a lot of emotional contact, but aren't we supposed to enjoy each other's company, at least sometimes, like most married couples? Aren't we supposed to make each other laugh out loud every now and then? Aren't we supposed to be interested in what the other person has to say or what the other person thinks?"

"I think you're being pretty dramatic," Luke said. "And I think you have an idealized view of what most marriages are like. But, okay, I get it. I'll try to be more attentive. Really."

"Luke, you're not listening," Alison said. Now Luke could see a tear in the corner of her eye. She wiped it away and her voice regained firmness. "What did I just say? Did I say I want to live in Fantasy Land? No, I said we should genuinely want and enjoy each other's company now and then. The point is you're offering to be more attentive, but you don't really want to be more attentive. So, no, I'm not asking too much from the person who's supposed to be my life partner. I'm not an appendage. I'm tired of pretending to be your happy girl-buddy.

"So, here it is," she continued. She knew, at that moment, she was finally ready to say what she came to say. "We've got too much invested in each other for me to just walk. And, I still care about you. I really do. I'll stick it out for your re-election. But, here's what's going to happen: Once you're safely in your second term, we're separating. I just can't do this for four more years, but I'll give you another 12 months."

"Wow, you've really been saving this up. I don't know what else to say," Luke said, buying time to think and trying to hold back his flaring temper. He didn't need this, another big complication that would be a field day for his opponents and probably late-night comedians, too.

Then he caught himself, knowing that, as usual, his first thought was a selfish one—how it would affect him. Maybe he really wasn't meant to be married. Old memories flooded forward and he pushed them back into the box where he usually could keep such thoughts locked. He wanted to share something about his deeper feelings with Alison but, as usual, he couldn't do it.

"I had no idea things were that bad, well, other than in the bedroom department. It's the stress, I think," was all he could offer his wife of 25 years.

"Dammit, Luke, this isn't about whether your Viagra is working," Alison said. "Maybe it'll be a relief to know we're on our last laps. Maybe without the pressure we can be friends again. Maybe I can help you more than just by smiling and waving at crowds and letting everyone dissect my wardrobe after state dinners."

"No one can catch a whiff of this," Luke Murphy said. "Not a whiff."

"Yeah, Luke, I figured that would be your priority," she said with a tone of total flatness. "Don't worry. As usual, the people around you won't let you down so you can do great things for America."

She left the room. The president of the United States stared at the door as it closed behind him, turned the television back on, picked up a triangle of pita bread and mimicked the way his wife stabbed the hummus. He noticed she had never eaten the olives from his plate.

13

Chicago | Late January Of Election Year

Bob Walters could feel the satisfaction, anticipation and excitement that came when he knew they had tons of good material for the next morning's show. It was a good enough feeling that both the guilt and the splitting headache from too much bourbon the evening nearly departed.

"Moose, this stuff is gold," he said to Scott Skowron, who had prepared talking points, statistics and trivia to show how unlikely it was the Cubs could repeat as National League champions in the coming season, let alone make it to the World Series or actually win the Series for an unbelievable second year in a row.

Every afternoon, before going home while the "Mike and Aimee Show" aired, Walters and Skowron met to compare notes for the next morning's show. It made his day longer, but it also meant he usually he didn't have to get up at 3 a.m. to go to work—the bad side of having a popular radio program during the morning rush hour.

Bryant's instincts had been right; the blend of sports and politics was working so far. "With these guys, we've got the best, most unusual morning talk show in radio," Bryant bragged when he was interviewed for an industry newsletter.

Today they were focused on sports. Skowron had been compiling advanced statistical information—what baseball data fiends called "sabermetrics"—to show the fuel for the Cubs' success included an unusually high number of balls put into play for hits instead of outs. They also won more close games than statistically likely. In other words, they were pretty damn lucky. Eventually, luck dries up like a desert pond in summer.

"The norms almost always level out over the course of a 162-game season," Skowron said. "This is something you can prove."

"Okay," Walters said, "but haven't they dramatically improved their team by adding Van Ohmann? Don't the data freaks have numbers for that?"

"Of course," Skowron said. "But they had to give up some good players to get him. And several other teams could be a lot better. They lost their manager, too. I know you don't think much of Mike Surrey and maybe he didn't make the most logical decisions at times, but he was a great leader, Bob."

"He's my new best friend now," Walters said. "Old news. I just hope we can have as much fun with the new one."

"Bottom line," Skowron continued, "they're a decent bet to make the playoffs, but you have a lot of ammo to argue they aren't going back to the Series. They'll be lucky to win 90 games or so. I project 87. You don't have to be the voice of doom. You can be a rational guy; a devil's advocate planting seeds of doubt."

Walters liked the idea of reciting a litany of memorably crazy, awful moments in Cubs' history, including some obscure ones that even many fans didn't know. He kept going, practicing his lines in front of Skowron for the next day.

"Oh, you laugh now about the curse. But, remember. They were a team so hexed that even when they traded people, the player took the hex to the new team. Consider: Bill Buckner was wearing his CHICAGO CUBS BATTING GLOVE when he made the error that kept the Boston Red Sox from winning the World Series. They were so hexed that at the end of last season, they barely won a game that FBI and Secret Service FIXED FOR THEM, and then nearly lost the real game because of a GODDAM COMET."

"You don't need to speak in all caps for me. Save it for the listeners, Bob," Skowron said, laughing. "Just use the material. They'll eat it up."

"Hey, maybe on the following day we can have a little fun with President Murphy, too. Maybe try to get him on the air," Walters said, seizing on a new idea. "My childhood chum spends way too much time rooting for the Cubs. We could get him a tape of tomorrow's show. The stats will piss him off. He'll get defensive and act all full of himself. I'll let him give his re-election a plug. Equal time since we already had Nicks on the show."

"Makes sense to ask Murphy," Skowron agreed. "I could reach out personally. The White House likes me more than they like you some days. Since we started talking more about politics, you've been pretty damn critical of your buddy."

"I've got to demonstrate I'm not playing favorites," Skowron said. "And we both know that most of the folks who listen to political talk wouldn't vote for a Democrat or a moderate Republican if they have a choice unless their guy molested a Little League team and some nuns on live TV. Even then, they'd probably just stay home. Murphy might be a Republican, but he's not the right Republican for a bunch of them."

Skowron then turned around in his wheelchair and rolled out of Walters' office to his office cubicle down the hall.

After Skowron left, Walters took two ibuprofens and contemplated, for perhaps the millionth time in the past month, why he had started drinking again and stopped going to meetings.

He had some theories and knew his triggers, but it was no excuse. He might've hit the bottom of the pit the previous night, finishing his tenth shot of Jameson's at a neighborhood bar and flopping into bed with a barmaid after closing time.

He had awakened in her apartment that morning, not sure how he got there and with no memory of what happened.

He knew her. Tricia was a regular barmaid at Flanagan's Near North, his second-favorite tavern—after Eger's in Wrigleyville—and Flanagan's had the virtue of proximity to his condo. The owner, Ian Flanagan, was enough of a friend that Walters had plugged the place on air a few times. Tricia was sexier than hell and she enjoyed giving the male customers something to think about when she leaned over in tight shorts that showed the thin strip of a thong and the wings of an eagle "tramp stamp" tattoo across her lower back. She always refused to tell the story behind the tattoo when asked. "I was young," was all she'd say. Her hair cascaded in wild, dark curls slightly past her shoulders, behind ears with large, gold-hoop earrings. She tied her Kelly-green "Flanagan's" t-shirt as tight as she could around her midriff and her breasts formed precise, desirable shapes underneath.

She also was at least 25 years younger than Walters. He wondered why she would take him home. While he was famous and financially secure, he didn't see Trish as someone who bedded down with the customers. She was a big tease who knew how to coax big tips, but not a hustler. *She certainly could do better than a middle-aged drunk*, he thought.

Lying in her bed in the small apartment, Walters noticed she wasn't naked but wearing the thong panties and a sheer top that left little to the imagination. He could see her standing in the bathroom, brushing back her hair, and he found it arousing to watch her slowly raising her arm and pushing her jet-black, curly locks across her bare shoulders with a stiff brush.

"Hey," he said, loud enough for her to hear. "Trish. I have a confession and a request."

"What's that, Bob?" she replied.

"Well, the request is for coffee. I think I had a little too much Jameson's last night. I really don't remember much. Hope I was everything you wanted. Hope we took some precautions."

Tricia laughed a hearty laugh.

"Bob, Bob, Bob. Now I know you were as wasted as we thought you were," she said. "When Ian and I saw how drunk you were, we didn't want you even walking home, let alone driving. You aren't supposed to be drinking at all, you stupid shit. I took you here and put you to bed.

"No worries, Bob. And no STDs in this apartment unless you gave me something when you slobbered on me while you were groping. I'll send you the cleaning bill."

***

Thinking back on the night, Walters checked his "rock-bottom" thought. Sad and pathetic as it was, he wasn't there yet. An alcoholic wasn't at rock bottom if he still had a job, decent relationships with at least some friends and family and could still convince himself at times that he could control his drinking. It scared him that he maybe he needed to dive more deeply into the hole before he could crawl out—everyone's life had a lot of irony, but nothing was more ironic than alcoholism.

He hit the speed-dial on his cell phone and called his ex-wife, Mickey.

"Bob?" Mickey Walters answered, no doubt seeing his name on her phone display.

"Hey Mick," he said. "I, uh, just want to say something."

"In other words, you're drinking again."

"You're right. But how the hell did you get from what I said to that?"

"Bob, who knows you better than I do?"

"Case closed."

"So, what is it you want to say? How's Aimee doing?"

"She's doing great. Just great. She's a natural on the radio and I think she's got chemistry with Surrey. She's got a great head on her shoulders, Mickey. That's thanks to you."

"Well, you've been there for her in the past few years, Bob," she said, sticking to a flat, matter-of-fact voice she learned to adopt years ago to block pain and keep her emotions from getting the better of her. "You've made a big difference. I gave up nagging years ago, so I'll just say it once: You shouldn't be drinking."

"I know, Mick, I know." He decided to make a joke, but it wasn't much of a joke, and it didn't lighten the mood.

"Maybe it's winter. I hate damn winter."

Before Mickey could say anything, or end the call, he suddenly decided to let it all out.

He said, "Part of it's the new job, Mick. You know me. I pretend everything's a piece of cake but hold it all in. And, well, I'm not trying to shift blame here, but I don't know any other way to say this. I thought maybe we had a chance to get together again. To take another shot. When you said you needed more time, I think that was a trigger. I think maybe I got my hopes up after what we went through during the World Series. I'm not blaming you. It just is what it is."

"Bob, the fact that you're drinking again proves that it wasn't time," she responded, her voice rising with flares of anger despite her best efforts to stay clinical. "You've come a long way. You probably saved Aimee's life from that madman. But I can't get past all the damage you caused and I won't be your shrink. You killed our daughter. You were drinking and probably coked up, too, for all I know. You were a cheat and a liar. Every time I see you or imagine you with a drink, it makes it harder to even contemplate another try."

Mickey Walters knew she needed to stop her monologue. It would go nowhere, but she also needed to put an exclamation point on her comments. She said, as firmly as she could, "Do you understand that?"

"It's a vicious circle," Walters said. "A Catch 22, whatever damn cliché you want to use. I'm drinking because of this hole in my life. But I can't fill the hole unless I stop drinking."

"It sucks for you Bob," she said. "It sucks for me, too. I don't know what else to say. We can be friends most of the time. We can be good parents for Aimee. But we just can't be together."

"Well, thanks for taking my call at least," he said with resignation. "At least we're talking."

***

Back in his cubicle, Skowron logged onto his computer and checked the email on the screen to his far right, one of three monitors at his desk. The subject line of an email that had landed about 15 minutes earlier, while he was meeting with Walters, quickly seized his attention:

Since I know this, Lydia Nicks will know it, too.

***

At that moment, Reginald Fox sat in one of the best offices in Seattle, with a view of Mount Rainier to the east and the Puget Sound to the west. It was a beautiful, crisp morning in the Pacific Northwest, but no mountain peak would command more attention than the email on his computer screen.

Since I know this, Lydia Nicks will know it, too.

It only took a quick skim to conclude that if all or most of this was true, it was more than a bombshell that would help his client's campaign. This could destroy Luke Murphy's career.

The text of the email read:

A husband and wife are dead because of Luke Murphy.

You will learn more from his daughter's notebooks. They're attached them to this email.

Since you won't know who I am, maybe you don't trust these attachments. Run them through every virus checker you've got. They're safe.

After you read this, you'll know what to do.

At almost identical moments, two time zones apart, Scott Skowron and Reginald Fox knew what to do. They started reading.

14

Taylor Pierce's First Notebook "About My Father And My Mother Who Had The Sparkle"

It's time. Time to write what I know. Do I really want anyone else to read this? Not sure. But I know it seems like it's something I need to do. If I wait much longer, the memories will fade too much, like ripples disappearing after you throw a rock in a pond. Maybe I'll want to tell my children, if I ever have any, if I hang around that long. Maybe I should tell the whole world. Maybe the world should know. After all, this is about the president of the United States.

Whatever. I need to do this. Mainly because it might help me shed my anger.

My name is Taylor Pierce. My Dad, Andy Pierce, told me what happened to him in college and then he told me what happened later. It took a lot of prodding. He was on his death bed, but I insisted that my brother Justin and I were entitled to the truth.

My Daddy never could really say "no" if I pushed hard enough. It's a dad-and-daughter thing. So, he told me and I think it felt right to him to unload before leaving this Earth, even though we're not Catholic. We're not ones to do much confessing.

"I guess you're my priest, Taylor. This is my confession." I still remember how he looked when he said that. He didn't say it with sadness or tears. And not much remorse. I think he was past that. He said it with a grin, just a crinkled-up whisper of a grin, but it was a grin that broke through the sunken craters where his cheeks used to be.

My mom, Gayle, was already gone; wasted away to nothing by the AIDS virus.

She got it from my father.

Pneumonia finally killed her, which was often what happened to AIDS patients before treatment improved, allowing most people to live with the disease instead of dying from it.

She died in 1993, almost the peak year for AIDS deaths in the United States. I looked that up. She was one statistic among nearly 50,000 known AIDS deaths in our country that year. More accurately, I should say deaths caused by conditions prompted by AIDS, as it usually didn't kill people as often as the pneumonia or cancer or other ailments that came with it.

But she was more than a statistic. I know that's a cliché, but it needs to be said. She was my mother. I was 10 years old and Justin he was only 5.

At 10, you remember your mother.

She was beautiful. She didn't think so, because she was a little overweight. "Oh my God, I'm my mother," she said one day, referring to my grandmother, a wonderful woman with what could politely be termed big hips. "I'm shaped like a pear," Mom said. She had thick dark hair that had just a hint of curl. Mom had bright blue eyes that seemed to sparkle the most when we did things that made her proud. Even at the end, she still had the sparkle. That's what I called it.

"You've got the sparkle, Mom," I said, holding her hand in that sad hospital room. I was the last person she talked to before she passed away that night.

Dad already was sick at that point, too, but his illness hadn't advanced as quickly and he had some years left. I think she knew when the moment was coming and she wanted to spend it with her family.

Dad, Justin and I were in her hospital room. One thing I remember was the smell. The other is the slow passage of time. Now that I'm an adult and I see the frenzy of our lives, I realize a hospital is the one place left where time still moves slowly. Glacially. You are on hospital time. You're hungry—well, ravenous actually—for the few minutes when the doctor shows up; when you optimistically want to hear encouraging words. "Hey, I have good news. The tests surprised us. The cancer is in remission." But, for the most part, you don't hear that. The doctor glances at the chart, asks the patient how he or she is doing, politely waits one or two seconds if there are any questions and moves on. Or he tells you about some specialist's opinion. Some doctor you never even met looked at the chart or the test results for maybe three minutes. (And, later you find out that costs you or your insurance company $500.) The next event: An aide will enter with a meal or a nurse comes into the room to do something. You're glad they came. You want anything to relieve the monotony of the walls, the mind-numbing drone of daytime television or the idle conversation among family members who have run out of things to say.

Of course, I didn't know what I know now. I knew she had cancer and I knew Dad had some sort of chronic illness. We got lots of sympathy for such "bad luck" befalling our family. Mom knew, of course, and now that I know he made her ill, her capacity for forgiveness and forbearance amazes me.

The one straight answer I could never get out of Dad was whether he confessed to Mom that he didn't get AIDS from a blood transfusion. She must have suspected that was bullshit. Wives know. He was no Arthur Ashe, the courageous tennis star who really did get it from a blood transfusion. But he always dodged the question like a gifted politician.

He came 99 percent of the way to admitting he never confessed to her. "Oh, I think she knew," he said, sighing. "But, you know, I was pretty careful about covering my tracks. There was no upside in coming clean; coming out, I guess, is the more accurate way to put it. It doesn't seem very courageous, but I rationalized. What was the point? How would it make anything better?"

It seems unforgivable, I know. But he was my father. Those were somewhat different times, and I choose to believe he made the decision he thought was best, and it wasn't just cowardice. Maybe you think differently. I say this: Don't be so quick to sit in judgment unless you were close to someone with AIDS during those years when people didn't even want to touch you or even let you go to school if you were ill.

In other respects, he was a great father to both of us. He could've been around more, but he was obsessed with his career and he provided. I think he regretted it later, but we always felt he loved us. Maybe Mom recognized that. She would have seen that as the most important thing. Maybe that's how she accepted him. Still, Jesus Himself would have a hard time fully forgiving, I think. Saint Mom. That should be her name.

Yeah, you figured it out by now. I'm still conflicted.

So, many years later, it was Dad's turn on the deathbed and he told me an incredible story that involved the president of the damn United States. Maybe I wasn't old enough to really handle the truth—sorry to steal a line from "A Few Good Men"—but I was certainly old enough to demand it.

I'll answer the question you probably have right now: He didn't get AIDS from Luke Murphy. It's not that simple.

But he probably got AIDS because of Luke Murphy.

I'll find another one of these essay-test notebooks and write down the rest.

15

Taylor Pierce's Second Notebook "About My Father And My Mother Who Had The Sparkle"

Dad told me that he met Luke Murphy in their dormitory, the 28-story Watterson Towers, during his freshman year at Illinois State University in Normal, Illinois, which apparently was anything but Normal in the 1970s.

"I'm not proud to tell you this, but we did a lot of drugs," Dad said. "It was that time and place. Luke and I were both from the Chicago suburbs, we liked the same kind of music, we both were majoring in political science and we kind of hit it off."

I was surprised. I asked him why that level of drug use never had come out about Murphy, given the fact that no one running for president seems to have any privacy.

"Luke was a good guy for the most part, but he could be very manipulative as I look back on it," was Dad's reply, or something to that effect. "I'm not sure he even realized that was so much his style. He just had a way about him. He always seemed to come out ahead and he was very careful in those situations. He could get other people to do things for him and only a few people knew he was more of a hippie-pretender. You know, he was one of those guys who wore his hair long, but not too long. He was one of those guys who would take a hit off a joint at a party but didn't want to do anything to ruin his future.

And, you probably know that he graduated early and joined the Navy. Otherwise, he would've been in the very last group of men to be drafted before the Vietnam War ended."

"I think he turned out to be a hero, or at least that's what they say," was my reply.

"Everyone has heard the story," Dad continued. "A pilot landed on an aircraft carrier on a stormy day. The boat was rocking. There was smoke in the cockpit, so the pilot couldn't wait for the seas to calm down. He almost overshot the runway and the plane nearly fell over the side, just sort of balancing on the edge, held by the tether the plane grabs when it lands on the deck of a carrier.

"Then a fire started in the cockpit. Luke was an officer on the deck. As everyone started to spray the fire, he was the one who got the unconscious pilot out, but an ocean swell made the boat move. That made the balance shift, so the plane starts to fall into the water as it begins to explode. Debris was flying everywhere and Luke took a big piece of metal like shrapnel in his hip."

Dad stopped at that point, needing a moment to catch his breath and I think to find his train of thought again.

"I kind of got ahead of myself," Dad said, turning back to their college years. "I could tell he wanted to experiment more. This would have been 1972 or '73.

"I guess I was more adventurous. We were stoned one day and I said, 'I'd like to try LSD. I'd like to drop acid.' And Luke agreed. Yeah, he said he had thought about it, too. And, as crazy as it sounds today, we got the stuff with a simple plan."

Dad paused to chuckle; then he had to pause to cough. It was a lot of talking for him, so I handed him a glass of water to give him a chance to regroup.

Dad said they simply walked into the student union, found someone "who looked like a hippie" and bought LSD from him. "Can you imagine that today?" he said.

And that's when my father described his first-and-only acid trip—at least that's what he said, although I suspect he said he only did it once to avoid encouraging me to try such a thing.

"It took quite a while to feel anything," he recalled. "We were playing cards. Hearts, I think. Then, all of a sudden the idea of looking at how many hearts I had in my hand seemed insanely, wildly funny. The queen of spades—I think she winked at me."

Dad described the rest of the night in amazing detail, from the music they played to the walks they took. He had vivid memories of looking at the stars, talking for hours and laughing until they had to stop. I could tell that these were important memories for him.

Then their night got weird.

Dad could see I was taking notes and didn't seem to care. My note-taking got really bad at this point as he told me what happened next. The truth is I was so stunned that I stopped writing. But, I definitely remember what he told me.

As they were starting to come down off the acid, they found themselves in Dad's dorm room, listening to "Aqualung" by Jethro Tull and both sitting on his bed.

At that point I felt a twinge of jealousy as I contemplated how he could remember the specific song that he played in his dorm room during his first acid trip. I wondered if he remembered nearly as much about my childhood. That sounds kind of bitter. Maybe that's unfair or irrational. Well, your childhood feelings aren't rational or irrational. They just are. And they stick to you like tar. Dad even made it a point to describe the damn bed in his room. It was one of those dorm beds that slides under some storage bolsters and turns into a couch when you slide it under the bolster during the day. They had smoked a lot of pot. It probably was around 5 in the morning. Luke said something like this, according to Dad:

"Man, I can't stop thinking about sex."

Dad said he murmured sort of an agreement. Luke asked if he had ever been curious about, "you know, expanding your horizons."

I definitely remember that line. It's hard to forget. "Expanding your horizons" was the way Dad quoted Luke. They both took turns repeating the phrase.

"Luke looked sort of dreamy," Dad said. "I still remember this. He stretched it out. We were both giggling like a couple girls. He says, 'Youuuuuuuuu knowwwwwwww Annnndeeee, we are ex-pannnnnnnnding yourrrrrr horizons, zons, zons, zons, zons.'"

Dad recounted he told Luke he was pretty exhausted at that point after tripping all night and probably said something back like, "Whaddaya mean?"

Luke still had sort of a glazed look in his eye as Dad recalled. He put his arm on Dad's shoulder as he sat next to Dad on the bed. He told Dad that he was a great friend and that friends you can trust and even love, yeah, maybe it was the acid talking, but, yeah, love, those friends were really special.

And Luke said again he was curious. He brushed the back of his hand against Dad's cheek and then dropped it down to Dad's leg. He kissed Dad on the same cheek and kissed him on the lips.

Then, for a brief moment, it was as though a gate holding back secrets had opened. Dad was talking as much to himself as he was to me, I think. It was pretty graphic. He started describing how Luke obviously had had some prior experiences by the way things happened after the kiss.

"He knew exactly where to go and what to do with a first-timer," Dad recounted. "Well, it's not that complicated, I guess. After some foreplay, he unzipped my pants and got on his knees next to me."

Then it was like Dad realized he was talking to his daughter. He stopped the details at that point, but I recorded this quote:

"You don't need to hear all the details of what happened next," he said, then showed another weak smile. "There's only so much you can tell your daughter, even when she is pumping you for information."

Then he laid back in the hospital bed and said he wanted to get some rest. That was okay with me. I was stunned and needed some processing time.

I picked up my purse from the floor next to the chair by his bed and started to leave the room when he spoke. I squeezed his hand and gave him a peck on the cheek. It seemed important to do that at that moment, but I felt a 100 percent kinship with my mom. My feelings were an emotional stew. Well, more like a hurricane. This man was a good father in some ways but not so much in others. What was this confession? Was it mainly pretend-acting so he didn't have to deal with my feelings at that moment about how living a lie might have killed his wife. My mom.

"Taylor, there's one other thing I should tell you about this."

I turned around and looked at him.

"What's that, Dad?" I said. "What is it?"

"I liked it. I liked what we did. I was scared about it, but in my heart I wanted it again."

It was time to go home for the night, so I left. I really didn't know what to say.

I've just about filled this notebook, so I'll finish in the next one.

16

Taylor Pierce's Third Notebook "About My Father And My Mother Who Had The Sparkle"

I need to say this right now, because I don't want anyone who reads this to get the wrong idea. I have a lot of gay friends and don't have any problem with it. I don't want to play into people's prejudices. But you have to understand: I had just heard that my father, whom I logically had always assumed was heterosexual, had a fling as a college student with the future president of the United States that led him to get a disease that killed my mom. *Would AIDS have happened to my family anyway? Is it fair to blame Luke Murphy?* You be the judge.

It's awful the prejudice and stereotypes that gays faced at the height of the AIDS crisis. Things have changed in my lifetime. For one thing, we know you don't get AIDS just by touching someone who has it or by breathing the same air or whatever. If you take care of yourself and get treated, many patients live pretty much normal lives.

Well, that's not how it was then, and if you weren't around, you can't appreciate the fears and prejudices AIDS inflicted on those unlucky enough or unsafe enough—or both—to get it. Imagine the Ebola crisis spreading in the U.S. beyond the handful of actual cases in our country. And imagine it not involving mosquitos but transmission by sex—and gay sex that. Is there anything that America has a harder time dealing with than sex?

Maybe if things had been different, if all my dad's "activity" had happened even a decade later, my mom and dad would still be alive. Or, at least, Dad could've faced his obvious conflicts more honestly in a different time and place. Of course, maybe I wouldn't have been born.

What if. What if.

Anyway, I visited Dad briefly over the next few days, but we didn't continue the story. He was getting weaker and didn't seem to be in much of a mood to talk when I tried to finish the conversation.

I sensed the end was getting close, so when I visited him the following Saturday, we mainly exchanged pleasantries. By this point, his skin had taken on a decidedly yellowish cast. His cheeks were sunken and there was an IV providing nourishment. He didn't have much of an appetite. He obviously as heavily medicated. The TV was on. I think it was a college football game—he was a big football fan—but he wasn't paying much attention.

We obviously were on hospital time again, with seconds going by that felt like minutes, waiting for a few doctor moments that quite obviously were not going to convey good news anyway. You could smell hospital smells and hear various machines doing hospital-machine-things in the room. The tinny speaker in the control next to his pillow announced that Michigan was beating Ohio State. Or maybe it was the other way around. I really didn't care.

"Dad," I said. "We need to finish your story. I want you to pick up where we left off.

"As you can imagine, I have some questions about what you told me," I said, having given some careful thought to how to approach this. "I know it's weird. It's weird for me, too, but I'd really like it if we could talk more about this. I need to get my arms around it. Do you understand? Do you mind?"

He opened his eyes, warily I thought.

"Why not?" he said finally, flashing a weak smile. "I'm not going anywhere—well, at least not at this moment—and I understand why you'd ask."

But I could tell quickly that this wasn't going to go smoothly. I figured he would be reluctant to go into much detail about his "needs" after the college incident. First, I asked him some more about Luke Murphy in the aftermath of that night.

"No," he said, anticipating my question before I could ask it. "We never did 'it' again." He put a feeble set of air quotes around the "it," then he continued.

"In fact, we drifted apart as friends and I got the feeling he wanted to drift," he said. "He was careful to be friendly enough, but he basically avoided any situations where we'd spend much time together."

Abruptly he changed course. "I love you, Taylor," he said. "You know that, right?"

I replied and sanded down my anger for his benefit. "I do, Dad. I think you did what you thought was your best under the circumstances." I wasn't sure if I meant that, but it seemed like the right, comforting thing to say.

"So," I continued, "did you ever hear from Luke Murphy after college?"

"Like I said, we drifted apart," Dad said. "I wrote him in Palatine, that's the Chicago suburb he was from, after I heard what happened in the Navy; that he was a hero. This was before he was a big-time politician of course. I just wanted to tell him his college friends were proud of him. But he never replied. To be honest, I would've liked to talk to him, to help sort out what happened that night. Later, of course, I realized it was way too risky for him to even acknowledge I existed."

"Did you vote for him when he ran for president?" I asked, not sure what spot in my brain came up with that off-the-wall question.

"No."

That's all he said to my question. Just "no."

"Did you ever try to contact him again?" I asked, feeling like the relentless cop in a bad "Law and Order" episode. "Did he even acknowledge you existed?" Dad remained willing to go along.

"I didn't contact him, but I know he knew about us. There was a college reunion that he attended when people were starting to talk about him maybe being a future president. Maybe he did it for political reasons or really wanted to go. Who knows? Anyway, there was another friend of ours, Kevin Knight. I know he talked to Kevin."

"I think I remember Kevin," I said. "I think he visited our house a few times."

"That's right," Dad said. "We've stayed in touch over the years. He's called me a few times here. Sometimes we email. He's been a real friend."

Dad continued from there.

"So, Kevin tells me that Luke comes up to him during the reunion and takes him aside. 'Say, whatever happened to Andy Pierce?' he asks Kevin. All very casual. Kevin says he tells Luke about your mom dying from AIDS complications and me going down the same road. He tells Luke that everyone thinks a blood transfusion or some other weird thing brought it on. Luke asks Kevin how to reach me. So, Kevin gives Murphy's aide a phone number and my e-mail. 'It would be kind of cool for Andy to get a note from a future president,' is what Kevin says he told Luke. But, no, I never heard anything."

Then my father seemed to find energy reserves I didn't think he had. He shifted gears back to the dorm room and the years that followed.

"Taylor, you do realize that I couldn't, couldn't, come out in those times," he said. "I wasn't even sure for many years whether what happened in that dorm room was more than an aberration. It would've been the end of our family. People would've shunned your mother. My career would've been ruined. And I swear. I swear. I didn't know I had the virus when your mom and I had relations. Obviously it happened after you guys were born."

I lost it at that point. It came out like a flood. I yelled at him.

"Damn it, Dad," I said, feeling tears. "You knew what you were doing was risky, right? But, you didn't stop, did you? Do you even know who the hell gave you the AIDS virus?"

Silence.

That's what I remember. Silence. It cloaked the room now with a thickness that felt dangerous to penetrate.

Dad looked exhausted.

"No, Taylor, you're right about all that," he finally said as though every word came from a deeper place. Maybe that's the soul. I definitely was the priest at his deathbed now. He pushed the words out in staccato fashion, as though he needed to make sure he said everything as clearly as he could in the time he had left. It was all very Faulkner-like now. Stream of consciousness.

"For a long time, I told myself I was just another guy cheating on his wife on a business trip here and there. No harm, no foul. Okay, that's bullshit, gay or straight. And, gay or straight, men are great at that sort of thinking. Inside, I knew it was risky. It was several years after that first time with Luke that I had another encounter. I'm not going to share the details. But I kept doing it. I never paid for sex, by the way. No, I don't want an award for that. I didn't do it constantly, but every now and then. Usually on business trips. You'd be in a bar. You'd get a vibe. It would happen. That doesn't make it right. And, no, I don't know who gave it to me. Whoever it was, he's probably gone, too.

"I truly loved your mother, Taylor. You have to believe that. But I killed your mother and destroyed our family. It's a burden I earned."

I stared at him. He seemed spent by this final confession.

"That's a shit pile of rationalization, Dad."

I saw tears making streaks down his cheeks. It was the last thing I got to say to him. I ran out of time. Well, actually, he did. So, some mysteries, especially about the relationship between my mom and dad, simply must remain. There's no one to ask. I know there was love in the house at times, and sometimes I seize some comfort from that.

We cremated him a week later. Kevin Knight came to the service and I took him aside. Long story short, he confirmed some of what Dad told me but couldn't or wouldn't fill in many blanks.

And that brings us back to Luke Murphy. His being gay didn't destroy my family, but the way he handled it sure contributed. I don't care if Luke Murphy is gay or not, but don't take political positions that make you a hypocrite. Living a lie helped make him president, so I guess he got what he wanted.

I think I can get over all of that. I really can. Sometimes it's the little hurts that linger. What I really can't forgive is that he was too busy running for office to risk being my dad's friend or even acknowledge his existence.

Luke Murphy might have been a military hero, but he'll always be a coward to me.

17

Dallas, Texas | Late February

Reginald Fox and Lydia Nicks stood on opposite sides of a dining room table in the candidate's suite at the Dallas Regency Hyatt, circling each other like caged cats, trying not to make their strong disagreement personal.

Nicks felt she had the upper hand. The election was going her way. For starters, she had exceeded expectations in the Iowa caucuses a few weeks earlier, always the first test of a presidential candidate. Her strong second-place finish was notable particularly because she had announced her candidacy "too late"—at least that was what all the political commentators said, even on normally friendly Fox News.

Well, she thought, *screw them*, and she had said as much in her speech at the Cedar Rapids Convention Complex.

"The media doesn't vote. You do," she declared, spreading her arms in a broad, flourishing gesture and then closing them around herself in a symbolic gesture to hug the cheering crowd. "When I'm president, we'll never forget how Iowa gave us such a great start."

Their suspicions that Murphy was vulnerable seemed true. Already there were whispers among major donors. A few Murphy supporters had started hedging bets, quietly writing checks to the political groups that supported Nicks and didn't have to report the names of donors.

Political analysts called it the "expectations game." If you beat expectations, you win even if you lose. While Murphy finished first in Iowa, he only won by three percentage points. Eight days later, he won the New Hampshire primary, something expected from the state's more moderate voters, but again Nicks did surprisingly well. Then Nicks won the South Carolina Republican primary the following week as voters in that conservative state apparently liked what they heard. The crowds had been large and enthusiastic from Myrtle Beach to Greenville and in between. The scent of momentum was intoxicating.

Now "Super Tuesday" loomed; twelve states voting on the same day, many of them in the south. Flooring Murphy in Texas was particularly important.

"Keep hitting him on the meaning of the Esaias comet and what happened in Bali," Fox counseled, tapping both fists on the tabletop for emphasis. "You say it's the sign that we've got to fight the Muslims wherever they stand. Then you hit him on how he let things go to hell with the Chinese. You hit him on compromising with the Democrats on way too much stuff."

"That's all fine, Reg, but it's time to bury him," Nicks said. "We should use all we've got. Leak the damn thing. It doesn't have to come from us. You know how to do it."

"No," Fox said. "It's too risky without verification. We haven't located Taylor Pierce. She might not even be alive. It could be all bullshit. If it turns out Murphy is the victim of a smear campaign, he'll benefit from sympathy and people will assume you orchestrated it. Beware of blowback. It'll be epic."

"But it's true," Nicks said. "It feels true. Once it comes out, he might even have to do an LBJ and drop out for the good of the country." She put air quotes around "for the good of the country" after the reference to President Lyndon Johnson, who shocked the nation in 1968 when he announced he wouldn't run for another term as president at the height of the Vietnam War.

She had recently re-read his announcement that stunned the nation on March 31, 1968, at the end of a speech in which he halted bombing of North Vietnam and described the importance of combatting the federal deficit. His words at the end were the ones historians recalled most often:

"I have concluded that I should not permit the Presidency to become involved in the partisan divisions that are developing in this political year.

"With America's sons in the fields far away, with America's future under challenge right here at home, with our hopes and the world's hopes for peace in the balance every day, I do not believe that I should devote an hour or a day of my time to any personal partisan causes or to any duties other than the awesome duties of this office—the presidency of your country.

"Accordingly, I shall not seek, and I will not accept, the nomination of my party for another term as your president."

Cynics abounded. Everyone knew that LBJ had a huge ego—what president didn't have one? Observers figured it was more than likely that what he was really saving was himself from an ass-kicking and the embarrassment of being a sitting president who couldn't get his party's nomination for a second term.

"You might not even need to step into this mud Lydia," Fox said. "It's a really bad idea this soon. We need more information. I feel very strongly."

"Strongly enough that you'd quit and cause a scandal by quitting if I just go ahead and do it myself?"

"Probably so," he said, unsuccessful at keeping his voice from rising. "I don't mean that as a threat, but I need to get your damn attention on how bad an idea this is. You're paying me to call it like I see it Lydia. Everyone plays to win. So will they. Believe me when I tell you this: Big-league dirt brings big-league risk. You don't use this stuff to seal the deal. You use it when you have no choice. You aren't in that place. You still have a choice. You've got him on the run."

"Okay, okay," she said. "No leaks from me. Not yet anyway. But I expect confirmation sooner rather than later. That way we're ready."

"We're on it," Fox said.

***

Nearly 1,000 miles away, in Madison, Wisconsin, Taylor Pierce awoke from a fitful, groggy sleep. Her first thought, like that of any fully addicted junkie, was whether she had stuff for the day. That's what she called it. Stuff. It was as good a word as any. She remembered there should be some heroin in the drawer next to her bed but knew it was possible she had used it all the night before and had forgotten. Still, her mind seemed pretty clear at the moment, making her briefly sad it had all come to this. Then she immediately focused on the quest.

Nervous to be out of supply, she slowly slid the creaky drawer open and immediately relaxed when she saw a syringe and plastic bag with a good amount of white powder, enough to last the day for sure.

"I'll get some coffee first and grab a smoke," she said out loud to no one in particular. Then she laughed, recognizing that there was no way this would be the order of things.

She prepared a relatively small fix. Carefully spreading two of her toes apart, she plunged the syringe into the opening and waited for the satisfying feeling of euphoria and, probably more important in her stage of addiction, the knowledge that she was avoiding the pain of going without.

The door opened and she recognized Meg Williamson, the woman who had sought her out and encouraged her to preserve her story in writing.

"Quite a welcome," she thought to herself, vaguely remembering how this pleasant, thoughtful college professor had invited her into her home to stay while she got oriented in Madison.

Things had a funny way of working out, she thought. Geo-Tech, a local consulting company, had interviewed her for a research assistant job. That was thanks to a tip from a new friend at LinkedIn. The reasons were unclear based on her rather skimpy resume, but that's what it meant to be a friend. She had been working in a Starbucks in Des Plaines, Illinois, between gigs after taking yet another break from nearby

Harper College. She had moved from job to job in information technology, explaining that she definitely intended to finish her nearly completed computer science degree. Depression that she medicated with drug use got in the way of that and was making it harder to keep jobs. She couldn't afford counseling, but she didn't a professional to vaguely acknowledge that had lots of "family issues."

She had always been drawn to Madison as a potentially fun place to live with a great quality of life as long as cold weather didn't bother you too much. She was excited about this opportunity and maybe the chance to finish her degree at a great school like the University of Wisconsin.

She recalled how she had met Meg by accident at the salad bar of an organic grocery on Madison's near east side shortly after she arrive. As the fuzzy warmth of the heroin began to take hold, she wondered if she should be angry instead of warm toward Meg, who seemed to have a lot to do with converting her depression-fueled flirtations with hard drugs into full-blown addiction.

Well, she thought, *at least there was plenty around and she certainly didn't need to know how it got there. And this cute little house near the university campus was a nice place to stay.*

"Hi, Meg," she said, her voice growing thicker. "What's up?"

"Well, I've been thinking," Meg Williamson said. "It's time, I think it's time, to provide some confirmation of your story about President Murphy."

18

Mesa, Arizona | Early March Of Election Year

Trey Van Ohmann and Mike Surrey had a few moments together before the "The Mike and Aimee Show," live from Sloan Park in Mesa, Arizona, the state-of-the-art facility where the Cubs prepared for the start of the baseball season.

Van Ohmann waited restlessly in the center seat in the broadcast booth with Surrey to his left and Aimee's seat to the right.

He looked down at his blue jersey in which a Cubs logo—a big "C" with a bear in the middle—dominated the left breast.

"Still seems weird to wear anything but a uniform that says Boston," he said.

"That's a perfect segue into the opening we have. It also has the virtue of being true," Surrey said. "I'll say something like this: Here we are, Trey. I'm used to wearing that jersey as the manager, not sitting here with a polo shirt and a microphone. And only in my wildest dreams did I see you in a Chicago Cubs uniform last year. If they'd traded for you then, I might've done a happy dance on top of the dugout and we'd never have needed a Game Seven. So, how does it feel to be a Chicago Cub?"

Surrey paused to give Van Ohmann a chance to react.

"That'll be fine, Mike," he said, offering a slight smile. "If you don't take offense, there's a good comeback line: If you'd kept your cool, you'd probably still be in that dugout."

"Touché. Hard to argue with that," Surrey said. "Go for it."

Van Ohmann usually cooperated with the media, but it was no secret he was introverted. At least with Surrey, he'd be talking to someone who had been on the field instead of just lobbing caustic comments from the broadcast bleachers.

It was a day in Mesa that provided better advertising for free than the local Chamber of Commerce could ever purchase. The cloudless sky was as the same shade of blue as Van Ohmann's Chicago jersey. A light desert breeze was just enough to dry any perspiration caused by the temperature—a perfect 77 degrees. In the background, mountains painted the landscape in pinks, browns and tans in sharp contrast to the lush, green grass on the baseball fields made possible by irrigation. Fans already were enjoying the day, even though it was an hour before the start, especially those who could sit on the outfield grass for a relatively low ticket price to watch a game that would create memories even if it didn't count in the standings. It was baseball in the spring, offering a vibe and a pace unlike any other sport that spoke of simpler times and clearer goals for both the players and the fans. All teams were created equal and every field seemed filled with future stars-in-the-making.

Van Ohmann and Surrey continued to make small talk as Aimee Walters came sprinting over.

"Hey, Trey," she said. "It's nice to finally meet you."

Van Ohmann returned her greeting with a nod and a slight smile. He hadn't come close to an ongoing relationship since the death of his father, and suddenly he saw the first woman who had really captured his attention beyond a few encounters that he had assessed and addressed by quickly retreating.

He noticed Aimee's trim designer jeans and the pleasing shape they made around her bottom as she slid into her seat. Her medium-brown hair had light-blonde streaks and she had tied it back into a short ponytail. She was wearing a sleeveless, brick-red polo shirt that had a WCO logo in blue with white bordering. The undone buttons revealed just a hint of cleavage with the bright gold chain of a simple necklace in between.

Aimee Walters caught Van Ohmann looking and made a quick calculation familiar to all young, single women: Was this guy a jerk or someone with a decent heart who might want more than a night in my pants? That was especially true when the voyeur was a rich, good-looking athlete who likely was used to commitment-free entertainment any time he wanted it. On looks alone, Trey certainly wouldn't have any problems. He was about six-foot-two with penetrating green eyes, light brown hair that was long but not too long and no discernible gut—unlike a lot of pitchers. His power obviously came from long legs that bulged against his uniform pants and his shoulders filled out the top of his shirt. She had honed her radar following years of bartending and even more years of just being an attractive young woman with the scar tissue from failed relations. This time her radar locked in, telling her that maybe Trey Van Ohmann had possibilities; maybe he was different.

Both their observations passed by in a flicker of time and she would have been pleased to know that Trey had gone through a similar mental rundown and felt the same way.

Aimee yanked her focus back to the upcoming interview.

"Trey, besides the usual questions, I'd like to ask how you and your family are doing," she said. "I'm so sorry about what happened to your father. It won't be long. Then we'll get into baseball talk."

"I don't like to talk much about it. I really haven't said anything since the end of the World Series. It's very personal," Van Ohmann said, then decided that since he was going to keep getting asked about it, he might as well address it for Aimee Walters. Others would pick up on the comments and he could just refer back to that when he inevitably heard the same questions again.

He looked at her directly, struck again by her presence; realizing some of his thoughts weren't exactly pure.

"You're going to be very good at this new job and I'm sorry about what you've had to go through, too," he said, offering a slight smile. "Here's what I want to say: It's been very hard on my family. My brothers and me; we've lost both our parents now. And there still are a lot of unanswered questions in our minds about how he died. That's what I'll say and I'd ask that we leave it at that."

"Deal," Aimee said. "Deal."

***

The interview with Aimee spurred Van Ohmann to do something he had been postponing.

The Cubs were off the next day, so he had requested an extra day to "deal with personal business related to my father's death."

He flew to Idaho, which was why the Van Ohmann brothers found themselves sitting in Travis Van Ohmann's GMC Yukon, sipping lukewarm coffee from foam cups. The gorgeous scenery was easy to take for granted if you were an Idaho native. Having been away for several years, Trey no longer did so.

He listened to the roar of the Lochsa River in eastern Idaho, near the Montana state line. "Roar" was no exaggeration. The river looked pregnant with the power of nature, running high and fast with March snowmelt from an unusually wet winter. Tall trees and mountains framed the scene, reinforcing a thought that occurred when he examined the area from the aerial perspective of Google Maps. U.S. Highway 12, the main east-west route through this section of Idaho, seemed little more than a nearly irrelevant, manmade ribbon as it snaked along the side of the river for hundreds of miles in the Lolo National Forest between Lewiston, Idaho and Missoula, Montana.

With the practiced intensity of a Major League pitcher, he studied the spot where Don Van Ohmann had lost control of his Chevy pickup truck. Trey could still see scar-like stabs of deep-blue paint along the edge of a guardrail that the nearly new truck scraped as it careened into the fast-moving river the previous October. The coroner's autopsy report said it was highly likely his father was seriously injured by the crash and couldn't escape the water filling the truck as it flipped on its side.

It seems like an unusually ugly, scary and lonely way to die, he thought. Even uglier was the notion that someone had tampered with the OnStar guidance system and took control of the truck.

"Now that I see it, I'm more certain than ever that it went down the way the FBI thinks," Trey said to his brothers. "He was too good a driver—a successful, retired race-car driver, for God's sake—to just plow into a river during broad daylight."

They also had stopped at the same Mexican restaurant in the small town of Kamiah where Don ate along his final journey—proven by the credit card statement that arrived after Don's death. Leftover bills had no regard for the departure of the recipient. They simply required payment.

"Dad had good taste," Trey had remarked as he swallowed the remains of a tostada. Knowing Don's affection for Mexican food, he had no doubt his father stopped there often during runs to deliver or pick up specialty auto parts between Lewiston and Missoula, Montana.

He had hoped to find some closure by retracing his father's last steps, trying to feel what his father felt and do what he did.

That night, he read an alarming article in the lodge where they stayed near Kamiah. The article made closure harder. Some computer hackers demonstrated it was relatively easy to take control of a Jeep SUV by gaining control of the vehicle through the connected GPS mapping system, which was always on if the car was operating. Jeep immediately announced that owners should go to local dealers for a free software patch.

"Hackers Show They Can Take Control of Moving Jeep Cherokee," said the headline of the story in the Wall Street Journal, which started like this:

> "Two computer-security researchers demonstrated they could take control of a moving Jeep Cherokee using the vehicle's wireless communications system, raising new questions about the safety of Internet-connected cars."

As the FBI had told him and the media reported in screaming headlines, Tommy Czerski, the crazed Cubs fan, probably hacked into the truck, figuring that Don Van Ohmann's death would prevent his son from pitching against the Cubs in the World Series. But Tommy misjudged him. Trey pitched anyway.

The trip helped in one respect. Trey finally accepted emotionally what he knew intellectually: It didn't matter if his father's death was part of some larger conspiracy. Dad wasn't coming back. In a vague sort of "I-had-to-see-it-for-myself" attitude, Trey decided the visit was worth it, especially since he did it with his brothers. Maybe that was the important part.

The Van Ohmann brothers took a last sniff of the damp, piney-scented, familiar Idaho air and headed back to Lewiston so Trey could catch his charter flight to Phoenix.

19

Madison, Wisconsin
Late March Of Election Year

Two big lakes, Mendota and Monona, squished either side of downtown Madison, Wisconsin, forming a narrow isthmus like toothpaste squeezed from a tube. The two east and west sides of the city and suburbs sprawled out from both sides around the lakes. If you were a funky college professor, aging hippie or a millennial seeking a more urban life, the east side was where you wanted to live.

Meg Williamson and her friend Frank Pfeiffer watched the "Super Tuesday" election results on a modest flat-screen TV in the living room of Meg's small but well-appointed house on Madison's east side, a few blocks from Lake Mendota and the downtown of Wisconsin's second largest city.

The scowl on her face told the story as she twisted her long, gray ponytail around her left wrist, a habit when she was lost in thought.

Her thoughts were focused on Lydia Nicks. After Nicks' great start in the early states, the predictable result was a volley of covert and overt attacks on her record, her character and her personal life. Just as predictably, Nicks had started to slip. The downward trend frustrated her supporters and, more importantly, raised small questions in the donors' minds that could become larger questions later.

With that in mind, it surprised Meg and Frank that Nicks and Murphy had resisted the temptation to leak Taylor's information before Super Tuesday. The notebooks would quickly ignite the media gossip train into a bullet train. Only ink-stained fuddy-duddies paid attention to the tried-and-true rules in journalism of, first, doing your own reporting, and, second, having two independent, credible sources before releasing information.

So, if CBS News or the New York Times wouldn't pick up Taylor's bombshell diary without confirmation, there would be no shortage of bloggers, hard-core "gotcha" websites and gossip programs to jump on it. Social media would go bonkers. Finally, the "traditional media" outlets would cover themselves by saying, "This hasn't been independently confirmed, but you need to know this is out there."

It was a toxic environment, which was why a lot of well-qualified, well-intentioned people refused to run for office. The price paid by the candidate, family, friends and business associates just wasn't worth it. Luke Murphy was performing exactly how Williamson expected: Acting presidential while carefully staying distant from a massive campaign to paint Lydia Nicks as a crazed, religious zealot who couldn't be trusted.

Williamson wanted him mired in scandal and Taylor's story was the perfect bring-down. It didn't come across as overtly anti-gay. This wasn't the 1950s, when it was perfectly plausible that the whiff of being homosexual could destroy a political career—the premise of a best-selling political novel and movie of the era, "Advise & Consent."

Taylor's story would provide another example of Luke Murphy's calculation, self-absorption and hypocrisy. His callousness helped cause someone's death, even worse than the Skowron incident because Murphy was that much older and should have been more than a fair-weather friend. Williamson was sure people would see it that way. And the delicious part was that the gay affair reinforced the prejudices of an important subset of Republican voters. It would even inflame the whispering about why Luke and Alison Murphy had no children. Lydia Nicks could win anti-guy votes without having to pander to them.

"Well, I'm definitely glad we put this in Skowron's hands, too. It's probably time to move forward," Williamson said. "That was our insurance in case Fox and Nicks surprised us."

"And, we have the advantage of proof. We have tons of Luke Murphy research and we know Taylor is as real as her diary," Pfeiffer said.

"A gift from the stars," she said, then laughed a laugh that was more like a muted chuckle. "Or comets, maybe."

"The real gift was Andy Pierce," Pfeiffer said. "What a break that we had someone check out Kevin Knight. Otherwise, we'd have never known about him."

Getting to Taylor had taken careful planning. With Andy Pierce deceased and her brother nowhere to be found, they wanted to find out what Taylor knew.

Taylor had no way of knowing that one of Williamson's colleagues consulted to Geo-Tech on hiring and human resources. The company always needed I.T. people. She had connected with Taylor on LinkedIn under an assumed name and tipped her about the job opening. Then she e-mailed a glowing, bogus "reference letter" to Geo-Tech to increase the odds that Taylor would get an interview. It was easy to arrange the "chance" meeting at the grocery store on the day when Taylor got the word that she'd have to look for a different job to stay in Madison. Somehow, Geo-Tech also had learned that Taylor had serious issues with depression and drug use.

Since Taylor had no money and a desire to stay, she readily agreed to crash with Meg until things squared away.

"I've helped a lot of young professional women get started in this town," she had assured Taylor.

At some point, they would need to decide what to do about Taylor for the good of the cause, but that would come later. For now, she was under control.

The challenge—to Meg Williamson, there were no "problems," only "challenges"—was that using Taylor Pierce created a high risk of exposure; higher even than their acts during the World Series. Taylor had no idea of the roots of Meg

Williamson's obsession with Luke Murphy, but Williamson knew that clues could become apparent to others if her name surfaced, though that remained unlikely.

One problem was a damn Wikipedia reference. Williamson hated its presence and checked it frequently to ensure there were no recent updates. She couldn't get it deleted, but she often submitted editing changes to make it as low-key as possible. The entry began like this:

> Meg Williamson
>
> From Wikipedia, the free encyclopedia
>
> Margaret (Meg) Williamson (born May 23, 1953) is best known as a childhood friend of president Luke Murphy in Palatine, Illinois. She, Bob Walters (see separate entry) and Murphy were present during a now-infamous childhood incident involving Scott "Moose" Skowron, who was permanently disabled after hitting his head on a sidewalk following a confrontation between him and the three friends, bringing Skowron's promising athletic career to an end. When Murphy became president, environmental radicals made an unsuccessful attempt to blackmail him by threatening to expose that Murphy was the one who actually pushed Skowron and let Walters take the blame, causing Walters to be sent to a juvenile prison facility for a year. Murphy refused their radical demands and survived an assassination attempt at Chicago's Wrigley Field during the seventh game of the World Series. (See entry on Thomas A. "Tommy" Czerski.)
>
> Members of the media have contacted Williamson many times over the years for insight into Luke Murphy in general and this incident specifically. She has consistently stated that while they were childhood friends, she lost touch with both Murphy and Walters after high school. As for the incident, she has said she only has a general recollection and doesn't recall who

> pushed Skowron or even if she was watching at that moment. "I was just a little girl," she told Politico.com. "All I really remember is screaming and crying after poor Scott hit the ground."
>
> Since the late 1980s, Williamson has been a tenured professor at the University of Wisconsin-Madison. She has a doctorate in environmental science. As a researcher, she has developed a number of patented processes related to energy industries……

She had used the wealth from her patents and her inheritance quietly. Only one other person, Pfeiffer, her friend and a philosophy professor at the university, knew how hard it had been for her to apply what she knew to help the coal and oil industries. But it was a necessary and clever cover. Few would expect that someone profiting from the fossil fuel industry was the leader of a loosely knit group of radical environmentalists.

Even Frank didn't know the full story of her connection to that fateful childhood day, how Meg had run out of the house trying to hold back tears after her alcoholic father hit her mother again. She had stopped Murphy and Walters on their way to school on a cold November day, setting the stage for Skowron's childish, bullying taunts.

Her life got much worse after the incident. She knew Luke and Bob were suspicious, but she never admitted the sexual abuse she endured from her father. It was no wonder she left Palatine as soon as she could. In Madison, she found refuge.

Her radicalism grew as Luke Murphy's career advanced and it became obvious to her that Murphy would never do what needed to be done to rescue Earth—Gaia, as she quietly called it, using the spiritual name attached to Earth as a living organism. America needed a president to lead the world in the right direction.

She thought that Matthew Leeds, the young senator from Ohio who was the leading candidate for the Democratic nomination, might be a good start. Williamson was doing her part to make sure he was well-funded.

"Leeds will never know what good friends he has in us," she said to Pfeiffer. "Murphy could beat Leeds. Nicks won't. But she can take votes from Murphy. We destroy Murphy. Leeds wins."

"It all sounds good," Pfeiffer said. "But, what if Nicks wins? She's worse than Murphy. She's not even sure the government should be involved in environmental regulation at all."

"Lydia Nicks can't win," Williamson said. "We can build her up and we can take her down if and when we have to. Right now, she's our secret weapon."

20

Citi Field, New York City | Late May

Like all great pitchers, Trey Van Ohmann obsessed what it meant to be a successful athlete who had to face the greatest hitters on Earth. But for all the reading, thinking and practicing he did when he was getting ready to pitch, one quote stuck with him the most. The speaker would surprise a lot of people. It was Charlie Brown, the sad character in the "Peanuts" comic strip and famous for being a frustrated athlete.

Van Ohmann thought that Charlie Brown said all there was to say about being a pitcher, "It's very lonely out here on the pitcher's mound."

It felt very lonely at this moment. He began the season slightly off form for the Cubs, winning more than he was losing, distracted by the death of his father, though he would never say that publicly. He simply wasn't as effective as usual. His fastball was just a tad slower; the location of his pitches was off just a little bit; the sharp break in his slider was just a little duller. With Major League hitters, that would turn a superstar pitcher into a so-so performer—a fellow fortunate to win more than he lost; a player who could still make a good living, because even pitchers of that caliber were hard to find. But, you weren't The Ace—the one guy everyone relied upon when the team needed someone to end a losing streak, and the guy who drew more fans into the park just because he was pitching.

Trey Van Ohmann was used to being That Guy, and at least on this day he was not only That Guy, but a guy perched on joining the elite group of pitchers of perfect games: 27 batters faced over nine innings and 27 outs.

So far, no one from the Mets had reached base. Twenty-four batters went up; 24 batters went down. It was the bottom of the ninth inning. He was ahead 2-0 and three batters stood between him and history.

The mound remained lonely. One of baseball's unwritten rules was that none of your teammates would mention a no-hitter in progress. Best to leave him alone with his thoughts, his ability and his competitive fire.

The first batter struck out. The second batter popped out weakly to the shortstop. Now it was between him and Miguel Pineda, one of the Mets' best hitters.

Pineda worked the count to three balls and two strikes. Van Ohmann took the sign from Armando Martinez, his catcher. He tried to stay calm and not think too much that one bad pitch would mean Ball Four and the end of the perfect game. Any rationalization that winning the game was all that really mattered, not a perfect game or at least a no-hitter, was pure bullshit at this point. This wasn't the World Series. This was one of 162 games in May during a season that wouldn't end until October. He wanted this.

He agreed with Martinez, who signaled for a slider. If Pineda had a weakness, it was for a sharp breaking pitch low and outside; a pitch that would scoot out of Pineda's hitting zone like a ball-bearing spinning crazily off a glass tabletop.

As soon as he released the pitch, Van Ohmann knew it wasn't going over the plate; not wildly off, but off just the same. It would be Ball Four if Pineda didn't accept the bait.

But Pineda couldn't afford to take that chance on a close pitch with two strikes. If the umpire called it a strike, he'd end the game with the bat on his shoulder. Screw that. He decided to swing. Because the ball was slightly outside, he hit the ball on the extreme end of the bat. A quarter-inch closer to the end of the bat and the New York fans would have had a home run to cheer. Still, he hit it hard and the ball kept rising as it crossed second base about 10 feet above the bag and headed toward the centerfield wall.

The Cubs got another break. If Pineda had hit the ball anywhere but almost straight at Chris Kronberg, the Cubs' center fielder, he would have had a double off the wall. But Kronberg easily stepped into the best spot to make the catch.

Van Ohmann pitched a perfect game.

About 30 minutes later, sweat still dripped off his face as he walked into the interview room at Citi Field. He noticed that there was a much larger media contingent than you'd typically see for a late-spring game, even in New York.

Well, that's what happens when you pitch a perfect game and you've just pitched your team into first place, he thought to himself.

He answered the usual batch of stock questions. Always courteous, Van Ohmann responded with obvious answers and a genuine mix of pride mixed with humbleness and thanks to his teammates. ESPN broadcast the news conference live. At the end, the network's reporter, Brian Bennett, said, "Trey, I think we've got a surprise for you," and handed him a cell phone.

Van Ohmann looked at him quizzically.

"Trust me, Trey," Bennett said. "You want to take this call."

"Okay," Van Ohmann said, turning his attention to Bennett's iPhone. "Hello?"

"Trey, this is President Murphy. I just want to congratulate you."

"Thank you sir. Thank you, Mr. President," was all Van Ohmann could think to say.

"Call me Luke," Murphy said. "You know I'm a Cubs fan and I think you know I'm also a fan of great performances by great people. Come and visit me the next time the Cubs are in Washington. I'd like to meet you and shake your hand."

"I'll try to do that, uh, Mr. President," Van Ohmann said.

"And Go Cubs," Murphy added.

"Absolutely. We want to do it again. I can tell you that."

Murphy ended the call and Bennett took the phone back.

"How about that?" Bennett said on the air. "Trey Van Ohmann just got an invitation to the White House from America's Number One Cubs Fan. So, Trey, will you go?"

"Of course, Brian." Van Ohmann said with a half-smile that turned into what was for him a rare, big public grin. "How do you say 'no' to the president?"

21

WCO Studios, Chicago | Late June

Skowron picked up the phone from the desk in his cubicle and saw on the caller i.d. that it was Davis Bryant, the station manager.

"The Bob Walters Show," he said in a low voice, playing coy with Bryant just for laughs. "This is Moose. Do you have a comment for Bob?"

"Funny. Very funny," Bryant said. "Listen Scott, I need you guys in my office. Now if you can, or at least before air time today."

"We're both here," Skowron said. "Bob just went out for and I quote, 'some goddam real coffee instead of that watery Keurig crap' and should be right back. What's it about?"

"Let's save it for the meeting," Bryant said.

"Chief, that doesn't sound so good," Skowron said. "Did we get sold? Are we converting everything to automated smooth jazz or something?"

That was everyone's greatest fear in radio. It always had been a tough business, especially in big cities with owners frustrated by the time and costs—both psychic and financial—involved in keeping high-maintenance, on-air talent happy. Consolidation, technology and cost-cutting had eliminated the need for costly personalities at most places except stations doing sports or political talk. Meanwhile, competition from devices, apps, Internet stations and satellite radio supercharged the urgency that both owners and on-air talent felt to make as much money as possible in the present.

"Threats to your survival will do that," Walters once remarked to Skowron when details of his latest negotiations had leaked to the media; something that Walters suspected—but knew enough not to ask—was the doing of his agent. A slight dip in the ratings could mean a general housecleaning; an ownership change could throw everyone out of work overnight.

"Nah," Bryant said in response to Skowron's query. "You aren't that lucky. You've still got me. But I do need to meet. Get up here as soon as you can."

Skowron hung up the phone and wheeled around the corner of his cubicle in his chair to see if Walters had returned. He caught sight of the door opening just as Walters entered with a steaming cup of coffee and a bag of pastries from Panera Bread.

"Bear claws. My favorite. One for you, too," Walters said, noticing how Skowron eyed the bag. "I'm rewarding myself for Day 30 without a cigarette. So, I'm wondering, if everyone thinks I'm such an asshole, how come I'm like Jesus—feeding others in need?"

"You're still an asshole. You're secretly trying to kill me until I get so fat my chair collapses or I have a massive coronary," Skowron said before taking a big bite. "Hey, Bryant wants to see us pronto. I have no idea what it's about."

Skowron started to roll his chair down the hall. In reality, he prided himself in maintaining his body above the waist like the athlete everyone thought he would become when he was a star quarterback and Little League star. He was everyone's first pick in wheelchair basketball and enjoyed a well-earned reputation as a fierce competitor in Paralympic events. He shook his head in a quick "no" when Walters offered to push, so Walters simply followed him past Bryant's secretary and into the station manager's office.

Bryant sat behind a black walnut desk. A window to the right dominated one wall, but the view showed little more than a parking lot in the scruffy neighborhood on Chicago's near-west side where the station had been located since the early 1950s.

The neighborhood had started to gentrify in recent years but still had a long way to go. As Skowron glanced out the window, he noticed two homeless guys sacked out in the small patch of grass next to the station's side entrance.

A series of publicity posters for WCO lined the wall behind Bryant. The most memorable poster if you were a Chicago sports fan was from the late 1950s with a promotional shot of Ernie Banks, the legendary Chicago Cubs shortstop, standing back to back with Luis Aparicio, the all-star shortstop for the neighboring Chicago White Sox. Both men were staring at the camera with one arm outstretched holding a baseball with the 1950s version of the WCO logo on it. Underneath the black-and-white photo was a quote, "We get our sports from WCO."

"I always wondered what Ernie and Little Looie got paid for posing like that," Walters said. "Salaries weren't much back then. They probably did it for $500 or less."

"No doubt," Bryant said, then quickly shifted gears.

"Look," he said, "I know you guys are following the news. Not the sports news. But the real news. You know, the stuff that average guys should care about more than food, sex and sports."

Bryant than pulled out two bright red flash drives, handing one to each of them.

"But this year is different," he said. "You need to look at this market research we just got back. Political talk is attracting more than just angry, half-crazed white guys with too much time on their hands."

"You just described a lot of our current audience," Walters said. Bryant ignored the remark and continued.

"We have a unique opportunity. The world feels like it's going to hell, right? Christians and Muslims are on the verge of armed insurrections in Indonesia and elsewhere in Asia. We have this woman running for president who sees signs of God and the damn end of days in the fiery cross. And she's doing well enough that maybe she could win.

"On top of that, Bobby, you are the only radio guy in this country who grew up as the best friend of the president of the

United States. No one can touch us. Surrey and Aimee are doing great with sports talk. Moose, think what you could do if you spent more time applying your skills to politics to feed material to Bob. We could go to national syndication if we get this right."

Walters said, "Are you saying what I think you're saying? You want us to shift more to political talk?"

"That's EXACTLY what I'm saying," Bryant said. "At least for the duration of this political campaign. You're a fresh voice. The Man Cub Fans Love to Hate becomes a political force. You guys can do it. Read this research. People are ready for someone new."

"Actually, Big D, I'm going to disappoint you," Walters said.

"How's that Bob?"

"Guess what? I'm not against it," he said. "Could be fun, maybe even helpful, and I'm ready."

Skowron fidgeted a bit in his chair, as though he was deciding whether to say something.

"You okay with this Moose?" Bryant said. "I know you love sports. Not that you have much choice. That's a joke. Sort of."

Skowron decided it was time to share.

"Well, you need to hear a story about a woman named Taylor Pierce. She has quite a tale that involves President Murphy. It was easy enough to confirm she existed; her late father went to college with Murphy. But I had no idea if these notebook diaries someone emailed me were real.

"About one hour ago, a woman called me. She said she's Taylor Pierce and gave me enough background to confirm most of her story. It's a bombshell. It could destroy Luke Murphy. And she said we're the only ones in the media who have it. It'll probably ruin any access we have to Murphy, by the way."

Skowron looked over at Walters, making eye contact.

"Bob, I know we go back a long way with Luke, but we can't ignore something like this," Skowron said. "We were going to have to tell Davis about this soon. It's a cliché but the public has the right to know about the character of the president. And, hey, you and I both know a little bit about his instincts for self-preservation."

Walters nodded but didn't respond to the rare reference from Skowron to the childhood accident and decided not to mention that if Skowron hadn't started the drama on that sidewalk in Palatine by bullying, he wouldn't be sitting in that wheelchair. It didn't change the reality that Luke Murphy knew how to salvage the best from bad situations. How would Luke get out of this one?

"Well, it'll certainly turbo-charge the ratings of our show," Walters said.

Both Bryant and Skowron looked at Walters. He had a look on his face that said "sad resignation" more than "excitement."

"At least this time, I won't be in the damn middle of it," he finally said after a long pause. "Let's get ready to do the job you're payin' us to do."

PART TWO
TREY & LUKE

22

Trey Van Ohmann

People say I'm pretty introspective and I suppose that's true. There's a simpler way to put it, though. My father always said, "Trey, you think too much." Guilty. Writing what's on my mind is often easier than talking for me. It's safer, too, if you are someone in the public eye as long as you don't share it or put it somewhere on the Internet where people can find it.

That's me, Trey Van Ohmann, the over-thinking jock from Idaho with a degree in political science from Penn State University. I've always been interested in politics and just what's happening in the world in general. I don't know why, but I can remember getting in arguments as a kid with my uncles about why Bill Clinton was going to be a better president than George Bush—the first one.

Here's something else I've thought about: Every great pitcher I've ever met thinks too much and most have some skills at introspection. A lot of us are introverts. No surprise really. It gets lonely out on that mound. And you're constantly thinking, because the battle with the batter means that if you are off by even a little bit, if you are the least-bit predictable to a big league hitter, well, that's the difference between the successful career of a millionaire professional athlete and someone who has a few good memories and a different job.

I liked pitching for the Boston Red Sox before I was traded and I've enjoyed pitching for the Chicago Cubs. I know I would've really liked to have pitched for Mike Surrey when he managed the Cubs. The new manager, Roberto Alvarez, is okay, too, and we play hard for him. He knows the game well, pays attention to the players without coddling us—an easy mistake to make when half the team makes more than you do—and hasn't caused any of us to question his decisions. He's also bilingual, which is a big help with the Latin players. Still, Surrey and I really connect. I've been on Mike's show a few times and I can see why players thought he was the real deal and could forgive his occasionally odd game decisions. None of that matters if you aren't aligned with those above you, so he's gone and we've got Roberto. And Mike's a little like me, I think. He has a college degree in history and thought about being a teacher. Actually, it's more interesting to talk to him off the air, because then we can get into things you don't touch on a sports talk show.

I should be honest about this. The other reason I go on Mike's show—and I know it pisses off some of the other hosts and reporters who don't get as much access—is Aimee Walters. I haven't been much for relationships, but I kept thinking and wondering if there were some possibilities.

I've never met anyone quite like her. She's positive and uplifting without being syrupy overly perky. Positive, I like. "Overly perky," I hate. She knows baseball better than most pros I know and she loves to get into political arguments with her dad. She always holds her own.

So, after we played the Nationals in Washington in July, I agreed to call into their show for a quick interview. It was a day I wasn't pitching. I had just finished with Aimee and Surrey. I was checking email on my iPad when my phone beeped.

"Mr. Van Ohmann?" the woman on the other end asked.

"Yes, this is Trey Van Ohmann," I replied. "Who is this."

"This is the White House," she said. "President Murphy is hoping you can meet him for lunch today. He has time from 12:15 p.m. to 1 p.m. Can you come?"

"Absolutely," I said.

She explained the security protocols to me, so that I'd be admitted. I also let Jake Martens, the team's traveling secretary, know where I was going. We were playing a night game and didn't need to be at the ballpark until later in the afternoon, so it was all good.

While I was waiting for my Uber ride, I picked up one of the free copies of The Washington Post in the hotel lobby. I usually like to keep up with the news, but hadn't paid any attention in the past 12 hours. We had lost the game, 5-4, in 15 innings the night before. I left in the seventh inning with us behind 4-2—it wasn't a night when I had my best stuff. We tied the score in the ninth but lost nearly two hours later. That's a long night and I didn't go to bed until nearly 3 a.m. by the time we got back to the hotel and I wound down.

The Post's headlines surprised and shocked me, causing me to wonder why the hell President Murphy would be making time for me on a day like this.

The top story was about how three American Christian outreach workers had been murdered while preaching in a prominently Muslim area in Bali in Indonesia, near where that meteor hit. Some radical group claimed responsibility. It was accompanied by a shorter story about how Lydia Nicks was campaigning in Tennessee and said that, as a Christian nation the United States needed to adopt a "muscular defense of its Christian heritage." She talked about that comet, too, and called it a "hugely symbolic, heavenly sign that sends a message all Americans must receive."

I'm not so sure about that. The Constitution and Founding Fathers I remember studying were very concerned about separating church and state. They were suspicious of any religion having too much sway over public policy. They recognized that many Christian principles influenced them, but so did a lot of other philosophers.

They were scared to death of demagogues—like Lydia Nicks, seems to me. On the other hand, she had a point, even if she smothered it with political posturing. We couldn't let the murder of three innocent Americans overseas go unpunished.

This also is why I need to write down my thoughts sometimes. I think too much and need to get stuff out of my system. Baseball is a team sport and distractions from the mission don't help. If I said what I thought on subjects like this, I'd be a huge distraction. Nothing to see here. Players on winning teams don't get into many political discussions in the clubhouse. Players on losing teams can be very gifted conversationalists when they should be talking about what to expect from the other team in the next few hours of their well-compensated lives.

"One game at a time" is not just a cliché, or maybe you could say that clichés become clichés for good reasons sometimes. As soon as you lose your focus as a player on winning the game at hand, you are much less likely to win at anything. It's the manager's job and the front office's job to think more than one game ahead; not mine.

The dominant story on the lower half of the page was the one that I read first, "Murphy tied to friend's AIDS death," was the headline with a smaller headline that said, "Daughter claims president ignored father after gay encounter."

The story noted the lack of "independent confirmation" for "some of the claims made on the new Bob Walters political talk show on Chicago radio station on WCO." However, the *Post* showed some impressive hustle in confirming that a woman named Taylor Pierce existed, though she was not available for comment, and that her late father went to college with the president and did, indeed, die of AIDS-related complications.

The headline verb "tied" gets to me. It's a weasel word. The dictionary says "to make a tie, bond or connection." I can find a common factor that "ties" anyone to anyone else, right?

Anyway, according to the Post, the White House issued a terse statement confirming that Luke Murphy and Andy Pierce were college friends. The White House noted that the two men had lost touch over the years, but that "President Murphy had been made aware of Andy's tragic passing and offered regrets to his family. The White House has no comment and does not wish to intrude on his daughter's recollections of conversations she had with her father while he was dying."

There was a link to the full text of the notebooks, which WCO had posted on its website. Ever the political science major, I pulled out my iPhone and looked at my news feed. The Murphy story was awash in commentary about how this would affect his campaign, the Nicks campaign and the Leeds campaign.

"It brings up everything we don't like about Luke Murphy," tut-tutted one writer on the Fox News website. "It gives Lydia Nicks a huge opportunity for those who believe in a moral lifestyle and standing by your friends."

All this was on my mind as I was escorted into the Oval Office. President Murphy got up from his seat as soon as he saw me enter. His suit jacket was off and his tie, a deep red affair with thin white stripes, was loose. I hadn't traveled with a suit, but had a deep, Navy blue blazer, gray slacks, a white shirt and the classiest tie I could find on short notice in the Marriott gift shop. I usually traveled with a Cubs tie—a silk tie in "Cubs blue" with the circular team logo repeated in small red-and-white dots. I had decided that would be a decent gift to give the president and the storekeeper had helped me box and wrap it. I might be able to throw a mean slider, but I can't wrap presents that look like anything but a scene of "wrapping paper gone wild." The wrapping didn't survive the encounter with White House security.

"Sorry, Mr. Van Ohmann," the guard had said. "We have to open and physically inspect any wrapped gift. I'm sure you understand."

I did understand and I noted by his monotone that he doubtless had said this many times before. Once the guard saw what the gift was, he folded it carefully back in the box and said, "I bet he likes the tie."

Murphy did like it, or at least he was good at pretending he did.

"I thought someone might have given this to you before, but if not, I thought it might make a nice gift, Mr. President," I said to Murphy, handing him the tie.

"Call me Luke when it's just the two of us," the president said. "We have some White House cufflinks for you, but I'd rather give you a 100 mph fastball."

"Now, that would be a present I could use," I replied, not imagining for a moment that I actually would call him "Luke" in the Oval Office. "The Cubs could use it, too. I might've won the game last night with that kind of heat."

We both laughed. Actually, we had a great talk for about 15 minutes, just chatting about baseball as they brought in lunch, a very American spread of corned beef on rye with stone-ground mustard, coleslaw and a small dish of fruit.

He also had been well-briefed about me to a surprising level. He made sure to share his condolences on my dad's death and assured me an active investigation was continuing to get to the answers. It all seemed normal at moments and we really got along pretty well. Of course, then you'd look down and see the presidential seal on the expensive china and realize where you were.

Murphy was obviously a big fan, but unlike a lot of fans, he had more than blind loyalty to a team he had followed since he was a little boy. He was a genuinely knowledgeable and interested baseball fan—and a fountain of trivia about the Cubs. It included a lot more than I knew, growing up in Idaho and—I must confess—rooting for the New York Yankees.

"You were on the Red Sox, so I know you've heard about Bill Buckner's famous error, right?" he asked me.

"Of course, Mr. President," I said, knowing he was referring to the sixth game of the 1986 World Series. Boston, a team almost as cursed as the Cubs, was a few outs from a world championship when Buckner made a fatal error at first base. The New York Mets won the game and then won the pivotal Game Seven to win the World Series.

"Way before my time, but I understand Buckner was a terrific player for the Cubs before they traded him to Boston," I added.

"Absolutely," Murphy said. "It sucks that he's remembered mainly for this. Do you know the real story behind Buckner's error?"

At that point he shrugged his head and crinkled his nose and mouth into a mock frown.

"Little-known fact," he continued, then raised his voice and lowered an octave so he sounded like a play-by-play announcer. "Buckner was wearing a Cubs batting glove under his first baseman's mitt when he made the fatal error! No way Boston could overcome that."

"That's a great story about Buckner," I said. "It almost makes me believe in curses. But I refuse to accept it, sir. I know we can do it this year. Is that story really true?"

"It's true indeed. Are you calling your Commander-in-Chief a liar?" Murphy asked with a mocking stern tone.

"Absolutely not, sir," I said, deciding to go with the flow. "I believe you are gifted with presidential infallibility, sort of like popes."

"I like the way you think, Van Ohmann. Maybe there's a place for you in my cabinet," Murphy said. "Or, better yet, I could send you over to Congress to convince them of my wisdom.

"Maybe even Indonesia," he added, somewhat wistfully.

He had pushed my button, so I shared what I thought.

"I don't know about that for sure, sir, but I have some pretty strong feelings about people using religion as a way to justify killing," I said, and then added something that I just sort-of blurted without thinking. "Or, people who use it to exploit people's prejudices and get ahead in politics."

I'm still not sure where that came from. It was a comment I'd never make publicly, let alone to the president of the United States, but I felt a connection. I think my candor surprised him a bit, judging by the wide-eyed expression on his face. He stared hard at me for perhaps two seconds, like a slide projector clicking on and off.

"Now I know there's a place for you," Murphy said with a half-smile and a serious tone.

As we sipped coffee and our time wound down, he looked at me and said, "So, Trey, do you follow politics as much as it sounds like you do?"

"Well, yeah, I guess I do."

He followed that by picking my brain on everything from terrorism to gun control to the famine in China and whether middle-class people like the members of my family in Idaho could really get ahead these days. Then, in the last few minutes, the conversation went in unexpected directions that would change my life.

23

Trey Van Ohmann

When you look at another couple, even if they're your parents, you're still an outside observer. Only they would know for sure, but I believe my parents never doubted their love for one another. That made it easy for Mom to laugh when Dad would do something clueless like forget their anniversary after weeks of her hints. She'd say something like this, "Don, once again you've proven that the term 'perceptive man' represents two words that never should be side by side."

"Women learn to take such things in stride," she would tell my brothers and me. Then she'd wink before reminding us to try to be thoughtful.

As usual, Mom was filled with wisdom. As a typical guy and somewhat self-absorbed to boot, I'm not very perceptive at times either, particularly in social settings and relationships. However, even I can't miss some of the signals between couples.

The next thing that happened in the Oval Office was that I heard a quick knock and Alison Murphy, the president's wife, walked into the Oval Office.

I had seen pictures of her, but she was more striking in person. She was classy and attractive with a commanding presence but not an intimidating one. That's not easy to pull off. Actually, that's sort of what I try to do on the pitchers' mound, because it's easier to surprise batters if they're not intimidated by you. Remember what I said about focus? They're a tad less focused if they're not intimidated and that gives me an advantage.

The second thing I noticed were signs of fatigue, particularly that her makeup couldn't hide the gray-blue semi-circles under her eyes. She blinked a lot and I could see her head tilting. A vein stood out on the side of her neck, suggesting a clench in her jaw. Fatigue is hard to quantify, but good pitchers are hard-wired to spot the signs, like "tells" in a poker game, while learning how to mask the signs on themselves. It's another advantage in your battle with the batter if you know he's tired—and you can pretend you're not.

This brought me back to the reality of what they both must have been processing and facing on this day given the scandal that had just erupted. I imagined an everyday, anonymous person dealing with the news that her husband had a homosexual fling that at least indirectly led to someone else's death. Now imagine it happening to someone who basically had no privacy, who was used to having her makeup, her hair color and her every gesture and inflection dissected on social media every time she appeared in public. That was Alison Murphy's life. No wonder she looked exhausted, making it even odder that I had just had a normal conversation with the president. Maybe he was good at compartmentalizing. Pitching a perfect game seemed easy all of a sudden.

Tired or not, her stare seemed to burn like a laser, especially when she made eye contact with Murphy. There wasn't a hint of a smile until she seemed to force an upturn in her lips.

"I'm sorry to interrupt," was the first thing she said. "Luke, they said you were in an informal meeting and it was okay to come in."

"Sure," the president said, giving the reply any spouse would expect. "Alison, this is Trey Van Ohmann, and I'm glad to say he's now pitching for the Cubs."

"Yes," she said. "Believe me, I hear your name a lot. It's all good. The president is definitely glad you're pitching for his Cubs."

When she said "his Cubs" there was an edge on the word "his" that was pretty hard to miss.

"It's a pleasure to meet you Mrs. Murphy," I said, opting to dance as far away as I could from the bad vibes. "We're wrapping up if you'd like me to go."

"No," she said. "No, Trey. I just need to talk to the president for a moment if you don't mind."

President or not, Murphy knew the husband requirement. He walked around his desk toward his spouse and said, "Excuse us just for a moment, Trey."

They moved to the large window to the left of the president's Oval Office desk from where I sat. They both turned toward the window and began talking. They obviously were trying to keep voices down with me in the room so I only heard sentence fragments:

Her: "When … plan to ever talk to me today?"

Her again: "… more interested in Cubs … … what about me … … …damn career?"

Him: "Sorry… … … You were asleep … … scheduled before today." (If the meeting had been scheduled before this morning, it was news to me.)

Her: "…media going nuts… … … know that?"

Him: "…meeting in next hour… … … damage control… Alison … so sorry."

Her: "…include me…"

Him: "Yeah. … … again … so sorry."

Then Alison Murphy made a rapid turn from the window and she looked at me. She seemed to consciously try to put some warmth into her gaze and words. "Trey, I'm very sorry to interrupt your meeting with the president. This is an unusual day," she said.

Before I could reply or even spit out a "nice to meet you," she turned and left the office. I noticed a small tear rolling down her cheek and she used her left hand to wipe it with a quick gesture as she walked out of the Oval Office.

Murphy walked back behind his desk and looked at me.

"Kidding aside, Trey," he said. "Reporters will ask you about your meeting with me today. My schedule is public record and The White House will issue a brief statement about it. From a 'spin' standpoint, one question that's sure to come is why we met today of all days. Well, first, you happened to be in town, right, and everyone knows that I talked to you after your perfect game and invited you to the White House. Right? My meeting with you also is a public example that we're staying to our schedule today and not getting distracted by media reports."

Then he paused for a moment before adding this, "I'm not telling you what to say, but I'd really appreciate it if you could keep things in that context. And if you overhead anything between the First Lady and me, I have to ask as a major favor that you keep it in confidence."

I recognized that he was saying without saying it that he wanted us to keep details of our stories straight. I'm sure he realized I was no novice when it came to living as at least a minor celebrity. I know all about what happens when you give reporters or bloggers anything to question or dissect. It's no different than what we often orchestrate when you work for a high-visibility organization like the Chicago Cubs, though his stakes were much higher.

Still, a lot of people care a lot more about who manages the Cubs than who runs the Supreme Court or the White House—or is the principal of their kid's school for that matter. I'm not saying that's right, but it certainly allows me to make an unbelievable living for throwing a ball every five days.

"I'm not operating at anywhere near your level in the public eye," I finally said. "But we've had a lot of coaching on what to say and what not to say in public. I'm pretty close-mouthed anyway. You don't have to worry.

"And really, sir," I quickly added. "All I heard were a few words and it's no shocker that this is a hard day for you and those around you. Actually, I have to admit I was surprised we were still having this meeting when I saw the news today."

"There's more to that story, Trey," he said. "You make a lot of tradeoffs to get to this office. It's the only way and it's getting worse."

I wasn't quite sure what he meant but didn't feel it was my place to probe. I also knew I did a few things in college that I wouldn't want out in public either, but I didn't say that either, figuring he needed to wrap up the meeting, and I certainly didn't want to know more about the scandal than what I read in The Post. It would just be another secret to keep.

"The honest answer for why we met today is this," Murphy continued. "It's not for cover or spin, Trey. I'd like you to really believe that. I've been wanting to meet you. First it was mainly because I'm a Cubs fan. Everyone knows that. But you're also an interesting person. I like interesting people who are in different worlds than the political circus. Keeps me grounded. This morning, I needed a brief distraction.

"I don't mean to call you a distraction," he quickly added, realizing how that sounded, though it wasn't necessary for him to do that. "But the Cubs are my passion. Win or lose, they offer a respite. We all need a break. Presidents get criticized every time they swing a golf club or take a vacation. I'd like to see anyone do this job without some down time.

"George W. Bush and Obama both liked to watch sports to unwind. There's something about baseball and presidents, too. Dubya was an owner of the Texas Rangers and once said he'd like to be commissioner of baseball. Obama was a big White Sox fan, probably still is, though truth was he liked basketball and golf even more," Murphy said, now on a bit of a roll as far as I could tell. "George Bush the First had his speedboat. LBJ loved his Texas ranch; Reagan recuperated at his ranch in California. Eisenhower played golf. Nixon had no discernible hobbies other than musing and being paranoid, which probably explains a lot. Teddy Roosevelt used to disappear in the wilderness and nobody knew where he was. Can you imagine that today?

"Well, I've played golf, but I stink to the point where it's embarrassing. We're not that big on vacations. I like baseball. I love baseball. And I love the Cubs. That's my passion. It's how I relax. And that's a big reason why I'm really glad you're here today."

"It's really a pleasure, sir," I said, sensing the meeting really was wrapping up. "I genuinely enjoyed the conversation. It's fun for me to talk about something besides baseball, to tell you the truth. People think we're cardboard characters. Baseball players worry about what's happening in the world, too. And I do plan to vote for you this fall. I'm not just saying that."

"Hopefully we'll be on the ballot in the fall," he said, obviously referring to his contest with Lydia Nicks but saying no more on that subject.

Then his expression changed, as though he had an idea that had just popped in his head. Was that true, was he just acting, or was this the plan all along? I chose to believe his look was genuine, though he floored me with his next words.

"Trey, one last thing," he said. "Tomorrow you're probably going to get a call or a visit from Charley Rayburn, my chief of staff. I'd really like you to talk to him and I'd again ask that you keep this in confidence."

"What do you have in mind?" I asked, not knowing what else to say.

"Charley will explain," was all he said. "Thanks, Trey. You made my day."

"Okay, Mr. President," I said. "I'll talk to him."

He stood up to shake my hand, looking me straight in the eyes, making me feel important. It was a practiced political handshake, firm enough to convey strength but not so strong that you'd think he was showing off; the kind of handshake you get from a lot of jocks. I had practiced it, too.

"I guess you're not going to call me Luke, are you?" he said, raising his eyebrows.

"Not a chance Mr. President," I said as I turned around to leave. "Let's go Cubbies."

"Roger that."

24

Trey Van Ohmann

After President Murphy told me to expect to hear from his chief of staff about "something" the next day, I figured a phone conversation would result. I made sure to place my cell on the nightstand next to my bed in the hotel.

My ringtone song is "I Gotta Go" by one of my favorite musicians, Robert Earl Keen, a Texan who combines swing, rock, blues, bluegrass and country. Why did I pick it? For one thing, I get a lot of calls from reporters and the title serves as a reminder to keep it short and to the point. ("Gee, I'm sorry James, but I gotta go.") When people ask about it, I tell people about Keen—a poet with lyrics. Baseball players have time to listen to a lot of music and we try to interest each other in the artists we like. In a room filled with young white, black and Latin ballplayers, you're exposed to a lot of great music if you keep an open mind.

When the opening notes of "I Gotta Go" sounded, the phone woke me up. I was groggy. It only was 9 a.m., early for a baseball player on night-game time and it always seemed harder to get out of bed after a loss, something we had "accomplished" again for the second night in a row.

What I didn't expect was what I heard the voice say.

"Mr. Van Ohmann?"

"Yes?"

"This is Mr. Rayburn's office. He'd like to meet you in the hotel restaurant in about 15 minutes if that's possible."

"Uh, sure," I said, still emerging from morning fog. "I'll be ready."

A personal visit from the chief of staff of the president of the USA? I expected maybe a five-minute phone call with a pitch to be in a commercial or make a few appearances on behalf of foster kids or youth baseball or something.

When I entered the restaurant, a security guy whom I assumed was from the White House noticed me, nodded politely and approached.

"Mr. Van Ohmann, the Chief is that fellow over there with his back to the window," he said. "Go on over. All we ask is that you keep your voice down and try not to refer to him by his last name. He doesn't mind if you just say 'Charley' or 'Chief' or 'Colonel.' This prevents unnecessary attention."

"Sure," was all I could think to say. "Thanks."

I wasn't sure I was dressed for this occasion either. In a hurry to keep the appointment, I tossed on blue jeans and an open-necked, green-checked Western shirt with pearl buttons; one of those shirts designed to have the tail out and still look good. Well, maybe the casual look was better for security. No one dressed like me would likely be meeting with Murphy's chief of staff, right?

Rayburn looked exactly the way I expected him to look. I keep up with the news enough that I had known who he was but not much else, so I did a little Google homework as I unwound in the hotel room after the game. The guy was a serious military hero and apparently the kind of leader who could inspire young soldiers and then politely explain the realities of war to a Senate committee a few hours later. Luke Murphy was lucky to have him around and Rayburn's loyalty to him was unquestioned, going back to when Rayburn began advising Murphy as a young member of Congress on national defense issues.

He was wearing the D.C. uniform—as much a uniform as what we wear at the ballpark: dark gray suit with faint pinstripes, light blue shirt, red tie. He was balding, but his hair was in a buzz cut that made him look like he was ready to lead a platoon into battle. The most compelling thing was that he sat ramrod straight, probably a habit from his military background. *His left foot is tapping a little nervously,* I thought, and he was circling the rim of his coffee cup with his finger while obviously reading a text or an email that didn't make him very happy as I sat across from him.

"Hello, Colonel," I said. "Your, uh, security people told me to just call you that."

"That's fine, Trey," he said, looking up and giving me a slight smile as he set the phone down on the table. Then he picked up the phone and slipped it into the inside pocket of his suit jacket, perhaps realizing that he might get a text or an email that he wouldn't want me to see.

"I suppose you're wondering why we want to talk to you," he said.

"Yes," I said. "I figured you didn't need my help getting tickets, so it must be something else."

Rayburn laughed. "People say you're introverted and don't say much," he said. "I think you're just careful about what you say and whom you say it to. That's good advice for anyone in the public eye.

"You're discrete," he continued. "You're smart. You care about the world around you. And you're famous. Those are all reasons why I want to talk to you in confidence today. Consider this a hard sell with short time."

I didn't know what to say to that, so I simply nodded and let Rayburn continue, which he did in the rapid staccato of a sergeant educating a fresh recruit.

"I want to talk to you about Luke Murphy first. He's a human being. He has flaws like everyone. He's not perfect. Like you, he can be kind of self-absorbed. People say he's calculating and he is, but that also can be a strength. Presidents must pick their friends very carefully. And I kid him that he definitely spends too much time following the Cubs."

Then Rayburn looked me straight in the eyes, making sure that I detected the direct contact. He slowed the pace of his speech and adopted a friendlier tone.

"But, really, so what? None of his flaws are fatal or make him evil. He's the best-equipped person to be the president of the United States, certainly the best person running, and he needs your help," Rayburn continued. "I've been around him a long time, Trey, and you need to see what's underneath. Our country, our world, is tearing apart. The other Republican candidate will bring nothing but more division. She might even set off a goddam war on behalf of Christianity that will make the Crusades look like a playground skirmish. They didn't have nukes or chemical weapons during the Crusades, but they would've used 'em if they had 'em. Look at the imaginative ways they tortured people. That's how religious zealots think and it doesn't matter what religion.

"Okay, now consider the Democrat, as I imagine you have. Matt Leeds is naïve. He has good intentions and, between us, even some good issues, especially on what most of us wish we could do to curb money and corporate influence in Washington. But it's all talk. The Democrats are too heavily in bed with Wall Street and Silicon Valley billionaires. He'll never deliver. Worse than that, he isn't clear-eyed about the rest of the world. He doesn't see some of the despots and sociopaths running some of these countries for who they really are.

"Luke Murphy is the only one of the three who can work with both sides in Washington and help the world get out of the mess it's in. I see what churns inside him; how much he wants to do the right thing even if he doesn't always show it. And until you've run for president and held the office, you don't appreciate the trade-offs that have to be made just to occupy it.

"Right now, Trey, we're not even sure he will get the nomination. I'm being very frank now. This is between us," he added, giving me a look that made me wonder if I'd be court-martialed or maybe just tossed into a plane and sent to Gitmo if I ever repeated his monologue.

Rayburn continued, "Okay, let's say he gets the nomination, which we believe he will. When we game-plan what happens next, we think there's a 50-50 chance Lydia Nicks runs as a third-party candidate. Once people get the taste for the race and the levers of power, it's damn hard to let go of the dream. Especially if they're zealots. Especially if they think they've been called by God. But, she'll divide our votes and hand the presidency to Leeds.

"That's not good for Luke Murphy, but more importantly, it's not good for the country."

I finally had to interrupt, mainly to collect my thoughts. "I don't disagree with anything you're saying, Colonel," I said. "But where do I come in?"

"We're asking one thing of you, Trey," Rayburn said. "The day might come—it might come soon to tell you the truth—when Luke Murphy is going to need all the help he can get. You're a celebrity in New England from when you pitched for the Red Sox, you're from the West and now you're a Cub. I don't mean to sound crass. We truly mourn the loss of your dad, but you're also a sympathetic figure for that reason. You and President Murphy are intertwined in a weird way, beyond his just being a big fan. Your father came to a tragic end because domestic terrorists made him part of a plot to manipulate Luke. As we all know, it was about a lot more than winning the World Series.

"So, Trey, how do you want to use the platform you've been given? Your public support of Luke Murphy might make a difference, particularly if Illinois is close on Election Day.

"I know what I'm asking is awkward and maybe weird for a professional athlete at the peak of his career," he added, returning to his staccato tone. "And we won't ask unless we need it. But we might. All I ask today is that you do two things. First, again, keep this between us. Second, just do what you're already doing with a little more focus—pay attention to current events, study up on Luke Murphy and think about this."

He then reached into a backpack next to his chair and handed me an unmarked manila envelope that bulged from being stuffed full.

"This packet includes a detailed biography, highlights of Luke Murphy's political career and our campaign positions," he said. "It's not just spin. You'll find it's a candid assessment of issues and strategy. It can't be traced back to anyone."

Rayburn glanced at his watch, an obvious signal that we were nearing an end. But he asked the polite "do you have any questions" that usually comes at that point in a meeting.

I did have some questions; questions I thought I had the right to ask if they were going to complicate my life this much.

"I'm stunned. I need some time to think about this," I said, debating whether to go down a very awkward road, realizing I felt compelled to make the trip. "But I have to ask about that stuff that just came out. Like, did the president really abandon that guy who died of AIDS?"

Rayburn surprised me with the directness of his answer.

"He did, Trey," Rayburn said. "Maybe not abandon so much as move on with his life, but that's a rationalization. He's not proud of it, but he did. He'd do it over if he could."

I had one more question.

"Not that it matters, except that maybe now it does: Is he gay or was that just a thing that happened?"

I didn't catch Rayburn off guard at all. He was ready with an answer, which is what you'd expect from a political pro.

"That's something you'd have to ask him yourself," Rayburn said. "And you have to ask yourself if the answer to that personal question would change your opinion about his fitness for the presidency. But one thing I can tell you for sure is that a lot of other people are asking that question, unfair or not and that's all the more reason why he might need your help—unless you want Nicks or Leeds to be the next president."

"I promise to think about it Colonel. That's all I can say right now," I said, reaching out to shake his hand.

"For right now, that's all we can ask," he said, ending the meeting.

25

Trey Van Ohmann

The team flew back to Chicago on a red-eye flight that was delayed two hours because some light in the cockpit either was lit when it wasn't supposed to be, or maybe it wasn't lit when it should be. I can't remember which, but it meant we didn't leave D.C. until about 4 a.m. Baseball players, even those who aren't part of the Cubs, are legendarily superstitious. You could feel the group trying to pretend that this wasn't a new curse omen versus the rational response that this was just an unfortunate shit-happens moment.

We were barely in first place after losing two out of three games to Washington. It's a long season. No other sport makes you play 162 games to earn a chance at the playoffs and a championship. But, even though there was a lot of baseball left to play, feelings nagged that we were hanging on instead of playing with the kind of swagger that successful teams have. St. Louis, always our biggest rival, only was a game behind. The Cardinals never seem to have a swagger problem either.

I had a lot more to think about, because the idea of sticking my neck out for a presidential candidate in the middle of a baseball season was jarring. I was too tired on the plane ride to look at the material that Rayburn left for me and I also didn't want to leave it out where people could see it. I really didn't want to answer questions. Still, my visit with Murphy had been reported. Our starting shortstop, Zach Mathews, went to

YouTube and found a heavy-metal recording of "Hail to the Chief." He played it loudly as soon as I boarded the team jet.

"Funny," I said. "Real funny."

That brought a cascade of catcalls. Fortunately for me, it was late, the guys were tired and snoring quickly replaced levity. Everyone tried to get at least an hour of sleep on the short flight.

I was driving back to my apartment from O'Hare Field, stuck in traffic on the Kennedy Expressway, when my phone rang. The display screen on the dashboard showed it was Aimee Walters. Normally I wouldn't answer a call from a reporter early in the morning after less than two hours of sleep. What could possibly go wrong by talking to the media when you're worried, confused and fatigued, right? But, I was able to rationalize reasons to answer the call by telling myself she had been fair to me and the team. All the while, I knew the real reason was that I had developed a serious crush. I think I could tell she was interested in me, too, but neither of us had acted on it yet.

"Hey, Trey," she said. "It's Aimee. Got a minute?"
"Sure. What's your quick question?"

"Well, I was wondering if I could get some audio about your visit with the president."

"Why?" I asked as I crawled east on the Kennedy in my Chevy pickup—actually the same Silverado model my dad had been driving. "He's a big Cubs fan; kind of a likable guy actually. Kind of sad what just came out. It's all been reported."

She paused at that point. I could tell she was working me, particularly since it was WCO that broke the story.

"Actually, Dad wants me to ask you how Murphy was reacting and whether he said anything about the new information that came out about him. You were one of the only people outside Murphy's inner circle to see him yesterday," she said.

Her pitch distracted me from the task at hand and I nearly drifted into a car in the next lane. The guy honked his horn and gave me the finger. I lifted an open hand and made sure he saw the universal "peace, man, sorry" gesture, but I'm not sure he bought it. Can't say I blamed him. I hoped he didn't recognize me and tweet about it when he got home, "#VanOhmannAsshole."

"I forgot your dad is nearly all about political talk now," I said. "That story broke out of his show, right?"

"It did," she said. "It's a big deal. Obviously. So, what was Murphy like?"

"He was like a president," I said, surprising myself by my strong desire to defend Luke Murphy from a talk radio attack, even with Aimee Walters. "I mean, he deals with all sorts of crap every day, so maybe this was just one more thing on his plate. I just don't have much to say about it."

"You're driving, aren't you?"

"Yeah. I'm on the Kennedy."

"I don't want to be responsible for you having an accident while you're trying to think through your statements for an interview that's not just routine 'how-did-it-go-on-the-mound-today' kind of stuff," she said. "Have you had breakfast?"

It really didn't make sense to agree, but I did. I guess you can figure out why.

We agreed to meet at O'Neill's, a diner near my apartment on the near-north side, about a mile from Wrigley Field. It was a good place that served the kind of breakfasts I remembered in Idaho and people would generally leave you alone. Plus, once I'm out of uniform and dressed normally, I'm not as distinctive as you might think for a quasi-celebrity.

Aimee was already there when I arrived, facing the entrance toward the back of the restaurant in a long row of green booths. She waved her arm when she spotted me.

"I hope you don't mind the way I look," she said. "It's not very professional. Actually, I'm supposed to be off today. Mike is doing the show solo this morning. I'm still having to learn to be a morning person."

No, I didn't mind the way she looked. The way she looked was outstanding. She wasn't wearing much makeup, but didn't need much. Her brunette hair was pulled back in a ponytail tied with a navy blue patterned scarf and I could see a few freckles around her small nose. She was wearing a pair of tight, blue-jean shorts that weren't crazy short, but short enough to show off her legs. For a top, she was wearing a rust-colored, fairly low-cut pullover with bikini straps.

She probably caught my "elevator eyes" looking her up and down. I couldn't help it. My excuse would be that I was operating on less than two hours of sleep. I made eye contact and blurted out, "You look great."

"You really are sleep-deprived then," she said, but I could tell from the smile crinkling the corners of her mouth that she appreciated the thoughts and, maybe, didn't even mind the scrutiny from Trey the Obviously Sleepy-but-Horny Guy.

"Trey," she said. "Look, I'm not going to push you to talk about this if you don't want to, okay? I'm just trying to help out my dad. He and I don't always see eye-to-eye politically and this Luke Murphy thing is really complicated for him. I can tell.

"On the other hand," she added, raising her eyebrows, opening her eyes and being a total flirt, "even a quote would be helpful."

"Even if it's a cliché, or something sounds like it's out of 'Star Trek'?" I asked. "You know, where Bones says something like, 'Jim, I'm a doctor, not a miracle worker!' Well, I'm a baseball player, not a politician."

"But, you pay a lot of attention," she said. "We've even chatted about that a few times off the record this season."

"Sure," I said. "My folks taught us it was part of being a citizen and I've always been interested in politics."

"Maybe," she said, "you'll run for office when you retire."

I laughed. "Probably about as far as I'd ever want to go would be county commissioner in Nez Perce County in Idaho," I said. "I can help my brothers and their neighbors figure out whether to add more livestock or plant more wheat. We don't grow potatoes in that part of Idaho, by the way. Just in case you're wondering."

"Another stereotype debunked," she said.

The waitress interrupted our conversation. I ordered ham and eggs with fried potatoes, not something I'd eat on a day when I pitch, when my diet is disciplined and plant-based. Aimee opted for a bagel with cream cheese and some fruit, which was as far as this place would go to be trendy. If anyone came to this place looking for quinoa or kale, they'd leave hungry.

At that moment, I decided to go for it.

"I'll give you a sound bite, okay?" I said. "Just one. But there's a price."

"What's that?"

"Today's an off day," I said. "Let me get some sleep and take you out to dinner tonight."

"Is that how you barter with all the media?"

"Do you want an honest answer?" I said.

"Absolutely."

"I can't even remember the last time I went on an actual date," I said.

"You have sort of an unusual life," she said. "You probably don't have to ask. I imagine the girls ask you."

"It really isn't that, Aimee," I said. "Honestly, there's too much at stake to do much of that; even if I wanted to. I've seen what happens to guys who pay too much attention to their social life and, well, let's say their after-hours skills. I just don't meet a lot of people who I feel like I really connect with."

"Well," she said, "then I'm really flattered. But now you owe me a quote—or maybe even two or three good quotes."

"Okay, here it is, but it really isn't too exciting. Turn on your recorder," I said.

She set her iPhone on the table and hit the voice recorder app.

"First of all, it's always an honor to meet the president of the United States. We mainly talked about the Cubs and baseball," I said, staring at the phone. "I could sense it was a tough day for him, which I suppose is obvious, but every day must have its challenges when you're the president. The scandal story never came up. What he did say and I remember this specifically, is that presidents need breaks like everyone else. Some like vacations to relax. Some like to play golf. Luke Murphy loves baseball and he's a big fan of the Cubs. But he really knows his baseball, too. He asks good questions.

"But, really, more than anything I think I was there to give him a little bit of a break in his day, to just sit back and talk some baseball for a few minutes. I was honored to meet him and I left with a lot of respect for him."

"Why do you say that Trey," Aimee asked, using her announcer voice; a slightly deeper tone with that subtle, increased emphasis on clear pronunciation beyond what you'd do in a normal conversation. She was learning fast, she was genuinely interested and she didn't sound phony or self-absorbed. Plus, all the players recognized that she really knew her stuff. She also had the looks to land a national gig. Talent matters, but, for women, looks come first. Plus, she already was a celebrity whether she liked it or not. In the clubhouse, a few of us had discussed her future and we gave her one more season, max, at WCO.

Actually, her question caused me to stop and think why I said what I said. The White House was a pretty intoxicating place and being asked to help the most powerful person in the world couldn't help but make you feel important for a second or two.

"Well," I finally said. "I had never been to the White House, let alone the Oval Office. You get a sense of history and sort of soak up the importance of the work. Whether you agree or disagree with him, you could tell he takes it very seriously and the responsibility weighs on him."

I had something else I wanted to say. There was risk to this, but I decided to say it.

"And, you know what, these stories that just came out about him? Maybe I'm more sensitive to this stuff as someone in the public eye, but we all make mistakes, especially at younger ages," I said. "We're all entitled to some privacy, even the president. We all want to be measured on what we are now, not what we were. I just don't focus on what happened to him in college. What I care about is whether he should be our president for another term."

"And, do you have an opinion about that?" Aimee asked.

I laughed and used my "Star Trek" line. "Hey, I'm a Major League pitcher, not a political commentator. I'll be trying to size up the candidates like everyone else. I certainly haven't ruled Luke Murphy out.

"Plus, he's a Cubs fan," I added, shamelessly playing to her audience with that not-so-witty aside.

"We certainly know that," Aimee said in her radio voice as the recording continued for a few more seconds. "This is Aimee Walters with Trey Van Ohmann, star pitcher for the Cubs, talking about his extraordinary meeting with President Luke Murphy in the White House. Thanks, Trey."

"Thank you, Aimee," I said. "It's always a pleasure."

She turned off the app on her phone and looked at me.

"That wasn't so bad," she said. "Actually, it was really interesting. You'll probably go from ESPN to Politico and some of the political blogs with those comments."

"I hope I don't regret stepping into this," I said. "I really should be concentrating on trying to beat the Pirates this weekend."

"I promise at dinner tonight we'll just talk about baseball," she said, then added. "Amend that. If we talk about other things, it won't be politics."

I thought I saw a twinkle in her eye and the freckles around her nose dance a little bit when she said that. A guy can always hope.

26

Trey Van Ohmann

It felt great to get needed sleep before my dinner with Aimee. I purposely left my phone in the living room on mute so I couldn't hear it vibrate.

When I got up, I checked the phone and it was filled with messages and texts. The first thing I read was a text from the 202 area code—Washington D.C. It obviously came indirectly from Rayburn, "CR says thanks for WCO interview."

Aimee hadn't wasted any time. Her dad must have played it on the air while I slept. I already was feeling twinges of regret for going beyond safe, clichéd sound bites. I knew my feelings for Aimee pushed me to say more than I hardly ever say to the media.

There was no changing it now and I didn't think I had said anything crazy. But I had voicemails from political reporters, Fox News and CNN wanting me to appear. I also had a text message filled with screaming emojis from Chuck Briggs, the Cubs' director of media relations, telling me to call him right away "before you talk to any more reporters."

In other words, I was causing problems. Well, I'm a team player. I called Chuck.

"Jesus, Trey," he said. "You're the last guy I ever thought I'd have to have this conversation with. Don't you know there's no upside in wading into politics. None. Zero. Zip. One part of social media wants to know how you can support Murphy for the way he abandoned his friend. The other side says you must be accepting the quote homosexual lifestyle unquote and maybe you're gay yourself by standing up for Murphy. Everyone wants to know if you have more to say."

Chuck seemed to be just getting warmed up. He could get pretty hyper whenever the team was in the middle of an unwanted controversy and most controversies are unwanted by definition.

"Slow down, Chuck," I said. "I was just trying to help Aimee out. She and Mike Surrey have been pretty good to us, which is quite a change at WCO as I understand it. I don't plan on saying any more at this point."

Chuck seized on the last part. He was just getting warmed up.

"Trey, what the hell do you mean 'at this point?' You're not seriously considering getting more involved in the election are you? You've got to trust me on this. I've seen what happens to my friends who do that work. You have no idea what a bottomless pit of bullshit politics is. Once you get dragged into a presidential wrestling match, you don't come out the same person. You'll get heavily damaged by people who simply do not care who they hurt and how much they hurt you to get what they want. It'll make you miss Bob Walters and the sports bloggers who question whether your arm seems tired, or if you're still more loyal to the Red Sox."

"Chuck, I want to win games for the Cubs," I said, firming up my tone. "You know I'm always careful about what I say and I'm not a publicity hound. But I have rights as a citizen to make a comment after I meet the president. His support certainly has been good for the team, right?"

With that off my chest, I lobbed an easy pitch to him.

"Look. Go ahead and put out a statement on my behalf that this is the full extent of my remarks on my meeting with the president," I suggested. "Say that I'm focused on helping the Cubs not only return to the World Series but win it. That also has the virtue of being true."

"That's basically what I was going to suggest," Chuck said, calming down audibly but making sure I understood he, not I, was in charge of the Cubs' public image. "We're on the same wavelength. We need to keep it that way."

Still, I couldn't resist a follow-up. What was getting into me today? And I honestly wasn't sure what I was going to do if Murphy asked me to get more involved. It seemed out of character, but maybe when your father gets murdered most likely by domestic terrorists it makes you feel like doing more than throw a baseball.

"Chuckie, if I decide to say anything else political, I'll give you a heads-up first," I said.

"You're going to give me a heart attack," he said.

***

Aimee looked even better at dinner than she did at breakfast. It was obvious she had gone out of her way to look great for me and I was duly impressed. Her highlighted brown hair was loose with light curls. She wore a pure white dress that ended about three inches above her knees. It had a high neckline with large cut-outs that showed bare shoulders and arms. When I pulled her chair out for her, I noticed that the portions of her back that were visible showed scars and I wondered if we would ever know each other well enough to talk about that. There was no question she put up an impressive front, but the scars must be emotional, too. She also was wearing ultra-high, thin heels and she laughed when she tripped getting out of my Silverado when I handed the key fob to the valet.

"I put these on just for you," she said, shrugging and tossing her hair back. "I don't know how any woman walks in these all day."

The dinner conversation wasn't exactly as promised after the initial small talk.

"Hey, I know we weren't going to talk politics," she said, as we both sipped drinks from the second bottle of Zinfandel I had ordered, a great "old vine" wine with a chocolatey taste and a quick finish. "But I just want to say I had no idea your comments on Dad's show would create this much frenzy."

"It'll die down," I said. "Let's keep our deal and not talk about it. What else do you want to talk about?"

"Tell me about growing up in Idaho."

"Is this on the record or between friends?"

She finally broke ice we had been skating on for weeks; maybe months.

"Trey, I'll just say it because you're too shy to say it first," she said. "Of course, it's between friends. Can't you tell I'm attracted to you? I know you can. I know you feel a connection. I don't just say that to all the boys and if it's a conflict of interest for me, I'll figure out a way to deal with it."

I stirred. I felt it down to my toes, though it seemed to stop for a spell just below my waist. "Let's, uh, finish this bottle and the appetizers we ordered and get out of here," I said, my voice suddenly dropping down half an octave through no conscious effort. "I probably shouldn't drive. We certainly don't want a story about you, me and a DUI. We'll call Uber. I'll tell you about Idaho on the way back to my place."

"I like that plan," was all she said.

***

The idea of sex had been little more than a fleeting afterthought for months, and it had been a lot longer since I had done anything that moved from a physical release between friends or casual acquaintances to something you'd call making love.

When we got back to the apartment, there weren't many words. We had put our feelings out there, and the wine reduced inhibitions.

With this woman, this beautiful woman, I felt a burning desire to do everything I could to make sure she understood the depth of my feelings. We held hands in the back seat of the Uber car as I talked about growing up in Idaho and shared more about my family. I told her about my brothers. I talked more in the cab than I normally talk to other people in a week.

Our first long kiss came as soon as we walked through my door. Her tongue immediately darted into my mouth and I responded by tightening my hold around Aimee's waist, wanting her even more.

We walked into the bedroom with arms draped around waists and slowly undressed each other as we exchanged glances and smiles. Once she was naked, I noticed she was sweating lightly. I guided her to the edge of the bed and sat her on the end with her arms behind her. I began by kissing her breasts and slowly worked my way down until I was on my knees. As I hit the spot with my tongue, I heard her moan. Then she stopped propping herself on her arms and laid back on the bed as I continued. First she flung her arms behind her head and grabbed the rails in the headboard. Then she brought one arm down to stroke the tops of my hands as they explored her breasts. The moaning and her movements accelerated as I moved my tongue faster and faster, slower and slower, then faster and faster again.

Then I stopped and I guided her to the front of the bed.

"Trey," Aimee said, almost gasping. "I think I'm ready already."

"No, not yet," I said, hoping this wasn't a mistake, because I was pretty damn ready myself. "Let's find another level. Let's wait a little longer."

"Well, if that's the way you want it," she said. Then she surprised me by sitting up so she should push me down on the bed, straddling me and then doing to me what I had been doing to her. She had me gasping quickly.

"Are you sure you're not ready?" she said, laughing.

Yeah, I was. It was obvious that this was not going to be like a phony porn movie where the guy somehow manages to hold back for an impossible length of time. But it was fun to try to make these delicious moments last as long as possible. I was still on my back. She sat upright, lowering herself over me. She began moving up and down as I stroked her nipples with one hand and tightened my hold on her lower back with the other. I sensed she had drifted to a place that maybe men can only imagine.

"Trey," was all she said. "Trey."

I gently lowered her back to the bed and we finished on our sides with our arms locked around one another. I needed to hold her closer and we gripped each other as tightly as we could for the rest of the ride. When we were done, we laid there for what seemed like a long time, lost in our thoughts, not letting go until we both fell asleep—naked, spent and contented.

27

Trey Van Ohmann

Climate change is real if you ask me. It was the hottest July I could remember. Even playing night games didn't seem to matter. The darkness only meant you wouldn't get sunburned.

The Cubs were winning again, widening our hold on first place, and I was pitching pretty well. We were in Miami, playing a day game against the Florida Marlins in the sweltering humidity of south Florida. Normally that wouldn't be a problem, but the ballpark's "state-of-the-art" retractable roof wasn't working. The mass of enclosed concrete captured the heat and held it like a prisoner. A field-level thermometer said 118 degrees. We were skeptical. That seemed too low.

The team said the afternoon start was the only way to ensure we could get to Denver for a game against the Rockies the next day without everyone being exhausted by the flight, the two-hour time change and the thin mountain air.

No one in power bothered to ask if maybe it would have been a better idea to have a Monday off instead of playing 20 days in a row in July. Don't get me wrong. I'm not complaining. It's still a life most people would take in a heartbeat. Well, maybe I'm complaining a little. Don't expect to see a team at its best when you spend $400 to take your family to a game on a sweltering July day in south Florida or the next night in Colorado.

I lasted six innings and 110 pitches and left the game with us ahead 4-2 and me seven pounds lighter from sweating. It wasn't my best performance, but I kept us in the game and we went on to win 5-3. Pretty uneventful. I went into the clubhouse, took a big swig of the green Gatorade G2 that was always waiting for me in my locker and got on the bus to the airport.

I watched CNN on the in-flight television. The news in the real world put my complaints about organized baseball into perspective.

The rioting in Indonesia was worse. The Mideast was crazy like it always is and now Indonesia commanded more attention than at any other time in American history. The Chinese were hungrier and their economy was declining sharply. Murphy had convinced Congress to sell wheat, soybeans and other grains to the Chinese. Actually, he brokered a deal in which the Chinese agreed to buy the wheat and also sharply reduce what we owed them in debt for all the billions in U.S. paper they owned. Pretty clever.

But Nicks had traction, too. Questions about the college scandal still dogged Murphy. Polling showed it definitely bothered a lot of potential voters. Then rumors had leaked that his wife had told friends she would leave him after the election. Nicks was doing a good job of raising questions that skillful politicians suggest about foes: Was Murphy tough enough to stand up for America while missionaries and other Christians were being murdered in Indonesia and other parts of Muslim Asia? Was Murphy's "domestic situation" going to be too much of a distraction for him to continue? She was very skillful at asking those types of questions in a thoughtful, concerned tone while ensuring they dripped with innuendo. Meanwhile, the shadowy political groups that had lots of money to get down and dirty with little accountability were tearing Murphy apart.

Adding to the anger in the Muslim world, members of Murphy's own party in Congress had blocked additional aid to help the Indonesian government, which was under increasing stress from radical elements as officials attempted to restore order. "Who knows what a Muslim regime will do with the hard-earned funds from American taxpayers?" Nicks asked.

The Republican Convention was next week in Cincinnati, coincidentally the same time when we'd play the Reds there. No one knew what would happen between Murphy and Nicks. Murphy had the edge in delegates but not enough to win on the first ballot. Meanwhile, he had to play the role of president.

We landed at Denver's airport, which is so far from the city called "Denver" that I think it's located somewhere in western Nebraska, when I received a text.

"Can CR speak with you in one hour?"

I knew CR meant "Charley Rayburn." I wasn't sure I'd be alone in an hour, given the distance to the hotel and the bumper-to-bumper traffic surrounding the bus on the east fringes of the Denver metro area

I texted back, "How about 90 minutes to be sure I have some privacy?"

"Okay," said the person texting from a number I didn't recognize, but who was obviously a Rayburn aide. Just "Okay."

Hotels are all pretty much the same, but the Westin Denver Downtown was one of my road favorites. It has nice rooms, a decent restaurant, a good bar and it's close to cool stuff like the 16th Street Mall. I'm really not complaining this time. In the big leagues, the hotels are four-star or better. If they're not, the problem gets fixed the next season. It's a long way from the lower levels. I remember bus rides in Billings and hotels with stained chairs and holes in walls; rooms that would tell you stories you wouldn't want to hear if they could talk.

I had just settled in my room, checking email on my iPad, when my phone rang. It was 89 minutes since the text.

"Trey," the voice said after I answered, not waiting for me to even say hello. "This is Charley Rayburn."

"Yes, Colonel, what can I do for you?"

"Have you been following the campaign? You know I've left the White House to work full-time on Luke's—President Murphy's—campaign, right?"

"I did hear that, sir," I said. "I would've been following the race anyway, but you sort of lit a fire in me after I read all that material you gave me."

"And what's your take on how things are going?"

"I have some thoughts of course, but, uh, permission to speak freely, Colonel?"

"Absolutely. And you really can just call me 'Charley' now."

I gave that a try. "Okay, Charley. I guess I'm a little befuddled as to why my analysis would matter much to you. Like I say, I'm a pitcher, not a political commentator."

"That's precisely why we're interested, Trey. You'd offer a unique perspective outside the bubble we're all occupying."

I suspected he was feeling me out, but for what reason, I didn't know. I said, "Well, between us, I've read every word of the briefing book that you left me and I did some independent research on President Murphy. I don't agree with him about everything, but I pretty much like what I see. He's the best choice."

"And what's your take on Nicks and Leeds?" Rayburn asked.

My real take was that Nicks was either pandering to the evangelical right or else she actually was crazy enough to think it was time to reboot the Crusades. I tempered my feelings a bit for Rayburn.

"Nicks just isn't for me," I said diplomatically. "I would worry a lot about what she'd do if she had the power of the presidency. And Leeds simply isn't ready for this job. I agree with him on some things, but his solutions seem thin. And, he doesn't seem to have many ideas that don't involve government spending more money it doesn't have."

"Do you remember when I said we might ask you to help?" Rayburn asked.

Here it comes, I thought. Yeah, I remembered. Of course I did. The notion still created so many potential issues that I had conveniently deposited the problem into the mental file folder I think everyone has called, "Things I Should Think About but Don't Want to Deal with Right Now." Maybe the short version of that file title would be "Death, Etc."

"I do remember that," was all I said.

"You're playing in Cincinnati next week, at the same time as the convention," Rayburn said.

I started to see what might be coming.

I said, "Yeah, that's right. I'm scheduled to start the night President Murphy should be nominated. If he has enough delegate votes of course."

He said, "We're working on that."

Rayburn seemed to drift off for a moment. I started wondering if Verizon had dropped the call. Then he must have decided he could trust me to say a little more, or maybe he just needed to vent with someone outside his usual circle.

He said, "Trey, this is the World Series of politics. You do what it takes. Just hypothetically, that's how a wavering congressman from Racine, Wisconsin, can achieve his dream to be the ambassador to Denmark if he helps the cause. If not, no one needs to tell this congressman that he'll face a quality, well-funded opponent during his next primary. And, after that, well, he'll be lucky to get elected to the city council. Anyway, I assume this means the day before you pitch is a fairly quiet day for you. Do I have that right?"

I said, "That's right. It's mainly getting rest and doing some light pitching and catching. I'll probably take a few minutes of batting practice, mainly because I like to hit even though I suck at it. (*Should you say 'suck' to the president's campaign manager,* I wondered.) I'll spend some time thinking hard about the Reds' hitters, you know, to make sure my memory of their strengths and weaknesses matches what they're doing at the plate. I'll repeat that the next day."

I realized that was probably way more information than he wanted or needed. "Sorry about that," I added. "I get into tangents sometimes once I start focusing on pitcher strategy."

Rayburn laughed. "That's fine, Trey," he said. "We like people who think things through. But you're talking to the wrong guy. The president would love to spend the next hour dissecting the Reds' lineup with you. You're probably too much of a distraction for a guy who loves baseball and has borderline

Attention Deficit Disorder—like most people who want to be president, I might add."

We both laughed. Finally, he got to the point.

"Well, here it is," he said. "We'd like you to publicly endorse President Murphy on your off day. We realize it's not appropriate for you to do it in uniform or as part of the team, but you could be a surprise guest at his news conference that day.

"This is a close nomination battle, Trey," Rayburn added. "You've been following this. You know that's true. If we don't win on the first ballot, everything's up for grabs. Most delegates can go anywhere they want. And you know the stakes. You just told me that."

I said, "Colonel, uh, Charley, that's a big ask. Even if I stick my neck out, it'll be a huge distraction for the team in the middle of a pennant race. I'm not sure it's even fair to the organization."

He said, "Trey, this is where I lay a guilt trip on you. There are two things that strike the president and me about you. First, you're really smart. Second, you're obviously looking for more purpose in your life and I can't think of a higher purpose than helping the one person—flaws and all—who has the best chance of keeping the world from falling into complete chaos in the next few years. I'm asking you the way I would explain a difficult mission to a soldier, but you're not a soldier, even if you have a soldier's soul. I can't order you to do it. But I can do all I can to convince you why it matters. You're in a unique position to help him."

A soldier's soul. I imagined he had used that phrase before. He must have known it would make me stop and think. He didn't become a successful leader without knowing what motivational buttons to push.

He had pushed mine.

"Okay," I said. "This is a tentative yes. I need to know exactly what you expect and the logistics. I don't want to give any long speeches. I'll have to give the team a heads-up. And they're not going to like it."

"We'll get all that to you," Rayburn said. "And we can help you with your talking points. We already thought of that. Some of our biggest donors are in Chicago. We can whisper in the owner's ear for you a day in advance. Jerry Landis donated to President Murphy in the past, by the way, though you should know his family gave some money to Lydia Nicks this year. Still, the statement writes itself and they'll surely be asked to comment. We've already worked on a draft. It'll go something like this: 'Trey Van Ohmann has free speech rights as an individual like any other American citizen. We respect those rights and respect his pledge to keep any distractions he may cause to a minimum.' Like you said to me, it also has the virtue of being true.

"Meanwhile, it goes without saying that you must keep this to yourself for a few more days," he added.

"I get that," I said.

We talked logistics for a few more minutes and then the call ended.

Rayburn had told me not to tell anyone, but he hadn't said I couldn't at least drop a hint. I reached Aimee on FaceTime.

"Hey," she said, "What's up? I'm doing some prep for the show."

"Are you going to be traveling with the team to Cincinnati next week?" I asked.

"Wasn't planning on it," she said before raising her eyebrows and scrunching her nose to one side. "Something I should know? They're not sending you down to the minors to learn how to pitch more perfect games, are they? Or, maybe you're quitting to grow lentils in Idaho? See, I remember what you told me about potatoes not being much of a crop where you grew up."

"No," I said, smiling and impressed that she had paid that much attention to my comments on Idaho's agricultural practices. "Nothing like that. I can't say a lot, but you should try to get down there for the Cincinnati series."

"Now I'm curious."

"Trust me on this, okay?"

"Is it sports or politics? With the convention going on, a hotel is going to cost a fortune and they keep cutting expenses around here. 'Repositioning to better compete,' is what they say. Repositioning, my ass."

I decided not to comment on the pleasant image that "my ass" immediately conjured. Hey, you can't help being a guy.

"I've got a college friend who actually lives in Fort Mitchell, right across the Ohio River in Kentucky," I replied. "You can stay with Ricky and his family I'll bet.

"Plus," I continued, "you've got sports, politics and geography coming together here. The president of the United States is from the suburbs. Those are your listeners. He's the world's best-known Cubs fan. The Cubs happen to be in town. You can do stuff live for both your show and your dad's.

"And, we'll get to see each other; at least briefly."

I could tell she was contemplating.

"I might be able to sell that," she finally said. "We've been feverishly arranging call-ins and stuff, but that's a crapshoot. People say they'll call and don't, especially politicians. We're pretty big by Chicago radio standards, but we're not exactly Politico, the New York Times or CBS News. Cincy is only a few hours from Chicago, so we can drive. Maybe the expenses would be manageable if I tell them I can stay with your friends. We'll say they're my friends, though, all right?"

"Sure," I said. "I'll let the Koenigs know you might be coming."

After I touched the "end talk" button, I sat still for several minutes, wondering what the hell I had just agreed to do, pondering a suspicion that Chuck Briggs, the team's media relations director, had been right when he told me I had no idea what it meant to wade into presidential politics. Chuck knew. In an earlier life, he had worked several years as an aide to a senator from Illinois before he ran for president. You might've heard of Barack Obama.

I knew one thing for sure: Chuck wouldn't like this one bit.

28

Trey Van Ohmann

I didn't visit Cincinnati much when I was in the American League other than for an All-Star game and one series the Red Sox had played there. Still, Cincy had potential as one of my favorite road stops. It's one of those cities that has the right scale of good restaurants and other amenities without the hassle of huge cities. Veterans told me it was getting a lot better, because the downtown was coming to life and the nearby Over the Rhine neighborhood was as cool a neighborhood as you'd find in New York, without New York's prices for eating or parking.

The more active party animals on the team felt differently and thought Cincy was pretty boring. Well, so be it. Then there was the famous Cincinnati chili, which to a non-local is much thinner than you'd expect and placed over spaghetti with an immense mound of packaged, shredded cheese plopped on top. Call it an acquired taste. On this visit, downtown Cincinnati was a zoo. From my window at the downtown Westin Hotel I saw protestors from every conceivable political persuasion filling every inch of Fountain Square across the street. I think the anarchists and atheists even got into a fight.

Before leaving my room for the game, I saw one group carrying signs saying "Defend American Christians in Bali." Several of them were screaming at another group with a banner that said, "Americans for Tolerance." Several of the presumably tolerant Americans were flipping birds at the Christians, who weren't acting very Christian in return. A lot of the signs had comets flying across them, symbolizing the bizarre event that caused the Cubs to nearly lose the last World Series.

I realized at that moment that I wouldn't be in this weird situation, or even a member of the Cubs for that matter, if not for these events. Was it fate, the hand of God or just random serendipity? Who could really say? But it was hard to escape the notion that events were twisting and turning into some sort of inevitable direction.

Every political media outlet was doing delegate counts to see if Murphy had enough votes to win on the first ballot. The wild card was a small subset of delegates who had the ability to vote for whomever they wanted. No one thought Nicks had enough votes to win in the first round, but if she had enough to stop Murphy, then the convention would go up for grabs.

Streets were closed for blocks around. There was no way for our team bus to pull up to the hotel entrance. To get to the Great American Ballpark only a few blocks away, we had to exit a rear entrance off Vine Street.

This was the convention's opening night. The next night would be the vote, so the news conference where I was supposed to join the circus would be tomorrow morning. Then, adding to the matters worthy of my consideration. I was supposed to pitch the next night when presumably Murphy would be on his way to the nomination if things broke his way—including, I guess, if Rayburn and friends had handed enough goodies to the unpledged delegates who could give Murphy a "W."

Meanwhile, the team hadn't played very well in Colorado. If we lost the first two games of this Series, we could leave Cincy in a first-place tie with St. Louis. I would need to be at my best on Thursday night.

The next morning, after we lost an uninspiring game by a score of 6-2, I was having second thoughts, sort of like a bridegroom with second thoughts—but the wedding takes on such a life of its own that it can't be stopped.

My phone played the start of "I Gotta Go." It was Aimee.

"Hey, Trey," she said. "I just got into town. You guys need to play better than you did last night. Any comment?"

I knew she wasn't serious. This was our typical banter. To play along, I offered up a classic, meaningless jock quote—the kind we're taught to provide so it looks like we're cooperating when we really don't want to say anything.

"We play 'em one game at a time," I said, deadpanning it. "I'm sure the team was giving 120 percent; maybe even 127 percent. We're looking forward to tonight's contest and expect the Redlegs to give us a real tussle."

Actually, the Reds were in last place after a promising start. The cliché "playing out the string" was more like "hanging from a rope" to describe their foul, depressed mood, which made last night's loss even harder to take.

"Oh, that's great," Aimee said. "I'm sure I can go national with those insightful comments. Tussle? Who the hell says 'tussle'?"

"Hey, you asked. At least I didn't use the most overused word in the English language. It was AMAZING!"

"Well, Mr. Van Ohmann, I guess we're going to have to schedule a coaching session."

"I'd like that, especially if it stays off the record."

"Well, we'll see how much coaching you need to perform effectively," she said, and if it's possible to hear a smile, I heard it and immediately started to imagine some possibilities involving a kitchen table and me on my knees.

Aimee interrupted my brief, imaginary trip into depravity. "Meanwhile, now that I'm here, can you tell me why I'm here?"

I said, "Are you following the political schedules as well? You know Murphy's got a news conference today, right?"

"I do."

"You need to be there."

"And that's it?"

"That's it."

Aimee was smart. She would start to put the pieces together. She asked, "Are you going to be there?"

"Now why would I be there?"

"Hmm," she said. "Answering a question with a question. A classic dodge. I don't have a journalism degree, but I'm catching on to this stuff. So, let's see: You had this interesting meeting with Murphy not so long ago. You urge me to come to Cincinnati. I think you're trying to help me be in position to be present for a damned interesting story that you know I'd want. So, stop playing Jedi mind games with me."

"More, I can't say. Be there, you must."

"You know, I've read and seen 'All the President's Men' several times," she said. "Dad encouraged me. He said it's a great film that will inspire me and he was right. Well, one time this Washington Post reporter, Carl Bernstein, really screwed up with a source as he investigated President Nixon and Watergate. Bernstein could tell that the source wanted to help him, but the source kept saying he wouldn't comment on the investigation. Bernstein thought he had a clever way so this guy could say something without saying it. The idea was that Bernstein would announce he was ending the phone call and whether the source said anything or stayed silent after that would be a signal. But they got confused on what it would mean if the source just hung up the phone."

I said, "And, you're going where with this?"

She said, "Okay, I'm going to do better than Carl Bernstein. This is simple; much simpler than he made it. Now, pay attention. I'm getting ready to end the call. If the ONLY thing you say from this point forward is 'I understand,' it'll mean you'll be at the press conference with Murphy."

"I understand," I said, and ended the call.

***

When it was time to go, I looked out the window, saw a sky greeting me with heavy clouds and turned on the local news. I regretted the decision quickly and realized I should've just checked the weather app on my phone. The TV weatherman finally offered the information I needed after five minutes of nonsense. The perky anchor apparently felt an urgent need to signal that this wasn't a smiley-face day as though we were all restless students in her kindergarten class. Then Mr. Weatherman said there was a threat of thunderstorms, including chilly winds and hail, for that night's game. Suddenly I felt pouty, too.

I had a suit with me on this trip; a medium gray job that Aimee said "doesn't look like you bought it at the Penney's outlet." We didn't wear suits much in western Idaho and had even less interest in worrying about fashion trends, though it's not true that all our shirts are preceded by the adjectives "flannel" or "T." I've figured a few things out as a guy in the spotlight. I don't want to look like a hick. I wore a white shirt with light-blue stripes and a red tie with small, gray paisleys that didn't clash with the pattern of the shirt. During one of my college classes on political campaigns, I had learned that red ties are called "power ties," because of the way most of us are wired to respond to different colors.

This seemed like a good day for a power tie.

When I'm dressed like this, I'm "out of uniform" and not that recognizable, especially outside Chicago and Boston, and it was too early for most of the diehard Cub fans in town to be wandering around after a night game. Between security, pedestrians and closed streets, it was much easier to walk the two short blocks to the Duke Energy Convention Center than grabbing a cab or an Uber ride.

The level of security shouldn't have been surprising under the circumstances. The president of the United States was going to hold a news conference during a time of terrorism and unrest after all. Still, it was overwhelming and I thought what a shame it had come to this. The bad guys know how to use our freedoms against us. They count on us becoming more like them to defeat them. Facing profound, misguided evil, it's hard to resist the urge to abandon human rights and hunt them down with reckless abandon, not worrying about collateral damage. Did Murphy have a better answer? Sincere or not, I didn't see one from Lydia Nicks.

These dark thoughts were interrupted at the first security checkpoint. I had received instructions to go to a southern entrance of the Center, along Fifth Street, not the main entrance at Fifth and Elm streets. Armed police surrounded three rows of concrete barricades and I had to show my pass and identification at each stop. I heard the swoop of helicopters overhead and when I looked up, I saw the barrels of sniper rifles poking out on the roof of the parking garage across the street.

After passing through multiple levels of Secret Service scrutiny, I was ushered into a small "holding room." I saw Charley Rayburn, who nodded a greeting, and I was surprised to see Alison Murphy when I first entered. She looked good; a lot more composed than when I saw her in the Oval Office.

"Hello, Mrs. Murphy," I said. "It's nice to see you again."

She laughed lightly. "You can call me Alison in this setting, Trey," she said. "Otherwise, you make me feel like I'm even older than you than I really am."

"Okay," was all I said, before she spoke again.

"I'm sorry about, uh, interrupting your meeting with the president when you were at the White House," she said. "It was kind of a strange day."

"I'm sure it was," I said, not sure that came out quite right.

Then she moved closer, making sure we had eye contact. She put a hand on my shoulder. She opened her eyes wide and I saw at that moment why people wrote that Alison Murphy had more charisma than her husband. At that moment, you knew you were the most important person in her life.

"Trey," she said. "Do you know what you're getting into?"

I gave her a half-smile back. I said, "That's exactly what Chuck Briggs, our communications guy, said to me. To be honest, the team wishes I wasn't doing this. I just feel as though, I don't know, that I need a larger purpose and I think your husband is the best choice we have."

"That's all true," she said. "I believe that, too. Just be careful. Everyone in politics uses everyone else. Users, abusers and enablers. That's what we are. You need to watch everything—and I mean everything—you say and do from now on. You're in a different game now. Even when you think you have privacy, assume you don't.

"Oh, one other thing," she added, grasping my hand, quickly tightening around it and then releasing it just as fast. "Watch out for diaries and notebooks."

There was no missing her point. A sad look passed through her face as she looked down for an instant; then she caught herself and focused back on me. I thought about the embarrassment and stress the Taylor Pierce revelations must have caused but thought better of saying anything.

"I appreciate that," I said but had to ask a question. "But, why are you taking such an interest in me? I'm just another guy supporting your husband."

"You're not, Trey," she said. "You remind me of me many years ago, when I met Luke, and we started down this road. You think you're prepared. You're in the public eye. So was I. It's a whole new level. They're going to come after you."

"They," I said, and repeated myself, turning it into a question to which I knew the answer. "They?"

"Everyone who doesn't want him to be president," she said. "Maybe even some who do. I'll go out there in a minute with him and smile like everything's okay. I'll pretend I don't hate most of them, because I made him a promise, because basically he's a good man despite whatever issues we have and because the country does need him. Then you'll be out there."

She touched my shoulder again, turned and walked away. I caught myself staring.

"So, Trey, what was that all about?"

It was Charley Rayburn, eyeing me almost suspiciously. He had startled me from behind, so intent I was on watching Alison Murphy walk away.

"She was sort of giving me a pep talk in a weird way," I said. "She reminded me that this stuff matters and to be careful about what I say and do. I think she was trying to say that being a sports celebrity might be a big deal, but it's not in the same league as this. Sorry about the lame cliché there."

"Apology accepted," Rayburn said, slapping me on my suddenly popular shoulder. "She gives good advice. You'll do great, Trey. Just read your statement and answer a few questions. We've got your back."

Did they? If Alison Murphy wanted to plant some seeds of doubt, she had done a good job. Well, there was no exit ramp at this point, and she had confirmed my instincts that Murphy was someone worth supporting. After all, if SHE could say that, after her husband's actions and all the hurtful crap raining down on her, I could do it, too. I reminded myself to extend the sweep and sensitivity of my mental radar beyond the usual range.

I had no way of knowing that my radar remained woefully underpowered.

29

Trey Van Ohmann

The script called for me to enter from the left of the podium after the president finished his remarks about how excited he was to be on the precipice of the nomination with his wife at his side. As was often the case, the First Lady would be addressing the convention. Rayburn had explained to me that the campaign had decided to hold an early-afternoon news conference "for multiple reasons." He didn't go into detail, but it wasn't hard to figure out.

First, they would get as many ugly questions about Taylor Pierce out of the way as they could, which wasn't made any easier by the inability of anyone to track her down.

Second, they'd subtly deal with rumors about the president's relationship with his wife, let them see Alison was with him and remind the public how much everyone liked the First Lady. This was the political game of, "Hey, she's great. If she married HIM, he can't be that bad."

Third, it would allow Murphy to once again express regrets that he hadn't paid more attention to his now-deceased college friend.

Fourth, they'd actually have a few minutes where Murphy could talk about policy and national problems. If the media insisted on boarding the gossip express on subjects like his sexual orientation—the likely scenario—he'd have a built-in applause line for his supporters, chastising the media heathens for their lack of interest in "the real problems facing this country."

And, then there was me. I was the last card they'd flip in a high-stakes game; the surprise guest whose job was to replace stale air with a fresh breeze, limiting the available time and space that the media otherwise would devote to Murphy's multiple flaws and sins.

I watched it unfold on the monitor in the holding room, reminding myself that the media horde wasn't that much larger than you see after the seventh game of the World Series. *If you can explain how your team handled a World Series, you can handle this,* I thought to myself.

I heard Alison Murphy say, "Successful couples work through their problems. The difference is that most don't have to do it in the public eye. But Luke and I have always accepted that this is part of our deal with the American people. That's why I want to talk about why I think it's so important to elect him to a second term."

Murphy nodded in appreciation with his arm lightly around his wife's shoulders. They were both such practiced political actors, there was no way to tell if this was a show, or if they really had worked things out and were moving forward.

Then Murphy went back to the lectern. "Now, I'd like to take a minute to introduce someone whose endorsement was particularly meaningful for me given what most of you know about my passion for baseball and a certain team," he said. "And he's also a special person who will forever change any unfair stereotypes you're carrying around about professional athletes. And, he's got excellent taste in the politicians he supports."

That got a modest laugh as people figured out what was coming. On the monitor, I could see Aimee in the second row of the swarm with a good sight line to the podium where I'd be standing.

This was my cue. Murphy said, "From the Chicago Cubs, here's their star pitcher and someone who has become a friend. Trey Van Ohmann."

In the old movies, this is where flash camera bulbs would start going off. Today, it meant that phones were held up by half of the media members for still photos or live-streaming while the other half busily began tapping tweets. Whatever insightful words I had to offer could reach the world in real time, as long as the insight neatly fit within Twitter's 140-character limit

My statement was brief.

> I'm here today to announce my support for Luke Murphy for a second term as president of the United States. I know that's a bit out of character for a baseball player to take a political position, especially in the middle of a pennant race; especially when my team is trying to win its second World Series since 1908. So, I want to address that head on.
>
> First, I want Cub fans to know this will not be a distraction. My priority is to do the absolute best I can to help turn the team's recent success into a dynasty. We're focused on not only getting back to the World Series, but also winning it again. So, I don't plan to regularly make political pronouncements or appearances. Today happens to be a combination of events with the Cubs in Cincinnati while President Murphy is here to accept his nomination.
>
> Besides, I'm not pitching today, so my day is relatively free.

That brought a few polite laughs as the speechwriters and I had hoped. I continued from there.

> But I do have some other things to say. Baseball is a great game, but it's also just a game. While we celebrate sports, all Americans also must take time to seriously examine the candidates when so much is at stake in our country and in the world. Whether your choice is President Murphy or someone else, I hope you will do so.

When I had the chance to meet President Murphy recently, I was struck by his focus and commitment. He asked me to seriously study his record and the candidates. He asked me to at least consider speaking out on his behalf if requested to do so.

As some of you may know, I was a political science major in college. Politics and public policy have always fascinated me. If I hadn't gone into baseball, I probably would've gone to law school and been involved in policy behind the scenes. Another reason I'm standing here, frankly, is that since my father's untimely death, I've spent more of my off time thinking about how I can make a difference.

So, I took the president's challenge and I concluded two things.

First, we are in terribly impactful and dangerous times. Second, President Murphy is the one best equipped to lead us. So, to the extent that my presence might make a difference for some undecided voters—or delegates—I would urge you to support President Murphy at this convention and in the election in November.

Thank you and I'll take some questions now.

I thought I was prepared for some of the questioning. I had done homework so that I could articulate Murphy's position on the economy, terrorism and his ability to work with Congress. Working with Murphy's staff, I had ways to deflect efforts to get me to trash the other candidates and stay positive. Others in the sports journalism world had been tipped, because Aimee wasn't the only non-political reporter in the room. Most of their questions were different; there was an air of almost anger from the self-appointed media guardians of sports purity about injecting myself into this.

Q: Have you talked to your teammates or Cubs management

about this?

A: Only briefly to management late yesterday and the honest answer is they respect my decision but would prefer that this hadn't happened.

Q: Don't you worry about being a distraction?

A: As I said in my statement, I've pledged that won't happen. It won't. My focus is bringing a championship to Chicago.

Q: What do you think gives you the qualifications to endorse President Murphy?

A: I'm a citizen like anyone else and I've tried to stay informed. I've done my homework, but my comments are more aimed at encouraging everyone to do that and reach their own decision. I didn't give up my interest in the world around me when I become an athlete. That's an unfair stereotype.

Q: Has the president made any promises regarding the investigation of your father?

A: No. None. We haven't discussed it other than he shared his sympathy.

Q: So, what reaction did you have to the recent revelations about the president's homosexual encounter and the death of his friend?

A: I processed this information like everyone else and finally concluded that this happened so long ago that it didn't have an impact on my choice now.

Q: Will you be doing other appearances for President Murphy?

A: Only if my schedule allows and if requested to do so. Again, I've made it clear that I won't let this interfere with my commitment to the Cubs.

Q: Do you think the president would have asked for your support if you were still with the Red Sox?

A: Well, that might have made his decision more difficult.

I did a good job of dead-panning that one. It brought a laugh and lightened the mood. Aimee asked that question. I owed her one for that.

30

Trey Van Ohmann

When I got to the ballpark, went to the locker room, assessed the mood and saw the expressions on my teammates' faces, two cliché words kept going through my mind.

Lead balloon. My ascent into presidential politics had gone over like the clichéd lead balloon.

I couldn't really blame them. I had said I wouldn't let my political side trip be a distraction, but it turned into one quickly. The looks I received in the locker room weren't exactly glares; actually, most of my teammates looked sad, not mad. But, you could tell they weren't very happy. I saw glances of curiosity and exasperation, as if to say, "Hey, man, we have enough happening right now. Remember THE FUCKING PENNANT RACE!"

Still, I was getting off easy; certainly easier than if I were the third-string catcher. They knew and so did I, they needed me to pitch well to get back to the World Series. Not that the job would be impossible if I collapsed or disappeared in the next 10 minutes, but it would be many-factors more difficult. That's not cockiness; it's simply true.

The room would empty shortly as players headed outside to warm up and take batting practice. Our second baseman, Justin Campanelli, my best friend on the team, spoke up just before a few players headed for the door.

"Look guys" he said, standing with one foot on the chair in front of his locker. "This needs to be said now before anything gets out of hand. We're a team and we face others as a team. There's no other way to get to where we want to go. As far as I'm concerned, if this is something Trey felt he had to do, we've got to have his back publicly.

"But, Trey. Dude. This has to be said, too. You need to cool it. I just hope you know what you're in for. I'm already getting texts from reporters asking for comments. Political haters are loading up on my Twitter. The other guys are seeing it, too. We really don't need this."

"I appreciate that," I replied, and then decided I should say more. This moment might not return. "Only you guys know what we go through. I just feel like my Dad would have expected me to speak up. This is for him. His death needs to stand for something other than him being a victim of some nutty fan. I meant it when I said I will not let this distract me from our goal. It just won't. And I'm sorry for the bullshit that's going to land for a few days."

"We're all hoping it's just a few days," Justin said.

Everyone shuffled out. A few teammates made it a point to tap my shoulder or touch fist-to-fist. There wasn't much more to say, but as soon as everyone walked out of the enclosed security of the clubhouse, it was obvious Justin had predicted the future.

All around the field, particularly at the batting cage, there already were four times more media members hovering than you'd expect for a mid-week game in Cincinnati, particularly since the Reds weren't going anywhere this season.

And, as predicted, my teammates were getting questions that normally don't go to athletes. You could feel the reporters sensing the opportunity to scratch the itch they get when they sense an irresistible story guaranteed to stir trouble and generate clicks.

Said one television reporter to a relief pitcher, Jonathan Ellsworth, unable to keep hints of sarcasm out of her questions, "So, Jon, are YOU going to be endorsing anyone for president? Do you think this is going to cause the Cubs to lose their focus?"

Jon was trying to kick his gross, unhealthy habit of dipping tobacco. He usually switched to gum once the game started. Not so at batting practice. He worked up a big, ugly wad and, like any artist who had mastered his craft, deposited a juicy hocker about two inches' shy of the reporter's fashionable blue heels.

Jon also was really smart and had a great sense of humor. He had a business degree from the University of North Carolina and shared stock tips with other players, but he enjoyed acting like he had just come out of a Smoky Mountains cave in overalls with the cousin he had just married slung over his back.

"Oops, sorry ma'am," he said in his soft drawl, raising an eyebrow. "I almost hit your shoes. Hope those weren't from Jimmy Choo."

She gave him a memorable glare and walked away. Five of us standing around the batting cage laughed out loud. For the moment, my teammates were laughing with me. But most kept some distance as well.

Roberto Alvarez, the manager, walked over.

"Front office is going ape-shit, you know, Trey," he said in his Spanish-accented English. "Not publicly, you understand, they don't want to look like they don't support your, you know, First Amendment rights.

"Behind the scenes, we just had quite a meeting."

I said, "How's that, Roberto?"

He said, "Well, they asked me how much of a distraction this was going to be. And they showed me something. Have you seen Facebook or Twitter today?"

"Not really, but I already got the word on what's happening. And, I gotta be honest, if I hear the word 'distraction' one more time today, I'll probably become a bigger one."

He said, "Well, you should look at Facebook for sure. You're already getting death threats. The Cubs' Facebook page is being taken over by people who don't have lives except to be jerk-offs on social media."

"And that would be different than people who have no life except to be jerk-offs about sports," was my witty response.

"Good point," he said, "except they're already thinking they're going to have to hire more moderators for our social media and they're wondering whether you're going to need security."

"Security?"

"There are a lot of kooks out there," he said, then underlined the obvious. "If anyone learned that last season, it was the Cubs. People almost died in our ballpark, man."

"Point taken," I said, maybe reflecting too late on all the implications of my debut in American politics.

31

WCO Studios
Two Weeks After The Convention

Sitting in his cubicle in the WCO office, Scott Skowron stared at his phone. It was a hard stare. He couldn't believe the tip he had just received from Jason Conkle, his anonymous source in the Cubs' data analytics department. But Conkle had always been right before.

This was crazy. Absolutely crazy.

He looked at his phone again. Had he dozed off? Was this one of his dreams? He often had vivid dreams—the kind that were so vivid you weren't sure what was real or not for several minutes as you awakened. He had asked his neurologist once if his paralyzing accident caused the dreams. He didn't know anyone else who had dreams like that; at least not so often or that they'd admit.

"Who really knows, Scott?" was the doctor's answer. "Nerves get all tangled up in these things. Your type of paralysis combined with that head injury is rare, too. New connections get made; new pathways emerge for all the chemical components and enzymes that make our bodies work. We've still got a lot to learn."

He liked or at least appreciated many of the dreams. In some of them, he could walk again. Plus, he had full command of everything below his waist.

His reality was different, though he did all he could to minimize deficits. Physical therapy and surgical procedures had come a long way in more than four decades. He'd just started a trial with electrical implants that might allow him to get out of the chair and walk short distances with just the aid of a cane. His male anatomy was another matter. There was no discernable stirring and probably never would be.

Skowron did a quick self-check. No, this was no dream. But it didn't make any sense.

He texted Conkle back. "R U absolute sure what you heard?"

Less than a minute later, he got one word back. "Yes. I'm not an idiot."

Well, then, who needed to know first? Bob Walters had just driven to Chicago's NBC station to do a live MSNBC feed to talk about the election. It couldn't have been a crazier two weeks in politics since the convention. After Murphy barely won the nomination, Lydia Nicks announced a third-party candidacy and seemed to be making headway. Leeds, the Democratic candidate, had his own problems. The Washington Post revealed that groups tied to the famine-stricken Chinese were funneling money to his campaign. Tourism had come to a standstill in many countries. Muslim extremists in Indonesia continued to torture and kill individual Christians and the contagion was spreading, providing plenty of energy for the Nicks campaign.

The latest polls, in fact, were extraordinary. Murphy barely led at 30 percent; Nicks and Leeds were in a statistical tie at 28 percent, leaving 14 percent undecided for everyone to fight over. With the margin of error, it was basically a dead heat. If Nicks could get on the ballots across the 50 states she might be hard to beat. For Skowron and Bob Walters, of course, an election like this equaled ratings gold.

Mike Surrey and Aimee Walters had just gone off the air. Skowron decided to start there. They might be able to confirm and break the story before competitors got a sniff.

Skowron wheeled down the hall, catching Surrey and Aimee Walters as they left the studio.

"Hey Moose," Aimee said. "How's it going. Do you have anything to tell me about the suddenly slumping Cubs?"

She was right about that. The Cubs had lost what was once a five-game lead and continued to stumble. The Cardinals were tied for first with less than six weeks to go. Trey Van Ohmann had lost a heart-breaking game, 2-1, the night before on a ninth-inning error by the usually reliable Justin Campanelli at second base. At least Van Ohmann had pitched well. He had slumped since the convention, including a terrible outing against the last-place Reds the night after his now-famous news conference that served a full meal to the social-media haters to digest and disgorge.

Maybe Trey Van Ohmann had no business getting involved in a political campaign, but political analysts figured that Murphy's slim lead had at least something to do with Van Ohmann's presence. It was a novelty; something that made voters take a fresh look. People also felt sympathy for him after the death of his father and it didn't hurt that Van Ohmann's presence reminded people of Murphy's leadership and courage in the events that followed the end of last season.

"Let's go in the conference room," Skowron said to Surrey and Walters. "It's important."

Skowron closed the door behind him as he wheeled over to the end of the table where Mike and Aimee sat.

"I just got the craziest tip," he said. "My source is impeccable. I believe him. But we should find someone else to confirm this, because this could burn him as a source otherwise."

He could tell Surrey was uncomfortable. He was still getting used to the shift from a manager to a sports program host.

"You know, I spent most of my career trying to keep stuff like this from getting out—whatever it is," Surrey said.

"Don't keep us in suspense," Aimee said. "What is it?"

"It's about Trey," he said.

Skowron looked at Aimee Walters and saw her eyes drop. Her relationship with Trey Van Ohmann wasn't openly known, but close to coming out. There had been a few hints in gossip websites and social media as they were seen together around Chicago.

"My guy says there was a meeting where the Cubs' general manager got an urgent text message. The G.M. was so shocked he set the phone down and ran out of the room. My source glanced at the phone. The text said that Trey Van Ohmann tested positive for a banned, performance-enhancing substance. The League got some kind of anonymous tip and ordered the test as part of their protocol. Major League Baseball will suspend him tomorrow."

"What!" Aimee shouted. "There's no way he would do that."

Surrey looked even more uncomfortable. Silence permeated the room for a few moments.

"Aimee, you're too close to this. Let me make a few calls," Surrey finally said. "Obviously I know some people. I feel sorry for Trey if that's true; for the team that fired me, maybe not so much."

Aimee Walters looked at the two men. She didn't want to cry, which was what she felt like doing, and she knew she had to talk Trey soon—for both personal and professional reasons.

"Okay," she said. "You're right. You confirm. But if Trey wants to say anything publicly, he knows he can say it through us on our show tomorrow."

******

An hour later, Surrey had confirmation. There was a lot of work to do. Since the station was an ESPN affiliate, they decided to break the story simultaneously with ESPN at 5 p.m. The Cubs wouldn't comment publicly but told Surrey as a courtesy that the commissioner of baseball, Craig Keech, was planning a news conference for the next morning.

Aimee couldn't reach Trey. She finally decided she needed a quick break and a Starbucks run, where her phone beeped. It was a text from her dad.

"Sweetheart, look at SportsCheese.com. Not good. Dad."

SportsCheese was a website specializing in the lowest form of sports gossip—but a must-see place for every sports talk-show host in America to reap useful material in the event what the site reported turned out to be true—or even if it wasn't in many cases. Some items were too juicy to just ignore while waiting for confirmation. The trick: Attribute the source as SportsCheese with a shrug and the catch-all atonement line of "We don't have independent confirmation, but are working to obtain it." Then they could go off to the races.

SportsCheese's editors were clever about knowing just how far they could go, and they were protected by federal law if the commenters on the site, and not them, were the ones saying or posting scurrilous items. Many people suspected SportsCheese planted some of those comments, but no one had ever been able to prove it.

Aimee went to the SportsCheese site and saw a click-bait headline that screamed, "Check Out Trey Van Ohmann's Latest Distraction! And She's Smokin' Hot!"

The text said this:

> Cubs pitcher Trey Van Ohmann has lost three straight games and that's contributed mightily to Chicago's disappearing World Series dreams.
>
> Just sayin' … maybe there are too many other distractions out there for the sexy slinger.
>
> First of all, we all know the noble Mr. Van Ohmann has other things on his mind, like reelecting liberal-squishy Luke Murphy as president, a RINO (Republican in Name Only) if there ever was one.
>
> But, apparently Trey has some other things stimulating him these days—like romping in Chicago's Lincoln Park with Aimee Walters, the steamy-hot sports radio personality in Chicago who seems to have recovered nicely from the wounds she suffered at the hands of a crazy fan last October.
>
> Check out this video snapped last week by an alert SportsCheeser.

(You, too, can be a SportsCheeser. Send your videos or photos to us and you'll enter a monthly contest that awards $500 for the best SportsCheese.com scoop of the month. Click the link here to register!)

Aimee remembered the moment the photo captured very well. They had gone for a walk in the park. It was sweltering, in the 90s, and she was in a silly, sexy mood. She wanted to see if she could turn Trey on. He usually posed in public as a master of self-control. She loved a challenge. So, she had let her hair fall naturally and put on some thong panties and her shortest shorts—a frayed blue-jean number that started below her naval and ended just below her crotch. Then, over a tight black bra, she slipped on a frilly black top with spaghetti straps that showed more of her cleavage than she would normally exhibit, but it was her mood at the moment. Like most of her tops, her back was mostly covered, better to hide the scars from the bullwhip lashes. She completed the outfit with open-toed platform heels, so she could stand a couple inches higher to Trey, who was at least six inches taller.

Trey, as usual, preferred to look anonymous, so he wore a faded, green baseball cap that said "Cabela's" that he pulled low along with a Zac Brown Band T-shirt, khaki shorts and flip-flops. He looked like any other young professional with some casual down time, walking through Lincoln Park. *Well*, she thought, *not just any young professional*. She knew she wouldn't be the only woman admiring the strong, long legs and upper torso of his athlete's body.

Amie could tell right away she had his number. He didn't just hold her hand; he began stroking it. They bought cold drinks and walked under a tree. No one else was visible as they leaned against the old oak, cooling off in the shade from the plush, green canopy above.

"You seem to have something on your mind, Mr. Van Ohmann," she said, smiling. Damn she liked this guy. "Spit it out."

"Actually, I was goin' over the best way to pitch to Philadelphia's hitters," he said, arching an eyebrow, but taking both of her hands and pulling her closer to him.

"I call bullshit," she said.

"Caught," he said.

He kissed her. Hard. Their tongues played together for a minute. She could feel herself getting damp already as his hand slipped behind her shorts and her panties and started stroking her in a slow rhythm. He pushed himself closer and she could tell he was hard, too.

"It's damn hot here," she finally said. "Hotter than I thought." Then she laughed. "Whoa, does that sound like a lame, porn-book line or what?"

Trey laughed, too. "Yeah," he said, though he was breathing heavily. "It does. Still, I propose we cut this walk short."

And they did. The lovemaking that followed was as delicious as any she could remember.

But, as the smartphone video at SportsCheese.com showed, they certainly weren't alone when Trey's hand slipped under her shorts. The hundreds of salacious comments accompanying the video didn't help either.

32

Chicago & The White House
The Following Morning

"I'm innocent!"

Chuck Briggs stared hard at Van Ohmann. The Cubs' communication director couldn't resist a sarcastic comment.

"I suppose you told that to the Murphy campaign, too, or are you going to be making more appearances while you're suspended?" Briggs said.

"Chuck, that's exactly what I told them," Van Ohmann said, missing his sarcasm completely. "And, no, I don't think they'll be calling. I'm pretty toxic."

"This is a damn disaster. You know that, right?" Briggs said, unable to resist a rant. "I warned you every which way not to get involved in politics. You're one of the biggest sports celebrities in the country now. You're making millions endorsing everything from sports apparel to Idaho potatoes and deep-dish pizza, right? You had to rock the fucking boat. What the hell did you think was going to happen? And, then, you get caught doping in the middle of our god-damn pennant race? And, then, you aren't smart enough to keep your hands to yourself in Lincoln Park? And, then, you have to be with Aimee Goddam Walters."

"I don't know what to say, Chuck," Van Ohmann said. "Except that I didn't do it. I'd never take PEDs. And I've got rights as a citizen."

"That's good that you don't know what to say, Trey. And you know why that's good? You need to shut up. You're supposed to be quiet and introverted, remember? Meanwhile, the team will issue a statement that says we're fully cooperating with Major League Baseball and we'll urge fans to reserve judgment until all the facts are known. Are all the fucking facts known, Trey?"

"Obviously not. I didn't do it. Someone is setting me up. Will the team help me get to the bottom of this?"

"Well, that's a step in the right direction," Briggs said. "Now you need the team. About fucking time. Before you go in with the brass, the G.M. authorized me to tell you that you're suspended indefinitely and to stay out of the damn limelight as much as you can."

Van Ohmann knew he shouldn't say what he was going to say next, but he couldn't resist.

"So, Chuck, I'm guessing you got your ass chewed on my account. Everyone knows Landis is a decent guy unless you push him too far. But our owner backs Nicks, right? I know he's donating to her campaign. Is that what this is about? Are you guys going to stand up for me?"

"Trey, don't even try to go there," Briggs said. "Your job is to focus on getting back in uniform and earn those millions Jerry Landis is paying you. That's it. That's the message. You do that, and we're with you. Understood?"

"Totally."

***

At WCO at that moment, Aimee Walters sat quietly in the office of station manager Davis Bryant. She had made sure to dress modestly on this day.

"I don't know whether to suspend you or give you a raise," was the first thing he said.

That surprised her. She decided to wait for his next comment.

"Aimee, that was stupid. You shouldn't be dating the people you cover. I really should suspend you, but this is sports talk. You're not Wolf Damn Blitzer and this isn't CNN or the New

York Times. Our ratings are going to be sky-high for a while," he added, contemplating an appealing upside of the situation. "Plus, you, Skowron and Surrey helped us get a great story first. There's that.

"So, I'm not going to suspend you," Bryant continued. "But you're going to have to address it today. It'll make news. I want to see what you're going to say beforehand."

She couldn't believe she was escaping so easily, but she appreciated it.

"I'm really sorry about this mess," she said. "I didn't mean to fall for Trey. We just kind of did. I should've told all of you."

Bryant smiled for the first time.

"Look, you have tons of talent, but you need to learn from this," he said. "Getting involved was really dumb. If a few things were different, I'd have to suspend or fire you. You need to understand that."

"I do."

"One other thing."

"What's that?"

"I wouldn't wear those shorts and that top in public again. Check out the comments on our website. I may need to hire more security to keep all the sexually starved guys in Chicagoland from trying to force their way into the studio like the walking dead or something."

"That's one thing you won't have to worry about," she said.

"I'm dressing like a nun, at least until the end of the baseball season."

She paused for a moment, collecting her thoughts.

She said, "I do have a favor to ask, because this whole thing is crazy, and I need to be there for Trey. After today's show, I'd like a few days off."

She paused for a moment, letting Bryant consider her request; then she flashed an impish smile.

"I just thought of something," she said. "You could call it a three-day suspension without pay for not disclosing the relationship to the station. You'll get some credibility. You'll even surprise some people."

Bryant saw the benefits. "Okay," he said. "That makes sense. We'll take some ethical medicine while you stay out of trouble. Just make sure you do that."

***

He wouldn't answer his phone. She drove past Trey's apartment and immediately realized it was a mistake as a media swarm camped on the sidewalk. She quickly turned around, hoping not to be spotted in her nondescript Nissan Altima.

Too late for that. One of the reporters recognized her as she started to make a turnaround in the alley. She knew if she stopped the car would be surrounded—in different circumstances, she would have been out there, too. So, she stepped on the gas before anyone could get in front of her car and drove away.

There were even a few reporters in front of her place, but Trey was the big story, not her. She was just the sex angle, as if the story needed more juice to become a bigger sensation.

That thought was confirmed as she walked past a reporter with an "ET" microphone for "Entertainment Tonight," and a free-lancer who said she was with TMZ, the gossip website.

"I'm sorry," Aimee said. "I know you have jobs to do, but I just have no comment for you right now."

"Do you think Trey is innocent?" the TMZ reporter yelled.

"I do," she said, deciding to give them a tiny sound bite.

"Are you and Trey still an item?" asked a reporter she didn't recognize.

"That's really our business," she said, and then walked inside.

And cried. Trey still wouldn't answer

***

Luke and Alison Murphy stared at each other in the private kitchen of the White House residence. "I'd like to talk to you about something," she had said to him a few minutes earlier. "Let's go to the kitchen."

Without ever taking a vote, they had designated the kitchen as their neutral zone—a private place to talk. They were on equal ground there without the symbolism of the bedroom, which they no longer shared anyway; a fact known only to the upstairs White House staff. That hadn't leaked yet, though it probably would at some point.

Alison microwaved some water for green tea; Luke rummaged around for some Ritz crackers and slices of Cracker Barrel cheese—a guilty pleasure—and grabbed a can of Canada Dry ginger ale.

They both sat and made a show of concentrating on the food and drink. There was so much unsaid, but what wasn't said rang like the clang of giant bells.

Publicly, they maintained the façade of a couple hanging-in-there while dealing with adversity. When they were alone together, they could remove their public masks, but that didn't happen much. Even in private, it was easier to play the roles they'd selected without ever really discussing why. Mask removal created too much danger of unproductive arguments and passive-aggressive games. There was too much danger of pain. Instead, one of the unspoken agreements was to wander down emotional roads as rarely as possible.

Instinctively, they both knew they still maintained powerful bonds, badly frayed but connected just the same. There even remained ill-defined love for the other person, but each was too scared and defensive to find out if the other held those feelings. They knew, agreeing silently, that to stop conversing completely was a bad idea. There were too many issues to navigate for two people who could make a powerful case for having the least amount of privacy of any couple in the world. Every expression on either face, every facet of their body language, even the way Alison applied her makeup or whether she looked tired or perky, was endlessly dissected wherever they went. If she looked tired, the bloggers said that was understandable. If she smiled and acted energetic, TMZ would find a "White House insider" to knowingly opine that she was "obviously moving past her marriage."

Maybe because of the intense, public scrutiny they shared, they were managing to maintain enough respect for one another to get through most days. Their memories were like old carry-on baggage, battered and worn but not quite ready to toss aside. In their hearts, they knew it was logically time for greater physical distance to match the emotional chasms and maybe in a different setting than the White House they could have contemplated it. Here, though, they still needed each other. They knew each other like no one else could. The hard part was to trudge onward with emotional armor fully deployed.

As a result, their relationship remnants were transactional—cold, clinical bargains; unspoken, mutual assistance pacts to help each other for a few more months. Alison, as most women would do, had spent more time thinking about this, and that was the way she imagined things now.

"You saw what happened to Trey Van Ohmann," she stated to her husband.

"I did."

"Do you think he did it, took the PEDs, or do you think this has something to do with you?" she said.

"I'm pretty sure you already know what I think," he said, offering the hint of a smile. "You just want it confirmed."

"Well, that's probably true."

"Here's what I think. We've been in this game a long time, Alison," Murphy said, tugging on his chin. "When these things happen, not to mention the spy photos of Trey and Bob Walters' daughter, well, that's no coincidence. I doubt if he ever took anything. He's too much of a Boy Scout. It doesn't matter. Someone wants to make him toxic. That way, he can't help me."

"So, can you do anything about it? You dragged him into this."

"I'm not sure what I can do, Alison. It's politics. It sucks. It is what it is."

"You could stand up for him," she said. "You. You and Charley could do that. You're the ones who pulled him into this world without much warning; if you guys gave him any at all."

"He's a big boy Alison. He's used to being in the public eye."

Alison couldn't resist a barb, though she regretted it as soon as she said it for allowing her feelings to occupy the main stage. She immediately knew where that would lead. And it did.

"That's bullshit," she said, her voice rising. "If you're a star athlete, no matter what you do, there always are people in your corner. In politics, the corner usually has a trapdoor in the floor. Trey was a pawn to benefit your campaign. You and Charley know it. And I know you're probably thinking of how you can turn this to your benefit instead of thinking about the toll on him and now this Walters girl."

Murphy flared back.

"Jesus Christ, Alison, I have to think about these things. But I feel like shit about Trey. I admit it again; like the thousand other times we've had this discussion. Yeah, I get pretty self-absorbed and self-serving. Sometimes it even serves us well. But, believe me, we didn't game-plan that something this crappy would happen to him. Give me a fucking break."

They sat, glaring more than staring.

"You owe him, Luke," she said. "Make it right. Then worry later about whether it turns to your advantage for once in your life."

"I can't get involved in an active investigation with Major League Baseball," he said with a flat tone that left no room for discussion.

Alison didn't care. She pressed on.

"You can and you should," she said, and then had a thought so calculating, and so insightful, that she felt ashamed. She knew Luke would grasp her point.

"Look, it might help you, but it certainly will damage you less than if you do nothing and have your press secretary spit out bullshit platitudes about 'letting the investigation run its course'."

Luke swallowed hard to keep from raising his voice.

He said, "How's that, Allison? Tell me. How the hell is that?"

"Let's both tone it down here," she responded, again in that flat voice, demonstrating to him that she was trying to move from emotional venting to clinical logic and he should, too.

"Think about it," she continued. "If you toss him aside you're being a fair-weather friend again. That's what they'll say. Luke Murphy is only out for himself, just like it was when Moose got paralyzed, just like it was when you didn't want to own up to a friend dying of AIDS. You know how to phrase this stuff. You have four brilliant speechwriters in the Executive Office Building. Stand up for the guy. Kick the shit out of the blog that invaded his privacy with Aimee Walters. Inspire your writers to write you a statement so good they'll talk about it as the turning point when they write about Luke Murphy's reelection. Short and sweet. You're fighting for your political life. Irony can be sweet. Maybe you save your presidency by doing the right thing."

He saw it now; saw the logic with radical clarity and it pushed his defensiveness aside. He didn't know what to say, so he looked at his wife in a way he hadn't looked at her for a long time. For a moment it was the way it used to be; the two of them brainstorming together about how they were going to do what it took to make a difference in the world, realizing there would be compromises along the way, maybe even unimaginable ones in which they'd have to weigh the cost to reach the outcome.

When he was a young Illinois state legislator, they'd stay up until 3 a.m. some nights, figuring out short-term and long-term plans. He'd sip his Maker's Mark bourbon; sometimes she'd polish off a full bottle of her favorite chardonnay. They'd usually end up laughing hard about something. Then it would just take a look or a comment that it was too damn late and they'd fall into bed. Often they were too tired and drunk to complete their amorous intent—at least that's what Luke would say—but it didn't matter. Those were great days. He just hadn't shared all his secrets.

Luke thought all of those things but couldn't say them to her. He ached to do it. He wished he could; wished so hard that he almost made it happen. Finally, he said the only words he could get out of his mouth to acknowledge appreciation.

"You're right, Alison. Thank you. You're right. That's what we'll do."

Alison felt better, too, but decided it was best to accept the moment and say nothing more. She touched his shoulder lightly with her left hand; then turned and left the kitchen.

33

Toledo, Ohio
Early August, After The Convention

Fifth Third Field in downtown Toledo, Ohio, seemed like an unlikely place for a campaign rally, but Reginald Fox insisted it was a good idea for Lydia Nicks to be there.

"First of all, it's a baseball park," he said. "Home of the Toledo Mud Hens. Good optics. You're not afraid to travel to what might be unfriendly turf: a troubled, Rust Belt Midwestern city that's trying to make a comeback. A place the Dems take for granted. We'll make sure people get the message that Toledo is friendly to Lydia Nicks. And being in a ballpark allows you to remind people that Luke Murphy spends too much time worrying about baseball, especially the Cubs and not enough time worrying about this great land of ours."

Nicks picked up on the theme.

"Yeah," she said, looking over the talking points her speechwriter had just given her. "It'll go something like this: 'I love baseball and I thank the good people of Toledo for bringing us to this beautiful facility. Just like your city and Lucas County, Ohio, we're coming back! We're coming back, folks! We need your support and the support of all of Ohio and our friends just over the border in Michigan, if we're going to accomplish our important mission. And I don't want to hurt anyone's feelings, but it's a mission more important than whether the Chicago Cubs beat, let's say, the Detroit Tigers in the World Series this year. I'm thinking this might just be a Tigers Year!' That might get a laugh, don't you think?"

"It should," Murphy said. "That's good."

Comerica Park, where the Tigers played in Detroit, was less than an hour from Toledo, making the city a rich reservoir of Tigers fans. The Mud Hens were Detroit's top minor league affiliate, too. A joke at Chicago's expense to boost the Tigers, who had a legitimate shot at winning the World Series for the first time since 1984, would hit Twitter right away and resonate with voters in northwest Ohio, southeast Michigan and even northeast Indiana. Those were all states that Nicks could win. Besides, once you got outside the city itself, there were plenty of Republican votes to harvest.

Her campaign team already had offered a zinger, which she'd dutifully memorized. The line had potential as a future commercial if it played well.

"And, speaking of baseball," she planned to say, "what do you make of a president who has homosexual affairs, abandons his friends and then tries to exploit the endorsement of an athlete who just got caught using drugs? What do you make of that, folks?"

They expected the crowd to boo loudly and then start chanting "Lydia," but they'd have their own people in the midst to encourage them—just in case.

***

About a month before the convention, Nicks, Fox and others in their inner circle began to quietly game-plan a third-party run if Murphy captured the Republican nomination. Meanwhile, a "dark money" political action committee, "Lydia First for America First," funded the research and documentation needed to quickly pivot and get on the ballot in 50 states.

Not even Fox, with all his connections, knew the sources of all the dollars, and he didn't want to know. What he did know was that it was extraordinarily difficult to mount a third-party candidacy and harder still to succeed. No one had accomplished anything like it since 1860, when the newly formed Republican Party of Abraham Lincoln won a four-party race—and the Republican Party already was a mainstream party. Leaders had splintered from the Whig Party in 1856 following the collapse of the two-party dominance of Democrats and Whigs.

Historians liked to point out that the Founding Fathers didn't want this system. They were leery of political parties. Few modern-day officials, let alone the voters, knew that originally the American system had the leading vote-getter winning the presidency and the second leading vote-getter becoming vice president. The founders hoped this would require the leaders to work together and move the country forward.

Noble idea but incredibly naïve, Fox thought.

Instead, by Lincoln's day, political parties and dirty politics were well-established. Whispered rumors of out-of-wedlock children and other sordid affairs hardly were modern inventions.

In 1856, many of the Northern Whigs became Republicans in a dispute over the anti-Catholic, anti-immigration policies of their Whig colleagues. Their candidate, John C. Fremont, nearly beat Democrat James Buchanan in that election.

"Fun fact: Luke Murphy, if he's gay, isn't the first gay president," Fox remarked to Nicks as they reviewed her options. "It probably was James Buchanan, who lived with a senator from Alabama, Rufus King, for 10 years and never married. People made jokes about their relationship. There are whispers about others, of course, but Buchanan seems the most likely. King even was vice president for two months under Franklin Pierce, the president before Buchanan."

The history of third-party candidacies made one point obvious: The odds were high that the insurgent would undermine the candidate who was closest philosophically. Dividing those votes opened a wide lane for the candidate most opposed to the reasons the insurgent was running.

"So, if we take this on, you're saying that we take a few votes from the Democrat. But, as much as we hurt Leeds, we hurt Murphy more and Leeds wins. But 'likely' isn't the same as 'impossible.' What needs to happen?" Nicks asked.

"It means everything has to break your way," Fox said. "Of course, if you assume that Leeds wins and will screw things up, you're in better shape four years from now maybe than if Murphy wins. You could give it another try. Age may not be a barrier for you. That's pretty hard to predict, though."

He added, "For sure, though, American history would be very, very different if you exclude third-party and even fourth-party candidates. Imagine U.S. history without Lincoln and Stephen Douglas winning in 1860. Abe only got about 40 percent of the popular vote with the other three candidates in the race. So, what happens in the Civil War? What happens with slaves?"

The most successful third-party campaign in U.S. history came in 1912 when former President Theodore Roosevelt ran as the candidate of the Bull Moose Party, getting 27 percent of the vote and 88 electoral votes. The incumbent president, William Howard Taft, lost ground as a result, helping Democrat Woodrow Wilson reach 435 electoral votes with only 42 percent of the popular vote. Wilson's presidency was highly consequential, including U.S. engagement in World War I and the collapse of his dream for world peace when Congress refused to join the League of Nations.

"Maybe a different president stops the events after World War I that makes Nazi Germany possible," Fox said. "Or, maybe we make matters worse. There's no way to know.

"Then, in 1968, you can make a strong case that an unrepentant racist, former Alabama Gov. George Wallace, peeled off enough votes from Hubert Humphrey to put Richard Nixon in the White House," Fox continued. "That was back when Democrats controlled the South. Thanks to Nixon, of course, that changed big-time."

"It's mind-boggling to even think what changes if Humphrey beats Nixon," Nicks said. "Watergate never happens. Maybe we get out of Vietnam faster. Or maybe we get in deeper. Like you say, who the hell knows?"

"That's right," Fox said. "Nixon would be way too left-wing to run as a Republican today. People forget he opened up relations with China, imposed wage and price controls on the economy and started the Environmental Protection Agency."

In 1980, moderate Republican John Anderson ran as an independent against Ronald Reagan but, in the end, had little impact on Ronald Reagan's landslide victory against an incumbent, Democrat Jimmy Carter, who was heavily damaged by a weak economy and the Iranian hostage crisis.

The last major third-party threat, Fox noted, was Ross Perot, the Texas businessman who probably took enough votes away from an incumbent president, George H.W. Bush, in 1992 to put Bill Clinton in the White House with less than 43 percent of the popular vote.

"Grass-roots groups got Perot on the ballot in every state," Fox said. "It wasn't easy and he made a lot of mistakes in the final months, including the pick of an obviously incompetent vice president. We've had bad veep candidates, but this guy, Admiral Stockdale, made Sarah Palin sound like Thomas Jefferson.

"Today, it's exponentially harder to even get on the ballot as a third-party candidate," he continued. "The two parties have made sure of that. First of all, you have to remember that the parties in power control the rules, and each state is allowed to make its own rules. They have no interest in making it easier for more challengers to emerge."

Nicks chuckled. "I wrote a few of those rules myself when I was in the Wisconsin Legislature," she said. "We purposely created a June 1st deadline for filing. It's not so funny now."

"You'll be called a hypocrite for voting for that," Fox said. "In fact, I think you were one of the leaders."

"I don't care. I'll just admit that I never anticipated we would have two other candidates this bad at a time of such national urgency. Besides, we have another out," she said. "Wisconsin is one of the states that has the Constitution Party on the ballot. Maybe I could be their candidate." She paused for a moment, checking Fox's expression, before adding, "Don't tell me I thought of something you haven't considered already."

"We're supposed to be the shining light of democracy," Fox said. "Other democracies and dozens of do-gooder groups have criticized us for making our ballot-access laws so restrictive. The courts are all over the map, too. The Supreme Court has never really ruled on how many restrictions are too many."

"Who cares what they think in Europe? And who the hell cares about Common Cause?" she said. "How's what they're doing working for them lately?"

"Well, things aren't so hot anywhere," Fox said. "That's why you're running."

"Touché."

Fox tossed a document on a table that summarized the laws in all 50 states, Puerto Rico and the District of Columbia. Standards involved filing fees, valid signatures on petitions related to percentage of total votes, difficult deadlines and numerous other requirements, all different in small and, in some cases, large ways.

In North Carolina, for example, unaffiliated candidates had to meet numerous requirements no later than the last Saturday in June before the upcoming election.

North Carolina could be a key state for Nicks, a place filled with angry conservatives and evangelical Christians; a populated state where she might win if enough people in the rural areas showed up at the polls unhappy with Murphy and if just a few moderates and liberals in Raleigh-Durham, Asheville, Chapel Hill and Greensboro stayed occupied with Starbucks, soccer games and school plays. She might even convince a few of them to come her way if Murphy seemed damaged enough, because a lot of the suburbanites weren't going to warm up to Leeds. He could end up with the black vote but little else. She might get just enough to win a three-way race in North Carolina. It was basic political math. They looked at their calendar and saw they had less than a month to get on the ballot. The Constitution Party wasn't an option there, either.

There really was no choice but to ignite the political reporters, bloggers, talk-show hosts and social media into a crazy frenzy. Nicks would announce she was mounting a third-party bid in "certain key states" as a "precautionary measure" in case Murphy got the Republican nomination.

"That's not such a bad thing," Fox reminded her. "You'll be the story for several news cycles. Murphy and Leeds will be fighting for attention."

Her prepared statement acknowledged the risk:

> I know this may cost us with some blind party loyalists. But we have no choice. For those states that won't let us on the ballot, we'll run write-in campaigns. I want to run as a Republican, but this election is too important to let Luke Murphy back into the White House, or to let Matthew Leeds move in. Way too important. World events tell us this. The cross made by the tail of the comet tells us so.

Meanwhile, Fox sent his business partner, Trent Schuller, to quietly approach the Constitution Party to see if the party leaders would be interested in Lydia Nicks as their candidate in the 25 or so states where they were on the ballot.

Schuller studied up. He came back optimistic. The party's mission statement was a good fit for Nicks. It read as follows:

> The mission of the Constitution Party is to secure the blessings of liberty to ourselves and our posterity through the election, at all levels of government, of Constitution Party candidates who will uphold the principles of the Declaration of Independence, the Constitution of the United States, and the Bill of Rights. It is our goal to limit the federal government to its delegated, enumerated, Constitutional functions.

A week later, Schuller called Fox.

"Reg, they've studied Lydia's record pretty closely," Schuller reporter. "Damn right they're interested if it comes to that. They're intrigued by the financial support that would come with this, too."

The last part was easy. Fox then called Nicks. "Lydia, 'Plan B' is a go. Brush up on the Constitution Party."

Then, a few days after the convention, an anonymous email came to the "Lydia First, America First" PAC with a "cc" to the inbox of the Reginald Fox Consulting Services LLC.

It was a draft copy of a news release that Major League Baseball was preparing on Trey Van Ohmann's suspension. The subject line of the email said, "You'll want to be ready to react to this."

***

Fifth Third Field got its name from Fifth Third Bancorp in Cincinnati, which bought the naming rights to ballpark in a 15-year agreement shortly before the new facility, often touted as one of the best in minor league baseball, opened in 2002. Nine years later, the bank had repaid $3.4 billion in taxpayer funds received in the bailout of troubled financial institutions following the collapse of the U.S. housing market and near-collapse of the entire world economy in 2008. The government made a $593 million profit on its investment to save Fifth Third.

As Lydia Nicks hobnobbed with banking executives and others from the region's Republican business elite during a brief reception before her speech, she decided not to mention that she was one of a handful of senators who had voted against taxpayer bailouts of big banks or helping the U.S. auto industry, which was important in Toledo, an area with two Jeep assembly plants. She was ready for the questions, though a careful listener would realize her words didn't really commit her to anything.

"Look, we have auto plants in Wisconsin, too," she said. "I was ready to help any way we could short of putting taxpayer money into it and I can document it. I must be honest: I'm still not sure about 'too big to fail' when it comes to huge financial institutions, knowing what we know now. Regional banks like Fifth Third just got caught in the crossfire, right? They were heavily penalized and publicly castrated for the sins of the big boys in New York. That wasn't fair."

She saw nods around the room, so she continued, tackling the more delicate subject.

"As for the auto bailout, I don't mind telling you my vote was not one I made lightly. It was unquestionably one of the most difficult votes I've ever cast. I'm always willing to learn and move forward. There's nothing wrong with that. But we can all agree that, wherever we stood at that challenging moment, we share in relief that Jeeps are still rolling off the assembly lines in Toledo."

From there she segued as quickly as she could.

"These are extraordinary times, too," she said. "If you don't think that comet was a sign, if you don't think that meteor means something, don't vote for me. To me, it means we simply must get our morals and values in order. These are signs that we can't stand still as a nation founded as a Christian nation while fellow Christians are getting tortured and killed around the world. And, finally, we need to let business do what it does best, without government bureaucrats picking winners and losers. We are blessed to be here. We are blessed to participate in an extraordinary, once-in-a-lifetime opportunity for our country."

The applause was solid but not spectacular, confirming Reggie's advice that she shouldn't say a word about auto bailouts in front of the everyday people waiting for her speech. However, calculated candor was important with the high rollers to increase the chance of big checks and discourage donations to the opposition. "They love it when they think you're letting your hair down," Fox had advised, though he was telling her what she already knew. "It's sort of like you're the opposite of Jack Nicholson in 'A Few Good Men' telling them that, yeah, you're the ones who can actually handle the truth. They'll wink at the masses with you."

She was ready to enter the main stage, which was erected behind second base to address a crowd of about 11,000 people on a perfect summer night.

"BNE," a Christian rock band, finished a 40-minute set as she readied herself. "BNE" stood for "Best News Ever," and the lead singer, a tattooed, handsome man with the unlikely name of Rory McCrory was getting ready to introduce Nicks as they played a perennial Christian-rock anthem, "Amazing Love," which the band covered in an over-the-top style.

"Why do most Christian rock sounds like U2?" Fox asked to no one in particular.

"Hey, that's not such a bad thing," someone said in response.

McCrory did the introductions, waving Nicks onto the stage. She felt the mix of excitement and tension that anyone would feel before giving a speech that not only would go out to 11,000 people, but also one in which every second would be recorded, edited and even altered to make her look good, bad or foolish, depending on the creator's point of view, or who was paying for the final product.

"For everything there is a season," McCrory said as he concluded his introduction, roughly quoting the famous verse from the Biblical book of Ecclesiastes, though perhaps better known by the masses as part of the song "Turn, Turn, Turn" by the 1960s rock band The Byrds.

"This. This, my friends. This, my friends, is the season. This, my friends, is the season of Lid-dee-ah Nicks!"

Nicks waved to the crowd, which roared in delight as she appeared, drowning out the shouts of scattered protesters in the back. She noticed some pushing and shoving between her supporters and the protesters before security intervened and escorted them out to hoots and hollers. It seemed like at least a thousand phones were recording every second.

A comet image with an artistically drawn cross was moving across a huge video board set up behind her. It had become the icon of her campaign. The words "Lydia Nicks. For America." were in block letters spewing from the comet's tail.

"I came here tonight to ask you to help me send a message," she began. "It's a message to Little Matty Leeds and the Democrats in particular. Ohio might be his home state, but a favorite son is nothing compared to a woman who can get things done!"

That got the crowd going even more than the fun of booing the protesters. Then, in one of those moments that even Fox couldn't script, a shooting star crossed the clear night sky just above her.

The crowd stood as one. The momentary silence was more powerful than any applause. Spontaneously, everyone started chanting "Lydia," alternating her name with "America," without any need for coaching from the planted supporters in the crowd.

Lydia. America. Lydia. America. Lydia. America. Lydia. America. It got louder and louder, filling the room, creating the atmosphere of a tent revival. Nicks held out her arms, palms facing down, in the universal gesture to "quiet down."

Finally, the crowd quieted enough in their chants for her to speak.

"Just this morning, Muslim terrorists in Indonesia killed more innocent Christians," Fox shouted, going off script to take advantage of the moment. "Is God saying yes, indeed, it's time for a change? Is that what He's saying?"

The crowd's answer was clearly a "yes." This moment would be all over the news.

"Reg, this is getting real," she said after she came off the stage to thundering applause 30 minutes later, shaking as she wiped sweat dripping from her forehead on this hot summer night. "I'm going to be the next president."

34

Madison, Wisconsin
Mid-August Before The Election

"Meg, I think I'd like to go home," Taylor Pierce said. She could barely speak the words in a rare moment of near clarity from her drug-induced fog. She wasn't sure there was even anyone else in the room, but she thought she saw Meg Williamson sitting in the corner. Maybe. A tear rolled down her cheek. Taylor knew she was unhappy, but it was just so hard to really focus.

With a clinical and curious stare, she looked at her scarred and bruised arms and seemed surprised to see an I.V. drip coming out of her left hand, leading to a bag with some liquid. Maybe it was nourishing her. She scratched at a bed sore on her behind. She was getting up less and less often.

With considerable effort, she sat up from the bed and stared across into a mirror on top of a chest of drawers painted in bright yellow with flower stickers. A ceiling fan with the blades shaped like butterfly wings twirled about her. Was she a little girl again? A scared little girl?

The gaunt face that stared back jolted her. It scared her. "What happened to Taylor?" she asked. "What happened to me?"

She tried a smile and noticed her teeth looked discolored from lack of care. She was missing one in the bottom row but couldn't remember when or how it happened. "I gotta floss," she said. "Meg, do we have any?" She recalled how dedicated she had been to white teeth and healthy gums, flashing to Dr. Nichols, one of her dad's best friends. Doc Nichols was a dentist who always teased her that he knew she'd be famous because "you've got a million-dollar smile. Like your Mom."

"Daddy," she said, suddenly remember her dead father. "Meg, can I go home?"

She stared again at the face in the mirror. Her hair seemed to be exploding out of her scalp at all angles. It had a dirty blonde, greasy sheen and was much thinner looking than she remembered. Her ears were sticking out in ways she didn't recall either and the freckled dimples on her cheeks—a feature so many boys thought really made her "cute"—had turned into sunken craters.

She shivered, an early sign of withdrawal.

Meg Williamson watched all this and knew it was getting near the time to decide. Keeping Taylor alive, at least until after the election, made sense; better to have her remain a mystery than all the investigation that would ensue if a body turned up. She would take no chances about a body or evidence. Too many carefully thought-out plots went awry once multiple people and bodies were involved. She was smart enough to know she wasn't smart enough to think of everything. She took pride in her modesty—at least in that regard—and believed this kept her grounded, focused and mindful.

The alternative was sad but necessary: keeping Taylor addicted. The I.V. provided some nourishment and the line offered a way to inject drugs as needed without creating new bruises.

"I don't feel good," Taylor whined, staring to shiver some more. "I'm cold, Meg."

"There, there," Meg said in a fake but convincing motherly voice. "Let's warm you up and make you feel better. You lay back down."

She grabbed a tan and rust-red blanket with a Navajo pattern and wrapped it around Taylor, who kept shivering. She quickly injected a fresh, measured amount of heroin into the I.V. tube, and it wasn't long before she heard Taylor say "ahh" as the tremors dissipated and she drifted into a fog that passed for sleep. Meg didn't know where Pfeiffer got this stuff and didn't want to know.

Her chore completed, Meg walked back into a screened sun room at the rear of her tidy house on Madison's east side. She admired her garden of herbs and vegetables and thought about the fresh vegetables she'd have for a salad and stew that night. It was important to eat right and she couldn't even trust some of the food at Whole Foods any more. This was the best time of year in Madison, because she could go to the square around the Capitol building every Saturday morning and buy fresh, organic goods grown by trusted local farmers.

She saw no disconnect in caring for her own body while inflicting abuse on Taylor. The cause required sacrifice. Too many people who shared her clarity about what was happening to the Earth weren't willing to go far enough to save the planet. What could matter more? Her real fear was that it was too late already; the damage irreversible. The evidence was anywhere intelligent people cared to look. And, so what if climate change wasn't real despite the overwhelming evidence she accepted as a scientist? Could people afford to take a chance on a one-in-a-billion chance that everything would be okay?

She certainly didn't believe in the Christian God and no God at all except for the unseen threads of Gaia, Mother Earth, that she believed science would one day prove as the link between all living things on Earth and beyond. Gaia would offer a new definition of life far beyond wildest imaginations.

That vision only would come to pass if environmental catastrophe or something else didn't sink humanity first. Who could argue that the world wasn't getting messier, uglier and more dangerous? The American government was so dysfunctional that the political leaders were incapable of even passing bad policy. Europeans wallowed in their benefits. Africa sank in corruption. Religious extremism showed no signs of abating. Now the crazed terrorists had the best-available tools of technology and destruction. Governments played whack-a-mole with the terrorist groups, but they always popped up again.

She didn't count herself as crazed, though it was a notion she had considered, acknowledging her actions were not those of most others. But you'd have to be crazed not to see the world for what it was. She accepted there probably would never be a public salute and maybe no knowledge at all of her efforts to save the planet.

When she first left for college, excited and committed to escape the ugliness in her parents' home, Meg Williamson decided emotions were distractions; distractions for losers; distractions from the calculations and perceptions that her genius-level intelligence provided.

Later, as she decided to take this path, she wondered if she was a sociopath, recognizing the superficial similarity between her and the textbook definition: a very intelligent person who believed the normal rules didn't apply to them and felt little or no remorse for their actions. Sociopaths lived in emotional dead zones. She spent considerable time studying the psychology of sociopaths and finally decided it really didn't matter. That helped her get past the rare moments when she experienced fleeting guilt about what they had done to people like Taylor and the children on the Ferris wheel they had brought down in Chicago to get Murphy's attention and compliance. She could make no time for emotions. Feelings only served as barriers to what she had to do.

Still, Taylor's presence tested her. Collateral damage no longer meant people far away. Now, she had to look in the eyes of a sad young woman in her guest bedroom. It generated feelings; feelings she had to work harder than usual to ignore.

Meg congratulated herself upon reflection. She felt sorry for Taylor. It was proof that she wasn't a soulless vessel. She was glad she actually felt it would be a shame if Taylor had to die.

Yes, Meg decided, she would be sad.

For a moment, Meg Williamson was a little girl again, betrayed by her own father even more than Taylor Pierce's father had betrayed his family. She laughed out loud at the notion as she compared her childhood to Taylor's. Random affairs, gay or straight, by your dad were nothing compared to watching your mother get beaten or getting on your knees to put your father's disgusting cock in your mouth over and over and pretend everything was okay.

Then the moment was over. Meg needed to focus on her goals.

Like making Matthew Leeds the next president of the United States without him even knowing it.

She had watched Luke Murphy rise in his political career. She saw that he acted out of the same characteristics she had seen in their childhood together in Palatine.

His intentions often were good enough. She could see that. He wasn't a crook or an evil genius. *But I can see he's calculating and self-absorbed, almost as good a manipulator,* she thought, *as I am.* Luke usually came out ahead, even when he didn't realize he was manipulating.

When Moose Skowron got paralyzed in that childhood accident, it was Bob Walters who paid the price, not Luke. Moose started it with his bullying, but it was Luke who threw the ice chunk that caused Moose to fall and nearly die when his head and neck hit the sidewalk. It was Bob who got sent away.

Still, Luke had been her friend. It had been more difficult than she thought it would be to launch the plot that almost got Luke killed during the last World Series. But the situation dictated her actions, just as the comet and the Bali meteor played into her hands. Luck was little more than the ability to be in the right place to take advantage of those things you can't predict. They had been ready.

She wondered where Pfeiffer was. He should have been there by now. She needed to think aloud with him. They had done a lot to prop up Lydia Nicks, but now Nicks was doing almost too well.

Then she heard a key turn the deadbolt in the front door, an opening creak and footsteps. It was Pfeiffer. He seemed out of breath as he pushed his long gray hair back across his skull. He tied it back in a ponytail. He wore cargo shorts and a black

Hawaiian shirt with a pattern of scattered bright, gold pineapples wrapped by red and green leis. As usual, he had a gold, cross-shaped earring in one ear, completing the look he cultivated of an aging, hippie college philosophy professor; someone not to be taken seriously anywhere but in a classroom or by a panel of obscure editors producing obscure journals with articles on the nature of reality and the results of thought experiments.

Pfeiffer had been thinking more about his mainly platonic partnership with Meg Williamson. His biggest regret was that it forced him to suppress a substantial ego. It would've been great to receive the recognition he confidently knew he could have earned if he'd publicly focused on mainstream political and economic philosophy instead of his attention to more arcane subject areas, such as French anarchists of the early 20th Century or the application of existentialism to ethnic art. It was better not to raise suspicion. Still, he would've enjoyed that spotlight.

He liked being blunt with the students in his "Introduction to Philosophy" class at the university. The class, like most intro courses, mainly was populated by students trying to desperately fulfill elective requirements. The numbers of seniors in an "intro class" symbolized that this was a last resort toward graduating on time when other, easier classes were filled.

He made an effort to help them realize they were driven by poorly formed, misunderstood beliefs and biased emotions. To get their attention, he usually opened the first lecture in the first class with eight words, "Most people dismiss philosophy as bullshit. They're wrong."

Reminded of the saying, "you're not a missionary; everyone can't be saved," he had learned after one or two frustrating semesters as a young professor to count it as a victory if he sparked a handful of the students to at least consider the value of exploring what drives humanity to do what it does. Today, most wouldn't even look up from their phones. You could pass his class if you displayed even a tiny amount of effort in that direction and string a few comprehensible sentences together.

The headaches of failing students and being more demanding than that weren't worth his time.

Every now and then, though, he lit that spark. And a few of the best students turned out to be very helpful as they advanced in their careers, never knowing the full extent of how they helped the cause.

Meg interrupted Pfeiffer's reflections. "We've got to start to bring Lydia Nicks back to Earth," she said. "We've done such a good job damaging Luke Murphy, she's gaining too much ground. And Leeds keeps screwing up. Having her win would be worse than Murphy staying in the White House."

"Hey, at least give me a chance to sit for a sec," he said, obviously out of breath. "I've been doing a lot of running around for you today. Not to mention what I had to go through to get this."

He tossed a plastic bag on the table that had about two dozen foil packets inside.

"Is this going to be a continuing problem?" she said.

"No," he said, knowing she didn't want the details. "I don't think so. Just say my source needed a new source."

They both knew she probably had it figured out. Pfeiffer's brother was a narcotics detective in Kenosha, Wisconsin, an old, industrial city on Lake Michigan where the epidemic was raging. Maury Pfeiffer wasn't averse to diverting some of the drugs he seized before they got inventoried for the evidence locker. He no longer spent much time trying to rationalize. He needed the money, the city had no money to pay cops what they were worth, and the junkies always were going to find it somewhere, whether he helped or not. Richard told Maury he was helping a young colleague. Because the mythical colleague was a poorly paid adjunct professor, he had no health insurance. He couldn't afford to have his addiction discovered but was saving for rehab.

It was plausible, but Maury had heard it all and didn't really care about the reasons. He acted like he believed the line out of sensitivity to his brother and he could see Richie was getting worried that the increasing quantities raised suspicions. That didn't matter either. Maury knew that addicts often needed more and more until they either crashed or died. Nothing unusual going on here. He knew how that story almost always ended.

"You're getting a bro' rate on this stuff," he reminded Pfeiffer during their last transaction. "Richie, I just hope this isn't for you."

"No worries, Maury," Richard Pfeiffer replied. "No worries. I wouldn't even know how to do it."

That was a lie; he had certainly learned how to do it to Taylor Pierce. But he was worried. Their plotting was getting more complicated and Taylor was an ongoing issue. He turned his attention back to Meg Williamson.

"I think I have a way to undermine Nicks," Meg said.

Pfeiffer asked, "And, what's that?"

She replied, "We can tie her to the PEDs given to Van Ohmann. People won't be surprised. And we tie her to Jerry Landis."

"Landis?" Pfeiffer said. "The Cubs' owner?"

"Yeah," she said. "He claims he's staying out of this one, but everyone knows he supports Nicks. I'll bet he's giving dark money to the groups backing her. People will figure that's how someone had access to the locker room. Everyone will put two and two together. We can buy time for Leeds to rehabilitate himself. Trey helped us cut Luke down to size and now his problem can help us with Nicks," she concluded, putting air quotes with her fingers around the word "problem."

Pfeiffer said, "And I assume you have an idea on how to do all that, how to point the finger."

"I do indeed," she said. "It'll take some time and some dollars to some good hackers."

***

Two weeks later, an anonymous text from an untraceable number dinged Moose Skowron's phone. It contained one sentence and an attached document.

Skowron rested his right hand on the wheel of his chair as he held the phone in his left hand to read the line of text. It said, "Tell TVO to check the Gatorade." TVO obviously referred to Trey Van Ohmann. He brought his lips together and curled them downward in thoughtful curiosity. Then he noticed the attachment.

"Okay my friend," he said out loud in his cubicle to no one in particular. His voice rose about half an octave with anticipation. "I'm interested. Just what is it that you want me to see?"

He clicked on it to enlarge the PDF file. It was a printout of PayPal transactions, showing multiple transfers of $5,000 from Jerry Landis and other members of his family to the Keep America Free Committee.

"Jerry freakin' Landis," he said. "And Trey Van Ohmann. All in one weird text. Guess I have some Google work to do."

35

Chicago
Early September Before The Election

Aimee Walters finally couldn't take it any longer.

"Trey, you just have to stop bouncing that damn ball," she said.

He was sprawled on the couch, slouching so that his head could touch the top of the back cushion, bouncing a tennis ball off the wall in front of him. The game was to change the way he fingered and released the ball. He could make it bounce off the walls in odd angles and still come back without him having to move anything but his arms. The game had been going on for a solid 20 minutes. A constant popping sound of the ball hitting the wood floor of Trey's condo and then the duller sound of it bouncing off the wall burned into Aimee's awareness. The wall was suffering, too, showing scars and marks from its role as a substitute racquetball court.

"Hey, lighten up," he said, continuing the game.

That was enough.

"Stop. Just stop. We need to talk," she said in a tone that wasn't loud but measured and obviously impatient. "We need to figure out a way to go on the offensive instead of you staying holed up in this apartment. And we're getting on each other's nerves."

Trey finally stopped and gave her a hard look, processing her comments and trying to resist the impulse to get defensive.

"Are we having our first big fight?" he said, settling for passive-aggressive as his mood du jour.

"No," she said. "No it isn't. This isn't a fight unless you want it to be. I'm just trying to get you out of this damn funk. I know you can't go more than a few steps outside without dealing with the media. But I have to believe there are actual things you can be doing to deal with your situation."

"Like what? All I can do is wait for the investigation to conclude and see what they do to me," he said. "It sucks."

"That's crap," she said. "We both know you're innocent. Don't you want to get to the bottom of what happened? Doesn't it make you wonder what's going on here? Your father is dead. You end up connected with Luke Murphy and his baggage. Your team needs you. And you can't help them."

"I'm exhausted," Van Ohmann said, not wanting to confess out loud that what he really felt was emasculated; like less of a man. What guy would ever admit that? He said, "It's all caught up with me Aimee. Finally, I guess. I need some chill time."

"You're just pathetic right now," she said, too annoyed to sense the pain lurking under his surface. To emphasize her point, she stretched out the word and changed the emphasis so it came out pa-thet-ICK. "I'm going back to work to help plan tomorrow's show," she concluded. "So much for a nice, extended lunch break. I'll call you later to see if you're ready to actually start helping yourself."

"You do that," he said, then bounced the ball off the wall again. "Wow, check out the curve on that," he said out loud, as the ball twisted into his pitching hand.

Aimee didn't even look back as she shut the door—harder than usual—and entered the elevator to the garage to head to the WCO studio on Chicago's west side.

***

As she pulled out of the garage, she shook her head in disgust as a creep with a cellphone camera yelled, "Hey, smile and look hot for me, Aimee," and took her photo, no doubt for some gossip blog, maybe even that damn SportsCheese site.

She looked straight ahead, determined not to make eye contact with an asshole, and started driving when her cell phone chirped. Her Nissan Altima was too old to have Bluetooth and she knew it was against the law in Illinois to use a hand-held phone while driving. She looked down at the phone, which was face up on the console, and saw the caller was Moose Skowron.

There was an officer sitting in a patrol car across the street. Normally, she'd welcome that, but the last thing she needed was a ticket for using the phone while driving with accompanying photos splashed all over the Internet.

"Shit," she said, pulling over to the curb quickly, which gave Mr. Creep a chance to take more photos of her. In one motion, she tapped the phone to the "speaker" setting, said "hello," and whipped into the street. If the cop hadn't been there, she would have made sure she drove close enough to the photo-bomber to make him step back on the sidewalk as she pulled out, but she resisted the temptation. Plus, he probably would have purposely stayed in the street so she'd hit him. That would cause a really delightful scene.

"Kiss my ass," she said out loud as she started down the street, pointing the Nissan toward the Eisenhower Expressway.

"Well, that's no way to greet a friend," Skowron said, his tinny voice coming from the phone speaker.

"Oh, hell," Aimee said, really laughing for first time all day. "I didn't mean you Moose. There was this asshole stalking outside Trey's apartment. He was taking pictures as I drove away. I'm sure I look lovely all over Twitter already."

"Hold on," he said "Let me check."

Aimee heard the clicks of a computer keyboard in the background, but only for a few seconds.

"Oh, yeah, you're there," he said. "You don't look that bad actually. Want me to read the tweet to you?"

"Sure," Aimee said, resigned to her fate, realizing she'd probably have to make light of the latest intrusion on the air the next morning.

"Okay," he said. "It says, and I quote, 'HASHTAG HotAimee makes quick getaway from Trey VO's Chi condo. HASHTAG ShowUsMore.'"

She said, "Well, HASHTAG EatShit. I won't be showing anything to this creep unless there really is a hell and that turns out to be my sentence in the afterlife. Hey, I think I'll save the line for the show, except for the 'eat shit' part. It's pretty good. And it could've been worse. What's up?"

"Girl, I always like your style," Skowron said. "Are you on your way to the studio?"

"Yeah."

"We need to talk if we can today," he said. "It's about Trey. Something that came in. It's really interesting. Trust me."

"Well, I guess I'll drive a little faster. See you in a few."

***

She pushed her chair to Moose's cubicle, which was dominated by an array of monitors and a computer work station that had more processing power than probably all the other computers at the station combined.

"What's up?" she asked.

He was so deep in concentration, staring at what looked like a long list of search results on one monitor, that it took him a few seconds to react.

"I got quite a weird, anonymous text," he said, wheeling around in his chair to face her. "It's like someone really wants us to pick at a big fat scab and expose what's under it.

"Look," he continued. "Your dad should be off the air pretty soon and I need to get back in there for the wrap-up bit. Go get some coffee and meet us in the conference room in, say, half an hour. It'll give me time to finish this. Is Mike going to be around?"

"Yeah, he should be coming back any time. This is our weekly planning meeting."

"Well, bring Surrey, too. The more the merrier," he said.

When Skowron said "finish this," he apparently meant all the text scrolling down two of the four monitors. He was using some search engine she had never seen and she caught the word "PED" in some of the text rolling past her eyes. There was an article apparently referring to the Cubs' owner, because she saw the word "Landis."

Aimee didn't quite know what to make of it.

"Give me a hint," she said.

"No," he said. "No hints. Meet us in the conference room. This could be real dynamite, but I want to be sure I have a good, working theory."

When all four were in the conference room, Skowron described the text.

"First of all, the news is that we might be sitting on an incredible story here. But, I need some help analyzing what we know," Skowron said. "So, let's recap. What has been going on now, for two baseball seasons with the Cubs?"

"That's easy," Bob Walters said. "Even more weirdness than usual. And that's saying something when it comes to the Cubs."

"Bob, be more specific," Skowron said. "What are the common threads. Or, who is the common thread? Is it really about the Cubs? I mean, it certainly seems that way, right? Last season, some crazy fan wants to do anything to make sure they win. This season, they're on the way to going back to the World Series and now Trey Van Ohmann is sidelined."

"So, someone is maybe telling us that Trey's Gatorade was spiked?" Aimee asked.

"Maybe," Skowron said. "Could be true, especially if you believe he's innocent, which I think we do. But what else do we know about Trey this season?"

"He's trying to help Luke Murphy," Surrey said, phrasing the words more like a question than an answer.

"Bingo," Skowron said. "Maybe this really has been about Luke Murphy. The Cubs are the means; Murphy's the end. They tried to blackmail and kill him last season. Even the death of Trey's dad was part of a larger plot to manipulate Murphy. Now, Murphy's running for re-election, gaining some traction even and suddenly Trey, one of his best-known supporters, is caught in a scandal. Oh, and that's on top of an earlier scandal about a gay affair and, oh, now we're reminded again how he tends to treat his friends like disposable diapers—useful for stopping crap until they're not—starting with you, Bob, when we were kids."

Skowron continued, "Oh, and now El Presidente has an unhappy wife. And let's not forget the whole damn world is going to hell between cosmic events, terrorists, budget deficits and millions of starving Chinese.

"If I didn't know better, I'd say Luke Murphy has some big-boy problems. How much scandal can one guy take?"

"Moose, find a few more of those stock clichés, and you might have a future in talk radio," Bob Walters said, unable to resist. "But you might be right. Someone is trying to destroy Luke. It makes sense. But how does Landis fit in? I can't make that work in my mind."

"That's what I've been checking more than anything since I got that text," Skowron said. "The contributions from him and his family to the Nicks campaign are only partially documented, but those PayPal downloads show they're ponying up for much, much more than what's been reported."

"Wait," Surrey said. "I know Jerry Landis pretty damn well. I might not agree with his politics, but he's a decent guy." Surrey could see he was getting strange stares from the group; then he understood why. He laughed.

"Well, except for the part about firing me," he said. "Hey, every manager knows there's only one way the story ever ends and he was pretty gracious about it. Really, I don't see him involved."

Skowron said, "Be that as it may, he runs the Cubs. If anyone was going to spike Trey's Gatorade, he had the means to get someone to do it."

"It helps Lydia Nicks," Bob Walters said, nodding his head in agreement with Skowron. "Trey is just collateral damage in a quest to destroy Luke."

"What about that, Aimee?" Skowron asked. "You've been in the locker room. Does Trey always drink the same thing? Does he always have Gatorade in his locker."

"He does," she said, slowly processing the information. "Always the green G2. He's like most pitchers. They're very superstitious and creatures of habit. They all have quirks. Trey is like an old witch doctor trying to control the mojo on the days he pitches. Like, he's one of those guys who won't step on the baseline when he walks between the field and his dugout. He always makes sure he walks over it. He told me once that he even expects the Gatorade to be placed in the same place in his locker with the caps of two of the bottles unscrewed and replaced. He was kind of embarrassed about that actually."

That remark broke tension for a moment and brought some light laughter.

Aimee said, "Or maybe, he just has a little bit of diva in him."

"Making millions of dollars a year to throw a baseball before you're 30 years old will do that to you. Trey handles it better than most. At least he's embarrassed by it. A lot of them never get it," Surrey said. "So, what do we do with all this? This is just speculation. Do we confront Landis?"

"No," Aimee said. "Not yet. If we can prove this, it all unravels and Trey gets reinstated. Maybe it exposes Nicks. Let me talk to Trey. He deserves to hear this."

"It's a great story," Bob Walters said. "It won't sit long. If we know it and nothing comes out, whoever sent this to Moose will send it to someone else. But maybe Trey can help us prove it. Move fast, my dear."

For a moment they sat in silence, thinking through the implications.

"What the hell are we going to do with this?" Surrey finally asked.

"Work our asses off, that's what," Walters said. "Aimee, let us know how Trey reacts when he hears we might have the key to his restoration. And, I know this is personal for you, too, but you've got to think beyond that. You know I'm always an old newspaper reporter at heart. Great stories get me jazzed. See if he'll go on the record."

"Yeah," she said. "First, I'll see if I can actually get his attention."

36

Chicago | Later That Day

"Are you in a better mood?" Aimee asked, speaking into the lobby's speaker box so Trey would buzz her into his condo.

"I guess I was kind of a dick earlier today," she heard him say in the shrill, scratchy squawk of the speaker. "Come on up. And sorry about that mess you had to endure when you left earlier. I thought you looked great in that tweet, though."

"Gee, your sense of humor is back," she said "I'm glad. It's old news now, so beam me up."

He was waiting at the door when she arrived, wearing jeans, a Cubs T-shirt and flip-flops. He looked at her, and with that one glance she was certain that, like her, he had been thinking about how they had been acting with each other.

Aimee decided to surprise him with a hug and he reciprocated. It was a long, tight hug, and what she really liked was that it wasn't sexual. It was simply a way of communicating they liked and respected each other, and a way of confirming the possibility of, well, real possibilities in this relationship; that maybe this could blossom into more.

"We've been bickering like a bunch of drama-driven teenagers," she said, making eye contact with him. "I'm sorry for my part in it."

He looked back and said, "I love what you didn't say there. You basically said I had a big part in it."

She started to say something and then stopped, realizing in his tone of voice that he was conceding the point and that she had blame-shifted even when she was apologizing. He was grinning by then—not a sarcastic grin, but an understanding one.

"I should've just said 'I'm sorry,'" she said.

He said, "No, you had the right. And, really, I provoked it. If we were having a contest for who was being more passive-aggressive, I won. You just fell into my dark hole. After you left and I realized how much bullshit you've been taking because of me and I stopped bouncing the damn ball against the wall.

"No promises, though," he said. "If things don't straighten out, I might have to go back to that."

"I grant you some self-pity," she said. "But now it's time to move on. So, tell me about the Gatorade in your locker."

"Say what?"

"Sit down," she said. "You need to know what we've been talking about at WCO today."

She described the conversation from beginning to end. He looked skeptical.

"Politics is a dirty business," he said. "I know that, but to do this? Jerry Landis? He's been nothing but gracious with me. He even gave me a contract that made it easy for my agent and me to agree. He could've squeezed harder, but he didn't. I know his family is all-in for Nicks, but I can't get my arms around it. I mean, he also wants the Cubs to win the Series, right? Why the hell would he want to screw that up?"

"I don't really know the guy, but people have different ways of setting priorities," she said "You only know him as Jerry Landis the team owner; you don't know him as Jerry Landis the hard-core Lydia Nicks supporter. You don't know about his family pressures. You don't know about 50 other things that probably are going on in his life. You only see one side of him. So, maybe helping Lydia Nicks is even more important. In his own twisted way, maybe he thinks it's more important to help Nicks than his own team.

"So, this Gatorade thing," she continued. "Could it be true?"

"Well, yeah," he said. "I mean, it's almost a joke in the locker room. Raoul—he's the clubhouse attendant—puts the

G2 in my locker before every game with a couple extra on days I pitch. It's all part of the ritual. So, could someone spike it? I guess so. I mean, over in the NFL, we learned someone can deflate footballs in a bathroom in less than a minute, right?

"I'll tell you this much. If it's true, I'm fucking furious. Beyond furious. The team is losing. They need me. And, every day I'm out, I'm breaking my promise that getting involved in the campaign wouldn't affect the Cubs."

She said, "So, the question is, 'What are you going to do about it?'"

He said, "I think I know who to call. I need to bounce this off someone who knows the political game a lot better than I do."

She said, "I don't mean to push you, Trey, but time is short. You need to get reinstated; and I won't lie. I'd like WCO to break the story."

"Agreed," he said. "Totally."

***

Charley Rayburn's day wasn't going well. He had lost confidence that any of the three candidates could win the minimum of 270 Electoral College votes to get elected, throwing the election into the House of Representatives for the first time since 1824. In the Republican-dominated House, the odds were growing that Murphy and Nicks would carve each other up, with Nicks likely to have the advantage in that conservative body. It would be an impasse of unpredictable, historic proportions. They'd never settle for Leeds, but the next president could even be "none of the above."

Of more immediate concern, there was the latest news. Every tap on his iPad seemed to land on something bad and incumbent presidents always absorbed blame for bad news. The stock market was sluggish at best and the "r" word—recession—kept coming up on the cable news channels. The "d" word—depression—even came from some economists' lips. Retaliatory attacks between Christians and Muslims were breaking out throughout the Third World; high-level security alerts in Europe, the U.S. and even Canada were common. And, this was what they shared with the public: Much was downplayed or kept secret to avoid widespread panic. On the campaign trail, Nicks' impassioned rallies were hitting new peaks and, perhaps more importantly, generating news coverage you couldn't buy with millions of dollars. One of the cable networks actually had bumped Murphy—a sitting president—from an in-person interview to broadcast an audio-only call from Nicks.

One saving grace was that the Chinese famine seemed to be getting better and Murphy earned some credit for the massive trade deal that saved the Chinese. And Leeds, the Democratic candidate, was trying to explain how millions of dollars from Chinese interests ended up in his coffers.

At that moment, the receptionist told him he could enter the Oval Office, so Rayburn walked through the door, sat on the couch and placed his iPad, which still displayed the headline on the latest Leeds story, on the coffee table.

"Charley, you look grim," Murphy said, glacing at the iPad and seeing the story. "The Leeds people think it was us leaking the Chinese stuff you know. I just read the same report."

"Is there something you want to know?" Rayburn said. "Actually, don't answer my question for your own good."

"Relax, Charley," Murphy said. "Why, I think it was just good, old-fashioned investigative reporting by a couple Ohio newspapers. They followed the money. They might win a Pulitzer. Maybe newspapers will survive after all."

"I'm guessing, let's say hypothetically, that someone helped the reporters a little bit," Rayburn said. "Once they started asking questions, maybe someone was helpful in educating them on the ins and outs of campaign finance. Maybe someone knew something about where to find records that might lead you to other records and people with certain histories."

"You're right," Murphy said. "I have no curiosity on this subject."

"Actually, I'm glad you could see me," Rayburn said. "Trey Van Ohmann is trying to reach me. Call it a rare moment of uncertainty on my part. Do you think I should talk to him? He's toxic for us."

Murphy considered that and replied faster than Rayburn expected.

"We both know he doesn't deserve what's happened to him," Murphy said. "Take the call. On your own time. On your own cell. But help him if you can. Consider it an unofficial request from a friend."

Murphy gave a quick nod of his head to the left and pointed his index finger at the picture on his desk of Alison holding Beckert, the presidential beagle. Beckert, named after a talented second baseman for the Cubs during Murphy's youth, was a shelter dog they had adopted as a recommended publicity stunt after years of a pet-free marriage by mutual agreement. The result was predictable: They both fell in love with Beckert, who was proof of the saying, "If you want a friend in Washington, get a dog." Naturally, now that they slept in separate bedrooms, Beckert slept with Alison.

"Oh," he said, making sure Murphy saw him studying the picture with mock intensity. "You're getting policy advice from Beckert the Beagle now?"

"Damn, you're funny, Charley. Really funny," Murphy said, then raised his eyebrows and pointed his finger skyward, as though he had a great idea. "The point is that dogs are loyal and Trey deserves our loyalty. Just help Trey if you can."

"Roger that."

***

That night, Rayburn returned Van Ohmann's call. He listened without speaking for five minutes while Van Ohmann explained what they had found and that Bob Walters was itching to break the story.

Rayburn decided to offer a guarded response, a long-held practice from his military training. Still, he sensed Van Ohmann needed encouragement and he was glad to provide it. If anything, he didn't want to sound too excited. The story didn't have to be true, though obviously that was optimal, especially if they could prove it. Enough evidence to raise serious suspicions would inflict serious or even fatal damage to Nicks.

"The G2," he said. "Do you think a bottle of it is still in your locker?"

"Probably," Van Ohmann said. "Why?"

"We have more than a few ways to test substances quickly. Do you still have friends on the team?"

"Sure, of course. They're disappointed in me. I know Justin, Justin Campanelli, is standing up for me."

Rayburn said, "Okay. Here's what I want you to do."

37

Northern Virginia & Chicago
Late September

At a small corner Starbucks in Alexandria, Virginia, two blocks from his apartment, Charley Rayburn recognized his old friend, Dr. Kris Shingleton, as she walked toward him holding a steaming cup of black coffee.

"Charley, you're aging very gracefully," she said, offering a warm smile and a peck on the cheek. "Must be those low-pressure jobs you have nowadays. You don't have to worry about how to infect the entire human race anymore—just whether to recommend that someone else does it. And how's Connie? I wasn't sure you'd ever get married. You're too ornery."

"You're too kind," he said, returning a whimsical grin. "Connie seems to soften me up a bit, but don't tell anyone. And I'm glad to see you still drink your coffee straight, like real military people do. If you'd walked over here with a pumpkin cinnamon espresso or something, I might've had to leave."

"In which case," she said, "I wouldn't be risking my career by getting in the middle of your political mess."

"Fair point," he said.

He was genuinely glad to see her. They had served together and dated briefly when he was attached to a classified bio-warfare unit. She was taller than Rayburn—she had played college basketball at Virginia Tech—and 12 years younger. Her brunette hair only had a few flecks of gray and her conservative dress couldn't hide inquisitive blue eyes and a natural sense of humor that often crinkled her mouth into a ready smile. After their second date, they had quickly concluded they liked being friends, they deeply respected each other professionally and they probably should keep it that way without the complications of something deeper.

Some experts in the unit developed top-secret protocols for how to deal with biological weapons launched by an enemy. Others researched drugs that could have positive or negative consequences in battle and other high-stress, high-impact conditions. Several unit members worked on procedures to determine when drugs, like many PEDs, with known long-term consequences were justified for short-term benefit.

The specifics were secret but not the nature of the work. Everyone knew that was necessary. It was Rayburn's full-time job then to think the truly unthinkable. His unit had a classified level so high that the unit members joked they only reported to God, which wasn't far from the truth. The president and the Secretary of State only knew about the work in general, benign terms, providing deniability if they were asked before a time everyone hoped would never happen.

Their job was to provide the operational detail and define the conditions, tactics and likely outcomes if American forces used biological or chemical weapons against others. They wrote a manual that officially didn't exist for the "what-if-we-had-no-other-alternative-to-destruction" scenario.

By necessity, all this research into the impact of chemicals on the human body required laboratories of world-class sophistication. Shingleton's lab specialized in understanding the impact of various substances on soldiers. Her scientists probably knew more about the subject than any others on Earth.

Checking a 16-ounce bottle of artificially colored, green Gatorade G2 was child's play.

"We still had to do some homework into some of the characteristics and interactions of the substances," she explained to Rayburn. "It wasn't hard. The military has been using PEDs for years. We have quite a bit of data."

Indeed, performance enhancing drugs had a long history with soldiers in the field—back to ancient times when Peruvian Indians chewed coca leaves for energy before battle.

For decades, many professional athletes had been swallowing pills, injecting fluids and even replacing their blood—the "blood doping" strategies employed by many bicycle racers—in the endless quest to seek a competitive edge. In baseball, old-timers told stories of dishes filled with "reds" and "greenies" in clubhouses to provide boosts as needed during the long, 162-game season. Owners looked the other way for as long as the fans kept coming.

Steroids and other performance enhancers were natural extensions of such a culture until things got out of hand—illustrated by once-skinny ballplayers suddenly looking like Olympic weightlifters and hitting massive numbers of home runs at an age when past players always had started to decline. Steroid abuse also was linked to the deaths of several prominent athletes, most notably football star Lyle Alzado and baseball's Ken Caminiti. The owners had to do something. Players who wanted to cheat needed to be a lot sneakier nowadays. Slipping something into a Gatorade bottle wasn't the craziest stunt a modern player might pull.

In the military, however, the ability to stay awake, alert and strong for long stretches of time wasn't just about winning a game. It could mean victory or defeat in battle. During World War II, soldiers on all sides ate amphetamines and methamphetamines like candy at times, barely conscious of the long-term side effects. People forgot that methamphetamines remained legal in the U.S. throughout the 1950s.

So, though it was rarely acknowledged in public, PEDs had valid, significant military applications. Shingleton's lab was equipped to seriously study and analyze the direct impacts and side effects of all manner of PEDs.

"The researchers don't mind this work at all. It's a cakewalk compared to some of the other stuff you and I know they have to do," she explained to Rayburn. "For one thing, they don't have to go through all the elaborate procedures necessary to handle bio-hazards, viruses and some new, nasty items that you probably don't even know about."

Rayburn glanced at his watch, knowing it was rude to an old friend but feeling the pressure of the day ahead. He asked, "So, what did you find?"

"It was definitely spiked," she said. "I wrote up a test request that just said an 'undisclosed official' was interested in the efficacy of certain PEDs in fluids. They're used to those kinds of requests. We found oral anabolic steroids in the G2, most definitely. We think someone had it in tablet form, crushed the tabs up into the drink and stirred it."

"And what would the effect be?" Rayburn asked.

"Well, in the quantity we found, it might be enough to give a male athlete of normal size a little buzz, but it was pretty diluted," she said. "I'm not sure he even would've noticed anything beyond feeling pretty strong that day. That kind of surprised me."

"Why's that," Rayburn asked, grimly satisfied he had heard the answer he expected but wanting to hear her say it.

"It's just that you don't typically go to that kind of trouble to hardly feel anything," she said. "I mean, why bother? You still have the risk of getting detected, so why do it unless you get the boost of running, pitching, hitting or doing whatever you have to do as an athlete more successfully? Or maybe someone made a mistake with the dosage. We can only speculate."

"Obviously, though, like you said, it was enough to be detected," he said.

"Obviously."

"And maybe that was the only point," he said out loud, knowing he could trust her. "I think the point was to have it detected after someone flagged the substance; to make it look like our guy was taking steroids without him being aware that anything was weird at the time."

"In other words," she said, "Van Ohmann was set up."

"Exactly," Rayburn said. "Now my job is to tell him."

She started to speak, but Rayburn made the "T" for "time

out" by holding his palm horizontally over his other hand, which he held vertically.

"Don't worry," he said. "You know me better than that. I'll just tell him I sent it to a lab for testing. He'll never know it came from the lab that only reports to God. I owe you one, Kris."

"I like hockey," she said after thinking for a few seconds. "So does my boyfriend. Have any ins for some seats behind the glass for a couple Washington Capitals games this winter? Maybe when the Rangers are in town?"

"You got 'em," he said. "I'll even throw in the parking. Thanks, Kris. I really mean it. You're one of the best."

He kissed her cheek lightly. She responded with a quick hug, a longer smile and the knowing glance that only people who do work no one else can understand can share.

***

Jerry Landis, the owner of the Cubs, didn't like direct confrontations and everyone around him knew it—including the players. His first reaction was shock when Trey Van Ohmann bolted from a chair and got in his face as soon as he walked into the reception area outside his office the next morning.

"Jerry. Mr. Landis," Van Ohmann stated with a no-nonsense tone and a stare he usually reserved for a hitter who got a little too comfortable in the batter's box during a close game. Such hitters needed reminders that the pitcher owned the plate. Nothing personal or dangerous; just a quickly thrown "message pitch," usually an inside fastball a whisker away from the offender's chest.

Landis felt like such a batter at that moment. "I need to talk to you," Van Ohmann said. "Now."

Landis had a rich, thick mop of unruly gray hair that formed curly ringlets. He prided himself on being trim and fit for a 66-year-old man and he was lightly sweating from his morning workout in a private area of the state-of-the-art fitness center he had built for his team across the street from Wrigley Field.

To the players, Landis was a distant, aloof figure, but they respected him for letting the baseball experts run the team without micro-managing by the billionaire owner or his family members who also owned a piece of the team. And they respected him for treating them fairly.

Still, underneath his affable posture, he carried a lot of stereotypes reinforced by years spent around professional athletes, back to when his father owned the team.

For example, he observed that many of the Americans often had a lot of growing up to do, even after making it to the big leagues. That was mainly because they had been coddled for years as athletic studs. So, it came as a shock to more than one college or high-school superstar to finally land somewhere where everyone was likely to be as good or better.

Many other players were from unimaginably poor circumstances in other countries and the most-depressed sections of American's cities and rural areas. Those players used sports to escape ugly circumstances and had a better sense of how the world turned. They might not be as articulate, or they might not even speak English, but they had survival smarts. Most of them were appreciative of the opportunity and had unreal work ethics—at least in the first few years of their careers. Their biggest risk was the challenge anyone faced who moved from being ridiculously poor to fabulously rich while surrounded by all the temptations of celebrity without the basic navigational skills of everyday life. And it could happen very fast. You could go from staring at a cane field in Cuba to pulling up to a nightclub in your Maserati in just a few turns of the calendar. Not every young man in his early 20s could handle it.

He always saw Trey Van Ohmann as an exception; a very grounded, mature young man. He was a great teammate with the talent that might help the Cubs build a dynasty his father only could have imagined.

So, Landis didn't recognize the "in-your-face" Trey Van Ohmann greeting him in his office.

He could see Van Ohmann was seething and didn't know what to say to lower the temperature, finally settling for, "Trey, this is highly unusual. Sit down. Please." He waved toward a chair and sat behind his own desk.

Van Ohmann had no interest in sitting down.

"You spiked my Gatorade," he said, emphasizing the word "you" and pointing two fingers straight at him.

"What?" Landis said, caught off guard, now finding his own anger replacing the initial shock of the encounter. "What the hell are you talking about?"

"You spiked my damn Gatorade to hurt Luke Murphy and help Lydia Nicks," he said. "You need to make things right."

"This is crazy," Landis said, deciding to placate Van Ohmann. "All I want is for you to be cleared, Trey. I want you to come back to pitch for the Cubs. We need you."

"Well, you're getting your wish," he said. "I've got proof my G2 was spiked."

With a quick, underhand flick, he tossed the lab report on the desk. The name of the laboratory was listed as Cassidy Chemical Testing LLC in Northfield, Illinois—just as Rayburn had arranged without Van Ohmann knowing the name of the military facility that had really done the testing

Landis looked at the report and read the conclusion that there was a PED in the G2.

"But, this doesn't prove anything," he said. "I can't show it to Major League Baseball. You could have had this done after the fact. Or done it yourself for that matter."

"That's why I have this."

This time he used a slower flick of the wrist and another document floated onto the top of Landis' desk. The owner saw it was an affidavit, signed by a private investigator hired to confront Raoul Pastore, the clubhouse attendant. Landis skimmed as fast as he could and still comprehend. Pastore swore under oath that he was paid $50,000 by a person he didn't know to put "something" in the G2 he always placed in Van Ohmann's locker. He felt terribly about it, but the people who contacted him had enough evidence to get his family expelled from the country and threatened to attack his wife and sisters.

"I'm told Raoul finally broke into tears and said he couldn't keep quiet about it any longer. You can confirm this," Van Ohmann said. "Major League Baseball knows the evidence against me is thin. First of all, if I was going to juice myself, why would I only use an amount that wouldn't have any real impact? Baseball wants me pitching down the stretch. It's obvious someone spiked it. Or, maybe it's more important for you to help Lydia Nicks. Do you deny you and your family are supporting her?"

"No, how could I deny it?" Landis said, shaking his head as confusion turned back to anger. "But that doesn't mean I'm responsible. I resent it."

"Resent it all you want," Van Ohmann. "Who could get more access to the clubhouse than the owner? No one will believe you didn't either hire or look the other way as someone else blackmailed Raoul. Who would have more motive to hurt Luke Murphy, even at the expense of your team's leading pitcher? When this comes out, you'll be a pariah, Jerry. No talented jock in his right mind will ever want to sign with the Cubs again."

Landis thought for a moment. He leaned back in his chair and firmed up his tone of voice. This was a confrontation he couldn't avoid.

"Now, you listen to me," he said. "I'm going to help you, because the team needs you. But, we're through after this season. Whatever it takes, you won't be a Cub next season. I don't give a shit whether you believe me or not."

Van Ohmann stared at the owner.

"Here's the deal. Get ready for some tough stories, Jerry," he said. "But I'll stand up for you. I'll say I don't believe it was you. I'll do it for the good of the team and the fans. That's the best I can do and still help my candidate instead of yours. It's not personal. Just politics. Isn't that what they say?"

Then he turned around and left the room. Before the door closed, Landis began to text Reggie Fox.

CALL ME ASAP. LANDIS.

Fox returned the call 10 minutes later. Big donors always were entitled to elite service. Landis explained the conversation with Van Ohmann.

"Reg, did you have anything to do with this?" Landis said.

"Jerry, I swear, we didn't, though I must admit I almost wish I had thought of it," Fox said. "Did you? It was stupid if you did or looked the other way for someone else."

"Reg, this is the second time in 15 minutes I've been accused of something I didn't do," Landis said. "I'm a big boy. I can take some grief publicly, but I'm not going to put up with this shit in private."

"Message received," Fox said.

"I still have a question," Landis said.

"And what's that? You know I'll help if I can."

"If I didn't do it, which I didn't, and the campaign didn't do it, which you say didn't happen, then who did?" Landis asked. "Who benefits?"

Fox said, "Well, that's easy. Matthew Leeds gains as Murphy and Nicks have a knife fight. But have you ever met Leeds? I think there's no way he'd have the balls to do something like that, but if he didn't, someone around him certainly had giant cojones."

"Well, this sure helps him out, just when he looked dead," Landis said. "It's going to look bad, isn't it?"

"Count on it," Fox said. "You need to be thinking about damage control."

"It's not fair," Landis said quietly, retreating into his everyday shell.

"Fair?" Fox said, with the question coming out as more of a loud exclamation. "You're worried about damn fairness? This is politics. It wasn't fair for Jesus to be crucified either, but it happened.

"Just remember," Fox added, "that after he suffered, Christ was resurrected. Praise the Lord. Have faith. At least that's how the story goes. Be a believer in resurrection my friend."

"Well, Reg, I'm Jewish. We haven't seen a resurrection we can believe in yet."

"Then you got a problem."

38

Chicago, Florida & North Carolina
Late September

A chilly, wind-blown rain, the remnants of a late-season hurricane, sliced underneath the umbrella that Lydia Nicks' aide held over the candidate's head. The rain stung and Nicks glared at him as she exited the auditorium following a speech at Stetson University in DeLand, Florida.

A Secret Service agent scanned the crowd as he opened the door of her leased car—the choice of candidates and political leaders everywhere—a solid black Chevrolet Suburban with heavily tinted glass. The car's color reflected her mood. Things were changing. The crowds seemed both smaller and less frenzied lately. Still, there had been people in the front row with signs that lifted her spirits such as "Hang in there," or "We're with Lydia!!"

Meanwhile, protesters were more pointed in their ugliness. "Cheap Shot Christian" was one sign. Several signs mocked her comet symbol with the word "CHEATER" spelled out in the comet's tail. The protesters and supporters nearly started a riot when one protester tossed a foam baseball at her as she came out; an obvious reference to the Van Ohmann situation. He was quickly arrested for assault while others came to blows. No one really got hurt, but there were just enough bloody lips and bruises to ensure the scuffle would lead the news.

Her denials about Van Ohmann mainly yielded mountains of disbelief. It made too much sense. The more reporters dug, the more links they found between Landis, his family and friends with candidates such as Nicks. Thus, Fox reluctantly changed the shading over Illinois on his computer map that calculated the path to the 270 electoral votes that could make Nicks president. Illinois was a state they thought they could win narrowly if Leeds and Murphy divided votes between moderates and liberals. Now, it was color-coded as "very unlikely" for Nicks. The large fan base and media coverage the Cubs had in Iowa, Indiana and southern Wisconsin also put those states at risk despite their earlier feelings of confidence. He changed all three states from "likely" to "at risk."

Landis, meanwhile, had purchased around-the-clock security and was rapidly learning the difficulty of proving a negative. Without an obvious culprit who wasn't him, denials fell short for many fans. He wasn't sure he could ever show his face at Wrigley Field again.

His other investors were restless, too. Several family members—particularly some of the wealthy, entitled nieces and nephews—were unfamiliar with being the objects of public scorn and social media shaming. He received quiet suggestions to sell the team with some minority shareholders noting that a huge profit would ease the pain of a sale quite nicely since the Cubs were now valued at more than $1 billion. Landis resisted. People would see a sale as an admission of sin. He'd always be remembered as the owner who spiked his star pitcher's Gatorade.

***

"I think today is the day," Aimee Walters said to Trey Van Ohmann.

"And what day is that?" he asked, knowing the answer but wanting to hear her say it.

"You're back in action," she said. "You'll be reinstated today by the baseball commissioner. Keech has no choice. He has to do it."

They were together in Aimee's bedroom. Trey rolled over and looked at her. She punched him lightly in the left arm.

"I hope you're in shape," she said. "Based on last night, it seems like you're in pretty good shape to me."

"Hey, watch that arm. That's what provides the thrills and pays the bills," he said. "But, yeah, I'll be ready."

"You better be," she said. "The Cardinals are coming to town for the biggest games of the season."

Van Ohmann was struggling for the words he wanted to say but finally got them out.

"Aimee, I couldn't have gotten through all this without you. After the season, I think we really should talk."

Surprised by his suddenly serious tone, she misinterpreted.

"Why?" she said. "What's wrong?"

"No, nothing like that. Relax. What I'm trying to say is that I want the dust to settle a little bit, but I, uh, really want to talk about our future. I was lost, really lost, after Dad died. Then I got traded to a new team. I put on a happy face but, really, I couldn't imagine being happy for a long time. Now I can't imagine whatever's next without you in the picture."

Aimee gave him a long look. She was very cautious about relationships and suspicious of this one, though she didn't admit it to Trey. She could tell he meant what he was saying. Still, their relationship was an intense whirlwind of, really, just a few months. Though she knew she loved him, she felt mixed up and scared.

"I think that makes sense," she finally said in almost a clinical tone of voice.

"I have to say, I'm not quite sure how to take that," he responded.

She could see her lack of emotion had hurt his feelings and that clinched a decision to see it through.

"No, Trey," she said. "That's not where I'm coming from. I love you. But I also know that good things can go bad. You're talking to someone whose sister got killed in a car accident. And not just a car accident. My drunken, alcoholic father caused it. Yet somehow I still love my dad. My parents got divorced because of that accident when I was little. You never get over that. Things are a little better now between them, but I don't think they'll ever be over it either, especially Mom. I've read books about being a child of an alcoholic. You sort of become the adult in the house, but you're not ready for it. You watch the real adults yell and scream at each other. They mutter under their breath to you about the faults of the other one. Or, they pass out in a chair, spoiling whatever plans your family had."

"For what it's worth," Trey offered in a quiet voice, almost a whisper, "I respect how you've handled it and maybe your dad has come a long way."

"Maybe," she said. "But you never know when he's going to slip. You've seen it. In my mind's eye, I'm always the little girl sitting in the car after the picks me up, late of course, from soccer practice. I'm sitting in the car in the tavern parking lot while he has what he always called 'a quick one' before going home. It never seemed very quick to me. And I'm thinking, how the heck can he do that, knowing it will make Mom furious?

"And then there was that other thing."

Trey knew that "other thing" was code for the kidnapping and brutal whipping she endured. The scars from the 10 lashes with the leather strap as they hung her nearly naked from a basement beam were still obvious on her back. Some would never heal, though plastic surgery was helping. He moved closer to her and put his arms around her.

He was surprised to see tears in her eyes.

"So, it's like this, Trey," she said. "My life teaches me that good things might happen, but they're like snaps of fingers. You hear the sharp snap and then it's over and things return to just the way they are. That's if you're lucky. Sometimes things get worse. Really worse. I don't trust this. It's not you. It's me. I wake up at night and figure that what we have will end up being a disappointment like my other relationships. Or, maybe something awful, something else I can't fix. I can't live in the moment like some people. I pretend I do. I should get an Academy Award for pretending, but I don't. In the back of my mind, I'm always thinking ahead; thinking about what might go wrong."

"It's not crazy," he said, if anything in a voice even quieter, trying to put faint light into the darkness of the moment. "You have a right to your feelings Aimee. But I think what we have is worth a shot."

She looked at him with a wistful look, the normal veneer of her good nature and wit stripped away. He saw what he needed to see in her eyes. He was relieved to see his calming tone was having an impact; that she could interpret his body language and realize that when he said he loved her, he meant what he said.

"Well, I'm not going anywhere right now," she said, forcing a small smile and perhaps deciding for certain only at that moment that she would see things through. "I can't imagine the alternative. Let's see what happens."

The ding of a text message interrupted them.

"ESPN Alert: Baseball commissioner reinstates Cubs star Van Ohmann. Cites lack of evidence."

His phone was ringing and wouldn't stop. The next text was from Adam Zerbey, his agent.

"Get your ass to the ballpark for a press conference. Your charmed life returns. Adam."

***

A few hours later, Matthew Leeds, the Democratic nominee for president, flipped between cable news stations in his hotel suite in Wilmington, North Carolina, with a sense of satisfaction that buoyed his confidence.

"I can't believe our luck," he said to the others in the room, which included his wife, Jackie, and his campaign manager, Belinda Weathers.

"I told you God was a Democrat," said Weathers, who knew all about weird breaks and twists in life as the first African-American female to lead a major presidential campaign.

Leeds was a 49-year-old senator from Warren, Ohio, who looked 10 years younger. His parents were both active in the United Auto Workers union, commuting to jobs at a huge, nearby plant for years until those jobs disappeared. For a while, his father had driven several hours to Toledo, for another auto job during the week, living in a small apartment and coming home on weekends for eight years until the company eliminated that job as well. He could have transferred to a non-union plant in the South, but it was too far away.

Paul Richard Leeds was luckier than most, though. His assembly job had allowed them to pay the mortgage on the ranch house just outside Warren where they raised four successful children. Then he retired with a decent United Auto Workers pension, though cutback threats always seemed to loom over what everyone assumed was an ironclad commitment.

For as long as he could remember, Matthew Leeds—everyone called him "Mattie" in Warren—had been around politics. When his father went door to door with candidate petitions, it never hurt to have his cute son with him.

Matt was the oldest and a tough act to follow. After graduating from law school at the University of Akron, Mattie Leeds returned home to nearby Youngstown and quickly became a partner in a mid-sized firm that handled a lot of labor law and worker compensation cases. As "Paul's kid," he found early backing when he decided to run for Trumbull County commissioner. From there, he jumped to the Ohio State Senate, then won statewide office as auditor, where he uncovered a major bribery scandal involving the state's Department of Education in Columbus.

High-ranking officials looked the other way in their oversight of for-profit charter schools—whose owners happened to be major campaign contributors to the other political party. The district attorney in Columbus didn't probe very deeply and wouldn't say why. So, Leeds used the power of his office to expose the scandal and ultimately force the state's attorney general to appoint a special prosecutor. Several education department employees, including the commissioner, were indicted and later convicted. The district attorney lost his bid for re-election.

Then Mattie Leeds exposed the sky-high fees that the state employee pension plans were paying politically connected hedge funds, even though the funds routinely generated lower returns than basic investments with lower fees. That was a subject that hit close to home for people with government pensions—everyday workers, including cops firefighters and teachers, paying the price for the greed of others. National publicity for "Ohio's crusading auditor" followed and he was in the U.S. Senate before he was 45 with a wife and three young children.

By then, his father had settled into retirement and took a part-time job at Advance Auto Parts, mainly for something to do with his free time. Paul stayed active in local Democratic politics, too, and was always ready for a good quote when the local TV stations were doing a story that involved his son.

Matt Leeds—he had abandoned the juvenile-sounding "Mattie" nickname—laughed when he saw his Dad on the national news. His Dad slipped and called him "Mattie," but that was okay.

"It humanizes you," Weathers said. "And he'll say something more candidly than you could."

Paul Leeds fulfilled her hopes a moment later when he said. "These other two candidates, they don't really give a BLEEP about working people. Mattie is going to show what he's got tomorrow night. Excuse my French, but he's going to kick some ass in that debate."

As soon as the brief story was over, Jackie Leeds looked at her husband. "Are you ready?" she asked.

Belinda Weathers cut into the conversation.

"We will be," she said. "We're going to use the entire plane flight to Springfield for final prep."

Leeds admitted, only to himself, that he was far more nervous than he would show others. He was used to the media spotlight, but this was different. Everything was on the line.

"We have a huge opportunity," he said out loud. "We can get past this Chinese thing. It's old news. The Van Ohmann mess is dragging Nicks down. That was a huge gift. I don't see how Murphy recovers from all the damage he's taken."

Jackie Leeds thought she knew her husband well enough to believe he wasn't responsible for the trickery with Van Ohmann. It was a despicable-but-clever maneuver that damaged both Murphy and Nicks at different points. Matt certainly was clever enough to think of it, she thought, but it was so out of character as to be nearly incomprehensible. Nearly. That was the thing. As a political spouse, she had seen how heated campaigns could make ethical standards very elastic. After all, these were people, for all their strengths, who had to be supremely ambitious and at least a bit narcissistic to even consider such a thing as a serious presidential campaign. No one could make it this far without a giant ego. She knew that Matt was just better than most at suppressing his; sometimes even from himself.

So, she wondered if the stakes were high enough that her husband would set his holier-than-thou ethical standards aside to make his peace with his good fortune. She knew there was no point in asking too many questions of those around him. That way, he could deny knowledge and not have to feign innocence when he was asked if the campaign had any role.

She looked at Weathers. She figured that Weathers, a seasoned political operative, would have had something to do with it or knew who did. Jackie renewed her decision not to ask. It was definitely better this way.

She looked at her husband and said, "You'll do great honey. The kids and I will meet you in Springfield."

39

Sangamon Auditorium, University Of Illinois Springfield The Next Evening

The president of the United States wondered why his brain wasn't working properly.

It was a gauzy sort of awareness, like he was afloat. He contemplated this and conjured an image: The ooze and stream of his thoughts reminded him of improvisational jazz musicians camping in his head, doing riffs off nearly forgotten themes, sending commands to his brain to process the vibe but not the reality. So, did that mean that somehow there were two brains, the one he was using and the one receiving his commands? Maybe he was dreaming. Or, maybe someone had slipped some LSD in his water, like someone did once in his college dorm. That made him smile, although he couldn't be sure anyone could see an actual grin, or that the smile really happened at all. Remembering college acid trips forced an image of Andy Pierce into his consciousness. That made him sad. It was so sad.

"Does this even make sense?" Luke Murphy said to himself before deciding that, yeah, maybe it did. And then he was thinking that he was thinking pretty slowly as he thought about what he had just been thinking about.

A moment of clarity intruded into the rhythms of the drifting, jiving thoughts.

"You've been shot.

"During the debate."

He wondered, "Is this what's supposed to go through my mind after I get shot? Where's that white light everyone talks about?"

That made him smile, too, even if maybe no one could see it. He decided that staying with this internal dialogue, thinking about his thinking, was the way to go. Back to the jazz. "Well," he said to himself, "I don't see the damn white light. Maybe it means I'm not going to die. Maybe it means I get to be president for a while longer."

The gauziness lifted a little more. His military training kicked in and thinking and feeling suddenly joined as if one were a plug and the other a socket. Okay, so be it. Now he felt pain. Problem was, he was badly out of practice with the injury drill. He tried to put his body through the mental checklist. Shit, the floor was damn hard. All his body parts seemed to be attached, but when he ordered his arms or legs to move, the only response was a little wiggle from his fingers. With blurry vision through the one eye that was working, it seemed as though he was watching a disaster movie without sound. His thoughts were all he had as he observed humans playing their assigned roles in the movie, scrambling in chaos and yelling words he couldn't hear.

He realized he was at the front of the stage by a podium with his gaze facing the stage's rear. He took note of the patriotic theme in the decorations; white stars forming circles and swoops of color in the backdrop evoking the flag. He remembered more about the debate; a rare three-way event for the presidency. It was him, Nicks and Leeds. *"Murphy, Nicks and Leeds,"* he thought. *"Sounds like a bad law firm."* He was winning the debate; he was sure of that. He would keep his presidency after all. He had been busy—was it only a few moments ago?—deflecting attacks from Nicks on the right and Leeds on the left, quite pleased and maybe too full of himself for his mistake-free performance.

Suddenly there was a muffled sound. In a split second he felt a powerful jolt like being cold-cocked by a sledge hammer, followed by a sharp pain in his right side. He collapsed where he was standing.

Now someone was dabbing around his face. He felt something warm, probably blood, under his back. He tried to say he was alert but wasn't sure anything came out. The person looked puzzled for a moment and mouthed something that included the word "okay." That much he could lip-read.

Damn, now he wanted someone to hear again. It frustrated him. Then, of all the things he could've been thinking about, from the state of the nation to his own mortality, Luke Murphy found himself wondering if he could come up with a wittier line or two than Ronald Reagan.

It took a special president to find humor in an assassination attempt.

"Honey, I forgot to duck," Reagan said to his wife, Nancy, after suffering two gunshot wounds in an attack by John Hinckley on March 30, 1981, just two months into his presidency as he entered his limousine outside the Washington Hilton Hotel. Actually, the president had cribbed a line from the boxer Jack Dempsey, who said it to his own wife after he was beaten by Gene Tunney in a famous 1926 bout that could have been a familiar, important event to Reagan.

The dangerous part of Reagan's walk to the limo, about 30 feet, was so brief that the Secret Service hadn't required a bulletproof vest. They made up for that oversight with quick action that probably saved Reagan's life, particularly a decision to rush Reagan to the hospital instead of an operating room in The White House.

Ever the jokester, Reagan also removed his oxygen mask in the operating room and quipped to the medical team, "I hope you're all Republicans."

Luke Murphy admired many things about Ronald Reagan—the real Ronald Reagan, not the gross distortion who was worshipped or vilified decades later. Murphy always hailed him publicly. Privately, he saw the flaws, too, and wasn't a member of the group that thought Reagan belonged on Mount Rushmore and had ascended directly to heaven propelled by red-white-and-blue angel wings. Murphy also felt a rivalry with the legendary president. The desire to top Reagan fueled his competitive engine, which immediately made the goal harder to achieve because one of the keys to Reagan's success was, whether you loved him or hated him, he was refreshingly uninterested in personal glory. Few politicians could follow the time-tested maxim: It's amazing what you can accomplish if you're not worried about recognition.

Now Murphy was fully alert; out of the fog. He wondered if he could be like Reagan right now: Spit out a wry, offhand remark to show the country he was still his witty self, or at least that a bullet or two wouldn't change things. He had a good line, too. It was what he had just been thinking about. He mouthed the words as best he could.

"The Cubs," he said, or thought he was saying. "Did they win today? Are they in first place?"

He saw Alison. His wife had a tear in her eye. He could see she was saying, "Luke," but he couldn't make out the rest.

She leaned closer, put her lips next to his left ear and wrapped her hand in his. He could see the "Luke" button on the lapel of her tailored pantsuit and smell the light dab of perfume she had used. He was surprised by how much her obvious concern touched him. It was the closest they had been to feeling deep emotion for one another in a long time. Well, that wasn't quite true. There was plenty of emotion at times. It was the closest they had been to having deep, positive feelings for each other in a long time. *How ironic*, he thought, *if bullets help us put a bridge over our gulf?*

Then all of a sudden, he could hear. It was muffled, as if someone had placed a sponge between his ear and her lips, but he could hear.

"Relax, Luke. Rest," he heard Alison order him in a mock military tone. Then he knew she had heard him.

"I see you still have your priorities in order," she said, speaking softly, directly into his functioning ear. "I checked and found out how the Cubs did. Tonight wasn't their night, but Trey is back. They're not out of it. They still can get back to the World Series and win it this time."

He squeezed her hand back.

"Ahh," he said as he felt himself being lifted onto a stretcher. "Now I have something to live for."

He mentally kicked himself for even caring whether his words would reach the media.

"That's pure Luke Murphy," they'd say with a chuckle on Fox, CNN, ESPN and every other network. "He never gives up on the Cubbies."

Murphy knew this for sure: Elections were won or lost in human moments at unpredictable times. *You play the cards you're dealt. You're shot, Luke. Sucks for you.* Still, the sympathy hand often won the game.

He was getting ready to tell Alison it was fine with him if she shared his words. She was a political wife. She'd immediately grasp the concept; she'd know how to play that angle. She would know that without being told. *No worries*, he thought.

Now, back to the jazz. Everything was getting gauzy again. A filmy, swirling mixture of whites and grays began changing to solid black at an accelerating pace. The combo played in the background, a song he recognized. Beatles. Sort of a cliché; almost disappointing that he'd come up with something so obvious, "And, in the end, the love you take is equal to the love you make." *Is that even true? Who the hell knows?*

Then it seemed like he could smell touches and touch smells. Was he holding his own heart for a final beat? Was that a black tunnel? Ah, but wait. At a moment too short to measure, he was moving; moving toward a bright light.

He wondered. Was this the bright light that comes at the end?

40

Trey Van Ohmann

The night of the debate was my first start for the Cubs after getting reinstated. I'd like to tell you it was like a scene out of "The Natural," the Robert Redford movie that would be the corniest baseball movie ever made, except they made "Field of Dreams," which is a better movie because it revels in its corniness—including scenes in an Iowa cornfield.

Not that I'm a movie critic, but Kevin Costner makes that picture work if you ask me. Even though you know you're being manipulated, it's still hard to watch the scene where Costner's character encounters the ghost of "Shoeless Joe" Jackson without a gulp in your throat. If you're a baseball player in real life, the movie touches you.

I felt fresh sympathy for "Shoeless Joe" after my experience with the PED suspension. Joe's career and reputation were ruined when he joined the others on the Chicago White Sox who conspired with gamblers to fix the 1919 World Series against the Cincinnati Reds. Judge Kenesaw Mountain Landis, baseball's first all-powerful commissioner, banned him from baseball for life in 1920. And, yeah, it's ironic that Jerry Landis claims to be a distant relative of The Judge.

I always just assumed that Jackson was as guilty as the rest of the "Black Sox" players, but I spent some time during my suspension reading up on the scandal for obvious reasons. Plus, well, I had extra time. What happened to Jackson is a book in itself—and several have been written. You can make a case that he was a partial victim and maybe not a conspirator at all. Uneducated and woefully underpaid in an era when players were little more than slaves under contract to the owners, Jackson had superstar talent. He'd make millions today. His .356 lifetime batting average is the third highest in Major League history. In the World Series that he supposedly was involved in fixing, he had 12 hits and a .375 average. Oh, he also threw a runner out at home plate and played error-free in the field.

The attorney for the team owner, Charles Comiskey, represented this nearly illiterate man in a classic conflict of interest.

Jackson's supporters cite evidence that Joe refused a $5,000 bribe and they say claims that he admitted guilt are untrue. Later, other players in the conspiracy said that Jackson's name was added to "the fix" to add luster and bolster their side. Others are dubious of Jackson's innocence.

They have a museum for Joe Jackson now, in the home where he lived and died in 1951 at 64 years old, called the Shoeless Joe Jackson Museum and Baseball Library in Greenville, S.C. near the Shoeless Joe Jackson Memorial Park.

I plan to visit Greenville during the offseason, but I have no intention of ending up like Joe Jackson.

So, I made sure I got to the locker room early. The atmosphere in the room was odd. Most of my teammates gave me a "Hey, Trey, welcome back" greeting. They said and did the right things, but I could tell that a few of them couldn't easily escape the belief that the Cubs would be in much better shape if I had never crossed paths with Luke Murphy.

How could I argue? I had broken the code by shifting my focus from 100 percent on the team. Even if your wife had a baby during the season, you were expected to be back as soon as possible and not become a months-long distraction. And, really, that's a fair trade for a career in which you and your family could be set for life for playing a game for just a few years.

Making matters worse, my first start after returning to action wasn't anywhere near what my teammates wanted, expected or needed to boost their confidence. I was rustier than I thought. I walked the first two batters I faced and then made an error by letting a line drive squirt out of my glove, loading the bases. The damn Mets scored two runs before I found a little groove and struck out two batters.

I wasn't awful, but I certainly wasn't the ace. I got yanked with one out in the sixth inning—much earlier than usual—with the score tied at 4-4. We ended up losing the game in the ninth inning, 6-5, which put us behind St. Louis with five games to play. I would be pitching on the last day of the season when we would be in Milwaukee.

As soon as I got back to the locker room, I learned that Luke Murphy had been shot a few hours south in Springfield.

I couldn't skip the post-game news conference. That would make things worse. No surprise, the media had more questions for me about Luke Murphy and politics than about baseball. I was a reporter's version of a two-for-one sale.

I had to remind myself to keep my temper in check a few times, as reporters found unlimited ways to phrase the same questions, "Trey, do you wish that you'd never gotten involved in the Murphy campaign? Don't you think the Cubs would be in better position now if you had concentrated on baseball?"

I said, "Let's focus on what's important. Our president just got shot. I'm sorry we lost a baseball game and I'm disappointed I didn't pitch as well as I can. I'm going to do everything I can to do better next time, but I'm even sorrier for the president and his family. And our country. And you should be, too."

I finally ran out of different ways to say the same thing. That was enough. Having fulfilled my obligation to the media, I turned and left quickly enough so they surely took notice. If they wanted to write that, "Van Ohmann stomped out of the post-game news conference," then so be it.

Back at the condo, I watched the news. Speculation about "who shot Luke Murphy" was rampant. No terrorist group had stepped forward to claim credit, but the speculation centered there, particularly Muslim terrorists with ties to Indonesia. Lydia Nicks had wasted no time suggesting that only she was tough enough to stop terrorism. The talking heads of cable news already were suggesting that new polls would show a shift of several points away from both Murphy and Leeds.

Everyone wondered about the gunman, who was killed immediately after he got off a single round. I assumed there must be terabytes of video from all angles of that moment. The media showed a blurry smartphone photo of a bearded guy wearing dark glasses and a Cubs hat. No one had made the identification yet. He looked vaguely Middle Eastern.

The coverage on the cable stations, having almost zero solid news to report, amounted to a speculation orgy by everyone granted face time. The one solid, fascinating fact that had leaked was that someone, maybe the gunman himself, used a 3D printer to make the weapon from plastic. That's how the shooter got it through the tight security. I watched a story that described how a plastic gun could be made with a decent home printer and then broken down into a number of small parts that would easily fit into pockets or a purse.

Being a curious person—and one who had done a lot of hunting as a kid in Idaho—I checked this out. Sadly, it was all plausible. Wikipedia had a reference to a chilling 2013 memo from the Department of Homeland Security:

> "*Significant advances in three-dimensional (3D) printing capabilities, availability of free digital 3D printer files for firearms components, and difficulty regulating file sharing may present public safety risks from unqualified gun seekers who obtain or manufacture 3D printed guns ... proposed legislation to ban 3D printing of weapons may deter, but cannot completely prevent their production. Even if the practice is prohibited by new legislation, online distribution of these digital files will be as difficult to control as any other illegally traded music, movie or software files.*"

About an hour later, my phone chirped the "I Gotta Go" theme song. It was Rayburn.

"Saw your comments, Trey," he said. "Just want to say thanks."

"Sure," I said. "How's he doing?"

"We don't know yet. We just don't know."

"Well, let me know if there's anything I can do," I said. "Today wasn't the greatest, but you probably saved my career."

"The best thing you can do for him—and probably the campaign—is win a World Series," Rayburn said. "I'm sure about that. How was the reaction of your teammates to your return?"

I had to pause for a moment with that question. "Uh, mixed at best," I finally said. "At least until I pitch better."

"Well, that's something we understand in politics. If the worst reaction is 'mixed at best' that usually makes it a good day around here. They'll come around."

41

Springfield, Ill. | Two Days Later

Alison Murphy knew this was a bad idea. A really bad idea. She stared at the second bottle of chardonnay on the table in her hotel room at the Springfield, Illinois, Marriott. She finger-rolled around the top of the first bottle then carefully lined it up next to the second one. The first stood tall but depleted. The second bottle was halfway to empty.

She wasn't just feeling "a little tipsy." She was drunk and she knew it. She needed to sober up to visit Luke. He was doing better, awake and mostly alert, but in a lot of pain.

She was alone in the room. In the background, the television was on ESPN, but she wasn't paying attention. She could no longer handle the incessant murmur and speculations of cable news, so she thought the tennis match on ESPN would be a welcome distraction. She had been a damn good tennis player, talented enough to get scholarship offers. But she couldn't concentrate on the match, so she sipped almost unthinkingly on the wine, unable to dig out of her emotional pit.

Everything was crashing around her. There was the embarrassment of playing the dutiful wife as the world dissected how she'd react to exposure of Luke's secret. She felt like she was holding her marriage together with emotional threads of baling wire and temporary glue of mutual self-interest.

Well, at least she knew now that Luke's serious deficiencies in the bedroom weren't just related to job stress or whether he found her attractive. His distance and lack of emotional support rankled much more. You never knew everything happening in anyone else's life, but she thought about Michelle Obama, Laura Bush and other First Ladies, and it certainly seemed as though other presidents maintained deep, supportive relationships with their spouses. The Murphys had lost their way.

What made things even more difficult, deepening the abyss, was the recent, surprising return of a small spark between her and Luke. They had worked through the initial anger of the latest events and her resentments from months of neglect and inattention. There were moments again when they were a team, working to accomplish something bigger than themselves. She didn't know if it would change anything—she still wanted to leave after the election—but it certainly created a possibility they could remain friends and maybe, eventually, become something more again.

She wondered if the recent, better moments would turn out to be just teasers. And now she had to play the role of stand-by-your-man First Lady to a wounded president of the United States facing new questions about not only his qualifications but also if he would be physically up to the job.

Lydia Nicks and Reggie Fox knew how to play the game. Nicks had issued a statement "sharing the horror we all share when our president is targeted" and added, "We wish him well as we continue our campaign," reminding everyone that Luke wasn't participating. Then she repeated her new mantra; that she was "the only candidate who was going to stand up to Islamic terrorists who wanted to destroy our religion and our country."

Leeds acted classier, but his handlers made sure he was publicly vibrant and active while his operatives were all over television, basking in the media consensus that he had held his own in the debate and probably won it, despite claims of victory from the other two campaigns.

Meanwhile, as the president fought for his life during the first 24 hours, she had to endure endless rehashing of Murphy's life and career. The media pundits overdosed on not only his accomplishments and military heroism but also, of course, on his "college experience," abandoned friends and childless marriage. The limited amount that was too sensitive or too speculative for the mainstream media was left for talk radio and the social media haters, who had no such scruples.

I think I understand PTSD. The next time I give a speech to a mental health group, no more pretending that I feel the pain, she thought.

The idea of even giving a speech in public pushed her deeper into sadness. Without thinking about it, she took another sip of wine and drummed her fingertips on the nightstand to the ironic beat of a commercial for Cialis.

Coffee, she thought. *Coffee. That'll help. And I'm kind of hungry.* She picked up the phone next to the bed and almost punched the button that would automatically connect her to room service. Then she realized what that would put in motion. For the first time in several hours, she laughed a little bit.

She knew the Secret Service was right outside her door, ready to do whatever she wanted. She imagined the poor hotel employee trying to even exit the elevator with an unannounced delivery of coffee, cheese and crackers.

She didn't want to open the door and let them see her. Besides being intoxicated, she thought she looked terrible. She hadn't fixed her makeup all day and there were dark circles under her eyes. Instead, she texted Renee Hawkinson, the agent in charge of her detail.

Sorry to bug u. Can you have them bring coffee and snack like cheese and crackers? FLOTUS

Hawkinson texted back to the First Lady of the United States almost immediately. *Will do. No prob.*

Well, Alison thought, *the coffee's coming. Why not?*

For just a flicker of a moment, she couldn't ignore the quiet voice in the back of her mind that tried to tell her when she was dancing to the rhythms of self-defeat and rationalization. In response, she shrugged. She carefully poured a few more ounces of wine. Then she nodded her head, trying to convince herself that she was in control of the situation, though she struggled a bit to push the cork back into the top of the bottle. She missed the opening completely on the first try. Finally, with the cork secure, she slowly and carefully placed the bottle on top of the mini-fridge, fully intending to put it into the unit for chilling—as soon as she got around to it.

***

Two hours later, the black Chevrolet Suburban carrying the First Lady stopped in front of Springfield Memorial Hospital.

The advance team made sure the lobby was empty. As Alison stepped out of the vehicle, the heel of her left shoe caught in a crack in the pavement, and she nearly fell, only to be caught by Hawkinson as her sunglasses tumbled to the ground.

"Thank you Renee," Alison said quietly to her as cameras and smartphones captured every second of the embarrassing moment. "I'm fine. Really."

Turned away from the media and other gawkers for the moment, Hawkinson looked quizzically at the First Lady. There weren't many secrets from the Secret Service and no agent training was necessary to connect the dots between wine bottles and orders of coffee.

An agent already had privately e-mailed a heads-up to Hawkinson to stay unusually close to Alison, both for her protection and to avoid embarrassment of someone they genuinely liked. When the agent had entered the room with coffee for the First Lady about an hour earlier, they saw Alison putting a partially full bottle into the fridge. Then when they carefully inspected the room after she left—a normal security procedure any time POTUS or FLOTUS cleared a hotel room—the agents noted that the wine in the mini-fridge only had about two fingers left. Apparently the First Lady drank something other than just coffee during the past hour. They found the first, empty bottle on its side next to the television, which Alison hadn't bothered to power off. A tennis match continued on ESPN.

"Are you okay Mrs. Murphy?" the agent asked, then decided to offer some encouragement. Unlike some presidential spouses, Alison Murphy always treated the staff and agents protecting her with dignity, respect and genuine appreciation. But, she was a private person by nature and recent events had locked her up even tighter. The last thing Alison Murphy would want is any public embarrassment.

"Is there anything I can do for you once we get inside?" Hawkinson added quietly, helping her stand up as she handed the sunglasses back to her. "There's a lot going on."

The agent was expecting a typical soft-spoken response like "no worries." Instead, Alison suddenly turned toward the agent, facing her head on and speaking in words loud enough for everyone to hear, punctuating each one with a pause or slurring them together.

"Renee, What The Hell Don't You Get About The Words 'I'm Fine'?" Alison said. Then, realizing she had made a scene that would be on Twitter by the time she finished the thought, her head fell forward in embarrassment and she nearly stumbled again.

"Sorry," the agent said in an even tone with a bit of firmness to get her attention, hoping she'd recognize a bad situation could get worse. "Please stay near me." The entourage quickly surrounded the First Lady and led her into the hospital lobby, which had been cleared of all but essential personnel or those authorized by the president's staff.

Once in the lobby, she tried to gather herself only to stop in her tracks when she saw Bob Walters showing his credentials to an agent.

They exchanged glances and Walters walked slowly toward her. The agents circled around Alison, tightening the open space around her and using body language to politely indicate that wasn't a great idea.

"It's okay," Alison said, forcing a smile. "This guy has been one of my husband's best friends for, like, forever. But I don't know why. He keeps making us look like crap on his radio show."

She steeled her posture and looked up, changing her mood abruptly and becoming overly effusive in the manner of drunks of any time and place; probably back to the time when

Egyptians honored the goddess Sekhmet during the Festival of Drunkenness.

"Bobby, Bob," she said, loud enough to cause every head in the lobby to turn. "I'm really glad to see you. Are you here to visit Luke?"

Walters looked at her and raised his eyebrows in surprise at Alison's unusual demeanor and tone.

"Yeah, Alison," he said. "I'm here to see Luke. I figured he could use a friend."

She pointed a finger at him.

"Don't you take advantage of Luke and talk him into an interview." She laughed loudly at the humor she saw in that.

"Well, actually, he had Charley Rayburn call me, to say I'm the first outsider he wants to talk to," he said. "But we'll start off the record and that's where it'll stay unless he agrees. I promise. And I've got orders not to push him."

Alison made a mock "thumbs down" gesture, shook her head and gave him a nod forward to join her on the elevator. Several other agents started to walk onto the elevator, too.

Walters said to them, "Hey, is it possible for Alison and me to have some private time. It's secure here I'm sure."

"Mrs. Murphy?" Hawkinson asked, looking directly at the First Lady. "It's your call. We know Mr. Walters well enough to know he's no threat—even though the president swears that anyone who rips the Cubs is a risk to national security."

The veteran agent made the last statement with a smile. Walters' actions during Game Seven of the World Series probably saved the president's life and he had visited Luke enough that he was as vetted as any guest could be.

Plus, Hawkinson knew Walters was a recovering alcoholic. The agent was no stranger herself to the destructive powers of heavy drinking in a family. With her training in body language, she was 99 percent sure Walters had recognized immediately that Alison wasn't in a good place. Maybe that was the motive for the elevator ride on Walters' part.

"Yeah, sure," Alison said, still speaking too loudly. "If Bobby tries anything with me or makes fun of the Cubbies,

I've got a damn sharp nail file here. Plus, by God, I'VE GOT SECRET SERVICE PROTECTION! So, don't get all touchy-feely on me."

"Hands off all the way, Alison," Walters said.

As soon as the elevator doors shut, Walters did just the opposite. He embraced Alison and hugged her as hard as he could. For the moment, she didn't know how to react.

"You're not fooling me," he said. "I can smell it on you. You don't want to go where I've been, where I still go sometimes."

Alison started to talk.

"Shut up," Walters said, knowing they only had a few seconds together. "Just let me hold you tight until the door starts to open. Let's be there for Luke and you're going to call me later, so we can talk about your problem and I'll be there for you."

"I don't have a damn problem," she said, speaking softly now. "I just have a shitty marriage." The last statement was a whisper by the time she finished.

Bob hugged her harder.

"Let me do this good thing for you," he said. "I completely fucked up my marriage. Micki will never take me back. I still slip up. I'm still a drunk. I just don't perform as often. Promise that we'll talk."

She gave in.

"I can't do this Bob," she said, and started to cry. "I can't do ANY of this."

"Yeah, you can," he said. "And then you can take care of yourself. You're not alone. Let me be someone besides an asshole for once." He hugged her harder. She kissed him on the cheek.

"So," she said, forcing a smile. "I guess we shouldn't go out for a drink to talk after we get out of here,"

"Starbucks at your hotel," he said. "I'm buying."

Then the elevator door opened as they pulled apart and a phalanx of Secret Service agents ushered them out. As they walked to the president's room, she hooked her right arm around

Walters' left elbow. He could sense her leaning against him and he decided that was a good thing.

***

"I think the Cubs are gonna make it," Luke Murphy said in a weak but positive-sounding voice, holding an iPad and using the "Watch ESPN" app. Rayburn sat in the corner, feverishly making notes on a legal pad, trying to decide what was essential to present to the president.

Murphy's iPad was open so it faced him vertically on the hinged tray table over his bed, which was adjusted so the president could watch in a sitting position. As he saw Alison and Walters enter the room, he quickly turned to face them and began raising his arm to motion them inside.

"We're ahead 6-1," Murphy said and then stopped in mid-sentence in an attempted yell that emerged as a scratchy croak, "Oh, shit." He had swiveled too fast, stretching the heavily stitched area where the surgeons had removed two bullets and saved his life—at least temporarily.

He winced in pain and carefully shifted to his earlier position. Walters saw Murphy push a button twice, no doubt for a morphine drip.

"Sorry," he said, gasping a bit. "That freakin' hurt. I'm trying to avoid the drip, but sometimes it can't be helped." He took a breath and then blew one out like a pregnant woman practicing Lamaze breathing. After a few moments, he seemed to relax.

"Alison, Bob. Thanks for coming. The nurses and doctors here are dictators. They'll throw me out if I talk and move too much. Charley's going to do most of the talking."

Walters thought his childhood friend looked exhausted. Murphy appeared to be in far worse shape than the public pronouncements indicated. He noticed a urine bag among all the other tubes and devices hooked into the president. He had read that there was some question whether Murphy would regain all his bodily functions but didn't want to ask such a delicate question. Plus, it was still very early, only the third day since the shooting.

Walters glanced at the other corner and saw Alison plop into a tired-looking blue armchair. Her head slumped forward a bit and Walters thought she looked almost as tired as the president.

"Alison?" Murphy asked. "Are you okay? I'm really glad you're here."

She looked up at him. "Anything for the Commander in Chief," she said, the sarcasm obvious.

Murphy processed the signals of his wife's drinking and decided it was best to move along. He carefully turned his head toward Rayburn, who was fully absorbed in reading something.

"Charley," Murphy said, and there was a faint slur in his words. "We're ready."

Rayburn looked at Walters and then eyed Alison Murphy, who had slid downward in the chair. Her eyes were nearly shut.

"Bob, the president wants you to have the first interview with him. The country needs to see that he's going to be okay and in control of things. You and Alison can both help send that signal."

Alison stirred at the mention of her name but didn't say anything.

"That's great, Charley," Walters said. "But, I can't do that by interviewing you. You're putting me in an awkward position."

Walters looked over at Murphy. "Luke, Mr. President, you understand that, don't you?"

"I do," Murphy said. "You might have to come back a couple times. Like I said, they've got me on a short leash."

"So, who's running the country? You or Vice President Campbell?"

Rayburn answered. "As you well know, Bob, the Veep is temporarily in command, but—off the record—we need that to end that as soon as possible."

"Because?" Walters said, putting a big question mark at the end of the word.

"I'll say what Charley won't say bluntly," Murphy said, summoning his strength to retain clarity of mind. "I'm saying this as a friend, not for your story, though I guess it's pretty obvious. If I'm out of commission too long, we lose.

"I'm not perfect," he continued. "God knows. But I'm the grown-up. Lydia might be crazy or ambition has turned her into a sociopath. Doesn't matter which it is. She'll push us into a religious war that plays into the bad guys' hands. They'll get the jihad they always wanted. Did you know they're close to getting a nuke? They already try to blackmail us through back channels. We can't tell the Saudis to go fuck themselves or anyone else who can help us—no matter what religion they are."

Rayburn added, "We give her the national security briefings with the least amount of detail possible. We're scared, frankly; scared that she'll either say we're making it up or not give a shit and find a way to go public."

"Then there's Leeds," Murphy said. "Honorable, decent guy. Don't agree with him about a lot of stuff but mostly good intentions. Pretty polished. Talks a good game. He's just not up for this."

"So," Walters said. "You're saying I need to make you look good, because the country needs you and the other two can't cut it? That might be the biggest bucket full of self-justification of all time."

"Well, you know my favorite saying—it has the virtue of being true and you know it," Rayburn said.

Walters thought about that for a moment. "Yeah," he said. "It probably is."

"So?" Murphy asked, slurring the word.

"So, I'll do a little story saying I was allowed a brief visit with you, and you said you were anxious to get back to work as soon as possible, but you still face a challenging recovery," Walters said. "I can't live with myself and make you look any healthier than that. In return, you give me the first real audio when you're ready and I can ask whatever I want."

"That's fine," Rayburn said. Walters scanned the room, focusing on Alison and Luke, and realized that only Charley Rayburn and he remained awake.

"I have one other question," Walters said, looking at Rayburn.

"Do you know who's behind the shooting? Is it terrorism? Is it political? Bad as things can get, political assassination from an opponent's camp would be a new low in American politics. Hard to believe."

Rayburn said, "Do you want an answer on or off the record?"

"Try both."

"On the record, we don't know and are working tirelessly to find out. Off the record, we also don't know, but maybe you should keep asking who the hell benefits from Luke Murphy being out of commission right now? It's not just terrorists. The shooter might be a gun for hire made to look like a true believer in Allah's jihad. That's off the record."

Walters said, "You look like you could use some rest yourself, Colonel."

Rayburn didn't say anything. He just looked worried. He turned back to his iPad, a signal to Walters that it was time to leave the room, call the station with his minor scoop and make the three-hour drive back to Chicago.

His last glance focused on Alison Murphy, now sleeping fitfully in the corner chair. Walters wondered how much longer she could star in her role of loyal presidential wife. He wanted to help. He figured he owed that much to a fellow drunk.

42

Trey Van Ohmann

I could tell I remained in purgatory with most of my teammates. I couldn't remember the last time I felt more stress about my performance and I had to consider the notion that maybe my presence was doing more harm than good. Team chemistry is a delicate thing, never more so than the end of a season when every game matters.

I was mindlessly stretching out, throwing a ball back and forth to stay loose before the next game, when our pitching coach, Wally Schweigert, stopped in front of me. He obviously had something on his mind and it was this: He thought I had some "mechanical problems." That floored me. Everyone always said my mechanics were textbook, going back to my second year at Penn State.

"Plus, you're thinking too much, Trey," Schweigert said. "I could see the wheels turning so hard they were smoking your last time out. Relax man."

I try to stay humble. Honest. But if you challenge my pitching mechanics, I guess I'm another know-it-all diva—even if advice comes from the pitching coach. Still, the one positive was that my teammates saw me working with Schweigert, a guy everyone respected. I decided to feign paying attention.

The cliché "chiseled veteran" certainly applied to Wally. There were thousands of minor league bus miles and hours of scorching sun etched on that face. He didn't get a chance to coach in the big leagues until he was well into his 50s. Now he was an acknowledged pitching wizard. It didn't matter if you were young or old, skinny or fat, rookie or veteran; it didn't matter if you had great stuff you couldn't control, or if you had great control that didn't match the quality of your pitches.

Some sportswriter had nicknamed him "The Pitcher Whisperer," and it stuck. The players shortened it to "Whisper," also because he almost never raised his voice. I'm saying the man spoke quietly. You usually had to turn an ear toward his mouth to even understand a soft voice thickened into a syrupy, husky stew by the drawl of his native South Carolina and decades of smoking—a habit his wife had finally convinced him to drop this season.

Sometimes, if he was out of earshot, his nickname became "That Fucking Whisper" when he asked you to do something you didn't want to do. Of course, the more you thought he was wrong, the more likely he was right. He spotted flaws that would be invisible to anyone else. If they had a Nobel Prize for the study of pitching, he would be baseball's Stephen Hawking, the famous physicist with Lou Gehrig's disease. Plus, he was almost that hard to understand. I thought more than once of getting him a voice synthesizer like the one Hawking had to use to communicate, but I wasn't sure he'd like the gag—or if the computer would be advanced enough to interpret Whisper's murmurings. The pitchers all suspected he exaggerated the whole thing, because he knew his soft mumbles would force you to try harder to listen.

Anyway, during this session, he insisted I had changed my delivery. He said my arm was dropping down too fast. That would alter the trajectory of my throws, flattening them out and making the pitches easier for the batters to see and hit.

Of course, since I already knew everything there was to know about pitching, I knew he was wrong.

"That's bullshit Whisper," I said. "I don't know what you think you're seeing. I've had the same motion since college."

Saying nothing, he shrugged his shoulder and twitched his index finger in the universal "come here" motion. Then he demonstrated what I was doing versus what he thought I should be doing.

"If you haven't changed, well now, let's just consider what that means. And here's what that means," Whisper said in his soft drawl. As usual, I had to turn an ear toward him to interpret. "It means that anyone using a motion this fucked up for that long, they'd be ridin' the bus in the Nowhere, Idaho, Almost Made It League instead of bein' fortunate 'nuff to be standin' here talkin' to me in the Big Show with the Big Dough."

If you didn't listen to him, you were always a candidate for the "Almost Made It League" in some remote place—like Idaho, where I came from. I pondered this, but I conceded nothing with my body language. Pride and conceit are amazing things.

He glanced at my buddy, Justin Campanelli, who was laughing as he stood next to the stands. Justin was staring at something on his iPhone, probably a cat video, along with several teammates. Whisper made a waving motion with his right hand for Justin to join our little party.

"Campanelli," he said. "I need you to do somethin' useful with that damn phone for a change. Mistuh Van Oh-Mann is bein' bullheaded."

He always thought it was funny to pronounce my last name as Oh-Mann, as in "Oh man, you best listen to me."

"Sure Whisper," Justin said. "You know me. Always glad to help. Especially if it annoys Trey."

"Trey Van Oh-Mann, of the Idaho Almost Made It League, is gonna throw his fastball and you're gonna record it and play it back for us. This will be a lot quicker than me takin' him inside to see the same thing I saw earlier in high definition. Can you do that, or are you too busy?"

"Just call me George Goddam Lucas. I'm the director you're looking for. Could be my second career."

Well, Whisper proved his point and fixed my delivery in a matter of minutes and the other players got a kick out of watching him find the flaw in the Cubs' star pitcher; something I would have caught myself if I hadn't been too arrogant and maybe too distracted to study video of my last outing. He had caught me taking for granted that making the big leagues wasn't the same as staying in the big leagues.

I noticed a weird little grin on Whisper's face as he walked away toward the dugout and he pointed quickly at the manager. Alvarez nodded back. I can't prove it, but I think Whisper also saw it as an opportunity to connect me with my teammates again. Maybe he was a brilliant psychologist, too. Nothing about that guy would surprise me.

The other thing the players must have liked was that I had 100 percent abandoned social media, which never appealed much to me anyway, and was refusing to answer any questions related to politics.

It wasn't easy. After Bob Walters' story ran, I was peppered with questions along the lines of, "Have you talked to the president, Trey?" I no-commented them all.

I had sort of talked to Murphy in the manner of most communication these days. He had texted me: ROOTING FOR YOU GUYS! REMEMBER CUB WINS = HAPPY POTUS. NO PRESSURE ☺

The reality was that both the Cubs and St. Louis were stumbling toward the post-season more than taking control. The division title and a possible bye in the first round of the playoffs could be decided on the last day with me pitching against Milwaukee and St. Louis facing Pittsburgh. After being three behind with five games left, we won one game of our next two while the Cards lost both, so now we were two behind with three left.

We would finish in Milwaukee for the last three games. Milwaukee was barely a road trip for Cub fans who lived in northern Illinois, so it would be like a home game for us. And it was close enough to Chicago that WCO, even on their skinflint budget, decided to send Bob, Aimee and Mike Surrey to broadcast live from a nearby bar where Chicago fans gathered when the Cubs played at Miller Park.

Whisper had kicked me when I needed it. I made a silent pledge that fixing my pitching problem would be my sole priority before the biggest game of the season. I had no idea what was about to unfold.

43

Springfield, Illinois
The First Week Of October

Charley Rayburn shook his head as he tapped and scrolled through a story from the New York Times, resisting the temptation to throw his phone against the wall.

"How about some good news?" he said aloud, then heard a tell-tale beep. He realized he had mindlessly pushed the button on the phone so that Siri, the digital assistant on an iPhone, could hear.

"Here's some news for good. Take a look," Siri said, and she promptly scrolled up a list of seemingly random headlines containing the word "good."

Since Siri certainly knew more about Rayburn's Web interests than Rayburn knew about himself—a weird thought to contemplate at another time—the headlines actually weren't random. Rayburn noticed that most of the headlines were related to politics and the military.

The first headline was this, "Campaign sources: 'Good chance' Murphy won't survive until Election Day."

Rayburn winced. Then he conceded defeat to the moment. The gallows irony of that being the first "good news" headline made him laugh. It was the best laugh he'd had in several days. But he couldn't laugh long as he reviewed the campaign's circumstances.

Election Day was less than a month away. Murphy was slipping in the polls, in third place with Nicks and Leeds in a dead heat. It was a close third, within the margin of error, but nobody put asterisks in headlines.

Media questions about Murphy's health were getting more pointed and skeptical. Violence kept escalating overseas. A domestic jihadist had just walked into a shopping mall in Wausau, Wisconsin, wearing a suicide vest. For an unknown reason, only part of the vest detonated, limiting the carnage, but 10 people in the blast zone died. The whole country remained on edge at high alert.

He knew that Luke would have to make some type of public appearance soon to satisfy the public that he was recovering and capable of carrying out his duties.

Right now, that would be a lie.

"They think it might be sepsis," he said to Alison Murphy as they walked down the corridor to Murphy's hospital suite.

"That sounds bad," she said.

Rayburn thought she looked terrible—almost as bad as Luke. While Alison didn't appear intoxicated, she seemed spent, like a partially deflated balloon that needed more air to firm up. Alison Murphy was smart, sensitive, savvy and sexy, and she knew exactly how to show any or all of that without flaunting. Rayburn had quickly learned that it never hurt to have her walk next to the president in public settings, especially on days with big messes to clean up.

Today wasn't such a day. Her cheeks were sunken and it was obvious her makeup had been applied haphazardly again. She had been chewing on her fingernails with little effort to cover it up. Her hair was tied back loosely instead of being pulled tight. Rayburn prayed that no one in the media swarm would be in position to snap a photo today.

She detected Rayburn's scrutiny, glancing downward but saying nothing. Silence filled the room.

"No sugar-coating the seriousness here. Most people get over it, but sepsis can be really bad," Rayburn finally said. "Here, you should take a look at this."

He handed her a printout from the Mayo Clinic website:

> Sepsis is a potentially life-threatening complication of an infection. Sepsis occurs when chemicals released into the bloodstream to fight the infection trigger inflammatory responses throughout the body. This inflammation can trigger a cascade of changes that can damage multiple organ systems, causing them to fail.
>
> If sepsis progresses to septic shock, blood pressure drops dramatically, which may lead to death.
>
> Anyone can develop sepsis, but it's most common and most dangerous in older adults or those with weakened immune systems. Early treatment of sepsis, usually with antibiotics and large amounts of intravenous fluids, improves chances for survival.

"Jesus," Alison said as she skimmed the description. "They kept saying he should start feeling a little better, but he has a fever. He's struggling to breathe. The doctors were saying he's not peeing, even with all the fluids they're pumping in him."

"That's a reason they think he has sepsis," Rayburn said. "He's in decent shape for a guy his age, but, you know, there are never any guarantees."

"So," she said, turning to Rayburn and looking directly at him. "What are you going to tell the public? Have you even told the Veep? Campbell deserves to know."

"The answers are 'I don't know' to the first and 'no, not yet' to the second," Rayburn said. "We both know Pete Campbell's limitations and his tendencies."

The reality, as they both knew, was that Murphy and Campbell barely spoke to each other. Campbell had been a purely political pick four years ago, a hard-core, conservative activist from a swing state, North Carolina, that Murphy needed to win.

Under Campbell's watch as North Carolina governor, the Legislature had starved funding for public education, made it harder for poor people to vote or get affordable medical care but made it easier to drill for oil, wear a gun anywhere and stop an abortion. To many of the voters Murphy needed, Campbell was a hero. Rayburn couldn't escape the suspicion that Campbell would prefer life as Lydia Nicks' vice presidential candidate.

They walked into the president's room and were surprised to see him on the phone. Murphy looked ashen and they couldn't understand his words as he was speaking almost in a whisper.

As he noticed Rayburn and his wife walk in, he put his index finger in front of his lips in the universal sign for them to be quiet.

"Yes," they heard him. "Yes. I appreciate that. You be well and thank you for taking my call."

"Luke. Mr. President," Rayburn said as soon as Murphy ended the call. "You should be resting. Give those antibiotics they're pumping into you a chance to work. What was that call all about, if you don't mind my asking?"

"Very interesting," Murphy said in a weak voice, pumping the button for the morphine drip and obviously feeling the effects of all the meds storming through his damaged body.

"Interesting. What's that mean?" Alison said, using a sharper tone than she intended.

He looked up at both of them.

"Kevin," he said. "I was talkin' to Kevin. Long overdue."

Alison spoke first. "Kevin? Who's Kevin?"

Luke said, "So sorry, Alison. Know it hurts you. Kevin Knight. My college friend. Guess I'm making amends for being a jerk, eh?"

The subtle barb hit Alison hard. "Making amends" was one of the key steps in the Alcoholics Anonymous program as the alcoholics coped with the impact of their drinking by apologizing to everyone they had affected.

Whether Luke meant to send a message or not, she was surprised that the remark jolted her so much. She resolved to read more of the material Walters had e-mailed her. It didn't seem possible to be unhappier than she was at this moment.

Luke spoke again. "It's all about amends." He paused, then continued. "I need you two to make sure I get better," he said, then grimaced from a burst of pain or fever. A tear rolled down his left cheek and made a silent splatter on some of his bandages. "Charley, Kevin has me thinking about some things. Come over here. I wrote something down that you need to make happen."

Rayburn walked next to the bed. He saw that Luke had scribbled a few words on the back of the hospital's meal menu. It said:

must be 100% off the books
Need Everything we have on
Meg Williamson, Taylor Pierce
+ Any major political enemies in Madison Wis
EVERYTHING!

Rayburn stared at the paper and turned back to Murphy, no longer looking at him as the president or someone he was serving as a paid consultant. He didn't have many close friends and he wanted to help this one.

"I don't get it," Rayburn said. "What do these two have to do with each other? What's with the political enemies?"

"Don't know yet," Murphy replied, sounding weaker. "You'll get an email that will start you on tracking Pierce and you're going to want to get some security cam footage from a hotel in Madison. Will explain after I get some rest. Also, almost forgot, when I'm up to it, get Bobby back here. Bobby Walters."

Murphy was nodding off. Then the blood pressure monitor set off an alert as his BP started spiking, causing the medical team to come rushing in.

A few minutes later, the doctor looked at Alison Murphy.

"He's close to slipping into a coma if he hasn't already," he said, then realized his bedside manner had been too abrupt. He put a hand on her shoulder.

"Look, this isn't hopeless," he said. "But, it's going to be touch-and-go for a while. Sepsis following gunshot wounds can be a challenge. We have the best doctors in the world on the case."

Rayburn knew there was no way to keep the seriousness of Murphy's condition a secret any longer. They'd have to go public, filled with encouraging words about his "likely eventual recovery," while they quietly pursued Luke's weird request.

44

Mount Prospect, Illinois
A Few Minutes Earlier

Kevin Knight tapped "end call," took a long pull on his vodka-and-soda and quietly uttered an expletive to himself. Once again, he had been dragged into the role of an unwilling actor in the drama of Luke Murphy's life. He tapped on the patio door to get his wife's attention in the kitchen and he motioned for her to walk outside and join him.

"You won't believe who I just talked to," he said to Cheryl as they both stood on the deck, oblivious to the Midwest chill in the air. It was the place where they always went to talk, a habit formed when their kids were younger and needed to be out of range when serious matters required discussion.

Cheryl Knight looked at him with a quizzical expression and a spouse's insight. She wasn't sure who had called, but she was confident she knew what it was about.

She said, "It's not another reporter? Not another question about that Taylor Pierce woman and you being in her damn notebooks?"

"Bigger than that," he said. "It was Luke. Luke Murphy. The president of the United States called to pick my brain."

That brought a pause. Finally, Cheryl said, "And did you politely tell him to screw himself for everything he did to drag you into this huge distraction and the intrusions on our family?"

He said, "Well, actually, you just told me the other day that our business is up with all the attention, so I guess we'll survive."

She said, "You know that's not what I meant."

He said, "I know. You're right. Bad joke, though it's true enough. I thought about saying exactly what you just said, but I couldn't do it. Couldn't tell him to buzz off. He was sort of working me. And, I could tell he was working me. He's still Luke. I even said, 'Hey, I know when I'm being worked,' and we both laughed about it. But I tried to help him out. Guess I'm too nice a guy."

"Well, we already knew that," Cheryl said. "It's your endearing flaw. So, what exactly did you tell him?"

***

Kevin Knight had inadvertently seeded the clouds for a huge storm months earlier in a Madison, Wisconsin, hotel bar; all because he had talked to someone he thought was a friendly fellow traveler.

He was excited about the business trip. It looked like a chance to land a big contract at a major university for a "green" solar demonstration project. He'd appreciated the anonymous tip "from a friend in the business" that the bids were going out, particularly since Wisconsin was one of his target markets. So far, they had minor footholds in Beloit, Janesville and Kenosha, but they needed clients in the big cities of Madison or Milwaukee. This project could get major attention. It could make "Knight Solar LLC" a national player.

He had bet everything on the business 10 years earlier, leaving an engineering job with General Electric with an all-but-assured path to stock options and a great retirement package. He was burned out by corporate life; weary of working for others and seeing a huge opportunity in green energy. "How often do you have a chance to be personally successful and do the right thing all at once?" he said to Cheryl during their first discussion.

Knight found a company that could manufacture solar panels that were a few percent more efficient based on his patent. That was a huge in an industry where incremental gains meant the difference between profit and loss. However, he had to spend $50,000 in legal fees to convince GE that he hadn't done the science on their time and was entitled to the patent, finally settling so that GE took a 10 percent stake in the business. There was an upside. Having GE as a partner gave him credibility.

Cheryl left her job as the chief business officer for their local school district in the Chicago suburb of Mount Prospect. Their oldest son, Kyle, had a marketing degree from Northwestern and made the leap with them. Then Knight's brother Troy, a construction foreman, came in for a percentage to supervise the work crews. They were off to a good start.

When Knight got to Madison, the initial meeting with the University of Wisconsin officials went well. He reviewed his ideas on meeting the bid specifications for a state-of-the-art solar farm on university farm property and offered some suggestions on how to make the footprint more compact and efficient by using his technology.

That night, he ordered a beer in the bar at the Isthmus Hotel downtown and struck up a conversation with "Bob," who introduced himself as a sales rep for a medical supply company. Bob said he was in town to finalize a contract with a large hospital group. He wouldn't say which one.

One drink led to another and they started sharing their life stories, including an exchange of college experiences. Both men were about the same age. They pulled out their phones and showed "Throwback Thursday" photos of themselves in long hair, looking wasted in 1970s college dorm rooms.

"Course, I never inhaled," Knight said.

"Yeah. Me neither," Bob replied. "But I could roll a joint with one hand. Only for others."

Both men laughed loudly enough that others in the bar looked up. Knight pantomimed passing a marijuana joint on a roach clip to his new barroom buddy and they both snickered.

Bob ordered a round of tequila shots, lemons and salt—another salute to the campus days. Each man went through the necessary ritual of licking salt from the top of the hand, taking a slug of tequila and enjoying the tart spurt of lemon juice from the wedge.

"So," Bob said shortly before 12:30 a.m. "What's something really crazy about your life that would shock me?"

"Hmm," Knight replied. "I've got a good one for you. I went to college with the damn president of these United States."

"No shit?"

"No shit," Knight said. "I knew Luke Murphy when he was just another hippie wanna-be at Illinois State. Peace and love would change the world, right? Guess that didn't work out the way we planned."

"Murphy?" Bob replied. "You mean Luke Murphy the war hero?"

"Oh yeah, but I don't think he ever really bought in. I mean, yeah, he saw the world as messed up, but his answers were different. Maybe he was right."

Bob said, "But he smoked pot, dropped acid and stuff? That's rich."

Knight said, "Yeah, some. He did some other things, too, but it'd be violating a confidence for me to talk about. Plus, shit, I wasn't actually there for some of what I heard about. We lost track of each other later, though I liked the guy. More him than me I guess. Whatever."

For the moment, Bob backed off. "Okay," he said. "I get that. Let's have another round."

When the next round came, Bob quickly poured his tequila into an empty water glass when Knight looked away, then acted like he was finishing the drink when Knight looked back. Thirty minutes and two more "tequila rounds" later, the stories came easier. Kevin Knight told Bob about another college friend, Andy Pierce, and what Andy told him about dropping acid with Luke Murphy. He concluded his recollections of Luke Murphy by sharing the odd conversation he had with Murphy about

Andy Pierce during the college reunion. Then he described how he had stayed in touch with Andy.

"But I guess you didn't stay in touch much with Murphy after college?" Bob asked after offering appropriate "holy shit" comments to key moments in the story. "This Taylor girl, that's maybe the saddest part of all. Wow. Do you know how she's doing?"

"Me and Luke, like I said, not so much," Knight said "But, yeah, Andy and I always stayed close. Shit, he was one of my best friends. I don't forgive what he did to his family, but you still must be a friend to your friends, right? Taylor's had some bumps. I think she's still around Chicago."

Knight was fading now. He yawned, then jerked himself back into a spurt of awareness as he reflected on the past. Between the alcohol, the late hour and the emotion of pulling out memories around the death of a friend, Bob saw tears form on Knight's cheeks.

"Sorry 'bout that," Knight said. "You can see that story doesn't have a happy ending. Actually I try not to think about it too much. Hey, I need to crash."

Bob didn't say it aloud, of course, but he thought that ending would be quite happy for his unknown client. As an experienced private detective and political operative, he also planned to charge a sweet $20,000 extra when he provided "bonus information" on the whereabouts of Andy's daughter, who would be easy enough to locate. He was confident the client would be extremely interested.

***

When Taylor Pierce's diary hit the news and media inquiries began inundating the Knights, Kevin thought about that night in the bar. Some of the memories were hazy, but he realized things didn't fit. Random, friendly business encounters in hotel bars inevitably led to at least an exchange of business cards or, nowadays, texting each other your contact information. None of that happened with Bob. And, as best he could remember, he had told Bob a lot more about himself than Bob had shared.

Knowing he could be naïve about politics as well as friendship, Kevin Knight couldn't escape a feeling that he had helped set things in motion. It bothered him. Luke Murphy might be an asshole in some ways, but, as far as he could tell, Luke wasn't a crook and he seemed to be a decent president. And they had been friends. Luke didn't deserve to have his college secrets exposed.

***

For Cheryl's benefit, he described Murphy's call and how he told the president about the guy he now called "Fake Bob."

Murphy had started the conversation like this, "Kevin, first, I'm sorry, really sorry, for the mess this has caused for you and your family. I'm trying to understand what's been happening. I actually have some time on my hands on this hospital bed while Campbell is running the country."

"Well, thanks, Mr. President," Knight said.

"Jesus, call me Luke. This is unofficial." Murphy hesitated at that point and then decided to be direct instead of manipulative. "I have two reasons for calling. One is to reconnect and say I'm really sorry. The other is to, well, fact-find. I've got to figure out what's behind all this and what to do about it if I have any chance of serving another term."

"Okay, Luke," Knight said with a slight chuckle. "You're working me a bit, but that's okay. I still voted for you, by the way. Andy, you and I were pretty close for a while. Everything changed later."

"We both know why," Murphy said. "I'll just say it. You probably knew something about me that was going to get in the way of my naked ambition. Best, I thought, to keep my distance from both you and Andy. My motives weren't pure when I asked you at the reunion what happened to Andy."

"It would've meant a lot to him to talk to you," Knight said.

"What happened at ISU was a major moment in his life and later for his family. Andy told me about it shortly after he was diagnosed. I think he felt the need to confess. Taylor spent a lot of time with him, too, at the end."

"What happened to her?" Murphy asked after a long a pause in which he let regret flow a bit. Knight recalled that the answer to that question was of great interest to "Bob" as well.

"She was still hanging around Chicago, working in some kind of I.T. job, then I sort of lost track."

Then Knight remembered a detail of something that happened after his drunken conversation with Bob.

He said, "Luke, I do recall getting a call from her that she was excited about a job opportunity in Madison. Just wanted me to know she was on a good path. And for some reason I remember she said she was using a friend's phone, because the battery was dead on hers."

"Can you pinpoint the time and place?" Murphy said. Taylor Pierce had been sought by both authorities and political operatives, but a quick phone call from someone else's phone would have escaped notice. "No one has been able to find her. Might help."

"Maybe. I'll check. Just tell me how to forward it," Knight said. "There's something else that's funny about it, probably just a coincidence."

Before continuing, Murphy texted private email addresses to Knight for "CharlesR" and "Beckert."

"Use these to reach me," Murphy said, slurring the words a bit, causing Knight to guess the president was medicated and in some pain. "What're you saying is this other funny thing?"

Knight said, "Are you okay? I can tell you're hurting, Luke. Do you want to finish this call another time? I don't want to be responsible for a presidential setback."

Murphy chuckled. He sounded tired but focused. "No, let's soldier on. Really, what were you going to say?"

"Well, I'm ashamed to say this, I really am. But, some months ago, I told the whole story about you, me and Andy to a guy I met in a bar in Madison. We got drunk, but that's no excuse. Well, at least he got me drunk. He might've been faking. I think I might be the one that started this mess for you. I think he was playing me and did something with that information."

"Shit," Murphy said. "That might explain a lot. Send me everything you can about where you were and when you were there with this guy."

Murphy hesitated. Knight heard him cough lightly and then issue a grunt of pain.

"It was the old Isthmus Hotel downtown," Knight said. "I'll send you the times and dates."

"Thank you," Murphy said before launching into a thinking-out-loud stream of observations. He sounded increasingly weary. "I've got to figure out what connections I have in Madison. I think an old childhood friend teaches at the university there. Lost touch with her. I have political buddies there, too, and the usual assortment of people who hate my guts, not to mention it's home state of Lydia's."

Knight was ready to end the call but Murphy, despite his obvious fatigue, wasn't.

"Hey, Kevin, one more thing before we hang up."

"Sure, what's that?"

"Do you go to church?"

"We do. Prospect United Methodist."

"Let's say the Lord's Prayer together. Let's say it for the Pierce family. You don't owe 'em, but I sure do."

45

Springfield Memorial Hospital
Two Days Later

"He's feeling better," Rayburn said to Alison Murphy as they walked down the corridor to Luke's hospital room. "Still a long way to go, but we think we can airlift him back to Washington tonight. We won't tell the media we're leaving until the last minute to avoid a feeding frenzy. We need to get the reins of the government back."

"That's good, Charley," she said in a distant voice, as though she was navigating through out-of-body detachment. "What's in the folder?" she added with a faint smile, pointing an index finger at the thick manila envelope under his arm.

Before answering, Rayburn tried to sniff the air without her knowing. If she had been drinking, telltale signs of alcohol weren't obvious.

"Busted, Colonel," she said, staying in her monotone. "No, I haven't been drinking. Can't say I'm sleeping well. Been doing some reading, talking to Bobby Walters of all people the last couple nights. Staying off the Internet and avoiding the news so I don't have a relapse. And, before you ask, my plans still haven't changed for after the election. Now, tell me what's under your arm."

"That's great, Alison. I hope you know that we're all rooting for you," he said before pointing to the folder and answering her question. "This is the stuff that Luke wants to talk to us about. We're going to get Bob on a secure video line from Milwaukee."

As they entered the room, they heard Luke yell, "Campanelli, you rock."

He looked up at his guests. "Cubs 4, Brewers 3. St. Louis is losing. Tomorrow's an off day. If they win on the last day of the season, they're in the playoffs. If they lose, they go home for the winter. And Trey's pitching."

"Have you seen the latest polls?" Rayburn asked.

"Oh, yeah," Murphy said. "Vegas has the Cubbies as 5-4 favorites to win the World Series."

"Ha-ha," Rayburn said. "You know what polls I'm talking about. We need to get you on your feet."

"Yeah, I know," Murphy said. "I was thinking maybe Alison and I could say something from Walter Reed when we get back to D.C. That would play well." He looked at his wife. "If you're up to it, of course."

"Sure Luke," she said. "We can do that."

The polls were grim. Leeds was rebounding and, in the inexorable math of the Electoral College, it didn't matter if Murphy got the most total votes.

"Leeds just needs enough votes to win in the states the Democrats usually win along with a few more where you're damaged. And they can both exploit your health," Rayburn said.

"But Nicks isn't getting any traction," Alison Murphy said in her same flat tone.

"I agree. She's still feeling the heat from the Van Ohmann steroid mess," Luke Murphy said. "But she still can hurt us."

Nicks, Fox and everyone else associated with her campaign repeatedly denied instigating it. Problem was, no one believed them. Rumors were rampant that Fox would take the blame and resign.

"I've known Reggie Fox for years and can't believe he would do something that underhanded and stupid," Luke Murphy said. "He's tough, but he's a real pro. It'll destroy his consulting business unless he starts representing Russian moguls and Third World dictators, which I guess you can't rule out."

"Maybe he's smarter than you think," Rayburn said. "It won't stop him from getting a six-figure gig on Fox News without the pressure of actually having to accomplish anything. Whether they actually did this really doesn't matter at this point. It's politics. The only truth is that perception trumps truth."

Both Murphys nodded. On that subject, they were united as a couple.

They knew Nicks could win several states as the darling of evangelical conservatives. Murphy recounted how Ross Perot's third-party challenge gave the presidency to Bill Clinton over the first George Bush. He needed a breakthrough. He turned and faced Rayburn.

"Charley, you're my friend and my campaign manager. You're going to need deniability on this one. So, connect us with Bob. Then, I'm ordering you to leave that folder and leave the room."

Rayburn made an untraceable video call to Walters, looked at Murphy, realized any protests to stay in the room wouldn't work and left as soon as Walters answered.

"It's like old times Bob. I need your help," Murphy said. "I'm not sure why yet, but we need to talk to Meg Williamson. You and Alison are the two people who can help me figure out what to do next. This is delicate."

With the mention of Williamson's name, Alison Murphy looked up as she skimmed through the material in the folder. Back when they shared far more with one another—though she knew now that Luke held a lot back—he had talked often about Meg, who was never a girlfriend but a girl who was a true friend when he was growing up in Palatine.

The last time Luke had seen Meg was at their high school graduation. She clearly had no interest in returning to the suburbs. Alison recalled Luke saying that he thought she had made a life for herself in Madison as a college professor.

Murphy recounted his conversation with Kevin Knight for Walters' benefit.

"That's wild, Luke," Walters said. "I was a decent reporter in my newspaper days, but I'm not connecting all these Madison dots."

"You need to see this," Murphy said.

Murphy was using an iPad for the video call. He took out his smartphone, started a video and held the screen to the iPad camera so that Walters could see what was playing.

It was obviously a security camera video of two women in a coffee shop. One woman had a croissant; the other a bagel. The images were hazy but the older woman, the one wearing a long print dress and thick gray hair tied back in a ponytail, looked familiar.

Walters said, "Luke, is that who I think it is?"

"Yeah."

"It's Meg."

"Yeah."

"Who's that with her?"

"We think it's Taylor Pierce."

"Shit."

"Yeah. Shit."

"But why? What are they doing together?"

"Hold on before I answer that."

Murphy teed up another video. Again, it was a blurry security video that showed two men sitting in a bar, slapping each other on the back and drinking shots of a clear liquid that likely was tequila since there were lemons and salt shakers on the table.

Walters said, "I don't know either of these guys, but I'm going to guess one of them is Kevin Knight. The guy on the right looks like him from the pictures I saw of him when the Taylor story broke."

Murphy said, "Exactly right. And the other guy is the alleged medical supply salesman named Bob. It confirms everything Kevin told me."

"So, what's it all mean?"

"That's what Alison is reading now, too. Let's say we found the resources to do a lot of digital digging and fact-checking."

"And I assume you're not telling this to me as a member of the media?"

"I'm telling you as my oldest friend. If it turns out to be a story later, you'll have it, but not yet," Murphy said.

Walters said, "I'll be so compromised that I can't be the one to break it."

Murphy said, "Bob, you're not bound by that journalists' code of ethics you used to talk so much about. You're an advocate now. You do it on the radio. I do it as a politician. I only ask that we worry about that later."

Walters thought about that and conceded. "Okay, tell me more."

Murphy then described what Rayburn's team had accomplished. Once they knew about "Fake Bob," it wasn't difficult to track him down in the Isthmus Hotel's vulnerable reservation system. "Bob" turned out to be Gavin Yost, a high-priced private investigator who specialized in political operations.

Yost's computer was more secure than the hotel's, but it yielded eventually. They found three large deposits in his bank account during that period and phone records of likely conversations with potential clients. None of the records belonged to anyone they could connect with Reginald Fox or Lydia Nicks, which surprised them and dashed expectations.

Instead, Murphy explained, some calls traced to a person who puzzled them. Why would this person, a University of Wisconsin philosophy professor named Frank Pfeiffer, be talking to a private investigator who specialized in dark political operations?

"The answer shocked me. He's a friend of Meg Williamson's," Murphy said. "The dots connect. For some reason, a college professor connected to Meg was pulling strings."

"I'm rarely speechless, but this time I am," Walters said.

Alison spoke for the first time in several minutes, still in her flat, matter-of-fact voice.

"Luke, this is all interesting and I'd like to see you win, but why I am in this room?" she said.

"Because I owe you that," he said. "I don't expect your forgiveness for living a lie, but there can't be any more secrets on the things I've done or plan to do that affect you. I also value your opinion on what I think we need to do."

"And what's that?" Walters asked.

Murphy said, "You're in Milwaukee, right? Tomorrow is an off day before the last game of the season?"

"Yeah."

"Maybe if Meg sees you of all people, we can find out what's going on," he said. "Maybe we find Taylor Pierce and we can figure out how to deal with that. Until we know the motivations here, whether it helps or hurts my campaign to be blunt, it's too risky to do anything but stay off the books."

Murphy added, "You could take Moose and Aimee with you if you want as long as they can keep this to themselves. That might mean something to Meg, especially to see Moose. They're both in Milwaukee with you, right?"

Walters said, "They are. My first reaction is that this is crazy. Luke, here we are again. It could blow back in a hundred bad ways."

"Do you have a better idea?" Murphy said. "What if Meg is helping Nicks? It could be criminal, maybe even treason, depending on how much she's been doing and how far it goes back."

There was silence as three people contemplated the choices. Then Alison Murphy spoke, looking up from the detailed reports she was reading.

"What if she's helping Leeds?" she said. "What if that's what it's all about? He might not even know."

The implication hit the three of them at once.

"Call it intuition. I think she's the one behind everything that's happened," Alison stated flatly. "We're just not sure why."

"What changed? We were childhood friends," Luke Murphy said. "Bob, I think you need to be really careful."

"I guess you've made a decision for me," he said. "Just like old times. You always were a persuasive SOB."

The call ended. Luke and Alison looked at one another with no need to speak.

They were united again, if only for the moment.

46

Trey Van Ohmann

Members of the Milwaukee Brewers marched to home plate one by one in my imagination as I sat in my hotel room, picking at a room-service breakfast of poached eggs and ham on our off day before the big game. I imagined exactly how I would grip every pitch in my arsenal, what delivery I would use and how to render each hitter helpless to my powers. Every pitch went exactly where I planned. I mentally went through the order, refreshing my memory on the strengths and weaknesses of each hitter I was likely to face.

Jaime Castrovenes, their big first baseman, would be the biggest problem. He looked fat and slow, but his wrists were quick. He hit 30 or more home runs every year and he had eye-hand coordination that made me think he had been sent to Venezuela on a rocket from Krypton. He was hitting about .800 against me. Well, that's a slight exaggeration, but the guy was one of the few hitters who always seemed to know exactly what I was going to do, no matter how much I tried to cross him up.

I decided on a George Costanza strategy, referring to an episode of "Seinfeld" in which Jerry's friend, George, succeeds by doing the opposite of what everyone expects. In baseball terms, that would mean throwing, say, a high-and-outside fastball in the circumstances in which such a pitch would be unusually dangerous.

I liked my plan quite a bit. Of course, for all I knew, Castrovenes was a fan of Spanish-language "Seinfeld," and was thinking what I was thinking. He was probably saying "él hará lo contrario" at that moment. Translation, "He will do the opposite." I'm telling you, this guy had an occupancy permit for my head.

The Brewers weren't having a good season, but they still were Major League players and they'd take great pride in beating us. Actually, this would be about more than pride. It always pissed them off when so many Cub fans made the short drive to Milwaukee to take over their stadium. That surely would be the case tomorrow for such a consequential game on national television. There's nothing they'd enjoy more than sending the cursed-but-lovable, media-darling Cubbies home for the winter as they ended their otherwise-forgettable season. If I were starting for Milwaukee, I'd pitch like it was Game Seven of the World Series, just to shut up the fans of Cubs Nation.

My advantage was that the rest of their lineup wasn't nearly as hard to fathom as Castrovenes. For example, Tommy Selma, the slim second baseman, was a good hitter, but I usually could fool him with slow change-ups that broke away from him.

DeAndre Williams, their catcher, was a guy with surprising bat speed who could adjust. However, he had developed a serious hole in his hitting zone, inside and down. Pitchers had an intelligence network that the CIA would appreciate and this was general knowledge, which was why DeAndre's batting average had dropped for three years in a row.

I mentally made it through the whole lineup, including most of their subs and even the abilities of their pitchers as batters. I felt better. I had a plan. Then Aimee called.

"Ready for me to come up?" she asked.

"Absolutely. I'm in Room 708."

She walked into my room looking great as always. We hugged. I noticed she was carrying her small backpack. We had made plans to go to the Milwaukee Art Museum. It was supposed to be a world-class gem with spectacular architecture that included a stunning pedestrian bridge leading from the lakefront to downtown. The visit also would serve a valuable purpose as a relaxing distraction from the next day's task. But I was startled by the serious expression on Aimee's face.

"Has anything else popped up on your schedule?" she asked.

"No. We're still supposed to have a late afternoon media availability," I said. "You knew that already."

I put air quotes around "media availability" and added an eye-roll at the same time; then continued.

"Other than that, we still have the day off. The manager says we could use the rest and if we don't know how to hit, pitch and field by now, it's too late."

"Good for him," Aimee said, then frowned. "As far as our plans for today, something came up."

"What's that?"

"Well, I'm going to Madison with my Dad and Moose," she said. "It's sort of a long story. I wouldn't be telling you, except that you need to know we can't get together. I hate cancelling a date, but you're on your own for the museum."

"Now I'm intrigued. It's not like you to keep secrets."

"Trey, trust me on this one. We should be back in time for the news conference. We need to be there. It's only about 80 miles each way. We should get there before 10:30 and be back on the road to Milwaukee by 1 p.m.; maybe earlier."

She paused, obviously deciding whether to say more. Then she continued, "If you really want to know, it's just a quick visit to a childhood friend of my Dad's, Moose's and Luke Murphy's who, uh, has some issues. It's kind of private."

I said, "So private you can't tell me? And what's the president have to do with it? This isn't like you and me."

Aimee sighed.

"Trey, look, I can't lie to you. There is more to it than that," she said, putting strong emphasis on the word "is." "It's complicated. I'll tell you more about it when I can. Right now, it would be a huge distraction for you and I can't promise we'll be back in time. You never know. It won't be the end of the world if most of the WCO team isn't at your press availability—we'll just get our asses chewed by the station manager. Besides,

Surrey will be there. But, what if you didn't show up? That's not good."

She was right. I needed to be there. As far as the baseball media was concerned, I was the current most-interesting-person-in-the-world. Failure to show up would be a far bigger story than any cliché I'd ever mouth at a press conference before a big game. More importantly, I really owed my teammates not to be a distraction again. They needed me at my best. Such obvious selfishness would raise questions in their minds about my commitment and affect our focus.

Besides, I trusted Aimee completely. She had been there for me at every moment in the past few months. Still, I had to add one other thing.

"Well, it'll also be a distraction to have you away on this mysterious trip," I said. "Make sure you keep your phone on. Call me when you're headed back."

I gave her a quick hug and smiled before continuing. "I'll just have to find some other attractive media personality to accompany me," I said. "Maybe I can give SportsCheese.com something new to say. I might even show the world that baseball players can appreciate French impressionists."

"I love you," she said. "And don't even think about finding a rebound date. Either go alone or take Campanelli with you."

"Now that would be something. He's a great friend, but I think he still has pictures of poker-playing dogs hanging in his condo," I said. "I love you, too."

47

Madison, Wisconsin | Late Morning

Skowron, Bob Walters and Aimee Walters didn't talk much as they drove on Interstate 94, which ran straight west from Milwaukee to Madison. Skowron drove in his Honda minivan, which held his wheelchair and had the special controls that allowed him to drive without using his feet. Their destination was Meg Williamson's home on Madison's near east side, about two miles from the state capitol building.

Finally, Aimee spoke up.

"So, what was Meg like as a kid? Why would she be involved in this somehow?"

"That's the mystery," Skowron replied. "We all kind of lost track of each other as the years went by. I still feel guilty in some ways for being such a bully to her. And Bob, I could have been less of a jerk to you and Luke, too."

"Water over the dam Moose," Bob Walters said. "Nothing to even talk about. At least your jerk time came as a kid. Mine came a lot later. We patched things up. I've learned a lot more from you than you've ever learned from me."

"It wasn't easy," Skowron said. "I had a lot of time to think going through rehab. I wasn't going to be the star quarterback. It was a big comedown and not much glory to becoming a star statistician. I definitely had no plans to ever connect with you after getting paralyzed by Luke's ice ball—even if I started it. Ugly memories for all of us, right? But it seems like we're destined to intertwine."

Walters said, "Aimee, to answer your question, Meg got more distant from us as we went through high school and then we lost track. We were polite and cordial enough to each other, but that was about it by senior year. Luke and I thought there was a lot going on in that house. Pretty nasty. Her Dad abused both her and her mom. It was as bad as you might imagine from what we saw him making Meg do one night. So, I wasn't surprised she left the 'burbs and never came back."

Walters hesitated for a moment as if a thought had just come to him. "You know, maybe we should've done more to try to help her. We knew she was hurting."

They continued in silence until they were about 15 minutes away.

"So, what's the plan?" Skowron asked.

"Now that we're closer, I'm thinking I can't believe we're doing this, but I guess we just knock on the door," Aimee said. "What else can we do? Maybe you should stay in the van Moose, just in case something weird happens. Don't know what that would be, but let's be safe."

"Let's get there, look at the house, and decide then whether to walk around a little bit or just go up to the door and knock," Walters said.

"Okay," Skowron said. "Just call us the WCO Strike Force. Go figure."

Skowron parked the van about half a block away from the tidy home on 230 E. Earl St., finding a spot that would allow him to watch the house the way he had seen police detectives observe in countless television dramas. The attractive neighborhood had homes from the early 20th Century along a narrow, tree-lined street. Several homes had peace signs in the windows and probably the majority of the driveways had election signs, many for local races. Probably half had signs that said "Leeds for America. Leeds for the Future," though Williamson's yard had no signs at all. Skowron noticed only one sign for Murphy on the street and none for Nicks. This was no surprise, as Madison was legendary as a bastion of progressive politics. A Lydia Nicks supporter would be lonely on Madison's east side.

As Bob and Aimee Walters exited the van, a light, cool October rain fell, just enough to create a damp chill; not enough to require an umbrella. It was a sign of winter that was sure to arrive soon in central Wisconsin.

"Be well," Skowron said. "I'm watching and waiting. Maybe I can get some work done on some stats for both your shows tomorrow."

He reached down between the seats and pulled out his laptop, wishing more than usual that his legs were working and wondering if he could ever find a woman like Aimee Walters. He envied Trey Van Ohmann for both reasons. Well, he wasn't going to give up the dream of walking someday. He pushed regrets and jealousies aside and booted up the computer, using his phone as a wireless hotspot. When he examined the Wi-Fi on his phone, a list of all the networks in the area quickly populated. It was a long list, which he would expect in a compact residential neighborhood in a university town filled with professional people.

The usual names of networks appeared—slang for pets and sports teams and such: BadgerFan1008, KrazyKat, MadCityMomma, GoPackersForever. Or, there were boring names like addresses or brands from cable and router companies that owners hadn't bothered to alter: 205EarlSt, Linksys1001, 2Wire447. But one caught his eye. GetAllInAllignment.

The network name sounded like something invented by an aging hippie. Skowron liked puzzles. Maybe that's what this was. He wrote down the four capital letters. They spelled a word, "GAIA," that seemed vaguely familiar.

He went to Wikipedia and learned more. Gaia was an ancient Greek God who symbolized the entire Earth. This had evolved into the "Gaia hypothesis, theory or principle." According to Wikipedia, the concept was that " … organisms interact with their inorganic surroundings on Earth to form a synergistic self-regulating complex system that helps to maintain and perpetuate the conditions for life on the planet." In other words, everything on the planet was somehow connected.

Many discounted the Gaia idea as a weird application of spiritual mumbo-jumbo to hard science, even though it was developed by a chemist and a micro-biologist. But yet, scientists had found evidence of fascinating relevance in many areas, including earth science, systems ecology and geology. Skowron noted that Williamson was a geologist and they knew Pfeiffer was a philosopher. Interesting.

The extreme believers thought that all organisms on Earth were linked aspects of one planetary being through biochemical and geologic processes humans only have a vague start on understanding. This presence, called "Gaia," reacts through the diversity and evolution of individual organisms. The Earth itself was some sort of living being.

"Get All In Alignment" neatly summarized the Gaia philosophy in four words. Skowron wondered if that was the Wi-Fi signal coming from Williamson's home. Another Internet search told him how to pinpoint a router signal. He narrowed the signal to three houses, with Williamson's house the most likely source. He also learned that the "GetAllInAlignment" network was unusually well secured for a residential network. It would take a dedicated, talented hacker a long time to figure it out.

Skowron had helped Walters gather talking points for the radio show on how the candidates stood on environmental issues. It occurred to him that if you believed in Gaia and believed that the environment had to be respected more harmoniously, Matthew Leeds would be the candidate you'd most likely want to elect.

He knew Leeds had made his reputation in Congress as a strong environmentalist—not that this was necessarily bad or evil by any stretch. The question was, how far and how fast should you go? Leeds didn't strike Skowron as a crazed zealot, but he made a strong case for short-term economic pain to achieve long-term environmental goals. And he believed climate change was settled science that demanded urgent attention.

Murphy, as usual, was in the middle. He often annoyed his fellow Republicans by acknowledging that climate change was happening and it was too risky to do nothing. Murphy admired how Germany had converted a large percentage of its energy use to "green" sources and kept trying to push Congress in that direction. But he also thought natural resources needed to be exploited for the good of humanity while better solutions were sought. He had worked tirelessly and personally to extract environmental concessions from the Chinese as well as debt relief in return for American grain as their drought intensified, often quoting the saying that no crisis should be wasted. But Murphy also had supported the Canadian oil pipeline through the central U.S., limited expansion of offshore drilling and a faster process to expedite use of nuclear power.

Meanwhile, Nicks wanted to eliminate the Environmental Protection Agency and leave most regulation to the states. She often said God put resources on Earth for humanity to appreciate but use as they needed. Where Leeds never saw an oil-drilling proposal he liked, she never saw one that was a bad idea with "adequate safeguards." She thought climate change was little more than a liberal hoax and probably part of a global conspiracy toward "one world" government and the loss of America's sovereignty. She argued that, at worst, climate changes were part of Earth's cycles that had little or nothing to do with human impact.

Skowron texted Bob Walters, "Will explain later: Meg might be an environmental peacenik. You'll probably get into nothing more than an argument with her whether Earth is alive. Seriously. She'll probably call it Gaia."

That didn't answer the larger question of what Meg was doing with Taylor Pierce or why her colleague hired someone to pump information from Kevin Knight. He guessed Meg Williamson was pretty messed up and probably needed some professional help, which wasn't a surprise if you knew about her childhood.

48

Madison, Wisconsin | Noon

Bob and Aimee remained uncertain of their next steps as they walked up to Meg Williamson's house. There were no cars in the driveway, which led to a garage behind the house. The garage door was closed. The neighborhood seemed eerily quiet as they looked around.

"It's really pretty here," Aimee said. "Look at these gorgeous, old trees. But where are the people?"

The trees showed vibrant fall colors, forming a canopy of reds, yellows and oranges over small but well-manicured lawns still showing green from late-fall rain. A few birds chirped. They heard someone's lawnmower in the distance. That was about it.

"It's a weekday," Bob said. "Kids are in school; people are at work. I imagine this is pretty typical for this time of year. Let's go up on the porch and see if we hear anything. If there's nobody home, we might have to go to campus to look for her. We knew that was a possibility. We've got that address, too."

"Well," Aimee said. "The quietness is an advantage. If there's anything to hear inside, we'll probably hear it."

There was a slight creak of the old steps as they walked up on the wooden porch, which was painted bright white with decorative touches of green. Flowers still bloomed along a beautifully manicured strip that framed the entire porch. A green-and-pink swing hung from the ceiling to their left. To their right was a screened area that had two rockers and a center table.

"That would be a really pleasant place for morning coffee. Maybe that's where she grades papers," Aimee said.

Bob lightly touched his daughter's shoulder just then and raised his left index finger to his lips in the universal sign to be quiet.

"I think I hear something," he said softly.

They both stood as still as they could, focused on voices that seemed to be coming from what might be a bedroom or a dining room window in the front of the house and to the right. The window was cracked open by about two inches.

"Where's Meg?" they heard a female voice say weakly, in the tone of a child.

"She'll be home soon," said a man. "Now, lay still, so I can fix you up here. You'll feel better in a minute. You shouldn't have gotten up. You're too weak."

"Where's Meg? Where's Meg? I need Meg."

"Lay down. I mean it," the man said in a sharper voice. "I don't want to hurt you with this. You pulled out your drip. We'll do it this way."

"Okay, okay," the female said, sounding pouty. They heard a sound of creaking springs, as though someone was getting in bed. There were random footsteps.

There was no sound for a minute or two. Bob and Aimee were starting to feel visible, standing on someone's porch eavesdropping in the middle of the day. Aimee mouthed the word "Taylor" at Bob and added a shrug so he could see it was a question. Bob shrugged back. There was no way to know yet.

Then, all of a sudden, they heard a large "ah."

Bob pointed to the door and made a motion of knocking, indicating he had decided they needed to talk to the person in there. Aimee was nodding in agreement when suddenly a man's voice shouted. They froze in place.

"What the hell," he said more loudly to the other person in the room. "Did you open this window? You can't be doing that. It's not safe for any of us."

Before they could react, the shade covering the window went up and they recognized Frank Pfeiffer staring at them as he was starting to close the window. Pfeiffer reversed course and pushed the window up. They heard another "ah" in the background before Pfeiffer said, "Who the hell are you people? What are you doing out there?"

Bob Walters was ready. "We just walked up!" he said in his perkiest, radio salesman voice. "I'm an old friend, from Palatine, outside Chicago, looking for Meg. I'm in Madison today and it would just be great to see her. We were really close friends back in the day. Oh, this is my daughter, Aimee."

"Hi," Aimee said. "Sorry to bother you. This means a lot to my Dad."

Pfeiffer eyed them suspiciously, obviously wondering what they had heard.

"You're an old friend? What's your name?" he asked.

"Bob. Bob Walters. She'll remember me."

Pfeiffer seemed to make a decision. He nodded his head affirmatively. "Yeah, she's mentioned you. You and the president, right? You guys grew up together."

"Exactly," Bob said. "Will she be home soon?"

"Soon," Pfeiffer said. "For sure. Hang on and I'll come around to the door."

The shade went down and the open window slammed shut, harder than necessary Aimee thought.

About two minutes later, though it seemed even longer, Pfeiffer opened the front door and motioned them in. "C'mon," he said. "Sorry it took so long. Had to make a pit stop. Let's go sit in the kitchen. We've got some tea, or I can make some coffee. It's chilly, eh?"

"Yeah," Bob said. "That would be great." He thought Pfeiffer looked really nervous.

"Call me Frank," Pfeiffer said, then continued, almost blurting out his words as though he felt an urgent need to answer possible questions in advance of them asking. "Meg and I are good friends. I help her out. Right now, I'm taking care of her sick niece. Maybe you heard her in there." He laughed slightly at that, but it sounded forced.

They entered the foyer. The door shut behind them.

Before opening the door, Frank Pfeiffer's "pit stop" had involved texting, not relieving himself. Meg was teaching a class and she couldn't leave. However, the students were taking a test, freeing her to text feverishly back and forth with Pfeiffer.

Her tone came through, even in texts, and it alarmed Pfeiffer. She obviously was surprised, puzzled and very concerned to learn Bob Walters was at her front door with his daughter. Meg said she couldn't get away from the university for at least another two hours without raising suspicions. But he had his instructions. These two wouldn't be going anywhere until she got here; that was for sure. Her last text definitely got his attention; "Biggest crisis we've faced. Don't F Up."

He did one other thing she reminded him to do before letting them in. Fortunately, they had already seen him wearing a green wool, zip-up sweater. The well-worn sweater, filled with fuzzy pile balls, was part of his uniform as the slightly whacky philosophy professor totally absorbed in a world few understood. They wouldn't see his concealed carry holster and the Glock 26 semi-automatic it held. Two years ago, Meg had insisted that he learn how to handle a gun. Just in case.

When they were both sitting in the kitchen, Meg and Bob could see Pfeiffer's hands were shaking. This was harder then he thought it would be. He had never shot at anything but cans or targets at the shooting range.

"What's wrong, Frank? You okay?" Bob asked.

Frank found his courage, particularly since he didn't think they were armed.

He reached into his holster and pulled out the Glock, pointing it at them. Aimee gasped, the fear of again being a prisoner bubbling up like an exploding well. Bob started to move from the table.

"Don't!" Pfeiffer said. "I mean it. I know how to use this. Shut up and listen."

He pointed at Aimee, waving the pistol at her. "You, get up and open that drawer."

She did.

"Now, take out that duct tape. Then open the cabinet under the sink and take out that rope."

She did again.

"Put the duct tape across your father's mouth and tie him to the chair."

"I suck at knots," she said.

"Did I tell you to talk!" Pfeiffer screamed. He knew he looked weak, which would give them added courage. If they both got up and charged, he wasn't sure he could shoot. He had to make a point to take control. He slapped Aimee as hard as he could across her face. She screamed in pain.

"The next time it'll be a bullet," he said. "Now do it. I'll check the knots after you're done and I tie you up."

Aimee could barely move. The scars a bullwhip had left on her back seemed to shriek along with the pain from the new bruise on her face. When she finished with her Dad, Pfeiffer told her to put duct tape across her own mouth, sit in the chair and use the duct tape to tie her feet together so that if she tried to get up, she'd fall over.

Aimee had no choice.

When that was done, it was easy for Pfeiffer to finish the job of securing both. Now it was matter of simply waiting for Meg. It was going to be complicated to figure out what to do next and they'd both have to work on that problem carefully. He'd spend the down time writing a list of everything they were going to have to deal with to preserve the mission. They didn't get this far by being sloppy. Then he remembered the open window in Taylor's room and cursed. He didn't realize the girl could still walk in her addicted fog. That was sloppy.

His first impression was that the best idea and safest course might be for these two to have an accident in their car. He realized he should've asked them how they got here. Well, the odds of anyone seeing anything unusual about whatever vehicle they had until Meg got here were nearly non-existent.

Down the street, Skowron had watched Bob and Aimee enter the house. He decided to give them 20 minutes. Then he'd text them with what would seem like an innocuous work question. They'd know he expected an answer and the text would provide a pretext that would raise no suspicions.

The problem was that if they didn't answer, he didn't know what he'd do.

Twenty minutes later, Skowron's fears came true. His texts went unanswered. He tried to call each of them, but achieved the same result.

49

Trey Van Ohmann

I tried going to the museum by myself but left after 40 minutes. Aimee's weird journey turned out to be too distracting; then I got more worried when she didn't respond to several texts and calls.

When my phone rang, I felt a wave of relief. It had to be Aimee. But it wasn't. To my surprise, Scott "Moose" Skowron from WCO was on the line.

"Moose, what's up?" I said. "I've been trying to reach Aimee."

"Trey, I am so, so sorry to get you into this, but I don't know who else to call. Aimee, Bob and I are doing sort of a personal favor for Luke. Luke Murphy. I know you care about Aimee and you're in Murphy's camp. I'm worried."

"I'm worried." Those words made it hard to breathe, but I managed to respond with two words, "Tell me."

"Look, if I tell you the whole story, it'll take too long. But she has been inside a house in Madison with her dad for a long time and I can't get them to respond," he said. "They went to see an old friend of Bob's."

None of this made sense. I said, "She basically told me that much. So, I don't get it. Why didn't you go in with them? Or, why don't you just go knock yourself if you're outside? I don't mean to be rude, but does it have something to do with your handicap?"

He said, "Well, not sure I could get up on that porch without some help, but that isn't it. I know this is crazy, but I need to know they're okay and I can't do that without help."

My practical side then briefly emerged, but I already knew I was headed to Madison. Still, I had to ask. "You know I have a so-called 'media availability' later today, right?"

"I wouldn't ask if I didn't think there might be danger to Aimee. Rent a car of something and get over here. I'll text you the address. And I'll call you back while you're driving and explain everything. That'll save time."

The obvious question was why not call the police, but Skowron wasn't stupid. There had to be a reason why that wasn't happening. And it involved Aimee. If everything worked out, I could always turn around and be back in plenty of time.

"Okay," I said. "There's a Hertz counter in the lobby. I'm on my way."

On the way down in the elevator, I texted Chuck Briggs, the team's director of media relations. "Chuck. Think I have 24-hour flu bug. Cover 4 me if don't make media avail. Should be okay to pitch." Oh, yeah. That would make his day. I also included Alvarez and Campanelli in the text so that my manager and best friend on the team wouldn't be caught by surprise. Campanelli would try to cover for me, too.

***

I was on the fringe of the Milwaukee suburbs when Skowron called and told me everything that had led to their visit to Meg Williamson's house. For me, any new insight the story offered into Luke Murphy's relations with his high school friends was far outweighed by worry over Aimee. Things still didn't make a lot of sense.

It was hard to concentrate on driving and I drove as fast as I could in the rented Malibu, which seemed to have a governor that stopped me from going over 85 mph. That probably was a good thing, because at some point I think they drag you to jail if you're too far over the speed limit and I was willing to set a record for the Milwaukee-to-Madison run. Don't forget, my dad was a race driver.

A trooper stopped me after I passed the exit for Delafield, for doing 83 in a 70 zone. I was in luck, though. He had grown up in Hoffman Estates, Ill., recognized my name and let me off with a stern cop-face and a warning ticket after I told him I was hustling to Madison and back to visit a sick relative who couldn't come to the game tomorrow.

"Go Cubbies," he wrote on the back of my warning ticket.

Following Moose's directions, I pulled onto Earl Street and slipped behind his parked minivan. I got out of the car and walked over. He powered down his driver's side window.

"Come in the van so we can talk. I still haven't seen or heard from them," he said, pointing to a house a few doors down on the right. "I need your legs Trey."

I got into the van on the passenger side and looked at Skowron. "What do you want me to do?"

"Walk up to the house, I guess. See if you hear anything. Decide whether to knock on the door. I'll watch for Meg Williamson. I don't think she's inside."

"Okay," I said. "I'm on my way."

I started to exit the van when we both heard the sounds of a car turning the corner.

"Wait," Skowron said. "Let's see if it's Meg."

It was. She was driving a brick-red Prius in need of a car wash. She pulled into the driveway, but she stopped next to the porch without going all the way to the garage. Although it's hard to tell with a quiet Prius, she appeared to leave the car running. When she got out, she moved quietly, taking delicate steps and making sure she closed the car door softly. We could see her holding a key ring in her hands. Instead of putting the keys in her pocket or a purse, she kept a tight grip on them.

Moose and I looked at each other, unsure of what was happening. Then she disappeared around the back of the house. Less than a minute later, she came around the corner, got back into the Prius, carefully closed the car door and backed away slowly, as though she again was trying to make as little noise as possible. Backing out into Earl Street, the car started to move away.

Moose surprised me and started the van. There weren't any cars parallel parked in front of him between his van and the front of Meg's house, so he quickly pulled forward and stopped behind her. He honked his horn, opened his window and waved his hand at her before holding his palm up, the sign he wanted her to stop.

I could see she was looking at both of us in her rearview mirror.

"Meg," he shouted, hoping the sound would carry through her open car window. "It's me. Moose. We need to talk to you. Hope everything is okay."

Instead, she made a different decision, ramming the gas pedal to the floor and speeding away.

"Trey, get out," Moose shouted. "Go ahead and check the house. I'm going to follow her."

I wasn't sure that was a good idea, but I did as I told. Moose was accelerating in pursuit before I even had a chance to slam the van door shut.

50

Trey Van Ohmann

It was getting darker as I nervously walked to the front of the house as the engine sounds of Moose's van faded into the distance. I shivered as heavy clouds seemed ready to convert chilly drizzle into harder rain.

I noticed that all the window shades were down and curtains were closed as I walked around the perimeter of the house to the rear, curious as to what Meg had been doing back there. Getting to the back yard eased my tension, because it was unlikely any of the neighbors would see me and wonder why someone was skulking around this pretty home.

I saw nothing out of the ordinary. Maybe Meg had gone in the garage, but the door was down and the side door was locked. Then I saw an exterior entrance to the basement, a pair of metal door panels mounted at a 45-degree angle that would open to reveal a stairway downstairs. But the panels were padlocked shut. I theorized that one of the keys on her ring would open that padlock, but I had neither the key nor the skills of a locksmith. Plus, it would make a lot of noise if I tried to do anything else, so I remained a shivering, nervous man without a plan.

I noticed some garden tools in a small bucket next to the back steps and more for the comfort of having something in my hand than any real thought of doing anything, I picked up a hand cultivator with four sharp prongs. It brought back a quick memory of teen years helping my Dad prepare his garden. I swear he took more pride in his tomatoes than the trophies he won racing cars.

Okay, I thought, *this is getting ridiculous*. My imagination was running wild as I stood in the back yard of someone I didn't know while armed with a garden tool. There had to be a reasonable explanation for why we hadn't heard from Aimee or Bob. Maybe the house was a dead zone for phone service, for example, although I had four solid bars outside.

If all else failed, I'd just knock on the door.

There really seemed to be no other choice. Still standing in the back yard, I saw what was most likely a kitchen window. The blinds were shut, but light leaked through the slats, something I wouldn't have been able to detect on a sunny day. I walked up to get closer to the window and heard music, some sort of classical concerto playing loudly.

There was a skinny gap between two of the window slats and I decided to risk taking a peek. That's when I saw two bare legs tied together with duct tape. I knew those legs quite well as well as the platform heels around those feet. They belonged to Aimee. For a moment, I had trouble breathing. Nothing in my life had prepared for this.

Then I heard words. A man yelled, "God dammit."

Did this guy know I was out there? I had done nothing to attract attention that I could figure. Then a loud pop of thunder caused me to reflexively look up and I saw my mistake. I saw the camera tucked into the top of the "V" where the sharply framed roof came together. No doubt there were cameras all over the place. Strike Three on me. Of course, they would have cameras.

I was performing live for Professor Pfeiffer. So much for playing the role of Trey Van Ohmann, amateur sleuth. Now I had to figure out what to do to get them out.

There was no time to call for help. I heard the back door open and saw the barrel of a gun.

Pfeiffer showed his face next. "You," he shouted looking directly at me, waving the pistol. His face was beet red, reminding me of how one of my uncles used to look when he didn't take his blood pressure medicine. He appeared to be under a lot of stress. This guy was about Bob Walters' age, too, and he looked like he was about 25 pounds overweight, but a flabby old guy with a gun is a hell of an equalizer against a younger guy holding a garden tool, even if he's a jock. This still made no sense, starting with the incongruous image of having your life threatened by an armed philosophy professor. Could either of us even prove this moment existed? Maybe he was one of the nihilists.

"Whoever the hell you are. You're coming inside right now," he said. "Move it."

"Okay, okay," I said. "Calm down."

And then I had an idea. It was dangerous, but it was something I knew I could do. Throw. Tossing a four-pronged cultivator at the guy wouldn't be the same as a 95 mph fastball, but it weighed about the same as a baseball and I figured I could get some force behind it.

"Raise your hands!"

As I started to bring up my hands, I whipped the cultivator at him as hard as I could with a sidearm delivery, sort of like you'd throw a Frisbee and dove for the ground at the same time.

The crazy-spinning cultivator caught him by surprise. Pfeiffer was as inexperienced at these games as I was, so he waited too long before reacting. Still, he was armed. As he moved to get out of the way, the cultivator slammed him in the head. One prong gouged an eye while the other prongs carved into the side of his face as he fired.

The professor turned out to be a good shot. I felt a bullet rip through my left arm, my pitching arm. Both of us screamed in pain and shock and I hoped I could react first.

With blood gushing out of his right eye onto his grayish-white sweater, Pfeiffer shot some more, but wildly. I rose up on all fours, hoping to find a second to take a deep breath, but

I forgot an important reality. I couldn't put any weight on my left arm and immediately pain spiked from my arm into my shoulder so intensely that my whole body shuddered. I knew I had to set the pain aside and adrenaline kicked into action. With my left arm hanging by my side, I was in a rough approximation of a three-point stance at that point, with all the forward weight on my good arm.

I dove at him, trying to remember the endless tackling drills from two years of middle-school football, though I braced myself for more pain if I succeeded in my plan for a textbook takedown that would wrap him up with both arms.

It worked. As I brought Pfeiffer to the ground, he fired again, but the shot went careening off the garage in the rear of the back yard. I chopped at his wrist as hard as I could. Maybe I broke it, because he yelled even louder, which I didn't think was possible. The pistol flopped out of his hand and I picked it up. Growing up in Idaho, I knew a little bit about handling a gun.

Meanwhile, Pfeiffer was in no condition to do much more than scream in pain, as he rolled around like a beached grouper on the paving stones that led away from the back steps. He was a threat no longer and I had more important things to do. I didn't care, frankly, if he bled to death out there, which appeared to be a real possibility and I hoped his screams would alert some neighbors. He already had spurred several neighborhood dogs to start barking.

When I entered the kitchen, I saw what I expected following my view through the slats of the blinds. Aimee and her father were tied to two chairs. Pfeiffer's laptop was on a nearby counter. Images from four security cameras showed on the screen—one in each quadrant. He must have been doing something else for a few minutes, or he would have seen me sooner, which would have been really bad.

I untied them both.

"Trey," Aimee said. "Thank God."

She needed a hug and I provided it with my good arm, but it was quick.

"We need to get out of here and call Moose," I said. "Let him know we're okay. He's following Williamson. My vote is to leave it to the police at this point."

Then she saw my left arm, which was throbbing like hell and bleeding as it hung limply on my side.

"My God Trey," she said. "You've been shot."

"Yeah, we need to do something about that. Another reason we've got to get out of here," I said.

Bob Walters went into a kitchen drawer and found a clean dish rag. He walked over and pushed up my sleeve. Even that hurt.

"You're lucky," he said a moment after he tore off the strip of duct tape covering his mouth. "I see a hole at both ends. Maybe the bullet went through your arm, but I've just exhausted what I know about bullet wounds other than I'm going to use this rag to tie it tight around the wound."

"There's one other thing," Aimee said.

"Geez," Bob said. "I almost forgot. We need to get her."

"Who?" I said.

"There's someone else here. Taylor Pierce," Aimee said.

"Holy shit," I said.

The three of us walked into the room in the front of the house that had been converted into a bedroom and we were disgusted and saddened by what we saw.

Taylor Pierce was sleeping fitfully on a hospital bed. She looked like a waif—that's the only word I can think of—skinny to the point of bony with stringy hair. Sores covered most parts of her body. Her arms were scabbed and she had a huge bruise on the top of her right hand where it looked like some sort of drip had been inserted. I don't think she weighed 80 pounds, even though she looked to be almost six feet tall.

The room also had a terrible smell, a combination of an antiseptic, hospital-room odor and the unmistakable smell of someone who couldn't control bodily functions. I noticed she was wearing an adult diaper.

"Taylor," Aimee said to her. "Can you hear me? C'mon wake up. We're going to help you and get you home."

Taylor stirred briefly as I heard sirens faintly in the background and tried to ignore the throbbing in my arm. The adrenaline rush was wearing off.

She opened her eyes and looked puzzled at our faces, which were new to her.

"Who're you," she said as though drifting in thick fog. "Where's Meg?"

"We're here to help," Aimee said, stroking her forehead lightly and brushing back strands of hair. "Can you get up?"

"Don't know," she said. "Don't want to. Where's Meg?"

"I'm not sure we should try to move her," I said. "I hear sirens. Help is coming. She needs an ambulance. So does the asshole in the back yard. I say make her comfortable and let's go outside and call for help if it hasn't arrived already."

"I think so, too," Bob said.

"Okay," Aimee said. "You guys go outside and I'll stay with Taylor. God, I feel so sorry for her. What have these people done to her? Dad, you can keep an eye on Trey in case he needs help."

Caring about Taylor and me before herself was just like Aimee. It was part of why I loved her. I had started fantasizing about having kids with her someday—after the wedding. We had started talking lightly about both things. The wedding would have to be in Chicago. We both laughed when she had the idea to serve Italian beef or deep-dish pizza at the reception instead of some boring chicken or overcooked tenderloin. She insisted that we find a real Chicago blues band instead of a D.J.

And, we'd already agreed kids would be in the picture. They would be really cool kids with Aimee as the mom. They'd be bright and quick-witted. They'd be compassionate most of the time but ready to call your bluff if you needed a kick. And, of course, they'd be beautiful in every way. If we had a boy, I was really hoping she wouldn't mind if we named him Don, after my Dad. He would've loved Aimee.

Bob had to help me move outside by grabbing my right arm as we walked out the front door. I was feeling weak.

"I guess you have the scoop that I won't be starting tomorrow night," I said. "It's another Cubs curse for you to have fun with."

The sirens were getting closer and I could see two people standing on a porch three houses away. I couldn't hear Pfeiffer's screams from the back porch. Maybe he had passed out or expired. I felt too weary to bother checking. Meanwhile, Walters took a long pause before replying to my sarcastic remark.

"I've spent a lot of my career ripping on the Cubs and now you since you joined them," he replied, "but I don't have any jokes right now. C'mon, let's find the fresh air and wait for help. We can direct the cops and an ambulance crew soon as they get here."

We walked toward the curb as I leaned slightly harder against Walters. We were almost to the sidewalk when I heard Aimee.

"Hey, wait up," Aimee said with a half-smile on her face as she came through the door and stood on the porch. "She's sound asleep; drifted back off. There really was nothing I could do for her, so I figured I might as well come outside with you guys. Plus, well, I'm ashamed to say this, but it didn't take much to convince me to get away from the smell."

Just as she took the first step from the porch to the sidewalk, the bomb went off. I was looking right at Aimee, back toward the house, and saw flames fly up into the first floor as the force of the explosion flung her forward into the yard. I saw her head hit the concrete walk that led to the porch from the sidewalk.

I screamed, "No!" I tried to run toward her, but I was too weak. Bob was still holding my right arm as I turned and we both tumbled as I started running. Then I couldn't get up. I heard Bob yell "Aimee" as he realized what was going on. Flames were licking out of the windows and already had jumped to one of the neighboring homes.

I saw Bob Walters holding up his arms with his palms facing outward toward the burning house as if this would dissipate the intense heat as he reached Aimee's limp body. Now I knew what Meg Williamson was doing in the basement. I should've broken the damn padlock. Maybe I would've found the bomb. The last thing I remembered before passing out was this thought: *How can I ever forgive myself?*

51

Trey Van Ohmann

I woke up the next morning in University Hospital in Madison. They didn't tell me about Aimee and Taylor Pierce right away, but the answers seemed obvious. Tears started rolling down my cheeks and wouldn't stop. My entire body ached, especially my throbbing left arm and my face felt like someone had set it on fire. I realized I had minor burns from the explosion and fire, but none of that mattered. The tears wouldn't stop.

I heard a snore, which surprised me. I started to move my head to the left and felt a stab of pain in my shoulder, so I slowed down and took a deep breath before turning my head more carefully this time. I saw a figure in a wheelchair. He had his head propped up with a pillow against the wall, sound asleep. It was Moose Skowron.

"Moose," I said, barely able to hold it together. "What's going on? C'mon. Wake up. I've got to know."

He stirred slightly, then realized I was awake.

"Trey," he said. "Good. You're awake. Hang on. Let me shake out some cobwebs."

"Aimee," I stated as loudly as I could. "Aimee. Tell me about Aimee."

Skowron looked at me and I could clearly see the concern in his eyes. I feared the worst.

"Tell me," I said. "Is she gone?"

"No," Skowron replied, and I felt a huge gush of relief, but only for a wisp of a moment as he continued.

He said, "But they don't know if she'll make it. She's in intensive care. Bob gave me the rundown. He's with her non-stop and I think her Mom just got here from downstate Illinois. Aimee's hurt pretty bad. Burns on a lot of her body, though I guess those will eventually heal. Not as bad as it could have been. Some broken ribs and a broken arm. The concussion from the fall is what they're most worried about. They put her in a medically induced coma to try to get the swelling in her brain to subside.

"Even if she makes it, Trey, it sounds like they're really concerned about brain damage," he said. "You need to be prepared for that possibility. I'm so sorry, man."

I spent some minutes processing what Moose had just said and he was smart and thoughtful enough to leave me alone with my thoughts. Finally, other questions and concerns began to intrude, though thinking about anything but Aimee made me feel guilty. So, I said the first thing I knew she would want me to say.

"Thanks for being here," I said. "I really mean it. Have you been here all night?"

"All night. Yes," Moose said. "I knew you had no family nearby, so I just stayed. Your brothers are on the way from Idaho. All of them. I made sure they were contacted."

"And what about you?" I asked. "Last time I saw you, you were peeling out like Dale Earnhardt chasing Meg Williamson in your minivan. What the hell happened?"

"It's almost funny in a way," he said. "A Honda minivan chasing a Toyota Prius through the streets of politically correct Madison. You can't make it up."

Then he erased the slight smile from his face. "Trey, I think I know the moment when Meg blew up the house. She must have had the bomb on some sort of remote timer. We were driving on the road that runs along Lake Monona, just east of downtown, probably going 70. It was crazy. I'm sure people were calling 911 by that point.

"I could see she was fiddling with her phone, but she couldn't make it work and drive at the same time, so she pulled off the road. She had sped up at least two blocks ahead of me, because I had to stop to avoid hitting a kid on a bike.

"I caught up to her, because she was stopped. I could see she was hell-bent on doing whatever it was she was trying to do with her phone. That's when I think she set it off. I pulled in front of her, trying to block. Meanwhile, I'm on my own phone frantically calling 911, because I realize I'm in over my head.

"She pulls out a gun, points it at me. I duck and she fires two shots through my windshield. I also tumble out of my seat, which means I'll need several minutes to pull myself back up into the driver's seat. I have these damn legs that don't work. I think this is it, I'm going to die. Instead, she steps on the gas and slips between the minivan and the railing along the lake where she's parked. Escaping was more important to her than killing me, I guess."

"So," I ask. "Is she still on the loose?"

"No, she isn't," Moose continued. "By now, half the Madison Police Department must be involved in the situation and the other half probably is headed to Earl Street to deal with the mess there. She really had no place to go."

"So, what happened?"

"They cornered her, of all places, at the scenic overlook where there's a plaque commemorating the death of Otis Redding."

"Who the hell is Otis Redding?"

"Ah, you're too young," Moose said. "He's only perhaps the greatest blues-and-soul singer of his generation; maybe ever. You've probably heard 'Sitting on the Dock of the Bay,' right? He died too young when his small plane went into Lake Monona, ironically on the dock of the bay so to speak. They had warned him about bad flying conditions, but he didn't want to let his fans down. I think it was 1967."

"And what about Williamson?"

"So, the cops chase her up to the terrace. She pulls a gun on them, they shoot her before she can fire and she falls over the terrace railing as she's backing up, refusing to surrender. She's dead, Trey, and I guess she destroyed a lot of the evidence of whatever she was doing when she blew up the house. Pfeiffer is barely alive; a detective told me he'll probably die in the next 24 hours from blood loss without talking. Unless he makes it, there might not be a lot of answers for a long time."

"It still makes no sense to me. It's all a mess. A blur."

"It never will; not totally. Bob and I talked about it. We had a lot of time during the last 12 hours. Somehow Meg turned into a psychopath with an obsession. That's our amateur theory anyway. She went through some horrible things as a kid. I certainly didn't do anything to help her then, so maybe part of the blame is mine. She wouldn't really reach out to Bob and Luke about what was going on in that house. Kids are embarrassed and easily damaged. They soak up everything going on at home but act to their friends like it's always sunny inside. They stop feeling much of anything, because it hurts too much, or it's too risky to have feelings. Eventually everything they've absorbed starts building up, like too much pressure on a dam, especially if there's no support. I've met a lot of troubled people coping with unbelievable stuff going through rehab. Most people figure out ways to navigate. Maybe Meg made other choices. Maybe she never really had any choice."

Again, quiet pervaded the room beyond the clicks, beeps and whirs of the hospital, and my thoughts drifted to myself. What was my future? What about the game tonight? I tried to put the thoughts in a box to concentrate all my thoughts and prayers on Aimee. But, I couldn't help wondering.

"And what are they saying about me?" I finally asked Moose.

He looked at me, again with sad eyes, but maybe not quite as sad as a moment ago, given the life-changing lesson we'd just had on keeping things in perspective.

"You'll have to ask your doctors about that," he said. "But it's safe to say the Cubbies need an emergency starter tonight."

"Duh. It must be a media frenzy out there," I said.

"Oh, yeah," he said. "Be glad they won't let anyone up here."

Then the fullness of the past 24 hours hit me and I started crying again. It wasn't just shock that brought tears.

"My God, Moose," I said, "not only have I let Aimee down, I've let my teammates down. I couldn't protect my Dad. Taylor Pierce died. This is all stuff that I could have stopped."

Aimee had told me one night about asking her father to explain the transformation of Moose Skowron from someone who was a spoiled, arrogant bully. He was a child football star who had coaches salivating before he even made it to high school. His parents stroked his ego by grooming him for stardom and seeing him as a kid who could do no wrong, even when he did.

After his childhood accident, somehow he found the power to avoid bitterness and channel his athletic competitiveness into academics. People whispered that his minister had a lot more to do with it than Moose's father, who never lost his anger or forgave Luke Murphy and Bob Walters. Moose often talked about meeting others in even worse straits as they dealt with disabilities, so he dedicated himself to being a role model. And, he was a great listener.

"He's the most thoughtful, compassionate man I know—even compared to you," Aimee said.

That was the moment when Moose Skowron showed me what Aimee had described. He said nothing as he wheeled his chair over to the side of my bed.

He hugged me—carefully, because of my injuries—but he hugged me. I put my good right arm around his shoulder. Then he spoke.

"You're being way too hard on yourself Trey," he said. "None of this is your fault. You did your best, just like when you pitch. Sometimes the other guys are still going to get a hit or two—even when you have your best stuff. What you did in that back yard is what got Aimee and Bob out of that house before it exploded. She's got a chance. Bob's alive. You didn't have to go to Madison at all, but you did. You did good. And you've got me and Aimee's got me, for any help either of you need. I know all about rehab. Trust me."

I acted as though I didn't want to hear it, but the tears said otherwise.

52

Trey Van Ohmann

By mid-afternoon, they had me up in bed with my left arm in a sling, but they didn't want me to move much more than going from the bed to the bathroom and back, trailing my glucose bag and morphine drip behind me. That meant I couldn't see Aimee. Besides, I wasn't family, even though I planned to be. She was still in a coma and I heard both her Mom and Dad were constantly at her side.

I finally convinced Moose to go to a hotel and get some rest, though I saw on the news that he held what amounted to an impromptu news conference as soon as he wheeled out of the hospital into the van he had to call since his minivan was evidence in a criminal matter with bullet holes in the windshield. The details of what happened were still vague to the public, but it was a spectacular story—particularly because it involved me.

The team and my teammates had exceeded my expectations and that really helped. The Cubs issued a statement they wished me a speedy recovery and they tried to quiet the nastier fans who were complaining I never should have made the trip. "Trey had his priorities in order to respond to a call for help, especially for the significant other of his life," said the statement signed by Jerry Landis. "The Cubs support Trey and any further investigation needed to deal with this tragic incident."

Given the last meeting that Landis and I had, when I pretty much told him to stick it and he told me I was done with the Cubs, that was damn classy. I texted my thanks.

Still, I figured it wasn't long before President Murphy would face questions about his connections to Meg Williamson and what his friends were doing on an off-the-books mission. As much as I liked and respected Murphy, I wasn't going to lie to the FBI or the police if asked what prompted me to go to Madison and I surely would face that. Once Taylor Pierce was publicly identified as the body found inside, it would be a political firestorm of historic proportions.

I was glad I was insulated from the fray; at least for now.

My teammates' support made me feel even worse about not being able to pitch. My phone filled up with private texts from them and almost every teammate had sent public tweets of support to "TreyVanO."

The Cubs announced that our Number Three starter, Zach Southern, would open the game on three days of rest instead of his normal four or five. Zach was a decent pitcher with an 11-7 record for the season. There was no questioning his heart, but he always had trouble with some of the Brewers' better hitters, because he had to rely too much on his fastball if his control was off. Several of them feasted on fastballs, especially Castrovenes. Man, I hoped Whisper, the pitching coach, was giving Zach the advice he would need.

What none of my teammates, the media or the owners knew yet was their positive vibes were for naught. The news on my arm wasn't good.

The doctors showed me the X-rays. Although it was fortunate the bullet had gone through my arm instead of lodging inside, it had done extensive damage, making a mess of the nerves, muscles and tendons just above my left elbow—illustrated by the fact that I still had no feeling from my elbow down to my left hand. They had immediately brought in a sports orthopedic specialist who worked with University of Wisconsin athletes. In turn, that doctor consulted with another expert on bullet wounds.

I knew it was bad when the two docs came in together with that look you don't like to see on doctors' faces.

The headline, stripped of the medical jargon, was that if I was really lucky, after multiple additional surgeries, I might be able to play catch with my kids, nieces and nephews someday. I should be able to sign my name and type with two hands again at some point. For now, though, their advice was to learn how to do a lot of things right-handed while the experts tried to figure out the best course of rehab.

I had to ask the pointed, direct question.

"I'm done as a Major League pitcher, right?"

They nodded yes and one said, "Miracles happen, but I honestly don't see one in your case. I'm sorry."

In a weird way, the diagnosis concluded something I had been thinking about, particularly since my confrontation with Landis.

I don't usually believe in signs from above, but this sure seemed like one. My involvement in presidential politics and my father's death had unleashed something; a call to do something more meaningful with my life perhaps. I already had plenty of money and millions more guaranteed in my contract. My casual contemplation of law school after my playing days now seemed like a serious plan to ponder.

Another text message beeped its arrival. I almost didn't bother looking, because the flood was exhausting, no matter how well-intentioned. I needed to rest before my brothers arrived from Idaho and they were due at any time.

I glanced at the phone. The text said "Call CR" and followed with a 10-digit number I didn't recognize. I called and Charley Rayburn answered on the first ring.

"Trey, the president and I want to thank you for what you did. It took incredible courage. You saved one of his best and only friends and his daughter."

"Where does this go?" I asked. "This is going to get even crazier between now and the election, right?"

"It will," he said. "We're going through a lot of damage-control scenarios and maybe we could cover up a lot, but Luke finally said, screw it, let everything come out, and what happens will be what it'll be. I kind of respected him for that. Might cost him the election."

"So, did Meg Williamson arrange to have him shot?"

"It'll be a long time before we know for sure. The dead shooter thought he was carrying out the will of Allah, but Meg's hand probably will turn out to be the one behind it," Rayburn said. "Somehow, in her mind, Luke was someone who could be sacrificed for her cause. Maybe subconsciously she felt Luke should have done more to help her when they were young. I doubt if we'll ever really know."

"And how about you, how are you doing?"

I said, "Well, it appears I need a new career. Right now, I'm more concerned about Aimee."

He said, "As you should be. I hope you can both come to the White House before the end of the year. Let's plan on it. Maybe after the Cubs win the Series."

I said, "I don't mean to sound too cocky about my skills, but that just got tougher for Chicago."

There was a pause. I could hear Rayburn talking to someone. He hadn't bothered to mute the phone.

"Trey?" a new voice said. I recognized the voice as Murphy's.

"Mr. President," I said. "How are you?"

"I'll be okay," he said. "Sorry about eavesdropping on the call. It's very tragic. We're going to make sure Aimee gets every imaginable medical support possible."

"Thank you," I said, then added, "I really wish I could pitch you and the Cubbies to the playoffs tonight."

"Well, maybe you can give Zach Southern a call and remind him how to throw to the damn Brewers," he said.

"Actually, that's not a bad idea," I said. "It's a small way I can help."

Just as the call ended, a nurse poked her head into my room.

"Mr. Van Ohmann?"

"Yes, that's me," I said.

"The Walters family insisted that I come down here and give you some news."

I couldn't read anything in her expression as she walked over to the bed. Inwardly, I already started preparing for bad news. She lightly touched my shoulder and then I saw the corners of a faint smile on her lips.

"We think it's good news," she said. "They are bringing her out of her coma and her vital signs are getting stronger. It's a long road ahead, but unless something really unexpected happens, she's going to live."

The relief I felt was beyond words.

The nurse started to leave the room. "Wait," I said. "Hand me a piece of paper and a pen."

I had to write right-handed, which was quite a chore. I scrawled out these words in block caps, "AIMEE: I LOVE YOU. WE'LL GET BETTER TOGETHER! TREY."

I handed her the note and she beamed when she read it. "Every girl wants a man like you," the nurse said with a wink. "I'll make sure she sees it as soon as she's awake."

"Thanks."

I was going to take a nap, then remembered I told the president I was going to call Zach Southern. I texted Campanelli, got Zach's cell phone number and made the call.

I owed it to my teammates to help the Cubs win another World Series.

EPILOGUE

January | The Day Before Inauguration Day

Charley Rayburn sat across from Luke Murphy in the Oval Office. It would be their last time in that room unless Murphy's successor invited them, which was unlikely, but you never knew when a crisis might make such a thing necessary.

"So," Rayburn said. "Did you do the letter?"

"I did," Murphy said, looking up from the historic Eisenhower desk that he wished he could take with him. "Just getting ready to seal it and put it in the drawer, like President Thompson did for me. You know, it's supposed to be private, so don't pump me for what I said."

"I would never do that to the Commander-in-Chief of course."

"That actually was a joke that didn't work. I'm going to break protocol and tell you what I said anyway, because I know you want to see it and I want your opinion on whether it sets the right tone."

Murphy opened the hand-written letter he had just finished in a scrawl he hoped was more legible than Thompson's. He read it aloud to Rayburn:

Dear Matt,

I've attached the letter President Thompson wrote to me about what you will be facing in this amazing office. That word 'amazing' is probably the most over-used word in the English language, but it fits this job.

I realized I can't articulate what you're going to face or provide any advice better than the way President Thompson said it. We all miss him. Please read his words and take them seriously, as I know you will.

The only other thing I will add is this: We have had our political differences. The campaign was tough. And weird. I hope you feel I did the right thing at the end. If you ever need my help, confidentially or publicly, you can call on me. Please count on it.

Sincerely,

Luke Murphy

"That's good," said Rayburn, who had read the Thompson letter shortly after Luke first opened it. "Short and sweet. You're right about the Thompson letter, too. It needs to be public someday. This place is quite a ride. He has no idea."

They both reflected on that for a moment.

"I assume you saw this, too?" Rayburn said, handing Luke a printout of a lengthy column from the Washington Post.

"I did," he said. "Monica was always a good reporter before she started writing her opinion column. I think she did good job with it."

POTUS: MEDIA CLIPS OF THE DAY

From the Washington Post. (Presented in full.)

Headline:

What's Next for Luke Murphy Following Bittersweet Year?

By Monica Lynch

As Matthew Leeds prepares to enter the Oval Office as the next president of the United States, it's a good time to reflect on the remarkable recent events that unfolded in Luke Murphy's life and probably cost him the presidency.

Murphy's main character flaws, being self-interested and manipulative, certainly aren't unique among politicians, but exit polls showed that voters reacted strongly and negatively to the "Madison mission" that resulted in the deaths of three people and major injuries to two others, including the career-ending bullet wound to Trey Van Ohmann, the star pitcher for Murphy's beloved Chicago Cubs. Aimee Walters, the daughter of Murphy's best friend from childhood, also faces a long and difficult recovery from burn and concussion injuries.

To Murphy's credit, he refused to let his chief advisor, Col. Charley Rayburn, take the fall for an ill-advised quest, as sources confirm Rayburn volunteered to do so. During a remarkable public mea culpa, Murphy admitted that he should have involved the authorities as his suspicions grew about Meg Williamson's role instead of quietly seeking additional information in case they needed to do damage control for the campaign.

And it was generous of Murphy to jointly appear with Democrat Leeds to state he was convinced that the Leeds campaign had nothing to do with Williamson's manipulations to make him president. It also would have been easy to raise questions and innuendo, but Murphy refused to drive down that dirty political road.

Of course, in so doing, Murphy also managed to undermine Lydia Nicks and advisors close to Murphy say the president would have had a harder time stomaching a Nicks' presidency than a win for Leeds. Such are the games of politics.

Maybe, on Election Day, it wouldn't have mattered, with Nicks' insurgent candidacy peeling off Republican votes from Murphy, leaving a wider opening for Leeds. Still, enough additional voters had grown exhausted by the intense, personal dramas of the Murphy presidency to tip the states of Ohio, Colorado and Florida to Leeds.

If the voters had known the drama that was still to come, they might have felt even more exhausted.

After the election, Murphy and his wife, Alison, made a joint announcement they wanted to "quell the rumors" and state that, yes, they would have an "amicable separation" as soon as they moved out of the White House. Not that it should matter, but questions remain about Murphy's sexual orientation.

The real irony is this: If things had been a little different, Murphy might have had a triumphant few months leading into a second term.

On the international front, voters didn't give him much credit for resolving the crisis with China and getting new concessions from the Chinese as their people learned how Americans step up in a crisis. Terrorism remains a huge problem, but the domestic economy is picking up and Murphy continues to push for "German-style" green energy objectives that make long-term sense.

And, much to the delight of their Number One Fan, Murphy's Cubbies repeated as World Series champs, turning a curse into a potential dynasty. No one thought it was possible after Van Ohmann got injured. But Chicago pitcher Zach Southern, who emerged as the star of the World Series, said it was Van Ohmann who quietly assisted him throughout the post-season. Southern said it was Van Ohmann's advice that helped him strike out Milwaukee's Jaime Castrovenes with the bases loaded in the bottom of the ninth inning to ensure the Cubs made the post-season. They were nearly unbeatable after that.

At his farewell news conference, a reporter asked Murphy what the Cubs' triumph meant to him and Murphy referenced Van Ohmann's pivotal roles "in both my life and the history of the Cubs" as he pulled out a "Cubs World Champions" baseball hat and wore it most proudly.

"Trey told me that most of his advice to Zach Southern was pretty basic," Murphy said with a wistful look. "One thing Trey recommended was to always at least consider the opposite of what instincts tell you to do at critical times. Guess that would've been good advice for me."

And that may be the most astute observation Luke Murphy has ever made.

It will be fascinating to see where this flawed-but-talented man goes next.

Murphy put down the briefing paper and couldn't resist a sigh. A portion of his sigh involved relief about escaping the unrelenting pressure of the White House, but it included deep regret that he left his job half-finished.

"Say, Colonel, how much of a break do you think we need to take before starting that consulting business we talked about; to help the right kind of people run for office and do the right things in the right ways?"

"I'd say about six months seems right," Rayburn said. "You realize that people are going to raise some eyebrows over you of all people doing this."

"Well, we'll have to find the right people and have some success. Maybe Trey Van Ohmann can be one of our first candidates. We probably could get him elected in Illinois and Idaho at the same time if only that were legal. I think he's got the bug."

"You might want to wait at least until he finishes law school," Rayburn said. "I hear that's where he's headed; probably at DePaul in Chicago."

"Maybe he can intern with us. And that reminds me," Murphy said. "Did you know we're invited to a wedding in Chicago the week before Opening Day?"

"I heard something about that. And our schedules look pretty damn open."

"Roger that. And you can come with me, because it's not like I'll have a date."

"Oh, yeah. We'll be the fun couple."

"Make sure you bring Connie. If your wife is along, people won't speculate about us as an item," Murphy said. "Well, you never know, come to think about it, and I'm not sure I care.

"Anyway, Jerry Landis has agreed to let Trey and Aimee get married at home plate at Wrigley Field. I want to be there. I'll sit next to Moose, watching Bobby Walters give away the world's most beautiful bride."

THE END

Author's Notes

Steve Bartman: You are free at last. And, I believe you made this book possible.

He loves the Chicago Cubs, though he lives in anonymity and reportedly has turned down serious money to speak or write in public.

Still, if you're a baseball fan, you have to admit that what happened to Steve Bartman could have happened to you.

I could've been sitting in the leftfield stands at Wrigley Field during a pivotal playoff game, listening to the radio broadcast. I could've reached out by instinct over the outfield wall and tried to grab a foul ball that maybe or maybe not was in play.

I could've set off a chain of events that caused the Cubs to lose the game and then lose their chance to win baseball's world championship for the first time since 1908.

Without the "Bartman incident," I believe the Cubs would have won the World Series in 2003. That sparked ideas that led to this book and its predecessor, "Killing the Curse."

But this raises a larger question. Why was Bartman the story and not the miscues and failures by the Chicago athletes that followed? What turned this story into one that loomed so large that merely saying the name "Bartman" evokes an image of almost Shakespearean tragedy among baseball fans?

I think it goes something like this: For those of us who grew up as fans of the Chicago Cubs, we learned to appreciate small victories and to view success of higher magnitude with great suspicion. Am I really worthy? When will disaster strike? Does the unexpected shatter your confidence, increasing the chances of failure, or strengthen your resolve, increasing your chances to succeed?

Steve Bartman's story is certainly not a tragedy on the scale of war, but a story that diminishes the rest of us for the way he was treated for simply doing what anyone would have done.

To fully understand this, I recommend a fascinating ESPN documentary, "Catching Hell," that describes how a few seconds changed Bartman's life.

To set the scene: Bartman instinctively reaches out to catch a foul ball that outfielder Moises Alou of the Cubs arguably would have caught during the sixth game of the 2003 playoff series between the Cubs and Florida Marlins. The Cubs go on to lose the game and the next one, too, blowing their chance to reach the Series in ways improbable to anyone but Cub fans. This includes a damaging error on the very next play by Alex Gonzalez, usually a sure-handed shortstop. This creates the opportunity for a Marlins rally that puts the game out of reach.

So, why doesn't Gonzalez get more attention—and blame? Or, how do you explain the collapse of the Cubs' star pitchers, Mark Prior and Kerry Wood for the Cubs, in Games Six and Seven?

More than a decade later, only nerdy baseball fans remember Alex Gonzalez. Yet, everyone "knows" Bartman. Those few seconds turned him into a pariah, despite his public apology.

The ESPN documentary argues that scapegoating Steve Bartman for the defeat is a case study in crowd psychology—fueled by over-the-top media coverage and a century of pent-up frustration. (By the way, there's an excellent argument that the Marlins' batter should have been called out for fan interference on the infamous play. Just search "Bartman play" on Google.)

The other driving force behind this book is my lifelong fascination with the people in politics. I've had a close view as a reporter, editor, newspaper publisher and, now, in the lobbyist portion of my role as president of the Ohio News Media Association. Politicians are complex creatures and most of them spend more time than you might think trying to do the right things. However, "party first, me first" thinking and the overwhelming influence of money often take precedence.

The parallels between the quest for success in big-time sports and national politics also are fascinating. When do you make ethical compromises? Some choices require major depths of self-justification—like taking steroids or fueling racial hatred on the campaign trail. Every choice extracts a price and the price you pay can cheapen both the thrill and impact of victory.

That's an issue I first explored in "Killing the Curse," which set the stage for the events in this book. You don't have to read "Curse" to enjoy this book, though certainly my publisher and I heartily encourage you to do so.

"Season of Lies" begins where the first book ends—the completion of a tragic and historic World Series between the Cubs and Boston Red Sox. Meanwhile, the real-life, 2016 Cubs exorcised past curses by winning the World Series. You might consider this book an "alternate reality" on how that could've happened—and what might happen during the following season.

You shouldn't have to be a Cubs fan or even a baseball fan to enjoy these novels. My goal always has been to use baseball and politics as platforms to a richer, deeper story. I'm flattered and humbled that so many readers have agreed.

Acknowledgments

This wouldn't have been possible without others, particularly my friend and award-winning political thriller author Rick Robinson. Rick was directly involved in *Killing the Curse* since we hatched the idea for that first book on a drive from Frankfort, Ky., to the Kentucky suburbs of Cincinnati.

Deep appreciation goes to many others for comments on various drafts, fact-checking and other forms of assistance, including moral support. I was buoyed by the suggestions and enthusiastic "yes" the manuscript received from Stephanie Storey—the author of the brilliant historical novel *Oil and Marble*.

I also thank Cheryl Hetzel, Jack Greiner, Heather Dugan, Fred Anderson, Craig Siewert, Chris Alexis, Linda Robinson, Belinda Jones and Steve Kirshenbaum, a Cubs fan and owner of a terrific independent store, Looking Glass Books in Oak Park, Ill. Kevin Kelly applied his great skills to the cover art. Finally, you wouldn't be reading this without the efforts of my publisher, Cathy Teets, and her team at one of America's great indie book publishers: Headline Books.

Notes On Fact Vs. Fiction

The events and characters in this book are fictional of course. When actual people, historical events, and settings intersected with the story, I strove for accuracy. Three examples: The "Leon Durham curse" that is part of Cubs' lore, the history of the desk that Luke Murphy uses in the Oval Office and descriptions of astronomical events under the unusual circumstances that begin to unfold in Chapter One. As the story notes, there is precedent for meteors to hit Earth without being detected. Any errors belong to me.

I took some fictional license in describing Lydia Nicks' efforts to succeed as a third-party presidential candidate. While I believe the processes I described are accurate, a real-world Lydia might face even greater odds to meet dizzying rules and difficult deadlines to get on ballots; let alone contend. A massive and unprecedented write-in effort would be her only alternative in many states.

This is largely because our two major political parties play extraordinary games to gain advantage, though it's not surprising when you consider the darker sides of human nature. Erecting big roadblocks to potentially successful third-party candidates is one of many ways they do it. Gerrymandering—adjusting the shape—of legislative districts to guarantee "safe seats" for your side is particularly destructive. The result: Few elections today are competitive and candidates on the extremes of right and left are more likely to get elected.

My fictional president, Luke Murphy certainly has flaws, but I also imagine him as a president who would say something like this:

"Just because an idea deserves to succeed doesn't mean it will, even what we call 'The American Idea.' We should spend less time telling the world how exceptional we are and more time showing by our actions how exceptional we still want to become."

Luke would use the real-world Cubs as an example of how to follow that challenging, inspiring path. May our political leaders do so as well.

Dennis Hetzel, January 2017

About The Author

"Season of Lies" is Dennis Hetzel's second novel, following the award-winning "Killing the Curse" (Headline Books, 2014) in which events precede those that unfold in the latest novel.

As a journalist and media executive, Hetzel has won numerous awards for writing, industry leadership and community service, including the 2003 Paul Tobenkin Memorial Award from the Columbia University Graduate School of Journalism for leadership in coverage of race and diversity issues. Since 2010, he has been president and executive director of the Ohio News Media Association in Columbus, Ohio, and president of the Ohio Coalition for Open Government.

He began his career as a weekly newspaper sports editor in the Chicago suburbs and has been a reporter, editor, general manager and publisher at newspapers including the Madison, Wis., Capital Times, the Cincinnati Enquirer and the York, Pa., Daily Record, where he was editor and publisher for 13 years. During that time, the York paper won national awards from the Scripps Howard Foundation in public service journalism and a Robert F. Kennedy Journalism Award. He also has taught journalism at Penn State and Temple universities.

Hetzel grew up in the Chicago area and inherited his lifelong affection for and frustration with the Cubs from his late father. He has a degree in political science and a minor in journalism from Western Illinois University, where he met his wife, Cheryl, a school psychologist and guidance counselor. They have three grown children and a home they love in Holden Beach, North Carolina, where he does much of his writing.

Hetzel also plays guitar and bass in an acoustic trio, "Phil's Five & Dime," which includes fellow author Rick Robinson on mandolin. He's still hoping "this guitar thing" works out when he grows up.

Follow him at his Facebook author page, "DennisHetzel" on Twitter and at www.dennishetzel.com.